Degrees of Freedom

A Novel

RICHARD LARSON

© 2020 Richard Larson. All rights reserved. No part of this publication may be reproduced, distributed, or transmitted in any form or by any means, including photocopying, recording, or other electronic or mechanical methods, without the prior written permission of the author, except in the case of brief quotations embodied in critical reviews and certain other noncommercial uses permitted by copyright law.

ISBN: 978-1-09830-452-2 (print)
ISBN: 978-1-09830-453-9 (ebook)

Cover photograph by Christian Begeman.

And if a lion spoke, we could not understand him.

– Wittgenstein

Bruce 1

It was the summer of the cicadas; yes, they were swarming that summer I arrived, the summer of 1964. The old-timers said to me, yep, it's been seventeen years all right since the last crop of locusts, just after the war. That was a real predicament, they said, even worse than this; you couldn't step outside without a dozen of the things landing on you. And the ugly creatures got into the houses, too, they'd find a hole in your screens and then the next thing you'd know you'd have six of them in your bathroom. They had a special scream then, when they were trapped and scared, not the one they used out in the open when sex was on their mind. And you had to decide what to do about them; you couldn't just ignore them (because they were too unnerving), couldn't smack them with the flyswatter (that would be too messy), and you couldn't open the window and let them out (because then more might get in). What I finally decided to do was to corner them, ignoring their squalling cries, and grab them with a paper towel. They'd stop struggling and screaming after a few seconds, and I could take them to the back door, open it just a crack, and let them go.

The summer I turned up, even when we couldn't see them, we could hear them for what seemed like miles. Their shrieking started with the first rays of dawn and lasted until well after sunset. As the temperature rose in the afternoons, the rasping calls became louder and more nearly continuous, until the clamor filled every corner of the countryside. The prodigious racket, at its late-afternoon maximum, made us feel as if the air itself had solidified and been transformed into a vibrating medium.

The summer I pulled in was also the summer of record-breaking temperatures and of the record-breaking dry spell. They all came at the same time; the locust population explosion and the heat wave coincided perfectly with the drought. I thought I knew how to handle heat -- it could be difficult to bear at times in the sweltering summers of the upper Midwest, where I had always lived -- but this drying-oven effect, apparently peculiar to this region of the country, was something new to me, and even the old-timers thought this was the worst they'd ever seen. We tried to bear the torment stoically; leaving the house in the glare of the early morning, when the temperature was still only 80o, it was easy enough to feel some faint optimism that things might not turn out too badly, but at the end of each day, drenched in sweat and cloaked in oily dirt and trying to feel the respite of a breeze in the sultry evening, we began to think that enduring another day like the one just past would put an end to our sanities. And we went to sleep, or tried to, naked and writhing on top of the blankets, and by morning our eyes purged themselves of their load of suspended grit as well as they could and deposited it in crusty trails running down our cheeks, and it was time to do it all over again.

And they kept coming that summer, the days, each new one a carbon copy of the last, and we discovered as each ended that our endurance had frontiers we had not so far imagined. The old-timers said to me, we might as well be in Hell as here, now; I don't know what made Grandpappy move here in '92, and I surely don't know why in tarnation I'm still sticking around.

Sometimes we would drive to one of the nearby state parks, where there was sometimes some water we could get into, although even this was likely to be as warm as and nearly as sticky-feeling as saliva. At least when we got out of it, since the air was so dry, there was a brief cooling respite while it evaporated. On the way to some of the parks, the road passed over high moraines of hills; we could see for many miles down into and across the valleys. On clear, still days we could stop our cars at the top of one of these ridges, look in either direction, and watch the few cars stirring up plumes of dust as they whipped along the long straight gravel roads.

The heat, oppressive enough when we were out of town, was intensified in the city as it was reflected from the sticky blacktop streets; seen through the scorching air, far-off objects near the ground took on an impression of fluidity, as their images undulated in the heat waves. Breathing and blinking and licking our lips in the hot, waterless air parched our nasal passages, and drained the sap from our eyes and mouths. Our eyes became streaked with red tracery, and we could feel the overheated blood pounding at our temples. We tried to keep our breathing shallow; taking a deep breath seemed to put too great a strain on the lungs and the heart, and made us feel dizzy and faint. It was the summer of record-breaking attendance at the movies, the only places that had effective air conditioning. All the cinemas had to do was hang up a banner that read "20o cooler inside," and it wouldn't matter what was playing, it could have been "Santa Claus Conquers the Martians," and we would flock to the flicks for a couple of hours of respite.

It was the summer of great and constant winds, but when a wind blew, rather than providing relief, it was as if someone had opened the door to an incinerator; the heat crackled as it impinged on us and made our skins feel as if they were about to scale off, blow away, and leave the denuded flesh to bake to gristle in the sun. Our hair, too, changed under the barrage of the wind and the dust, becoming as brittle, bleached, and lifeless as stems of dead grass. When washed, it stuck out in all directions as if it had been charged by a Van de Graff generator; only when liberal applications of grease were applied did it submit, and then only for as long as the sun could boil off or the wind evaporate away whatever we smeared or sprayed up there.

At its strongest, the wind did not so much howl as hiss, the sound of gritty, stinging particles being driven against objects, including us. We tried to protect our eyes by any possible means; handkerchiefs, shirt sleeves, newspapers, even hats. To walk along the streets of the city in an episode of one of these sizzling winds was to walk among the blind, as pedestrians temporarily ducked away from the fusillades, men clutching their lapels to their pinched faces, women trying to hold their skirts in a seemly position and also to protect their faces at the same time, an ultimately unachievable undertaking.

The wind also stirred up a hazy yellow dust from the surrounding hillsides; this less-noticeable intruder penetrated all the cracks in our homes and settled in a grimy film that destroyed the shine on glassware and tabletops, and gathered in little drifts in all the corners. The sun, filtering through that suspended dust, gave off a smoky, poisoned yellow light, more or less the color and texture of a poached egg yolk. Outdoors, the acrid smell and taste of the dust filled everyone's lungs, especially after a fitful shower, which seemed to release trapped, volatile acids from the pores of the soil. On especially turbulent days, fine dust would settle in our eyebrows; it filled the pores of our skins so that we never felt clean. If we wiped our faces with handkerchiefs, the white cloth would stain yellow.

Ponds that had formed in the spring rains dried up in that summer of dust, their mud forming a powdery crust that crumbled into a checkerboard pattern of irregular concave scales. These bygone ponds were also a source of fine dust, as the wind scoured and lifted their sediments into the air. The dust seemed to have a toxic effect on plants; after standing for weeks coated with a film of brownish-yellow powder, unwashed by rain, the leaves of trees would decide "wait till next year," become chlorotic, and shower to the ground in a freak early autumn display. Annual plants, if not watered regularly, buckled and lay at full length, stunned, moribund but clinging to life out of habit, like terminally ill relatives. We knew we were in for grave trouble when even poison ivy began to wilt. One old-timer said to me, it sure has been dry; I just seen two trees a-fightin' over a dog.

Not even the cicadas were ever quite free of dust, although they never completely lost their metallic sheen. In addition, the cicadas seemed to be synthesized by heat, like miniature dragons or phoenixes; the warmer the days became, the more abundant the locusts seemed. On the hottest days, they were apparently too dog-tired to fly, and mostly remained stationary, but occasionally we would see one walking, lurching comically along on what seemed like tiptoe, apparently trying to raise its body away from the blistering pavement.

DEGREES OF FREEDOM

That summer, we never got used to seeing those huge green clumsy creatures fluttering toward and past us, with glossy red billiard-ball eyes staring at nothing. Like tiny wind-up buzz bombs, they hurtled from their hiding places in the short grass and, after bouncing off unsuitable impediments like our bodies, came to rest on flat, conspicuous perches, usually vertical, where they launched into their vocalizations. There were not many trees in the city -- mostly a few old cottonwoods and box elders near the river -- but those were highly desirable resting places for the cicadas and became covered with them. Walls, fence posts, tree trunks, screen doors, every artificial and natural vertical barrier also displayed them, as well as bisected, desiccated pupal skins where the adults had emerged in the dead of night, and were now screaming into the teeth of the wind. I saw one of the pupal skins on the rear tire of my car; lucky creature, that I did not decide to drive off somewhere in the middle of the night as it was straining to burst into adulthood. And to drive over their living bodies or their corpses on the slickened streets in our cars or (worse) our bicycles was deeply disquieting; we continually heard and felt the unsettling whisper of the tires, reminding us of thousands of tiny deaths, lives crushed out without qualms or laments from anyone.

Some, even some old-timers, professed not to notice the cicadas or their sounds. To me, this was unbelievable. It was like being unaware of a thousand gnats covering your face, unaware of the outcome of an explosion which has just blasted a hole in the pavement ahead of where you are walking.

I am an ecologist. I couldn't stop thinking about the cicadas and how they could support such huge populations. I am not an entomologist and I didn't know the details of their life-cycles. I guessed that the insects I was hearing were the adults, perhaps only emerging to mate, lay their eggs, and die. Perhaps in their frenzy to breed, they didn't eat at all. How many of them were doomed to die without breeding? Did something eat them? I never saw a bird or squirrel or mouse go after one. Were they just so unpalatable, like monarch butterflies, that any animal fool enough to bite one turned away, in disgust, vowing "never again?" Or was it just that there were so many, emerging at once, that they overwhelmed everything that might eat them?

My colleague Ellen Gould told me about a parasitic wasp, a predator on the cicada. The adult female laid its eggs inside the larva of the cicada, and when they hatched they would eat their way out of the body from inside, leaving a shell, but a still-living shell, at least for a while. There clearly hadn't been enough of those wasps to control this year's population of cicadas, anyway.

I continued to try to think about what it must be like for a bird, for example, to try to eat the adult insects. It was unsettling to contemplate; as Thomas Merton had said,

> "And who shall dare to look when all the birds with golden beaks
> Stab at the blue eyes of the murdered saints?"

Needless to say, since I harbor such sentimental notions, I am almost certainly not a very successful ecologist. In the eyes of my professional cohorts, I ought to be able to take a cold look at death and the needs of the world ecosystem to turn over carbon in order to function. All of us animals and plants are just about ready to die and immediately become part of the required nutrient input for degraders, those ugly but essential species that gnaw, tear, shred and ingest dead things, be they leaves or lizards or people. As I once told Dean Pfaff, we are all members of the class of incipient detritus. So if I know this intellectually, why is it so hard for me to accept the fact of my own imminent dissolution, and those of my family and friends, and even to feel distress over the inevitable fate of the cicada population? Obviously, I lack the potential for success in my trade.

Maybe just being on the staff of Cimarron State College and having stayed here for eight years precludes thinking about success in one's chosen profession. I suppose Cimarron State is a sort of purgatory of academia, a place where scholars with insufficient talent or drive or balls to make a go of it at the bigger schools wind up. Or perhaps it is more like a sort of settling basin where those with inadequate kinetic energy finally drop out into a pool with others of similar thermodynamic histories.

No, I certainly do not exclude myself from my comments. At one time I had ambitions, as God is my judge I did, but now I feel the same enervating chronic disease of the spirit that affects most of my colleagues; I feel it creeping coldly up my loins, as Socrates felt the approach of death after he had drunk the hemlock. We old-time faculty members greet each other cheerfully enough in the halls, but our eyes and our spirits are numb. We bustle about with our meetings, our seminars, and our classes, but it is all a sham to cozen outsiders. We do not need to address this issue among ourselves; it is an affliction we live with without needing to mention, as lepers do in their colonies. We have given up and are only putting in our hours, loiterers biding our time until someone finds us out; or until we retire, cackling and drooling, to the old-timer colony in Arizona; whichever comes first.

At times, I feel our institution is doomed, and at some time in the not too far future the wrath of the state shall rise up, and the fury of that great beast, the people, shall be revealed, and the whole campus shall be plunged into darkness at one stroke of the governor's pen, and there shall be an orgy of blame (faculty, administration, and students all calumniating each other), and a weeping and a gnashing of teeth shall be heard among the merchant classes of the city, and wild beasts and birds, entering through the broken glass of the windows and doors, will colonize these deserted halls. And finally will come the time of the great flames and explosions, as the former campus falls into the hands of warring bands of savages, and the desks and the chairs and the very books in the library will be consumed to ashes.

At any rate, for the moment, matters are still outwardly calm. I am still (family, genus, and species respectively) an educator; a professional biologist; and a member of that still-unusual class of ecologists who like to think about Nature as an abstract set of overlapping grids, square randomly-chosen plots if you will, obeying mathematical rules and subject to reductionism. In this role, my professional wants and pleasures are few. I admire the cold precision of tables of numbers printed on glossy paper; the look of a graph in a peer-reviewed journal, with a nicely fit straight line and close-set error bars, can evoke a sort of bliss in me. I love the sound and the feel of peeling a crisp new issue of such a journal out of its brown paper sleeve with my name and title printed in block capitals on the mailing label, and I love the smell of its fresh unweathered ink and the feel of opening my new copy for the first time and running my hands over its cool shiny pages. I love data; I adore the designing of experiments to collect data, and I crave the mathematical analysis of data. I love computers. I am not ashamed of these tendencies in the least. I hate many things, though, and for these hates, if I am to call myself a biologist, I feel some embarrassment. I hate death, such as the endless deaths of the cicadas, and the rapacity of predation, and the cold commingling of genetic material by mindless, animal sex, (though I do not hate the sociology and physiology associated with human sexuality, don't get me wrong) and the mechanical greed of organisms for energy (the demeaning, continual wheezing and gulping required of us all by the universal energy-yielding metabolic cycles of oxidative phosphorylation and respiration, and the filthiness and sloppiness of ingestion and defecation).

I suppose the unusual combination of these qualities was part of the reason Dean Pfaff and his august search committee hired me in the first place, even when I didn't get a chance to snow them and the rest of the staff with my carefully prepared seminar full of matrices and differential equations. A year or two later, after a couple of whiskies too many, the Dean told me he'd never seen a life scientist who spent so little time on living things. Hardly a fair statement, even then, but I wasn't in the mood to argue with him. He admitted that he hadn't understood anything about the details of my research, but he still recommended that I be hired because he thought I would bring some **rigor** to the department. Rigor, or rigor mortis? I wanted to reply, but I hadn't drunk sufficient brandy to ask.

Although I am not sure what role the rest of the academic staff had in my joining their number, I think most of them were glad I had come. It took the onus off them and their more traditional approaches to biology, which could then continue without them having to go through the pain of having to learn anything new. However, for me, as a new faculty member just being provisionally admitted to full membership in the hierarchy, I had to suffer through exposure to new types of ignorance I didn't even know I had. I suppose it was a type of hazing, more subtle than having red pepper sauce smeared in one's pubic hair by one's fraternity brothers, but no less demeaning in some cases.

All my cohorts were only too eager to expose the gaps in my knowledge, especially when they were able to fill them.

For example, my friend and colleague, Professor Pyke McKenna, would have had an explanation about the cicadas. The full explanation. He wouldn't be overbearing about sharing it with me; he wouldn't have exposed my ignorance in public, the way many of the others did; but neither would he have stopped until he gave me the full benefit of his encyclopedic knowledge. He would feel that it was a professional duty to enlighten me, a novice, and to pass on his hard-won wisdom to me. Thus could a simple question to Pyke McKenna become a two-hour discussion with ramifications ranging from genetics to cytology to behavioral science. You could look up the story later, if you should have any doubts, but it would have been all there, right down the line. There might even have been information you couldn't find in any book or journal article.

Pyke was unique; he had a way of seeing nature and understanding it directly; seeing what was important and true, and ignoring what was anthropocentric or sentimental; and although he would talk to us, his immediate colleagues, at great length, he didn't often feel the need to write anything down for the rest of the world, the scholarly world far beyond our provincial borders. I think his approach would have been, "I found it out just by looking, and you can do the same. If you don't have sufficient insight to see, then I can't really help you."

Pyke was no ecologist, at least he denied being one, although he had done some early ecological research during the war; but he seemed to think ecologically. By that I mean that when confronted by a question, he would take the time for it to sift through all the categories of his knowledge, until it came to rest in not one, but several of them in an interlocking fashion, and only then did he analyze the problem and offer an answer. Of course, for him, this could be a nearly instantaneous process, so perhaps it would be more accurate to say that he thought like a stroke of lightning that hits several things at once. Or maybe the sectors of his memory, the ecosystem of his brain, had become linked together in some different way than they are for the rest of us, so that by pulling on one corner of the net of his intellect, he could shake loose what he needed from a distant section.

As should be obvious, such metaphors are grievously imperfect, and I freely admit I don't know quite how to get Pyke's character across to those who never knew him; but he was so important in my life and in my spiritual development that I have been driven to write this memoir. I am going to try to get across something of what he was like; I have assembled some taped interviews with people who knew him, a few letters from and about Pyke, some of his taped lectures, and manuscripts I found in Pyke's desk and files after he died. I'll try to put these together in some sensible order. I know it won't be enough, but it's important for me to try.

Let me introduce myself first; I hope it won't take too long. My name is Bruce Francis Cahill, and I happen to be a short (5'8", 155 lbs), blond crew-cut, serious-looking man of 35. I was born in Valparaiso, Indiana, on March 4, 1937. I wear heavy black-rimmed glasses, the kind that Dave Brubeck started wearing in the early 50s and that I immediately adopted. Dave doesn't wear them anymore, but I still do, and I still think they look as cool as they did then, although it is harder and harder to find a pair now. My taste in clothes runs to the conservative, what they used to call Ivy League, chinos, button-down shirts with short collars, penny loafers. The peacock revolution has passed me by. I have taken to wearing tweed and corduroy sport coats in various shades of brown with the above wardrobe. This makes me look like what I perhaps am, a middle-aged professional trying to recapture my fading youth.

I enjoy singing, swimming, jazz music, gardening, and teaching Sunday school at the Methodist Church. I was a married man until recently, but now I am legally divorced; in many ways, I feel guilty about it, wondering if there might have been a way to salvage things, but my wife has already moved back to Indiana, to the town where her family lives, Ft. Wayne. We didn't have any children, which is a blessing, I suppose.

In high school and college I was the kind of guy who was usually a class officer, president of the science club and the honor society, list of activities as long as your arm in the school annual, voted most likely to succeed. Succeed. What do high school seniors know about success? What happens to all those voted that honor by their peers? If I am in any way typical, God help the rest of them.

I met Pyke McKenna eight years ago (in 1964, the year of the cicadas), when I came to the campus of Cimarron State College for a job in the department of biology. I was a fresh Ph.D. at the time, coming out of the ecology program at Michigan State. I wasn't really sure what I wanted to do with my life (I still had the romantic and adolescent notion that life was mine to shape as I saw fit); I knew that I was never going to get rich (there were no ecologists in private industry in those pre-Earth Day days, and none of those in government, then, earned a decent wage). So that left academia, unless I wanted to become a postdoctoral fellow and subsume my individuality for a year or two to some big star at Cornell or Caltech, and postpone my decision until then. That would also have been the best way to get a faculty job at a prestige school, but I had come from a small-college atmosphere as an undergraduate, in a Lutheran college in a northern Indiana town, so when my thesis adviser at Michigan State told me in a sort of offhand way that there was a job open at Cimarron, I went for it.

I called Dean Pfaff that very day, within minutes after Jim had mentioned the job to me, and he invited me to come as soon as possible for an interview. On the phone, he sounded like a friendly sort of guy, with a slow southwestern accent, and didn't seem pretentious or sanctimonious at all. I was so eager I didn't even try to make airline reservations (the dean hadn't mentioned anything about reimbursement of travel expenses), but just hopped in my antique Rambler American before daybreak the next morning, along with Viola Henderson Cahill, my bride of six months, (ah, wonderful times, when one could do such impulsive things, not worrying about the obligations of tomorrow, the next day, and forever); and we drove that day all the way from the cherry orchards and quaking bogs of central Michigan, across the wheat, corn, and soybean fields of Illinois and Iowa, and then across the tall grass prairies, what was left of them; and past the High Plains Museum, General Store, and Amusement Park (where we stopped for a late lunch; the place was sixteen acres of kitsch; I remember especially a ten-foot-square American flag, made entirely out of Indian arrowheads); there we saw our first magpie, that piebald harbinger of the West.

Somewhere along our journey, about here, we noticed (I think Viola noticed it first) how the sky became more and more dominant in the landscape. Towns and cities, even isolated buildings, were no longer commonplace events but something to be noted. The population of trees began to drop, and even the shrubs and grass thinned out. Thus, the number of obstacles between us and the horizon decreased greatly. Man-made objects also appeared further from the edge of the highway, and the occasional distant farmhouse and windmill began to take on aspects of model-railroad accessories, to become incongruous interlopers into a pure, mineral landscape of sandpaper earth and sapphire sky.

And as we continued our journey across the ever-changing natural backdrop, the human intrusions seemed to compensate for their infrequency by taking on a new ferocity; we drove past the World's Largest Prairie Dog (a yellow-fanged, thirty-foot-tall plaster monstrosity, with protruding wires, and badly in need of a paint job); and past the oil fields in the central part of the state, with their pump jacks a few hundred feet apart, nodding endlessly like a mechanized display of prehistoric birds -- and through the acidic, mephitic stench that had been forced up by them out of the bowels of the earth; and past the state penitentiary, a formless granite bastion the color of excrement, with a fence sign warning us not to pick up hitchhikers, who might be escaped inmates. But despite this, Nature kept interpolating occasional breathtaking intimations of her ultimate sovereignty, most conspicuously by bestowing upon the landscape sweeping pure stands of sunflowers, imperceptibly and uniformly pivoting away from us throughout the afternoon to point their incandescent faces westward into a sunset the color of blood.

Finally, toward evening, we reached those rolling hills covered with short, gray-green grasses, the foothills of the Rockies, and suddenly, there it was, Pawnee Springs, the home of Cimarron State.

We were in the middle of April. The weather was cool and dry (although there had been spring rains), and the air was crisp and pure. On the horizon, fringing the sunset, was the scarcely discernible deep violet of a range of distant high peaks. It had been a typically miserable and wet early spring in East Lansing, and the contrast was refreshing. I rolled down my window as we coasted into the outskirts of town from the east, and I distinctly smelled the perfumes of sagebrush, although I thought we were still a few hundred miles from that biome. That smell, as much as anything, began my seduction, the development of a love-at-first-sight for the vicinity; much of it has stayed with me for these eight years.

We stayed in one of those old-fashioned motels, the Moonglow Motor Court, on the east side of the city, one of those with the separate cottages. For some reason, we opted against staying in the Wigwam Lodge, just a few blocks down the street, which advertised "Sleep in a Tepee Tonight," and featured whitewashed, conical reinforced concrete cabins in red, white, and blue. I think we were put off by seeing the words "Braves" and "Squaws" on the two tepees nearest the road.

Our cottage at the Moonglow may not have been noticeably better. We shall never know, since the Wigwam was bulldozed in '68 to make room for a bank branch. Our Moonglow room had a ceiling fan, which I started up but stopped, two minutes later, when it started to squeal uncontrollably. The musty smell in the room (it seemed as though it hadn't been occupied for years) hadn't been markedly affected by the fan, in any case. Viola and I, despite being tired out by our fourteen-and-a-half-hour drive, made love between the gritty sheets when we first arrived; then, after about an hour's nap, we went out for a hamburger.

We ate at a picturesque, working-class establishment, covered inside and out with posters and neon signs for all known brands of tobacco products and soft drinks, called "Lloyd`s and His Mom's." A young gentleman, very possibly Lloyd, with a pack of Camels stuck in his rolled-up T-shirt sleeve, brought us our meal on a cork tray, giving us a flourish, a bow, a wink, and a big smile. At the Safeway next door, I bought two quarts of Schlitz, expecting to continue our debauch at the motel, but Viola went to sleep after one plastic tumblerful. I was too nervous to sleep, even after consuming all of the rest of the beer, which I finished at about two a.m.

I set the alarm for seven, and also left a wake-up call for the same time. I was leaving nothing to chance. Unfortunately, I forgot to push the alarm button on the clock, and the wake-up call never came. It didn't matter, though, because I couldn't sleep and was out of bed at six; I turned on the TV and watched first a syndicated country music show and then, at 6:30, a local farm program which told me, with graphic details, how to prevent mastitis in my cattle. During a singing commercial for urea nitrogen fertilizer, I also stepped outside for a moment, in just my pajama bottoms, to watch the sun rising over the highway; the truckers were not out on the road yet, and the only sound was the distant barking of farm dogs and the exultant crowing of young roosters. Viola slept through most of my wakefulness, though she moaned and muttered once in a while.

After brushing my teeth into the cracked, salmon-colored sink, I put on my best and only suit, a white button-down shirt, and a narrow wool tie in an Argyle print that my mother and father had given me for high school graduation. I think this was the second time I had worn it since. I took my leave of my bride, kissing her delicately on the forehead without waking her, and stepped out into the prairie morning, a glorious festival of rosy light; a thin rim of violet-pink clouds shaded to russet at the horizon, where a sun (still the color of blood) had just risen.

I drove over to the campus long before any sensible academics had arrived; it was easy to find, just off the main highway, a long curving arc of a street going up to the unmistakable red brick buildings at the top of a hill. Of course, there was the inevitable bell tower, with its inevitable clock, perpetually showing the wrong time, donated by the class of 1941. In fact, in place of numbers on the dial, the clock had the letters and numbers, CLASS OF 1941, going around the face clockwise, with a dot at the 12:00 position to take the place of the missing letter. Actually, the first "1" in 1941 was gone, having fallen off sometime in the past (it has still not been replaced), and as a consequence the clock gave the fleeting impression that the college dated back to the days of Erik the Red.

I drove up the hill and explored the small campus. The biology building was smaller than I expected, a squat two-story structure in mud-colored brick, announced by a mud-gray sign; MURCHISON HALL, and in smaller letters underneath, DEPARTMENT OF BIOLOGY. The structure was dwarfed by a huge adjacent parking lot, which also appeared to serve the fieldhouse (whose presence was announced by a two-story-high illuminated sign with changeable letters; the sign announced that the finals of the state Class AAA basketball tournament had been held there March 26-28.) Mine was the first car to enter the entire lot that morning. As I pulled up into a metered parking space with the word VISITOR stenciled on the asphalt, I noticed a faded grafitto on the wall of the building in red spray paint: the single word FEAR.

I looked up at the wall in front of me, with its row of identical and equally spaced darkened windows, topped by rusticated stone arches, and wondered what human dramas had taken place behind them -- what storms of passion, what delights, and what moments of insight those shuttered casements had concealed.

I sat in the car for nearly an hour, reviewing my presentation package, rehearsing my exposition of myself, imagining questions I would be asked and the best way to answer them. Also, I was waiting for a respectable number of employees to arrive. The first did not arrive until more than forty minutes had passed, but thereafter they started showing up in small bunches, at more or less regular intervals. As each went into the building, I amused myself trying to place them in their jobs; this one, in boots and green coveralls, carrying a black steel lunchbox, was no doubt a janitor; that one, a frowsy middle-aged woman in butterfly glasses, carrying a canvas bag decorated with raffia gladioli, was clearly a secretary; and that large gentleman in coat and tie, carrying a full briefcase, he must have been the Dean. Finally, I could put it off no longer, and walked through the front door.

Even if I would not have known this was the biology building before, it would have become immediately obvious that instant, because of the smell of formaldehyde, the faint sting in my nostrils that I knew so well from too many years of class work with preserved biological specimens. The building was rather gloomy, with only a few bare bulbs dangling into the narrow hallways. The floor was of worn linoleum in a dark green and brown diamond pattern, and the walls were of beige stucco broken at intervals by unwieldy walnut-varnished wooden pilasters in a Corinthian column design. All of the room doors were closed, and each had a frosted glass panel with a number and a designation tidily lettered in its upper center, delineating its exact function; CLASS ROOM, STOREROOM, SHOP, CUSTODIAN'S CLOSET -- I observed them all. After pacing restlessly up and down the halls for about five minutes, I decided I had to make my move and opened the glass-fronted door bearing College insignia and the label ROOM 144 -- DIVISION OFFICE -- DR. J. M. PFAFF, DEAN.

The door creaked loudly and a startled middle-aged man peered up at me over the tops of his half-framed, rimless glasses. He was not the one I had earlier pegged as the Dean; in fact, I had not seen him enter the building at all; perhaps he had been there all night. He cleared his throat and continued to gaze at me over his wire-rimmed Lyndon Johnson spectacles as if he was surprised I'd shown up so soon. I introduced myself, and after an awkward pause, he said "Oh, yes, you're Jim's student." He remained behind his desk, not getting up to shake my hand. He looked at his watch and asked me to sit in his outer office while he took care of a few matters. As I closed the door, I noticed a directive, in tiny print painted at the bottom of the glass, that I should have entered the office through Room 142. Great start, I muttered to myself.

I sat watching Miss Freemartin, his secretary, type virtually nonstop for at least half an hour (yes, I was at least partially vindicated, she was the one with the gladioli-bedecked handbag). She was terribly efficient, rigid in her straight-backed chair; staring at her text, moving her lips almost imperceptibly, and making the keyboard chatter in an unchanging rhythm. She'd only stop once in a while to offer me coffee or some Danish cookies, but I was really too nervous and hung over to eat or drink. She looked quite disappointed that I wouldn't accept her hospitalities, but returned at once to her clerical tasks.

Finally, Dean Pfaff emerged, smiling broadly and shaking my hand robustly, as if the other Dean, the first one I had seen, had been someone entirely different, someone whose job description did not include working with people at all and proscribed the expression of any form of hospitality. His smile, however, seemed to me just a little bit too false and hail-fellow, exposing his long horsy teeth. He asked me to step inside and sit down, and then asked

Miss Freemartin to hold his calls, although to tell the truth I had not heard the phone ring while I was waiting.

The office was smaller than I expected, but sunny, with a bay window and maroon velvet curtains held open by gold fabric cords. I perched on the edge of a straight-backed wooden chair in front of his huge teak desk, while he sat in a massive leather recliner on wheels, leaning forward, squeaking his chair rhythmically, humming quietly, reading the letter I had brought, with my curriculum vitae on the second page. He appeared to be poring over this section of the letter, reading it over and over again, as though he could not quite believe or not quite understand what was printed there. His glasses slid quite regularly down his long nose, and he replaced them in their original position by grasping both earpieces in his hands and jiggling them backwards. Occasionally, he stopped to rub his ear, close one eye, and scowl, all at the same time.

Finally, after a minute or two, he put the vita down, smiled at me again, and asked, "So you're a Michigan man, eh?" I assured him that I was, although I had been born just across the border in Indiana. He nodded and put his hands together, fingertip to fingertip, steeple-fashion, under his chin. After a long pause in this position, he asked me if I knew Ralph Tyler, the pioneer plant ecologist who had worked in the Amazon in the twenties and early thirties. I responded that he had come to the MSU campus for a lecture in my first year in graduate school, but since he was on the faculty at the University of Michigan in Ann Arbor, I hadn't had any real contact with him. He asked me whether I had finished my dissertation; I indeed had, and my final examination was scheduled for the middle of May. And what were my plans for publication? My adviser, Professor Watford, was considering a paper in Ecological Monographs, I said, in which my thesis would only be changed slightly. He felt, I told the Dean, that my work on the altitudinal variability of sedges in the northern Rocky Mountains was a pioneering attempt to apply mathematical techniques to population biology. I was one of the first to use matrix algebraic concepts to examine large populations of a single widespread species.

I did not tell the Dean that, in fact, Jim Watford had fought my ideas every step of the way since I became mature enough as a graduate student to argue with him, but toward the end he was grudgingly convinced that my data probably deserved to be published. All that he asked me to do was to publish the paper under my own name; he said he never wanted to be associated with the direction my work had turned, and would never put another graduate student to work on the topic. As far as he was concerned, I could have the field to myself. As for me, the long arguments I'd had with him, together with the thought of those endless field notebooks filled with laboriously gathered data on those scratchy, stringy plants -- their heights, aboveground dry weights, root dry weights, numbers of seeds in the heads, distance to the next nearest sedge, chlorophyll, protein, carbohydrate, silica concentrations -- that I had to put together again and again in different ratios to try to make something significant fall out, had turned me away from research. The thought of returning to those northern Idaho mountains, as beautiful as they were, and struggling with mosquitoes, biting flies, logging roads, and drunken California campers, likewise made me shiver somewhere deep inside.

Anyway, all the Dean did was nod. I told him that I had presented my data at the annual symposium on arctic and alpine research held in Golden, Colorado, last September, and had spent most of the rest of the time until now putting my dissertation together (and, I might have mentioned, waiting for Jim to read it). I was prepared to give a seminar to the department, I said; I had brought my slides.

He paused after I said that, muttered something noncommittal, and then asked me about my teaching experience. Here, I thought, I was on solid ground, since I had been a teaching assistant for the second semester of every year (spending most of the rest of the year in the field), and had taught general biology, plant systematics, plant ecology, and statistics. I had taught in large classrooms, in small discussion sections for the bigger classes, in the laboratory, and I had given seminars on mathematical biology in the new-graduate-student introductory course. I told him that I enjoyed teaching, which was true enough, but that I wasn't sure how I would handle very heavy teaching loads. To that, he responded with a slow smile and said that I would find that out soon enough.

Then, he tapped the bottom of my letter sharply on the desk top with both hands, stood up, and said there were some people he'd like me to talk to. He asked me to wait in the outer office while he made a few more calls, so it was back to Miss Freemartin's care again. She was no longer typing, but was painstakingly cutting file-folder labels out of strips of different colored papers, smearing glue on them, and affixing them in place on the tabs. She was humming quietly, something classical-sounding, and she only looked up briefly from her absorbing task to flash me a toothy smile. After a minute or two, I finally accepted some of her coffee out of politeness. It was strong, bitter stuff that probably would have given me quite a buzz, but before I could take more than a few sips the Dean was bounding out of his office and asking me to come with him.

With a stride that suggested a man trying to keep up with a trotting horse, he walked me around the building, knocking on office doors and introducing me to everyone who happened to be in; he stopped students and non-academic staff in the hallway and introduced me. I must have gone through the same set of pleasantries with twenty-five people.

One description will suffice to give the flavor of these encounters. The Dean stopped a stumpy woman of about sixty-five, wearing sensible shoes, an indigo dress, and plastic pearls, and introduced us. "Dr. Bamberger," he said, "I'd like you to meet Dr. Bruce Cahill from Michigan. Dr. Cahill, this is Dr. Hattie Bamberger, who is one of our long-time teachers; in fact, she's retiring next year, which is one of the reasons we will have an open position. Dr. Cahill (he said to Dr. Bamberger) is looking for a job in our department." She looked up at me with a quizzical smile that exposed only her upper teeth. "How wonderful to meet you," she said in a wheezy voice (as I wondered what it was about me that was so wonderful), "I am sure that you know well my dear old friend Ralph Tyler." Before I could explain, she continued, "This is a very interesting institution. I have taught here for nearly thirty-five years. My specialty is the blue-green algae, an extraordinary group of organisms. I try to find some time every day to look through the microscope at them. I have described nearly eighty species, most of them in my younger days, but I still love to observe even the commoner specimens; I feel almost as though they are my old friends, that I know them on a first-name basis. My colleagues sometimes laugh at me when I talk to the algae, saying things such as 'Why, Anabaena flos-aquae, what are you doing in this temporary pond?' but I have learned to ignore their laughter. Well, young man, it has been wonderful to have met you, but I must hurry to prepare for a laboratory class. I wish you luck in your job-hunting." And she was off, thumping down the hall at a surprising pace, and disappearing around the corner.

The encounters continued like that, one after another, impromptu meetings of three minutes or less in duration. I doubt that anyone at all had known that I was coming. How could they? The Dean was the only one I'd spoken to and obviously I hadn't given him clear travel plans. Here I was and they had to do something with me. It must have been embarrassing for them; it certainly was for me. My jaw was starting to hurt from the constant smiling. I started to shake hands with people I'd already met.

These whirlwind talks must have consumed about an hour and a half. Finally, the Dean handed me over to Jack Dombrowski, a slender, bald, fiftyish entomologist with thick glasses and a perpetual half-smile, and asked him to take me to lunch. I was to report back at one sharp for a "final interview" with the Dean. I asked him again about a seminar on my research, but he told me that due to an important faculty meeting at 3, it would not be possible to schedule me for one.

Hearing this, I was devastated. I thought that surely I had done something extremely stupid. Why was I getting this bum's rush? Why not just tell me straight out I wasn't the man for the job? How could I have been so bone dumb as just to rush down from East Lansing without making definite plans? I must have seemed a real oaf to barge in as I had done.

At least I could make lunch enjoyable. Since it was just Jack and me, we decided to go to a working-class Mexican restaurant off campus. He drove me over in his old black Ford pickup, probably about 1950 vintage. I noticed that the original gearshift knob had been replaced by a huge black rubber stopper. I shoved collecting nets, killing jars, buckets, and beer cartons aside to make room for myself. The usual interviewee, I learned, was taken to the seedily genteel Faculty Club, a place with overpriced sandwiches and oversalted soups and no liquor until 7 p.m. At least this way we could get a couple of Carta Blancas.

We drove about three blocks off Kearney Street, the main east-west thoroughfare through the city, into a district of low warehouses and concrete-block buildings. This older section of town had a certain gaslight ambiance, with Belgian block streets and green-painted wrought iron street lamps with Tiffany leaf motifs. Tired-looking, greyish men, leaning in shop doorways, craned their necks to watch us as we drove slowly past. The restaurant, called "El Campesino," was in a stucco building the color of adobe; it was small, dimly lit, and smoky. The few other customers appeared to be American Indians. A jukebox played country music at a low volume. Jack spoke Spanish to the waitress. I let him order for me; Mexican food was virtually an unknown quantity for me at that time in my life.

After clicking our beer glasses together in a toast, we talked briefly about Jack's work; he was a specialist in cockroaches, and spent three months every year at a national park in Panama. "It's not much to write home about as far as the rugged accommodations, the malaria, and the celibacy are concerned," he said, "but it's a paradise for a natural historian, particularly one interested in insects." He collected quite large numbers of the more abundant species and brought them back (he must have created a sensation at Customs) to his laboratory at Cimarron, where he studied their growth and reproduction as it was affected by various dietary and temperature regimes.

Finally, in a break in our conversation, I decided it was time to cut the crap with Jack. I told him I didn't think I was having a very successful interview; the Dean was practically ignoring me and I hadn't had a chance to discuss anything professional with anyone before our discussion here. Jack was surprised I felt that way; he got the impression I was doing well. Was this my first interview trip? "You'll learn," he said, "that you can never read the minds of people who are taking stock of you. The Dean is actually quite a shy person; he doesn't move in the circles you do. We actually don't get many active researchers, such as yourself, to stop in here; most of them fly overhead, without even looking down; we're just a sip of a cocktail on the way from St Louis to Denver. We're more than a little ways, I'm afraid, off the beaten path from

California to New England. Anyway, the Dean doesn't go to professional meetings and present exciting research. He goes to the state academy of science meetings and sits with his old cronies in the bar of the Holiday Inn-Downtown and grouses about the way he's treated by his faculty, by his secretary, by his wife and kids, by the president of the college, by the president of his bank. You are a bright young guy, you're respectful, and you're eager. I think he's already made up his mind, and I think there's a good chance you're in. Speaking for myself, I hope you do decide to come; it's been a long time since we've had anyone around here who might shake us up."

Well, I didn't know if it was the beer talking (he'd had three to my one), and I was pretty skeptical. I was wondering what in hell I was going to do with myself when we got back to East Lansing, since I had no other hot prospects for work and I was going to be an unemployed Ph.D. soon. At least Viola had a good job as an insurance adjuster, so our standard of living would not be significantly affected by the loss of my research assistant's salary; but what was I going to do around the house all day? I decided I would hang around the off-campus bars and watch the Tigers play all summer on television. I'd gain twenty pounds from the beer, but it would be worth it in terms of destructive self-pity. Or maybe I'd have a tempestuous affair with one of my fellow students who was in the same predicament (I had my eye on her; she had a hungry way of smiling at me), even though it was a little early for the seven-year itch. At least I wouldn't gain much weight that way. Or possibly I'd move to Detroit and drive a taxi, hanging my diploma from my rear-view mirror, hoping for sympathy and extra tips from the customers, and maybe a last-page writeup in Life magazine. Ah, the self-abominating reveries of the scorned scholar; there's been nothing like them since the flagellants of the plague years disappeared.

Jack paid the check and we drove back to the campus. We got back late to the Dean's office, and I had to wait once more. Miss Freemartin now had doughnuts, and I took one, although I was stuffed from lunch; I passed on her coffee again, also. It looked like the same stuff I'd seen in the morning, by now well along in the process of brewing itself into an evil black paste. Finally, the Dean called me in and started to talk seriously about the job -- the responsibilities I would have inside and out of the classroom. He warned me that, at least at first, I would have to work harder than I ever had before, and the rewards were likely to be minimal. "Not everyone is cut out for teaching in a small college," he said, "and it's no disgrace to admit it." I think he may have been waiting for me to say that I really wasn't interested, but instead I told him that I thought the challenge of teaching was what I needed in my life, that I was not a stranger to hard work, and I thought I could motivate and excite the students with the special perspective I would bring to the department -- a perspective that, as far as I could tell, would be something brand-new on the campus. And that, really, was the end of the conversation; he smiled, (fairly genuinely, this time, I thought), we shook hands, and he told me I'd be hearing from him as soon as possible.

So I went back to the motel. The whole interview process had lasted about five hours. Viola was lying on the bed in her underwear, reading Newsweek. She stretched and yawned when I came in, arching her back and forcing her breasts and pelvis up against her restraining garments. I reached for her in an embrace, and leaned forward to kiss her and to rub my body against hers, but, still yawning, she put a restraining arm against my lips and body. "Well, Dr. Cahill, my darling hubby," she asked me, "when do you start and what are they going to pay you?" I realized I didn't know the answer to either of those questions. "It doesn't seem like an auspicious beginning for your academic career," she said, and I had to agree with her. I set her back down on the bed, and she turned over and continued to read, bending her knees so that she could desultorily caress my chin with her toes.

We left late that afternoon, getting as far as Rapid City, a strangely misnamed and sleepy town -- at least it was then. In the morning, we drove through the Black Hills and the Badlands, and visited Mount Rushmore, which struck me as a terrible thing to do to a perfectly good mountain. Viola liked it, though, and insisted on paying good money for a souvenir Mount Rushmore brass ashtray, a foot across, with the faces of the presidents projecting in bold relief and against which I assume one was supposed to stub out one's butt. She thought it was a "hilariously funny and typically American" object.

We got back to East Lansing late Friday, and damned if there wasn't a telegram stuck in the door. OFFERING YOU POSITION ASSISTANT

RICHARD LARSON

PROFESSOR BIOLOGY CIMARRON STATE START AUGUST 15 ACADEMIC YEAR SALARY $7500, it said, fifteen words in all, carefully and economically chosen, fifteen words that were to change our lives; and there was even a check for $98, with no further explanation, but which I assume was intended to cover our travel expenses. So now you finally know me as well as you need to and we can move on to the action.

To begin with, Pyke McKenna was not one of those I met that April morning in my non-stop tour of the biology department. It was a little early for him to be around. I am not sure how I would have responded to him. I know he would have skipped the small talk and gone straight to the serious questions; how has your research helped you to be a better scientist? Do you think anything in your life, particularly your graduate education and training, has given you a philosophy of teaching? How are you going to face the overwhelming majority of students at this college who are only here because they or their parents can't think of anything better for them to do? How are you going to handle the transition between the beachhead of thought that is Michigan State University and the backwater that is Cimarron State College?

If I had the chance to think seriously about some of those issues, maybe I would not have come at all; but I did, and I am tremendously glad that Pyke was here to help me out. After I started that August, he was always close to me, both physically (in the next office over) and emotionally, as a friend and mentor. It is hard for me to believe that I knew him for less than six years. Oh, there were times when I thought I hated the man, times when I thought he was using or cruelly mocking me, but there were other times when his insights changed me forever. I think I was good for him, also.

No one else on the staff was really close to Pyke, possibly for good reason. I'm not sure that the typical scholar could stand up to the sort of sustained crossfire attack on cherished beliefs that Pyke was capable of mounting and discharging in your direction. Or maybe it was more like a siege, a continuous sniping away at the weak points of your personality, a repeated dropping of cynical remarks just sharp enough to raise your hackles but never quite insulting enough to make you raise your voice or fists at him.

Anyway, I survived his assaults, learning to surmount his scorn with insolence of my own devising; and now I think like Pyke (I try to, anyway), I write like him, I even blow my nose like he did. His presence still infects, yes, that's the right word, the way I look at things and the way I arrange my life.

Before I turn this memoir over to the words of others, I will give a few biographical details for the man in question. Pyke Gladstone McKenna was his full name, and he was born in 1921 in Pittsburgh.

His father, James Raphael McKenna, was Irish, having left the Republic as a young man just after the Easter rising in 1917; he had been an apprentice printer for the Dublin edition of an English newspaper, a royalist, and a Protestant, and he hated Parnell's followers and everything that was happening in his country. He settled in Pennsylvania, first taking a job as a copy editor on a small farming magazine published in Rittenhouse Square in Philadelphia, of all places; and after a year or two in that job, he married the publisher's daughter, Felicity Kiplinger; and by way of family connections they moved west to Pittsburgh, where he became an executive in a medium-sized steel company.

Their picture from this period shows a handsome couple; Mr. McKenna, seated on the right, looks off to the right of the picture, away from the camera. He smiles shyly. He has a small sandy moustache, his hair is parted rigorously down the exact center of his head, he wears a tiny rose in the lapel of his pin-striped suit; he is holding a cane, just below its duck-shaped handle, at a slight angle from the perpendicular. His legs are spread; he is wearing high-top black button shoes that look surprisingly worn. Mrs. McKenna, leaning slightly forward, looks directly into the lens. She is a slight, dark woman with short hair arranged in ringlets about her face. Her eyes are accentuated with heavy kohl makeup; her mouth is parted as if she is about to say something but has momentarily lost her train of thought. One of her hands is in her lap and the other is touching a strand of pearls at her neckline. There is a large lacy object, perhaps a hat, in her lap. Her legs are pulled back under her chair so that her feet cannot be seen.

Pyke was their firstborn. During the twenties, on the advice of his father-in-law, Pyke's father became very heavily involved in real estate and in the stock market; the crash of 1929 ruined all of them financially, and Pyke's family moved to rural southeastern Ohio where they rented land and raised vegetable crops for cash, kept a few cows and chickens, and essentially kept their family together on a very small income. His father became embittered with his fate, and apparently took increasingly to drink.

His mother, when she was able, took a variety of demeaning jobs, waitressing, small-time assembly-line work, and a little accounting-clerk activity. She had chronic asthma. After the birth of Pyke's younger brother Tom in 1931, she never really recovered her health, and died of pneumonia a year later, when Pyke was 11.

He was a gifted child; his aunt still has more than a hundred annotated drawings of common wild plants and insects from his family's farm and the surrounding woods. She is sure there were at least that many more that he discarded at some stage. He began making them when he was about 9, and must have worked for hours over each one. They are done in black drawing ink, using pens of several widths, on rather large sheets of coarse paper, and are painstakingly detailed; the wing venation of flies and moths is especially carefully rendered. His notes reveal where he found each specimen; in the case of the insects, he records what plants they were found on, whether they were feeding or laying their eggs, and what other insects were in the vicinity. He seems to have stopped doing these drawings at about the time of his mother's death.

Academically gifted, also, he finished high school in 1938, a year early. One of his high school science teachers, a Mr. Renfrew, appears to have encouraged Pyke to pursue a scholarly life as a biologist. Although he is no longer living, I was able to visit with his son, who has kept some of his books and some biological models. He had several very beautiful 19th-century German books on entomology that I am certain Pyke must have seen.

After graduation, Pyke never wanted to go anywhere except Ohio State, and of course he was admitted with no difficulty. He even got a scholarship that paid for most of his expenses, and that was no small feat in those late-depression years. He majored in biology, of course, and moved through the undergraduate curriculum with no particular stress. His transcripts show A's and B's in all his major subjects as well as in his liberal arts courses, and in all his core and required classes except for advanced mathematics, physics, and chemistry where he managed C's.

By the time he graduated, in May 1942, we were at war, and like many other college men he immediately went into the armed services as an officer. He chose the air force, and naturally since he was a life scientist they put him to work managing a motor pool. I really cannot imagine him in this role but apparently he discharged it responsibly. He was mustered out in August 1945, within a day or two of V-J Day, and within a few weeks he was back in Columbus to enter graduate school. Here again, he showed his skill in an academic setting, taking only three years and a few months to finish the Ph.D. The title of his dissertation is "Mineral Requirements of *Salix lucida* Seedlings and Those of Related Species in the Family Salicaceae." Within a few months, he was hired on as an assistant professor at Cimarron State College, and that, as they say, is where our story begins, although I expect we shall need a few flashbacks periodically.

Physically, he was a huge man, about six feet four and weighing about 260 pounds, I would judge. I understand that he had gained a great deal of weight at one time. His face was long and full, with a high forehead from which the fine reddish-brown hair was combed back into an irregular tumulus. His beard was lighter, almost sandy, with blond and grey streaks. He wore it in many different styles, ranging from a neatly trimmed goatee to a disheveled, Ivan-the-Terrible forked design; but he never shaved it off completely. By the time I met him, he was balding, but only at the back of his head.

His hands were large and pale and soft, always in motion and expressive when lecturing or arguing. His eyes were remarkable, clear bluish-grey and changeable in an instant from twinkling and merry to bright and ingenuous to hard and challenging; the brows were thin but energetic. His voice was marvelous, a sensitive, delicate instrument, that of an actor rather than a professor, ranging from almost a purr to a great roaring shout; he had a great command of American regional speech, being particularly devastating when he took on the local prairie patois; and he also had a great laugh that came easily, and when it came it seemed to fill a room.

His wardrobe was eclectic, mostly out of style, probably usually obtained at the Salvation Army and Goodwill. He favored proletarian clothing such as coveralls and foreman's coats with oval name patches on the chest (never with his name), plaid shirts, and steel-toed boots. I doubt if he owned a tie. He had obtained an astonishing assortment of hats and caps, and he especially favored flashy ten-gallon models with feathers or brightly colored ribbons. He even had a Chinese army cap, of heavy green wool with a big red star in front, that he wore when he was feeling militant.

We taught, as I mentioned, at Cimarron State College, in Pawnee Springs, a small city in the western half of a large, nearly rectangular state in the Great Plains. Place names have been changed slightly to protect the innocent. Pawnee Springs has grown somewhat faster than the usual city in our region, and now numbers nearly 40,000 residents; it is now the fifth largest city in the state, and in the 1950 census it wasn't even in the top fifteen. As the triple-A guide says, it is "the educational, cultural, and commercial center for the surrounding rural area," and as the tone of that description implies, it isn't very good at any of these things, but it is all we have.

Pawnee Springs was rather poorly named, since as far as I could determine the Pawnees were located mostly to the east, before they were practically exterminated by the more warlike tribes, such as the Cheyennes and the Comanches. Those of them that survived this fate were further decimated by the white settlers, who introduced liquor and smallpox; and the remainder was moved to a reservation to the south which was completely unsuitable, as it bore no resemblance to their ancestral lands, and rapidly filled up with missionaries. Furthermore, there are not even any springs in the immediate vicinity.

The arid surrounding landscape is made up of rolling hills, constructed of an alkaline soil of a sandy, yellowish-brown character. Occasionally the grassy hills are broken by stretches of rocky cliffs, isolated buttes, box canyons, and escarpments; it is largely treeless except for substantial old cottonwoods growing near the banks of the intermittent creeks, which run in muddy torrents after summer thunderstorms but are normally dry. The principal vegetation is short fuzzy grass, interspersed with tough, spiny plants like cactuses. The countryside is mostly devoted to cattle raising, although some farmers grow winter wheat, sorghum, and alfalfa. Their land is largely irrigated; you can see the rotating sprinklers, mounted on massive tires rolling in endless circles, from the highway as you drive past. From an aircraft, the resultant green circles are striking against the grey-brown background.

Most of the city is in the valley of a sizeable river, which flows vigorously for most of the year but is reduced to a trickle, thanks to irrigation and evapotranspiration, in the late summer; but it hardly counts as a stream, at least within the city limits, because it had been channelized by the Corps of Engineers during the 30s. The basin is solid concrete a foot thick. The roar of that sterile watercourse dominates the whole center of town. It is hateful to any biologist who has ever worked in or loved a body of flowing water.

The first group of residents of our area mostly arrived in the United States between 1865 and 1900, during the great wave of immigration that took place after the Civil War; land was free in our region, too, for a time -- to anyone who would promise to plant ten acres of trees on a quarter-section of land. I see no evidence, however, that any settler actually did this, or if one did, that their trees survived. Somewhat later, the free land offer was withdrawn, but land was still very cheap, and immigrants from Europe and from the eastern United States continued to pour in. The populations of Centerland County (our county) and Muspell County (the next county over to the east) increased by a factor of twenty between 1860 and 1910. The early settlers were principally Germans, although there were also many Scandinavians, Bohemians, and even some French Canadians.

Cimarron State was founded in 1926, when the state legislature, prodded by the legislators and building contractors of the sparsely populated districts in the western counties, decided that the youth of that remote region needed a local campus so that they wouldn't necessarily have to attend the state university, in the more sophisticated eastern half of the state. Data had shown that these youth, when confronted by the huge classes and metropolitan distractions of the capital city, performed quite poorly and had a dismal frequency of graduation. There was also a feeling, rarely enunciated as such, but always present, that the foothills youth became disaffected, irreligious, and difficult to manage following their exposure to the urban culture and somewhat more liberal standards of the flatter eastern city. Yet there was a demonstrable need for educators, dental technicians, management trainees, agricultural extension personnel, and other college-educated individuals for the businesses and schools in the fast-growing west. It was also hoped that the faculty of such an institution would also be drawn from the more conservative stock of educators and scholars of the American South and West; that the setting of the campus would be of little interest to big-city leftists, wine-drinkers, and chamber-music lovers. Thus, the staffing of the new institution was conducted with some discretion; the search committees looked first in their own backyards, among the senior teachers and administrators of the local secondary schools, and also among the elder professoriat (just possibly including some of the dead wood) of the two state universities, particularly that of the smaller, more practically oriented land-grant school in the state's second-largest city. The new college had few Ph.D.'s, but a large complement of Ed.D.'s and many faculty with various master's degrees. Ergo, Cimarron State!

The older buildings of the college occupy an area of perhaps nine city blocks of reclaimed grazing land, on a hilltop at what had been the westernmost edge of town, but naturally the presence of the new institution stimulated growth in its vicinity, and soon it became nearly surrounded by rooming houses, fraternities in art-deco buildings, and one-story brick-framed businesses selling weak beer, insignia shirts, phonograph records, condoms, and fried sandwiches - all the essentials for an educationally-minded community. The campus itself is dominated by a large classroom building in red brick with grey molded concrete details; this is the building with the clock tower. It is universally known as "Old Main," although it had been renamed Mundelein Hall in the fifties, after a wealthy alumnus who had donated $300,000 to repair some defective construction. This had led, among other things, to the collapse of part of the cornice and the near-fatal injury of a fraternity brother who, with his girl friend, had been lying naked under some shrubbery. The girl, who was underneath, suffered only minor bruises. It was never in the paper, but every student and staff member knows the story.

In a large room in the basement of Mundelein Hall is the extraordinary Quincy Bible Collection, bequeathed to the College by its first president,

DEGREES OF FREEDOM

Norman Hardegree Quincy. President Quincy was an indefatigable collector of various editions of the Good Book, as well as a credulous purchaser of Bibles said to belong to the famous. It was fortunate that he possessed independent wealth. Thus, our college was bequeathed Bibles supposed to have been owned by Napoleon Bonaparte (a purported lock of the Emperor's hair, also obtained by Quincy, is also on display adjacent to it), Lincoln, Disraeli (a dubious probability at best), Meriwether Lewis (damaged by water), and Simon Bolivar. Also on display are copies of the Smallest Bible, the Wicked Bible (where the typesetter forgot the *not* in the Seventh Commandment), and a Bible said to be engraved on the heads of 6,636 pins.

There are, of course, other notable structures on our campus, in particular the football stadium, completed in 1929. In essence, it is a pile of red brick, except for a few arbitrary Ionic columns, in native sandstone, shoehorned in somewhere around the middle, and a sandstone inset in high relief depicting a farmer shaking hands with a World War I soldier; "Geek Revival architecture," Pyke McKenna called it. There, most of the students and a good fraction of the townies meet on four afternoons every autumn for home games between our "Bears," in their green and gold uniforms, and their opponents, barbaric rivals from similarly-sized schools in the high plains. I always thought the games were just an excuse to get together for fun and some serious drinking and celebrating afterwards, but Pyke assured me that something much more consequential and elemental was at stake, a sort of fierce totemic rite of manhood in which the rising youth of our home district, suitably armored, could test their mettle in a ritual struggle against mighty strangers with different totem animals.

By the time I joined the staff, in 1964, there had been a phenomenal growth of the student body, from about 1500 in the middle 50s to about 6000. Although we always had a master's degree program in education, in 1958 and 1959 there was also a great expansion of the graduate program, and now practically every department, including ours, had a curriculum in which you could get an advanced degree. We had a surprisingly large graduate enrollment, too, although I could never convince myself that a master's from Cimarron would impress prospective employers greatly.

The faculty had not undergone such a dramatic expansion in numbers, and there was much grumbling about the increase in our teaching loads; but at least our salaries were going up, in general, as the fear of Russian educational and scientific domination was still very much on people's minds. The state board of higher education entertained fewer questions from the floor of the legislature about just what it was these professors were really doing with the handsome salaries the taxpayers were forking over to them; how some of them could get away with working only nine or twelve hours a week, and spend the rest of their time reading magazines in the library. The Russkies were coming, and by God, they had ten, or twenty, times as many engineers and physicists per capita as we did, and we needed hard-nosed hard scientists to keep up with the knowledge gap. Biology, by that time, was considered one of the hard sciences at last, and was no longer a nebulous, fancified cousin of gardening and birdwatching. DNA was on everyone's lips, the key to the mystery of life was now available, and most importantly, there was money in it. The students were pouring into our classes and the instructional units were piling up. It all seemed very exciting.

As the new boy on the teaching faculty, I was of course to be given the heaviest loads, and no one seemed to feel it was anything extraordinary for me to be assigned classes to teach about which I knew nothing whatever. There was, luckily, a sort of general camaraderie about such matters, and those who had taught the course in previous years were usually quite willing to share their lecture notes, and such expertise as they had on the subject. And, in truth, the students seldom seemed to be very critical about the kind of education they were being given; although that did begin to change as the 60s went on.

I now want to introduce the first of many people I was able to interview on the subject of Pyke McKenna. I have done very light editing on these interviews, preferring to let the subjects tell me in their own words how they communicated with him and how he affected them. Thus without more ado:

Millicent

(A tape-recorded interview with a lady who will introduce herself.)

Is it on? Oh, dear, these things make me so nervous. I hope I don't sound too foolish. I suppose I should just start talking; my name is Miss Millicent Freemartin, and I have been the secretary to Dean Pfaff, and to Dean Slye before him, and to a lesser degree to the rest of the Biology Department, for twenty-seven years. I came here from the East, from Virginia, where I was born and raised.

The way it came about was this. A girl friend of mine, whose name was Frieda Thrasher, and I were feeling very adventurous back in '45, with the war over and everyone feeling like a new spirit was sweeping over the country. So we took a vacation from the shipyard in Newport News, where we both worked as stenographers, and set out in her car, an old 1938 Buick. Let me show you a picture of us from those days. Here we are; she's standing by her car. She's the one with the braids. That's me sitting on the running board. I haven't changed a bit, have I? Her mother took this picture of us not long before we left.

We said we were going to drive to California. She was about 25 and I was a little older. We were both single and I have a feeling we were thinking about all the returning servicemen from the Pacific Front, who were descending by the thousands on the west coast. We had been working so hard, putting in extra time every week for the war effort, and had hardly any time for fun; and finally, it was all over and we felt so tremendously relieved and happy, and we were overdue for a fling. I don't think we realized how long a drive it was going to be -- we were supposed to be back in two weeks. And the car just gave us fits, it kept overheating, especially in the mountains of Tennessee which were much more of a challenge to drive through then than they are now. They always seemed to be so full of foggy patches, so that you had to keep driving at no more than twenty or you'd either go over a cliff or run into some farmer driving a mule-drawn wagon, with no lights, from behind. And the switchbacks seemed endless; we just kept twisting the wheel and shifting the gears over and over again, for hours, to get through the things. All we could do was stop when the radiator started to boil and wait for half an hour to let the thing cool down. And once we even ran out of gas up there, and one of us, it turned out to be me, had to walk four miles down the mountain to the nearest station, and I was given a ride back by the mechanic to where our car was, and there was Frieda, surrounded by about five Cherokee Indians, young men, laughing and drinking beer with them. Some people have all the luck.

Eventually, as it turned out, after many adventures and seven days of travel, this was as far as we got. Pawnee Springs, I mean. We pulled in here on a Sunday, around noon, a miserable day with the rain coming down in sheets. My shoes were practically ruined from having to push the car out of a mudhole early that morning. We were both feeling surly, snapping at each other and feeling particularly sorry for ever having undertaken such an unpromising trip in the first place. And, we were running out of money; so, as we sat together over not much of a lunch, she decided to turn back, even though it would mean that she would never get to California and she might be getting back late to her job. It was actually not made entirely clear to us if we'd have our jobs waiting for us, anyway, we only had one week of vacation coming. But we just told the boss, a man named DeWeese, we were leaving for two weeks, and he grumbled and muttered something about us being ungrateful. I didn't really hear exactly what he said, and I think I'm glad I didn't.

DEGREES OF FREEDOM

But I told her I didn't want to head back east with her. I wasn't so ready to give up on my California odyssey, and besides, I thought to myself, I was getting a little tired of her company on this trip. So I told her I'd stay here for the moment, take a temporary job until I had enough money saved to go the rest of the way to California, and then I'd send her a postcard from Hollywood and she could tell me how things were going. So we left the restaurant; at least it had stopped raining, and we walked over to the car and said goodbye, embracing each other and crying just a little, and she turned the car around and headed back out of Pawnee Springs the way we'd come in. And I stood there on the sidewalk, waving and blowing kisses and watching the mud flying in the air as she disappeared. I was feeling a little bit lost and very much alone, and not knowing what in the world was going to happen to me, but knowing I had to find a way to get hold of some money in a hurry.

Well, amazingly, the first job I heard about was this one; from a waitress who worked at the old American Cafe down on Hollister Street. It's been closed now, heavens, it must be over ten years. I suppose the food wasn't really very good but we maybe didn't know much better in those days. The pies were always good, I thought. Her name, the name of the waitress, that is, was Rosanna Papadopolous. She was small, and had a little mustache and hairy arms and a big Middle Eastern nose, altogether very Greek-looking. But of course she was very clean, and so was the restaurant. They were always coming through and spraying for bugs.

I had bought a hamburger and a Coke from her, and she could tell by the way I spoke that I wasn't from around here. It was still unusual in those days to see somebody in Pawnee Springs that you didn't recognize. So we started talking, since she was about my age. Her younger sister Evangelina, as it turned out, had just quit this job in the Biology Department to get married, and they needed someone right away; so the next day I went in and talked to the Dean about it, Dean Slye, that is, a wonderful old man who still dressed in stiff collars and wore a pince-nez. You may have seen his picture in the display case in the east hallway of this building, in there between Professor Murchison's brass German microscopes and the killdeer eggs that Professor Turnbull used to collect. And Professor Grimthorpe's platypus used to be there, too, but it got infested by beetles and we had to throw it out. He had a little thin mustache, Dean Slye did, that is. I was so afraid in that interview I had scheduled with him; I'd never met anyone with an advanced degree and I didn't know how you should talk to them. Wasn't that silly? But that was what I was thinking, that he'd use big words that I wouldn't understand and he wouldn't be impressed with me at all because I was so ordinary. So I went in there, into his office which is the same one Dean Pfaff uses now, but he didn't have the airy window with the nice curtains, and Dean Slye had so many more bookshelves, all the way up to the ceiling so it was really dark in there. Dean Pfaff seems to work mainly from file cabinets, I think. Also, Dean Slye used to work on his research in there, something to do with fossils, I don't really remember now, but he had rocks and jars of chemicals and little forceps and knives all over the tables that were in there then. So it was quite dark; the only light was a little gooseneck lamp shining down on his work table. And he came out of the shadows, said hello to me, and shook my hand and smiled so nicely. He was always smiling and polite to everybody. He had beautiful teeth. I still remember his high-pitched voice, gracious me, I almost had to laugh to hear him speak. But he was really the kindest gentleman I have ever known. For example, even before I took the job, he told me about an inexpensive apartment that was available, in the basement of the Reverend Danvers's house, he was the Baptist minister in town back then. That's where I lived for the first three years. And we had a nice discussion, very relaxed and friendly, and I felt so happy when I went out of his office because I'd thought I'd made a very good impression and he seemed like he'd be such a nice man to work for. So I went back to the hotel and lay down on the bed and hugged myself and wished for the job.

And wouldn't you know it, my wish came true. I felt as if the sun was shining only for me that day. He gave me the position, he came over himself the next day to the Mueller Hotel where I had taken a cheap room for the duration of my work-seeking odyssey; he had walked the whole way, it must have been ten blocks, the poor man was wheezing so badly as he walked into the lobby where I was sitting reading a novel. I had been down there for a long time, and he had tried to telephone me but I was out of my room, so he came over himself. So like him, that was, it never occurred to him that he might be putting himself out unnecessarily to do something nice for a stranger.

I still remember that lobby so well, with its big red high-backed mohair chairs and potted palms, oriental carpets, and twisted arches that I suppose were supposed to be sort of Moorish, painted pale yellow. The place was torn down in '63, I guess that was the year before you came, to make way for the new First National building.

But to get back to Dean Slye and his asthma, it was always such a problem for him and he had a bad spell of it that day. I could hear him coming all the way down the hall. I can still see him so clearly the way he looked that day, June 16th, it was, I remember so well, yes, heavens, all dressed up in his grey tweed suit and his straw hat, standing in front of me all out of breath. I had been sitting there up against the Moorish wall, reading an Irish novel, as I may have already said, yes, full of dark-haired handsome princes and maidens with perfumed breasts and roses in their hair meeting in out-of-the-way castles, yes, and I in my flowered cotton frock, I stood up when I saw him coming over toward me and I could tell he had something important he wanted to tell me. And when he finally had caught his breath enough to tell me I had the job if I wanted it, I was so happy and excited that my heart started going like mad; I wanted to jump up and put my arms around him and kiss him, yes, I did, but I didn't think that would be appropriate, so I just told him, "Yes, yes. Yes, I will. Oh, yes." He must have thought there was something wrong with my vocabulary!

I started working the very next day, only two days after my interview. I didn't dare to tell the Dean that I only intended to work for a short time. And the work was very hard, I had to put in extra hours almost every week with the increased class loads we had then. And there was even some talk about pressing me into service to teach a class on shorthand, clear across the campus in the business school. At night. But nothing ever came of that, for which I was just as glad, really, because I'm sure I'd be terrified, my stars, I know I would, if I ever had to get up in front of a big group of people I didn't know. I suppose they found someone else to teach that class, although no one ever told me about it.

So here I still am; this has become some temporary job, hasn't it? I still haven't made it to California, although I've gotten as close as Tucson, where my twin brother lives now. And I don't know what ever happened to my friend from Newport News, although I surely would like to know. I wrote her back at the shipyard, but never got any response; so for all I know she never did get back.

Anyway, as I say, here I still am, as I have been since September of 1945. As such, I knew Professor McKenna from the first day he came on the job, it must have been January of 1948 or maybe 1949. I remember the Dean introducing us. Professor McKenna was wearing an old-fashioned double-breasted dark-blue suit, with the arms and the legs a little too short; it looked like it could have been a hand-me-down from his father. He was wearing a little red pre-tied bow tie and a tight white shirt with a little collar that made his neck look especially long and gangly. He shook my hand and said that he was ever so pleased to meet me and that he hoped we could achieve great things together.

He was fresh from the Air Force; he wore his hair so short then, like almost all the returning military men. And he was such a nice man, so very polite to everyone, not just the other faculty but everyone, even the janitor; he would always call out with a cheery good morning to everyone he met. He even liked my coffee, which not everyone cares for; I put eggshells and salt in it, as my mother had always done, and I thought it was delicious.

It seemed as if Professor McKenna was always smiling and full of joy, you couldn't help but feel a little bit bubbly when he was around. He was so witty and funny too, some mornings he'd come in and start telling about some amusing things that had happened to him, and my stars, he could make me laugh. Sometimes I was just reduced to a giddy hysteria, and I just had to grab him by the arm and tell him to go away from me before I had to leave my work behind. He would have been a wonderful comedian.

Also, he seemed so much younger than most of the veterans; in fact, he was very often mistaken for a student. In those days, though, he was much more businesslike than the students, always carrying around folders of lecture notes; and it seemed as if he always had something preserved in a jar, some organ or slimy animal. He was forever thrusting his repellent specimens under the Dean's nose, smiling the whole time, as if he was some mischievous kid playing a trick on his betters (but I think it was just exuberance and the joy in what he was doing); the Dean would never say anything outright to Professor McKenna, but I could tell that he was upset because he began to stammer. And also, he would go into his office and not come out for a long time. My sakes, I know the poor man had a nervous stomach. When he came out, he would sometimes look a bit green about the gills. But he would never say anything, at least not to me.

Well, as I was saying, Professor McKenna was a very serious scholar and lecturer in those days, not like he unfortunately became later. And since he was new on the staff, the Dean would tend to give him the introductory classes to teach, the ones everyone else on the faculty had done over and over and over again; and Professor McKenna did the most yeoman service year after year on those dreadful classes with the huge enrollments, that is, the students from other divisions who just needed one science class for their degree in sociology or whatever, and were accordingly not that serious about the subject matter. But Professor McKenna never complained, in fact he tried all the harder to make his lectures interesting, to get through to them. And sometimes he would have signal successes, really he would, more times than I could count I would hear shouts of applause or screams of laughter coming from the big lecture room down the hall. I never heard anything like that, ever, for any of the other teachers. Many times I would hear the students chuckling among themselves about something Professor McKenna had said or the way he had expressed something in class.

Some of the other professors were a little bit jealous, I think, I would overhear them grumbling about circus-like atmospheres or unprofessional behavior in his classes; but it was mainly sour grapes that they weren't loved by the students as he was. So the almost universal opinion was that the man really had a gift for teaching, and it is really such a shame that he lost it and lost it so irretrievably.

I don't think I mentioned Professor McKenna's singing, did I? He was the most wonderful basso profundo, I really think he could have sung in the opera if he hadn't decided to become a teacher. It seemed that he was always singing some aria in Italian or Russian, the first thing every day when he came up the stairs to check his mailbox. Yes, he came in early those days, never later than 8:15, often a lot earlier. My sakes, I loved to hear him sing; it really started the day off nicely. I wish I could remember some of the numbers he used to perform. I would ask him and he would tell me, but I really don't follow classical music, the names just went right out of my head. The only one I remember for sure is Eugen Onegin by Tchaikovsky, with lyrics by Pushkin. That was his absolute favorite and I got to the point where I could recognize and remember certain numbers from that one. But his singing stopped at about the same time that all his other troubles were starting to happen.

I really can't put my finger on when it started, but I think it had something to do with women. Not the students, heaven knows, at least not at first. Not the female professors, I don't think they interested him at all. Not me, certainly not, although when he first started he would put his arm around me sometimes when he'd give me something to type. You must remember, Professor Cahill, I was a lot younger and better looking then. I was thin, too, just like a rail; but Professor McKenna and I both put on a lot of weight over the years. Yes, I always had some sort of boy friend back then, although none of them ever seemed to want to get married. I don't think he really meant anything about it, Professor McKenna, embracing me, that is, I mean he would do the same with some of his men colleagues. But I didn't enjoy it and I would sort of stiffen, I suppose, when it would happen, and as a result he didn't do it any more. It may have been another secretary in our department, heavens, more than twenty years ago now; I don't even remember her name. She was sort of a mousy little thing, at least that's how I would characterize her, and there was nothing really explicit between them, nothing anyone really saw. Just a sort of feeling I would get when I would go in there when they were together. They would stop talking the minute I came in and usually stay quiet until I left again.

I remember her laugh; she had a sort of machine-gun giggle that she'd start up at the end of each sentence, a nervous titter, all on one pitch for a while and then dropping at the very end. She laughed through her nose, too, that was so big and sharp. And other times she'd come up weepy, sniffing and dabbing at her eyes with a little silk handkerchief, for no reason she would ever admit to me. She'd always wear spike heels and tight dresses, some with wide stripes, that I would never wear and that I thought made her look like a tart. And she even made her mouth up to look like Betty Boop, if you are old enough to remember her from the cartoons, using that bright red lipstick you could get then. Well, she didn't stay long, and in fact I think she just didn't come in one day and never showed up again. And Professor McKenna was very quiet for some time after that. Well, there may have been nothing to it at all, but I think I'd lay a dollar to a doughnut on it, if there was ever any way to prove anything, which of course there isn't. But it was just about that time that that Professor McKenna started to do somewhat odd things that weren't really characteristic of how he'd behaved before.

Although he had flashes of his earlier good humor, he seemed to spend more and more time sitting and almost sulking in his office. That was the time he started to grow his beard, too, I think it was in 1956; even before any of us had even heard of Fidel Castro and all the left-leaning young men started to try to look like him. It was even before beatniks started to be in the news, at least out in the sticks where we live, although I suppose there've always been people like that in the big cities like New York. Anyway, we didn't have them in Pawnee Springs, that's for certain. And sometimes Professor McKenna would do things that were just crazy. For example, one day I went into the ladies' room and met Professor McKenna coming out, just zipping himself up and not concerned in the slightest about what he'd done. Well, I was really quite shocked and asked him, "For goodness' sake, Professor McKenna, have you made some sort of mistake?" and he simply glared at me, and, I remember this so clearly, he said, "I am a human being, and my urine is chemically similar to and very likely biologically indistinguishable from yours, Miss Freemartin, and therefore in my opinion the answer is no." Well, I had never heard him or anyone else say anything like that before, so I was too flustered to say anything. I did mention something to the Dean, that was Dean Pfaff by this time, but I don't know if he spoke to Professor McKenna. In any event, after that there was sometimes a hand-lettered sign on the door of the ladies' room that said "Out of Order." And although I was never sure that it meant Professor McKenna was in there, I never went in to check up. And the sign was never there for very long, so I don't think anything really needed repair; it has always taken so long to get anything repaired or painted around here, even before the unions became so powerful back around 1950.

Another thing was, I just thought about this, when he first came to work here and handed me something to type, it was neatly printed and I almost never had to ask him what something was supposed to mean. But gradually his written papers got messier and more disorganized, with sections struck out and arrows going everywhere and all kinds of paper stuck together with tape, or clips, or staples, in odd lengths, no pages really, just a sort of scroll that I imagine I was supposed to unroll as I went along. And the misspellings, heavens, he had always been so careful about the way he spelled, and then it seemed suddenly he didn't care about how a word looked. It was so ludicrous that I almost had to laugh when he brought in one of these concoctions, but he was so serious and he never was apologetic. So it was obviously not a joke; I don't think so, anyway.

Another thing, when he first came he used to run me ragged. He had so many things he wanted typed up, and especially Multilithed. And his drawings were so beautifully done, in fine black ink right on the pages I typed for him. He was a great one for handing the students big stacks of those blue and white pages that smelled like ink when they were fresh off the roll, that smell we never have anymore now in these days of Xeroxing. It was a sort of sweet-and-sour smell, not like that burned bacon smell the dry copiers put out. And then, after a few years, it seemed that his need for this material sort of dried up. I asked him about it once and he said that he didn't teach that way anymore; he said the students just threw all that paper away and that it was very wasteful. A lot of trees were dying for nothing. He relied on sheer lung power, he said; it made the students listen to every word if they wanted to do well in the class. There was no tomorrow, was the way he put it.

And then his teaching methods changed in other strange ways, too. For example, he'd march his classes out of the classroom and have them meet out on the mall, and especially in the spring there was no way of knowing where they might be found. He'd meander around restlessly all over the campus, wandering from one tree to the next, pointing out things like buds and leaves as they were coming out. And the class would stalk him like a pack of ducklings, just skittering along behind with him striding off in the lead, enticing them off to only he and God knew where. I heard that sometimes he didn't even lecture to them, just led them to a bed of flowers and sat them down, then picked a blossom and held it up to them, smiling away in silence, for minutes at a time; or else he'd find something long dead, like a ground squirrel or a baby starling, practically nothing left but bones, and he'd do the same thing with that, pick it up and show the disgusting thing to them with tears streaming down his face. My lands, I've no idea how I'd have responded to such a scandalous display if I'd been in the class; I'd probably think he was out-and-out crazy; but I know for certain that some students were absolutely fanatical about Professor McKenna, they loved and idolized him like a mighty hero.

I love my job and I love the people I've been able to help down through the years. I'm going to retire in a year or two but I shall never forget the interesting people I have known here. I think I've known examples of all human types, but I have never met anyone who was as hard to figure out as Professor McKenna. People like you and Dean Pfaff and Dean Slye before him, God rest him, are straightforward people to deal with. There is never any doubt about what you mean, and everything is straight from the shoulder. But gracious, Professor McKenna was so very different; you could never tell whether he was serious about what he said. He'd say something outrageous with a straight face, something that mocked you or someone you both knew, and it was like he was just waiting to see how you would respond. If you should get upset, he'd laugh and say he was only joking. It would really get infuriating sometimes.

Also, he was sly, and liked to play tricks on people, which I thought sometimes was very cruel. Once he called on the phone and pretended to be a visitor from France, an agronomist working on crops that could grow in salty soils, whom we did in fact expect that day. He said he'd gotten off the train one stop too soon and was trapped fifty miles away and wanted someone to come and get him. His accent was pretty good, and he'd even stop and pretend to forget some word in English. I was just about to run around and try and arrange something when the real visitor showed up! Well, at that point I knew what was up, and I was so mad, so I picked up the phone and told the phony Frenchman that the Dean had decided he didn't want to see him, so he shouldn't bother to come in at all. And Professor McKenna just started laughing, he knew what had happened. But I just hung up on him.

Still, although he would waste his times on these silly, and I think petty, trifles, he was such an interesting man, especially in his younger days, but even just before the end he always had many worthwhile things to say. So of all the people I will remember, I suppose he will be one of the last ones I forget in my old age. Oh, I have rambled on, Professor Cahill, but I hope I have been of some help. And good luck on your book, I shall be sure to buy a copy, that is if I am still alive when it comes out! Just kidding, Professor Cahill, I was just remembering how late you used to be with your annual self-evaluation forms. Dear me, I hope I'm not turning into a joker like Professor McKenna!

Bruce 2

So I had the job and an apartment near the campus, and we moved down the first furniture we ever owned, some of it (blocky, fake Danish-modern stuff) bought on time from the Big Boss Discount Furniture Emporium in Lansing. The owner, puffing on his big cigar, had told us that since we were students he'd give us a special deal if we bought two whole roomsful. He'd been a student once, too, he told us. It came to $650, more than we had in the world, and it hardly seemed possible we could ever pay it back. Some other furniture (puffy overstuffed balloons of chairs in pale oak, mid-Thirties relics) were given to us by friends and in-laws. We moved it all down, all by ourselves in a rented van, dragging the Rambler behind, in the middle of August, into the furnace heat of these western plains; in that summer of '64, the summer of the cicadas and the drought and the heat. The last hundred miles of the trip it was so hot that we removed every article of clothing except for the flimsiest scraps of underwear that we owned, the ones with a few unmended rips that we were almost ready to throw out, and drove as fast as we could past the farmers on their tractors and truck drivers looking down on us from the high cabs of their ten-wheelers, fast enough to prevent them from getting a really good look at our exposed flesh.

 Once we got here, I found I even had an office all of my own, not much to speak of; although I have never measured it carefully, I think it is actually an even smaller area than what was assigned to me in graduate school. But at least it was an office more fitting for a professor; I always thought so, anyway. At MSU my desk had been in the middle of a big, well-lit room on the ground floor of a brand-new building, with tall square windows overlooking the busiest part of the campus, and shared by six other people; here I was up on the fourth floor of an old red brick building, Musgrave Hall, Room 432, about a block from the main biology department offices and classrooms, with wooden floors that creaked whenever anyone came down the hall, which was seldom, because there were no classrooms up here where the roof slanted down.

The facilities have a musty, senescent flavor; for example, the odor of the building is that of the long-abandoned clothing of a deceased uncle, a mixture of mildew and formalin. The walls in my hall were all at one time painted a greyish yellow up to a height of about five feet; above that was a color which may have been a light green at one time but had become a sort of khaki over a period of many years of neglect. There were only a few inconsequential light bulbs, the few that had not burned out, high up on the ceilings. It was nothing if not somber. One practically expected a knight in chain mail to emerge from a dark recess and cry a halt to the intruder into her majesty's precincts.

My office is fitted with a very solid door, without a window, in heavy, dark-stained oak. When I opened it for the first time, it was if I had disturbed a fragile and complex ecosystem that had existed in that enclosed space for millenia; the very motes of dust, it seemed, must have hung in an immutable position, perfectly at equilibrium and unmoved by breath or draft. But opening the creaking door out into the hallway changed all that. A rush, almost a moan, of stale, sharp-smelling air poured past; a beam of pale greenish light lurched out of the room as though it had been propped against the door; and I heard a brief, brittle patter that I took to be the suspended dust, suddenly tumbling down in a thin blanket to cover everything in the room. On reflection and further experience of the office, however, it may have been the footfalls of hundreds of roaches and beetles running in panic into the darkness.

When I was in the office, later, and the great door was closed, I couldn't hear anything from the outside. I was sealed away from the hubbub of the world in my timeless cubicle. Sometimes the only sound I could hear was the scratching of my fountain pen on paper. It was quite monastic, really.

The office had a slanting ceiling, so it sloped from maybe nine feet on the side nearest the hallway to no more than five feet on the outside wall. The room did have a small window, very narrow and dirty, with greenish streaks down the outside, looking out onto a ledge where pigeons would sit and coo and fluff up their feathers and defecate, and mate if it was in season. If I looked very carefully, I could see some of those same pigeons lying dead on the flat-topped roof of the annex, one story below; the roof had just been freshly tarred, and the tar had been poured indiscriminately over everything, including the carcasses of those pigeons, now decaying away in unthinkable hideousness inside their airless asphalt coffins.

I think the architect of my building had been inspired by tenth-century castles with their hollow tower windows carved out of the thick walls, where a defender with a longbow could rain death down upon the enemy hordes. At least I, unlike the yeomen of old, had glass; but it was of little use, first because of the dirt, and secondly because the frame was so corroded that I didn't dare try to open it. The pane on the lower half of the window was cracked all the way from one corner to the other. I had called to have it replaced, but was told by the man who came to inspect that it was an odd size and it would take months to be specially ordered. So I forgot about it and trusted that it wouldn't break in the middle of the winter.

One long wall of the office was completely lined with shelves, nine running feet of two-foot-deep pine boards fifteen inches apart. The only object on the shelves when I moved in was a dusty stuffed great horned owl, lying on its back. The other wall featured a local service station's calendar for 1962; it showed a fetching blonde woman wearing cut-off bib overalls and nothing else, lying on her side on a mechanic's creeper and fondling a grease gun. Also along this wall was an archaic wooden desk that I half expected would be infested with death-watch beetle larvae and crumble into sawdust when I touched it, and three battered file cabinets in mismatched light and dark grey (two) and beige (one). The desk contained a few paper clips, a few broken pencils, part of a deck of cards, several long blonde hairs, some fingernail clippings, and a 1960 Cimarron State student handbook. On the desk was a brown plastic cup with a dead beetle in it.

The file cabinets were completely empty except for a hundred feet of faded chart paper in one drawer, with a single meaningless line of grey ink down the center, drawn by an electrical recording device, and no human writing on the chart to indicate what it might have represented. One of the four drawers in each cabinet could not be opened; it was a different drawer in each case.

My chair was of grey metal, upholstered in coarse straw covered with a primitive celluloid-like material to which the years had not been kind. The yellowish surface of this material adhered to my clothing, especially on warm days, and left ineffaceable stains on light-colored fabrics. The chair was mounted on a four-wheeled platform, but one of the wheels was broken, making it impossible for me to move the chair except in a broad arc. This was not such a problem once I got used to it; in the first place, a deep hole in the linoleum would have trapped the functioning wheels, anyway, and besides the office was so narrow that I could sit at my desk and reach behind me to get something off the shelf without spinning my chair around or straining for it.

Being just beneath the roof, which was dark green, the room was extremely hot, even in the winter (I was to discover) when the ancient and unregulatable steam radiator clanked and rumbled. But in the summer, it was hellish. An air conditioner was out of the question because of my window and the fact that there had "never been one in that room before, and no one has ever died in there" -- so said Dean Pfaff, denying my request for one, made in all innocence on my second day on the job, Tuesday, August 25, 1964. This he said just before he slowly polished his glasses, spraying them with a milky-white fluid drawn from a plastic atomizer, and using a separate tissue to remove it from each lens; and then he used still another tissue for the final polishing job. Finally, he put them on, seating them carefully and firmly against his eyebrows, leaned back, put his hands behind his head, lowered his jaw almost to touch his chest, and looked me straight in the eye for the first time during that particular discussion. (I understood that this was my dismissal from his presence.) Not incidentally, that was also the day I had my first conversation with Pyke McKenna.

After meeting with the Dean that day before lunch, I went back in the direction of home to have a bowl of soup and a glass of iced tea. Yes, back to visit Lloyd and his mother, who were really nice people, merry and ironic. Their food was cheap and filling, if not especially Epicurean. That day, my soup was more of a stew, thick with generous chunks of potatoes, cylinders of carrot with the peel still attached, and succulent nuggets of fibrous beef dripping with gravy. Our drought was still running along in full gallop, and the temperature was somewhere in the upper 90s; although the humidity wasn't high it was still enervating to move about. Mom and Lloyd had only one small air conditioner for their whole restaurant, and it was back next to the kitchen, which made sense for the help but was of little consolation for the customers.

I would just as soon have taken a long nap afterwards, but I had a lot of things to move into my office -- books, file folders, my new electric typewriter -- and I wasn't looking forward at all to the labor, particularly since the immemorial elevator had wheezed to a stop on the second floor with its door forlornly open. Luckily, hardly anyone else was around, and I was able to park right outside the front door, so I didn't have to carry my heavy things too far.

It was on my third trip up the creaking stairs with an armful of papers, in boxes cadged from the Spartan #1 Liquor Shoppe, that I ran into Pyke coming down; literally ran into this huge man, as I turned the corner behind my armful of boxes and hit him square in the chest. My pile of boxes came crashing to the floor and Pyke said he was sorry! I said that it was my fault, that I didn't know anyone was up here, that I was just moving in. "Oh yes," said Pyke, "the new man on the job. I'm sure we haven't met, my name is Pyke McKenna, and I have taught here for what seems like a very long time, and I am glad to meet you. Do you have much more to move in?" "No," I said, "just about two more loads." So Pyke said, "Let me help you and that'll make it one. It's terrible to have to move in on a wretched day like this. Why haven't you been using the elevator, are you one of those fanatical energy conservationists?" "No," I said, "it doesn't seem to be working." "Oh," said Pyke, "I think you'll merely have to show it who's boss." So we went down to the second floor and Pyke struck the **Down** button sharply with his fist, and we ducked inside just before the door hissed shut. And he helped me move up the last of my stuff, carrying up truly heroic loads of junk (since I'd underestimated the amount of garbage I still had to bring in).

As we rested in my office after we were finished, I complained about the stifling heat, and mentioned that the Dean had turned down my request for an air conditioner. Pyke said that was just as well, that the electrical system was overloaded as it was, and if you blew a fuse (as you undoubtedly would with a thing like that up here), that you would have to walk all the way down into the basement to change it; there were no newfangled devices like circuit breakers in this building. "Besides," he said, "it is a blessing that it's so miserable up here. It keeps you from spending too much time behind your desk, and it keeps you away from the telephone. You find yourself spending time out in the world, either in Nature itself or in that other great Forum, the open space on the campus, out among the students. You will learn far more out there among the rabble and the rattlesnakes than you will in this converted sheep barn."

"If you are anything like me," he said, wiping his brow with an enormous red bandanna, "you become weakened when you lose contact with the soil, very much like the Greek god Antaeus, who lost a wrestling match with Hercules when the latter held him up in the air. In addition, I have a serviceable electric fan which dates back to the Harding Administration; it is not at all silent, it has several types of more or less annoying squeaks which vary in pitch and intensity as it heats up. Nevertheless, it helps move the air around, but you'll have to be careful not to stick your fingers into the blades, because even the flimsy cage it had to begin with disappeared long ago."

"Well," he went on, we have achieved much here today, my friend; I will treat you to a beer or two at the local if you are so inclined." I was, of course, so we ambled through the hazy heat the two blocks to the Cambridge Arms. A mock Tudor exterior gave way to Eisenhowerian sleaze as soon as we went through the front door, a creaking door hung on ponderous wrought-iron hinges and studded with big brass rivets. Through a muggy haze of cigarette smoke, I made out pool tables with patched and faded baize tops, a massive jukebox silently flashing its rippling colored lights, pinball machines featuring Day-Glo cowgirls flaunting their panties from beneath fringed buckskin skirts while blowing smoke suggestively from their six-shooters, a few distressed tables and unmatched chairs, and, most important, a forty-foot galvanized bar. Behind this a huge, bald, impassive barkeep, a black man of uncertain age and improbably named Cyril, had been installed to keep things under control.

He was one odd-looking cat. First, his heavy-lidded eyes seemed to look in two different directions; his left eye was much lower on his face (almost buried in his cheek) than his right. Secondly, his ears were small and set very low on the sides of his head. Finally, he wore a fixed smirk that appeared to have nothing to do with mirth but was rather a product of bone structure, like the regal smile of the African lion. Pyke greeted him by name and inquired after his health; he replied with a grunt. Pyke introduced us, and lazily Cyril raised a bloated arm from its position of repose on the zinc-covered bar, took my hand in his dark, cold one and shook it phlegmatically, looking just past my ear with at least one of his eyes as he said "Haryah."

Pyke selected a booth for us. We sat on elaborately carved, high-backed benches like church pews or seats in some oared Nordic ship, facing each other across a heavy walnut-stained table some three feet wide. Both the benches and the tabletops were covered with crudely carved initials, dates, hearts, and obscenities. We ordered a pitcher of Drewry's, the cheapest beer the house had. Cyril brought it to us, puffing with the exertion, and accepted a quarter tip by rapping it on the table and stuffing it into a carpenter's apron at his waist.

The barroom was humid, probably because of the huge beer coolers; two large floor-mounted fans at either end of the room stirred up the air in complex patterns, but provided little or no relief from the heat. Our glasses of beer left deep pools of water on the dark wood tabletop. Since no students were in town yet, the tavern was almost deserted, but Pyke still spoke in his ringing, declamatory style, making everything he said sound heightened and urgent, a little like it was being spoken from a stage. I asked him if he had any advice for a beginning teacher with a heavy classroom load to look forward to. Should I try to lead a discussion group -- let the students do more of the work? "Good heavens, no," shouted Pyke. "The caliber of student you get in this institution has no notion of how to think, how to distinguish one idea from the next. And they can't write, or even speak; according to an old proverb I just made up, out of the mouths of babes cometh bullshit.

"Just wait until they all arrive on the campus, all at once, next week. You'll be able to tell from their guileless, refined faces that they're as unformed as neonates -- they don't look like authentic humanity, they're still only approximations of functioning adults. If you turn your class time over to them, you will have even less chance of influencing the few who do have a glimmer of ability into becoming something other than wage slaves."

"No, run your own class;" he continued, "talk only about what you, yourself, deem important. You are the lecturer and the state is paying you to educate them. Answer questions if you have confused them, but don't let yourself be drawn into anti-scientific arguments. For example, I know that at least one person, usually a girl, in every introductory biology class will get up and argue with you about the theory of evolution. One hundred and five years after Darwin and thirty-eight after the Scopes trial, and there are still some who haven't heard the word yet. Professor Cahill, she will say to you, I have sat patiently through your lectures and you have not once mentioned God. Don't let yourself be drawn into a creation-evolution debate; some of these kids have had the crap drilled into them by unscrupulous high school biology teachers trying to curry favor with the fundamentalist community, and they will argue irrelevant points with you all period. So close down those arguments firmly when they start. Just tell them that you are going to present the facts of biology and the concepts that explain them as best as we can understand them, and that if she (it's almost always she) wants to do the same, she can start her own discussion group. And if you want, you should say, I will come to your meetings and we can argue about religion and biology all night. It's still a free country, tell her, even though it really isn't, and academic freedom necessitates the giving of ample time for the evaluation of complex hypotheses. That is usually enough; I think they normally only want to speak out once when they fell uncomfortable, and after a time they will come around to the truth."

"So how can I make a little less work for myself," I asked him. "How can I bring the students into the educational process a little more actively? Should I expect them to absorb everything I say without question or complaint? How about the Socratic method?"

He practically turned purple. "You mean pretend not to know something?" he exploded. "I thought you were a scholar, damn it. You have to show them your world. It may not suit them, but they are too immature to have their own. They need to try on many philosophical concepts for size before they go parading off on their own. Socrates, shit! That bastard was the biggest fake in the history of philosophy. He was an anti-thinker. I can't believe that the same man who died so well could have been such a smarmy, bullyragging creep. I think Plato just used him as a foil for his fascist ideas."

He took a long drink of beer, draining more than half of his full glass, and went on; "There are no philosophers that I trust. Artists, scientists -- those are my kind of people, those who deal every day with real objects and objective phenomena. I never wanted to be a philosopher. I never wanted to formulate timeless truths; I could never tell anyone that my world was credible as a universal principle. That's why I'm a teacher. I can present the students with my views on a subject, a sort of work in progress. If they're mature enough, I can ask for comments, give them some help to get them started on their own individual world views, then step back and let them go. Because in the final sense, as I implied, you can't take another person's world as yours. You have to forge your own, step by step. Every once in a while you have to tear most of it down and start over with just the framework of the old one. And unfortunately, you have to do it in the full view of your colleagues and your students."

"Well, this is new to me," I replied. "I never realized a teacher's job was quite that hard. I'm sure most of my professors were more like journalists than the fiercely independent scholars you are describing. None of them ever told me I had to start my academic career at the beginning. Is this what you're telling me -- me with three classes to start teaching in two weeks?"

"It *is* hard," he said. "You do have to be a journalist at first, a sort of cub reporter, even. You begin with the simplest facts; you go to the library and get down journals and books, and find out what other people know, or think they know. You copy down the information these sources give you, and arrange it in a coherent fashion. These written-down words about plants and animals will help you get started, and you'll have a temporary framework for putting your own world together. For a while, it'll be all right. Then you find yourself one day telling things to your classes that you don't really believe. You've repeated other people's ideas year after year, and you realize you really haven't lived in those ideas, you've only visited them and looked at the antique furniture in the rooms behind the velvet ropes. That is the crisis. Then you have to sit down with yourself, either behind your desk or out in the field, and decide what it is you really have to believe in."

He finished his glass of beer at that point, with a large gulping swallow, and then looked over my head out the window of the Arms, gazing at nothing for some time. "Well, Bruce," he said after this pause, "you have a lot to do. I envy you just a little bit. It will be terribly hard on you, but it will be exciting, and I'm sure you'll make it. Now let us have just one more stein of beer and you will need to get on with your work."

So we did that, and we left the Arms, squinting in the late afternoon sun, and he sauntered off in the direction of his apartment, and I went not back to work, because I was weary from the alcohol, but home to my wife; I could get on with the job of reshaping my life later.

Linda

(Linda Norquist Porterfield graduated from CS in June of 1968 with a major in music and a minor in biology. She was not in any of my classes but I remember her very well from departmental seminars, where she often sat with Pyke and occasionally asked questions of our visiting speakers. Pyke never spoke of her to me, but it was common knowledge that they were lovers; often, they were seen holding hands together on the campus, having a drink in town with eyes only for one another, or walking into her apartment building or Pyke's. Later, the two of them parted without apparent rancor and were seen with others. She stayed in Pawnee Springs after graduation to work in her new husband's tobacco store. She is a slender, pale, redheaded girl, about five feet five, with very long straight hair a la Joan Baez. She used to wear granny glasses, but has recently gone to contact lenses. Her eyes are heavily made up now, so that they resemble a fawn's; before, her face was relentlessly scrubbed and artless. In addition, she has started to dress more neatly, the torn jeans and basketball shoes of her undergraduate days beginning to be replaced by skirts and loafers. I interviewed her in January of 1972, over cups of herbal tea, at the student union.)

I would just put my head down on the desk and stare at him while he was lecturing. He was the most beautiful man. Something about him really got to me, even though big guys with big beards and a lot of hair all over never really turned me on before he came along. He really was amazingly hairy, he had hair right down his back like a streak. That was quite a surprising discovery for me. It really made me feel a little weird at first. When I would hold him, later, he was just like a wonderful big teddy bear that was all yours. But I guess I'm getting ahead of myself.

I don't know if you realize it, but I'm not from around here. It took me a long time to get used to the rhythm of life in this area. I think I fit in pretty well now, though. I was born in Tulsa, just after the war, in the middle of the baby boom. That town grew tremendously during the war, because the needs of the military for gas and oil were so huge, and my father moved there right after he got out of the Navy. He'd been a radio communications officer stationed in San Diego, but he was an Oklahoma boy too, from Muskogee, and he wanted to get back. So he found a job as a radio and phonograph salesman, and just at that time television came on the scene, and he decided to move on into his own business, selling and repairing TVs. He was really raking in the money about the time I was born, and he still is; he owns eleven electronics stores, last time I checked. They're spread out all over Oklahoma, Kansas, and Nebraska.

So eastern Oklahoma, that's where I am from. My mother (she's English, that's where my red hair comes from; my father is Swedish) is from San Francisco, and she used to grouse and complain about how provincial Tulsa is; my father would take it for so long, and finally let her go back to California for long stretches, usually without me, but once in a while I'd go along with her. I haven't been out there now since I was 13. We'd usually ride the Southern Pacific trains; I have very clear memories of those two-and-a-half-day trips. I remember the hot mohair seats that were impossible to sleep in, the curmudgeonly conductors, so serious in their black suits with their little punches, the black porters, so friendly to little girls like me, with their big smiles and funny way of speaking, the dining cars where you had to write your orders on a little green card with a little yellow stub of a pencil, and finally the smell of steam in the station in San Francisco when we got off the train and an uncle or aunt or cousin would meet us. And it is a beautiful city, I remember a little about the hills and the water and the elegant greenery in the early summer, so different from home. Mostly, though, I remember the people, the nicely dressed women striding purposefully along Market Street, and also the food; the special breads and little cakes we couldn't get in Oklahoma, and the wonderful fish and shellfish we would eat down on the wharf. And once in a while one of the natives of California would ask me whether I was from "back East," and I would say no, because to me Oklahoma was not the East; it was part of the West, much more so than that strange misty Oriental place I was visiting. There were no cowboys in San Francisco, were there? I never saw any. And stuffed pompano and sourdough bread, eaten in a little restaurant on Fisherman's Wharf, gotten to by cablecar, what did that have to do with the frontier?

So I was a child who was torn between home and exotic, faraway places; I suppose I was never really satisfied with my life as a kid, and it's probably caused me a great deal of emotional stress in my life. I'm OK now, though; I am completely fine and dandy, really I am. I hope the rest of my life is as placid as it is right now.

For a time, though, like right after high school, it was a little rough. My parents had conflicting ideas about what I should do. My father wanted me to stay and help run the business; he said that I was someone he could trust not to rob him blind. But that I really didn't need, I know I'm not tough enough to succeed in that kind of dog-eat-dog stuff. And my mother wanted me to do something in the arts, or the "ahts," as she called them; to become a cultured and refined person, the person she couldn't become because of the war and her marriage and me coming along. But here also I think she missed the boat, because I couldn't stand the thought of having to take any old job to tide me over between gigs or gallery openings. That would have been a little too much anarchy for me.

No, I decided, I wanted to do something useful, to be a teacher; and to teach what I enjoyed, which was music. And after perusing all the catalogs of all institutions of higher learning within 700 miles, I settled on Cimarron because of its music education curriculum, which was unusually complete and didn't place all of its emphasis on classical music. My father was pleased because Cimarron is cheap; my mother was pleased because I couldn't help but acquire some veneer of culture; and I was reasonably pleased, because it got me out of the house and far enough away so I could be more or less my own person.

So in the fall of '64, I drove into Pawnee Springs with my nifty new little Dodge Dart and moved into the dormitory, the brand new one down the hill, MART, we called it; Mulholland Avenue Residence Tower. And I lived there for a year, struggling with my classes and with the stress of living with six hundred other students, and then I moved out and took an efficiency apartment, living all by myself in a room-and-a-half, a box, really, hardly any more room than I had before; with no air circulation and a shared bath, further away from the campus. All because I had fallen in love with a boy in the next dorm over, a blond boy named Alan, who was shorter than me and usually wore numbered football jerseys for shirts, and canvas shoes with no socks. And we decided we needed a place where we could be alone. And then in the middle of the summer, after I'd lived there six weeks, he decided he didn't want to go to college anymore, and moved back to Topeka (and took up with his high school sweetheart there, I found out); and I cried in my lonely little cubicle for the rest of the summer; and then I sublet my place to another ex-dorm resident and moved in with my good friend Molly Derwent in a much newer, nicer, two-bedroom place; and that's where we stayed until we both graduated. And I still drive by the newer place every day on my way to work, and I always sigh and think of the good times I had there with Molly and our friends, and especially with Pyke McKenna.

I never really wanted to take biology. That seems to surprise you. What I like, as I said, is music, folk music generally, but I listen to all kinds. I like to hear people singing. I like to hear the words of the songs; I think electric guitars are a terrible invention. So I was majoring in music education with an art history minor, but we had to take a science course and I heard biology had no math whatever. I'm terrible with figures, my head just clogs up even when I try to balance my checkbook. I trust the bank, I really do, though I suppose I shouldn't. So I signed up for Bio 103 and Dr. McKenna taught it that year. It's a big class, as you know; there are a lot of people like me who have no head for science, so I decided to get it over with before it was too late. I was signed up for the 8 a. m. section; I don't know what came over me at registration. Anyways, I stagger into the big lecture hall in Old Main, and there aren't any seats except right down in front. And, I'm in here with all these pimply and smelly freshmen, and I was a junior by this time, sophisticated and worldly, right?, and I know nobody at all in the whole class, so I am vacillating between thinking I'd made a terrible mistake and maybe I should have gone for astronomy, and thinking I ought to be able to leave those freshmen behind in the dust on the exams. And meanwhile the bell has rung and there is no instructor in sight. Professor McKenna is late as he nearly always is, as we find out soon enough.

Then there is a commotion in the hall, we hear someone shouting in a loud voice to another person, and then laughing, and then the great man himself comes through the door, rumpled and wheezing, a mythic figure, carrying his old triangular black briefcase that looks like a Victorian doctor's bag, which he slams on the floor by the lectern. He throws his arms over the top of the lectern, turns off the light which throws his hairy face even more into shadow, he composes himself, and looks at us all, looks every one of us in the eye. It takes a long time. All the while, I'm looking straight up into his face, ten feet above mine, as if he's the priest and I'm a penitent. Finally, he speaks. He sounds like Orson Welles. He uses lots of dramatic pauses. He says, "Biology is a science. At least it is a sort of science, or can be studied as a science. But biology is also a religion. You can live, you should live, by the code of biology. Biology is pure ethics; it will tell you how to live. It will reveal itself to you if you will only let it. And the glory of biology as a religion is that you do not have to struggle to understand it. You do not have to memorize facts or agonize over, heaven forbid, concepts. Biology is not abstract, it is real, as real as a candle flame, and as pure. And all you need to do is live it. Thus, all my lectures may be unnecessary if you are the right kind of person. But most of us have lost touch with nature; we haven't taken notice of living plants and animals since infancy. So I shall play the role of nursemaid for you, try to open your eyes and your hearts to the obvious. And when I am done, most of you will not have understood. But if there be out there a few who will respond to this terrible beauty which is life, my time will not have been wasted, and I shall be blessed."

So in the first minute of the lecture I know this class is designed for me, and the professor has won my intellect, and my heart, and my body, if he wants it, and the conquest has taken less time than it takes to tie my shoes. Nobody ever said that the subject they had to teach had a "terrible beauty." But coming from him, and the way he approached biology, I immediately felt it to be true. Nothing like this had ever happened to me before; I felt chilled, dizzy, stunned, it's like everything the guy says follows so logically and so beautifully on what he's said before, I just sit there enraptured. I think I know the kind of effect Jesus had on his disciples.

Well, not every minute of every lecture flows along quite as beautifully as that, and he does have a certain amount of factual information he has to convey, but every lecture seemed, at the time, to make a lot of sense. Of course, I didn't have any knowledge coming in, half of what he says may be utter crap, but I don't think so.

Well, some of the kids in the class can't take McKenna's style, for a while there's a lot of muttering and snickering in the class, especially in the back of the room, and I guess about a third of them drop out after two or three weeks, but I didn't pay any attention, and I'm positive McKenna never noticed them. The muttering level drops off to nothing, it's like a cathedral in that room while he's lecturing to those of us true believers that are left. For my part, it was like he is talking only to me and none of the other bodies in the room are of any consequence whatever. I'm not sure if the class was very logically organized or not; I don't know if it prepared us very well for any of our future classes. He certainly never had a syllabus or handed out any lecture outlines. He never used any notes at all. Some of the guys in the class thought he memorized everything, but it always sounded too spontaneous for that. I think he just knew so much that he was ready to let it spill out any way it chose to come. Anyways, I never had any problems with any of the other biology classes I wound up taking.

Yeah, I guess you could say his lectures were strange. I stopped taking notes after a few weeks. We never knew what he was going to launch into once he got going. I remember once he was talking about mimicry, talking about these two species of butterflies; one of them was supposed to taste bad to its enemies, and the other didn't taste bad, didn't have these toxic chemicals in its body, but just looked like the bad-tasting one. After he had said this, he looked up and sort of smiled, and said, "But at least to me, they taste the same!" And no one doubted that he had in fact eaten these two kinds of butterflies, testing out the theory for himself. It was never good enough for him to accept what the biological authorities told him was true. I think he was saying to us, "You shouldn't believe what I say, either. If this is important to you, you have to go out yourself and eat the butterflies, or whatever else matters to you."

His class had an immediate effect on the kind of person I was becoming. He influenced me right away, directly, not like anybody else had ever done. He made me think about what mattered to me, and to put it into context with other concepts. For example, McKenna had said in class that Nature played according to the rules, but that our copy of the rulebook was out of date, and had a lot of smudged and torn and missing pages, besides. Part of the game, for us, was to discover what the rules were; and then we could make a lot more headway in the game, it would seem, but then we would discover that there were even more complex stages with their own sets of guidelines. He said that the game was so fascinating, though, that we wanted to go on playing it even though we knew we couldn't win; the best we could hope for was a sort of draw. This made me think, for some reason, that biology was really a lot like music. Music had rules too. You took some materials, just a few of all the possible sounds in the case of music and biochemicals in the case of biology, and arranged them according to quite fixed rules, and you could come up with marvelous and meaningful patterns. And there was really no end to the possible combinations that made sense. It made me feel better about composing songs -- at first I thought that all the good ideas had been taken, but when I saw what nature had done over the millions of years with organisms, I was encouraged over what people might be able to do with something simpler. You play the piano, I think you may know what I'm talking about; when you're fooling around with your instrument, the guitar and voice in my case, at first everything you try to do sounds no good, or winds up being just like some other song. But if you stick with it, your own voice begins to come through, and in some magical way the melodies start to fit what the words are saying. I really don't understand how it happens, but I'm convinced that it all fits together like with nature and biology and organisms somehow. I'm sure that's the way God, or evolution, or whatever, does with plants and animals. Anyways, I actually wrote a song about meiosis, not very good but I had fun doing it, and it helped me in writing other songs that were more personal and more important to me. For example, songs about Pyke, of which there must be nearly twenty, and which no one but him has ever heard, or ever will hear. So in my case, science was helping out with art rather than driving it farther apart. And it was only Pyke that had helped me to see how it worked out.

I really wanted to know him better, so I made an excuse to meet him. I was really nervous. It took me weeks to get up the courage; I never thought he would take any interest in me or want to hear anything I might have to say. I stopped after class to ask him about something or other he'd said in class, early in the semester. He said he had to rush to make a meeting in Murdock Hall but that we could talk as we walked if I was going his way. He was all sweaty, especially down the back of his hair. I think lecturing took a lot of effort for him. Then about halfway to Murdock he suddenly asked me what day it was. So I says it's Monday. He says he'd forgotten that his meeting was on Tuesday and would I like a cup of coffee. He said one day was a lot like another to him since he worked every day. Well, I don't drink coffee but I agreed to let him buy me a glass of lemonade. I really don't know if he had a meeting or not; I never found him, afterward, to be very excited about attending scheduled gatherings that might involve work.

We made the usual small talk that professors and students do, how do you like the class, can you hear me when I lecture, what is your field of study, blahblahblah. I felt myself blushing terribly as we were talking, and I kept fidgeting, fiddling with my hair, you know, tossing it back over my shoulder with a seemingly casual flip of my hand, and swirling the ice around in my lemonade glass with my spoon. When I spoke, I kept using bigger-than-normal words and phrasing things in a very stilted way; "in that regard," stuff like that, I'd hear myself saying, but for some reason I couldn't stop. I thought he must have been thinking I was a real twit. But he wasn't laughing at me, at least not overtly. He leaned across the table toward me, though, stretching his arms in my direction.

Suddenly he said he'd noticed me in class, which surprised me because I had taken to sitting close to the back of the room and way over to one side. He said he always noticed redheads, that there was something quite special about us. I suppose he was thinking that he was one himself, though I always thought he was darker, practically a brunette. Anyways, he said that he thought I was very beautiful, and that I could have looked exactly like a movie star if I'd use more makeup and look less "ingenuous" (at first I didn't know what he meant by that, but he explained, he was a great one for explaining). And that I shouldn't get the wrong idea, that he loved beautiful and complex things for their own sake; that he wasn't trying to seduce me any more than he had sexual designs on the butterflies he used to collect. Well, I didn't really know how to take that line of conversation, but it didn't go anywhere else for the moment, so I let it ride. I can't say anyone had ever come on to me like that before, though, and it was very flattering coming from such a good-looking guy, even if he was a lot older.

So I suppose that's how things got started with us. When he was talking to me, not just then, but practically always afterwards, I just felt like I was the only person in the world for him at that moment. His eyes wouldn't leave my face. I'm sure I never stopped blushing the whole time at first, but somehow I liked it a lot. I felt like I was really hitting it off with him and like both of us just never wanted it to stop. But now when I look back on it all I don't really know whether there was a woman like me in every class he ever taught. Maybe more than one, in some, who knows. I would hear these stories, but somehow it didn't matter to me at the time.

We started meeting regularly for coffee (yes, I stopped drinking lemonade under his influence), usually after class but once in a while he would call me up at my apartment and meet me in the evenings. I was tremendously flattered; what did this great man see in me? Molly, my roommate, of course, said he just wanted in my pants, but for months nothing like that happened. I was starting to wonder if the guy was normal. Then we started to change the subjects of our conversations from music, art, and biology to our feelings about ourselves and each other.

One Tuesday evening we arranged to meet at a little hole-in-the-wall Italian restaurant off campus, quite late for us, I think around ten. I took the bus, since it was drizzling just slightly. There was no one else in the place. The waiter said to me, "Will you be wiss ze genteelman?" and I suppose I nodded, and he beckoned me to the back of the room. I didn't even see Pyke at first, but he gave me a little tiny wave that I only just saw out of the corner of my eye. He was sitting at the table farthest from the door, backed into the angle of the wall; he had ordered two glasses of wine for us. The room was quite dark, and his face was lit from below by the flame of a stubby little candle in the middle of the table. It reminded me of the first time I'd seen him, behind the lectern on the first day of class. I remember that for some reason I had put on heels and quite a tight skirt that evening, and as I clicked and clacked insecurely across the brick floor, he didn't even crack a smile at my outlandish attire, or come running up to hug me, as he had been doing lately (but like a friend, not a lover); he sat still and looked straight past me and didn't move anything except his right hand, to swirl his glass of red wine. I wondered what the hell was up. When I sat down across from him I saw something completely different about his eyes; they seemed to be richer, incandescent and wet, as if he had a fever.

I said hello, and he reached out and took both my hands in his, and closed his eyes, and pulled them up to his mouth and kissed them, slowly and tenderly, one at a time. He'd never done anything at all like that before. I stared at him as if he'd lost his senses, but he didn't look into my eyes, just started right out, talking into the checkered tablecloth, as if he had a lecture all outlined.

He started by saying that it was easy for strangers to become lovers; that intimate conversations came easily to people who knew they would never have anything to do with each other again. That was why strangers in bars got it on so regularly, both in folklore and reality. He said love was much more difficult to incubate between close friends.

Then he raised his eyes, took a small sip of wine, and was quiet for a long time, just looked off into space at a point past my right ear; so I finally spoke up and said, "Well?" And he finally looked at me, piercingly, dead serious, and said, "I did not love you as a stranger. It has taken a long time for me. You have become a very close friend, and I love you now. Yes, don't look so shocked; I'm serious as I can be, I mean it sincerely and truly; I love you. It is difficult for me to say this, and I have no idea what you feel about me, but whatever you feel it will not affect my love for you."

Well, I don't know whether I said anything at all in response, but I know how I felt; it was that same dizzy sensation I'd had when I first saw him, and I distinctly felt my heart speed up like a motorboat, and I felt a hot blush run down my front, and my hands got cold, and I started laughing and giggling like I was eleven years old, and I grabbed him by the neck and kissed him square on the lips, a really big smack, and he pulled me away and beamed at me with the biggest smile I'd ever seen on him or anyone, and he paid the check and we went to his place and we kissed and hugged and moaned and fucked for the rest of the night.

Oh, God, I remember the instant his cock went into me I felt such a raw surge of bliss that I just screamed in pure delight. At least Pyke told me I did, afterwards; I remember the feeling, but not my response to it. I remember the way his strong hairy arms and legs felt, as they squeezed me so hard I almost wanted to cry out. But it felt so very, very good.

Another thing I remember, for some strange reason, were the two blankets on his bed; the lower one was olive drab-colored and coarse, made out of stiff fibers like the kind you'd find in welcome mats. I remember that one because Pyke pulled it up behind me as I was sitting on top of him, and rubbed it all over my back. It was a sensational sexy tickly feeling, like having an army of slaves all scratching my back at once. The other blanket was completely different, pale blue, thick, and soft and light as a Persian cat's fur. It must have cost a thousand times as much as the first one. I remember lying face down on top of that, with no clothes on, feeling just as contented as one of those Persian pussycats, while Pyke stroked and petted me all over, making me gush out in goosebumps all over my whole body.

That evening, we didn't just make love all the time, don't misunderstand. I poured out my whole life story to him, there in the dark, and he returned the favor for me by listening, mostly, and telling me how he loved me so very much. I've never had such a concentrated emotional experience as I had that night. I cried, and laughed, and sometimes both at once, for that man -- with that man. We even sang together for about an hour, his dark voice and my high clear one raised in songs we both loved -- hymns, folk tunes from Appalachia, and English ballads. I didn't sleep one wink, nor did I want to.

That night, and later, we spent a great deal of time talking about love. Pyke was very analytical about it; I sometimes think he wanted to treat it quite mechanistically, as just another physiological function -- oh, I don't mean the mechanical, you know, hump-and-pump aspects, but the mental and emotional attributes. He believed that love was a stable state, that two individual humans who were with each other and not (or not yet) in love, had a very high energy level, tense and uneasy. But when love came it was as if its energy was like a great change in a physical property, an organizing force, like when a liquid freezes to a crystal. He thought that it ought to be possible to develop a predictive theory of love. He was convinced that certain personality or physical types had something that would bring them together, almost inevitably, the way a magnet attracts an iron nail with invisible force. He told me that the first time he saw me, just the moment or two he'd looked at me in his class, he'd felt a sensation that was just like a tiny electrical shock, a twinge going down the back of his head; and he knew then that something could happen between us. Well, I told him that although I had also been somewhat attracted to him in those same few moments, I couldn't quite believe in something as deterministic as all that; for me, I said, there had to be a certain mistiness around the edges, a few romantic instants when anything could happen; when love and hate were about equally possible. But he said that was his point; there was an initial attractive force, bringing the couple together in a sort of high-energy or excited state, that then had to release this energy, and that could happen in a number of ways, and the two could fly apart violently just as easily as they could settle down into a loving, paired system.

Oh, Pyke was some talker, after sex as well as at practically all other times. We'd talk about anything that came into our heads, but he had a way of structuring our conversations so that I found myself learning things without even knowing it; only later, when I had a chance to reflect on what we'd been saying, did I realize how differently, and with how much new insight, I was able to look at some phenomenon. I remember one day, a Sunday, when we spent the entire day in his apartment, talking just about him -- his life, his failures along the way, and his eventual development into what he was now. And I wasn't the least bit bored and didn't feel like he was being egotistical or domineering; it was like a fascinating lecture about someone else, some intriguing and renowned personage, which I suppose he was, at least to me.

He was always amazing to talk to; he would start off on something and then we'd drift off the subject, and then a long time later he'd make some incredibly apropos remark that would bring everything back to where he started. I would just be floored. And although he seemed to know everything about art, literature, and politics or whatever, he would usually see things in terms of biology. If I told him I had an argument with Molly about who should scrub the toilet, he'd make a remark about some similar type of territorial disputes among ants or weaver birds or something. Sometimes it'd seem so remote when he'd talk like that, it was like he was examining you, looking at you like some specimen under his microscope. But still he had this way of making you feel like he really cared about your problems. Plus, he remembered what it was like to be a student, he'd been through the same ludicrous angst you had, and he'd sympathize with you and say the same thing had happened to him "when he was a child," and it made you feel better to hear he'd gotten over it. He wasn't like some of these sanctimonious professors you'd swear weren't even in the same species with you. Like I couldn't imagine casually telling Dr. Dombrowski about my monthly cramps. But it seemed so natural with Pyke. Even before we started to ... before we became lovers.

So he was a great friend. He was someone you could barge in on any time, whether you had a problem with one of your classes, or needed to be cheered up, or just wanted to waste some time. I was good for him, too, when his black moods would come over him and he just wanted to get into my car and drive out to where no one lived. He could rail at the world and he could be with me, just him and me alone, and we could walk out there among the buttes and the cliffs and the rattlesnakes and listen to the wind blow the dust across the state and hold each other for as long as we wanted.

And he was very good at sex too, outstanding really, even if he was sometimes very mechanical in a way, he wanted to make me feel good; so he would hold back somehow for a long time if I was slow in coming. I asked him how he could possibly do that, because the other guys I'd been with just popped off and that was it, and he smiled at me real lazily and said that he could control his body. He couldn't explain it exactly, but he told me he'd worked out techniques where his mind could drift away and deal with something else while his body went on fucking, but the mind could still control some of the things his body did. He wanted us to come as nearly as possible together, so when he would observe that it was about to happen for me, he would let go the controlling mechanism (those were his words) and off we'd go. Damn, it really worked! And yet there were other times when he was like a hungry animal, frenzied, like a shark, and I felt like a piece of meat that he was attacking again and again. He would scream and moan and squeeze me hard, digging his nails into my shoulders, and pull my hair until I had to tell him to stop, and finally he'd explode. But those times were exciting too even if I was the one who felt a little detached. Maybe if I didn't love him so much I would have felt used, but I loved to make him feel happy, so often he seemed to be so glum and full of negative feelings.

Other times he was like a crazy kid, a sixteen-year old out where his mother didn't want him to be, doing illegal and antisocial things. Like the episode of the cat and the grass.

I had this cat, a real pretty calico who didn't care much about most of my visitors, but was really friendly toward Pyke. He really admired cats. Dignified animals, he called them, not like dogs who reminded him of salesmen for Carolina Biological Supply. He liked to sit around barefoot and let the cat attack his toes. He had big feet with really flexible, long, practically prehensile toes! He almost never wore shoes inside my house, or much else, some days. I used to worry about the neighbors seeing him parading around naked but he told me there had to be more light inside than out for anyone to see. I suppose he was right but it still made me nervous.

So anyways, one time he brought over this big grocery sack completely full of grass. It scared me to see it, because back then we still had the death penalty for possession. But Pyke just didn't give one shit, he said it was local stuff and that he'd collected it himself from the unmowed strip between the cemetery and the air force base. No money had changed hands; he was just doing a little primitive hunting and gathering of the native flora, nothing in the least illegal. He said he wasn't sure if it was any good, but after he'd chopped it all up and dried it in the lab oven (the crazy shit!), he noticed that Jack's cockroaches had all gathered on one side of the cage, the one next to the oven. He thought that cockroaches would be a lot more efficient and cheaper than dogs, for the U. S. Customs. He said that he thought about writing to our congressman about it but that he was afraid they'd find out it worked.

So anyways, he wanted me to help him sort out all the seeds and stems, so he just dumped the whole bag on the kitchen table and we went at it with tweezers. I was trying to get it all in a plastic garbage bag, but Pyke just tossed a lot of it on the floor. I was just about to get paranoid about it, because you remember what kind of cops we had in Pawnee Springs in those not-so-long-ago days, when I noticed my cat was chewing on the stuff. Pyke said it wasn't surprising, that cats were very susceptible to all kinds of drugs. If you want to kill a cat, he said, just give it one aspirin. So right then, he rolled up a huge joint, lit up, took a big drag, and blew the smoke into his empty grocery bag. Then he put the bag right over my cat's head. Well, that cat was tense for about ten seconds, and then he just mellowed out; his legs buckled, and Pyke turned him over on his back, and he just stayed that way. I don't think I ever laughed so hard over some animal.

Well, we finished the joint. It was really good shit, and we went to bed for the rest of the afternoon. I saw visions, really, while we were fucking; I saw Pyke as a beautiful dragon, all covered with glossy green scales. It was fantastic. Molly, though, was really pissed when she came home about 6 and found us snoring away, all balled out, and the table still covered with grass.

God, we had a lot of crazy times together, he and I. The man had real style, a sense of rightness about what he would decide to say or do. Most of the time, anyway.

One weekend we went canoeing, just the two of us, in the La Garita Mountains in southwestern Colorado, right up by the Continental Divide in the San Juan National Forest. I will never forget that trip as long as I live. I was a very inexperienced canoeist; all I had done was paddled around a bit in reservoirs as a teen-ager. But I knew how to steer, and Pyke said that was all that was necessary, even in the white water of the high country. Pyke had made his own canoe out of Fiberglas and dull red plastic resin from a kit he'd bought years ago in Denver. It was even named and signed, big blue enameled letters on the front saying "RINGHORN; MC KENNA, 1957." He wouldn't talk about the name, just said it had something to do with his brother.

We left Pawnee Springs on a Saturday at about three A.M. Having crammed all our things into Pyke's little car, we headed off at top speed across the eastern Colorado desert. As dawn broke I was dozing, and Pyke woke me up to see the first light striking the Rockies west of Colorado Springs. They were an amazing shade of pink at that hour. "The biggest one's mine," he said, and it took me a while to realize that he meant Pike's Peak.

Just after dawn, we rolled through the almost deserted streets of Colorado Springs itself. The only vehicles we saw were military transports -- trucks, jeeps, and personnel carriers full of faceless men clutching rifles. It was frightening. I don't know if they were just off on maneuvers somewhere or if they were about to be shipped off to southeast Asia. Neither Pyke nor I said anything, but I knew it was something he didn't want to see. I felt like crying.

As soon as we got out of Colorado Springs, though, things improved dramatically. Almost no other vehicles were on the road with us. The highway soared to the tops of razorback ridges, giving us one melodramatic vista after another, and then repeatedly descended steeply via switchbacks into canyons and ran zigzag along rushing streams full of boulders. The wildlife, also, was magnificent. As our car entered one canyon, it disturbed a golden eagle by the roadside; he rose slowly and regally into the air with deliberate strokes of his mighty wings, ignoring us as we jumped out of the car and followed him for as long as we could with our binoculars. That was my first golden eagle, but we saw many more that day, although none so close and magisterial as that one.

Finally, around noon, we pulled off the main highway and started going up and up on increasingly narrower and bumpier roads. At the boundary of the national forest, the commercialized world suddenly fell away. No more billboards, no more tacky ski condominiums, no shopping centers hiding their rapaciousness under the guise of historic preservation of gold-rush towns, no more rich Californians with $25 haircuts, in down vests from L. L. Bean; just the two of us, our car, and the wild high country all around. Alpine meadows, the first ones I had ever really seen, were a flourish of color; columbines both yellow and red, monkey flowers, chiming bells; mountain bluebirds, pure blue, not those business-suited species from the plains; gray jays, "camp robbers", completely tame, flying up to snatch popcorn from our hands as we laughed; and once, almost as far away as we could see him, a grizzly bear, romping in pure joy across a high saddle meadow, surrounded by the sky.

Finally, we came to the end of the trail, a place called Lost Canyon, as far as we could drive; a sheer cliff, topped by misty clouds, confronted us. Pyke told me we would have to carry the canoe for about three and a half miles toward it. I couldn't believe, first of all, that we could be that far away; and secondly, that we could even make our way through that jungle. But we unfastened the canoe from the car top where it was roped down, and after putting on our knapsacks and boots, heaved it onto our shoulders and set off. Pyke was in front, slashing through the brush at a high rate of speed, and I brought up the rear, gasping and trying to keep up. We were yoked together like slaves by the necessity of carrying the boat. The trail, such as it was, meandered up and down, though mostly up. The downward stretches almost seemed refreshing after the agony of climbing with our heavy load, but the load wasn't any lighter going downhill. My shoulders started to throb and my neck muscles to ache. The trail was quite rocky, and I kept banging my knees and ankles on stones when I slipped. It was hot and dusty with my head inside the boat, and it seemed to amplify my panting. It was strange to be in these gorgeous surroundings and not to be able to see them, or at least only that part directly underneath my feet, since my vision to the side and above was completely blocked. I only fell once, cursing and tripping over a root, and the canoe pitched off to the right and tumbled about twenty feet down the slope; but luckily it was stopped by a rock just before it was about to plunge into the stream. I jammed my thumb against a tree when I pulled that maneuver. It stung for a while but I kept bending it back and forth and it was all right.

Finally, by some invisible sign, Pyke determined that we had come as far as we could. I was glad that we were finally there, because I doubt that I could have gone fifty feet further. My legs were quivering uncontrollably; there were shooting pains in my calves. My jeans and socks were torn, ripped up by the stones we'd been stumbling through. My arms and shoulders felt like they were about to pull loose and slump to the ground. We threw ourselves down on the grass for a rest.

After a few moments, Pyke sat up and looked around, then shook me by the shoulder, saying "Hsst! Sit up very slowly and look straight ahead." And right in front of me, about twenty feet away in the fast-flowing stream, was a family of harlequin ducks; the male with his Picasso head in bold green, red, and white, and his drab brown-striped mate, and their little ones darting about like flies. The sun was dancing in the ripples, and the ducks looked like they were dabbling for the light.

We waited for the ducks to move off, and then it was time to go into the water. We put on our yellow life jackets and stuck the paddles into the boat. It was a tricky start. I sat in front, and because the stream flow was so fast, Pyke had to hold the canoe back from the bank and jump into the rear seat from the water. I don't know what would have happened if he hadn't made the maneuver; I suppose I would have swamped within a few yards and hit my head on a rock and drowned. In any event, it worked out fine; we set off at a good clip, picking up speed for about two hundred yards, and then I saw, or rather heard, the first rapids coming up around the bend. They looked like a waterfall. I screamed out "Now what?" and Pyke said, "Take it by the right channel." So we headed into it, not exactly straight, and I felt the water taking us for a ride like a cork, jerking us powerfully first to the right, then thrusting us to the left, around a colossal boulder, and I felt the nose of the canoe diving, and a jet of water splashed into my eyes and nose and blinded me, and then the rear plunged down and I was lifted up, feeling suddenly sick, but then we hit the end of the riffle and the roller-coaster ride was over and things were calmer again. Pyke shouted out "Well done!" and I didn't say a word, because it seemed to me that I hadn't done anything but react, but it still made me feel better about the next rapids. And they came along rather quickly, in less than a minute. If anything, they were longer and bigger than the first, but we took them in a straight shot right down the middle. It was like falling off a cliff at first, but instead of accelerating, we slowed smoothly down and knifed along through the next calm stretch like a giant Fiberglas fish. I screamed out inadvertently from the thrill; it was orgasmic.

I don't know whether those first two rapids were the biggest ones we encountered, or whether I just got used to dealing with them, but the rest of the ride didn't seem quite so thrilling, or so intimidating. We did take one spill, when the canoe grazed a rock that we couldn't see below the water surface; we just keeled over gracefully and pitched out into some shallows near the left-hand bank. We were soaked but not hurt, and the boat was fine, just a little scratched, and we hadn't lost anything except for two bottles of Coke. I couldn't believe it when, very shortly afterwards, the car came into sight and we had to pull out. Pyke said we'd been on the water for nearly an hour, but it seemed like no more than five minutes to me.

We got a blanket out of the car, hiked off up the hill for a hundred or so yards, took off our wet clothes and hung them on tree branches, and had a bite to eat (naked and wild as apes, slapping biting flies off one another). The sun shining through the branches made dappled patterns on our bodies. We ate yogurt (homemade, by Pyke) from a wide-mouthed quart jar; he'd added the fruit and syrup from a can of pie cherries. The stuff was thicker and more astringent than the kind from the store. Because we had forgotten to bring spoons, we took turns lying back on the blanket and being straddled by the other one, who tried to scoop yogurt by hand into the open, laughing mouth below. It was pretty messy, but fun to lick it off each other when we spilled, especially for me, tracking it down in the crannies of Pyke's beard with my tongue. Pyke asked me if I'd ever practiced gursha before this; apparently that's a kind of African custom where lovers feed each other.

Then we made love, of course, and took a nap, and it was almost dark and time to head back. That night we stayed at a motel in Salida, sleeping on a water bed in what I suppose was the motel's version of a honeymoon suite. The clerk, a woman of about forty in a beehive hairdo and butterfly glasses on a chain, sniggered at us about hoping we would be having a restful evening; I think she thought we were going to spend the whole night screwing; but we were both so tired that we slept the whole time. We didn't even have any supper. In the morning, though, we did spend some time bouncing and sloshing back and forth, having a good time, before we went out for an enormous breakfast; we ordered pancakes, cereal, ham, scrambled eggs, bacon, coffee, and two kinds of juice. The waitress rolled her eyes at us and kept it coming. We just laughed and scarfed it all down. Like wow, what a trip.

I still believe Pyke and I truly loved each other, but he seemed to have different needs than I did. I wanted to be with him all the time; when he was gone, I felt like half a person. Pyke was a lot more self-actualized. He could be by himself for days, going for a whole day without speaking a word, probably. Other times, he wanted to be with people. Sometimes me, but he had a lot of friends he could call on. Especially women. Sometimes I think he had six women he was in love with at once - honestly, from his perspective - and sometimes he'd need none of us, sometimes one, sometimes several in a short time. I don't mean just sex, even though he did have a great capacity for fucking. But it would come and go, his needs to be with me, I mean. And after a while I wasn't always willing to drop all my plans to be with him, and that seemed to bother him more than I thought it should, and maybe that drove us apart even more. The man had a lot of problems, I began to realize after a while.

When I was able to think about it rationally, I recognized that I loved him at least in part for his youthful and rebellious attitude -- his refusal to put up with bullshit from anyone, whether the president of the United States or the mayor of Pawnee Springs -- but he seemed to believe, sometimes, that rebellion had to be on his own terms. He seemed to think he was the only one in fifteen states who couldn't stand the war in Vietnam. Anyone who doubted what he was doing or what he thought was automatically an enemy. And that included me, of course, when I would get exasperated at some dumb thing he had done or was planning to do. It's hard to be yelled and screamed at and told what a moron you are for just wanting to talk something over, and if I would start crying, to be told to grow up. And then it always fell to me to be the one to apologize, to want to get back together on good terms again. Although I couldn't really stay mad at him -- I loved him, you understand -- it's hard to keep up a love like that for very long. And so, we never formally declared that we weren't going to see each other again, it's just that the times we did see each other got to be less and less frequent; and when we did meet, it was like, "hey, how've ya been," just very casual and no deep feelings expressed either way. So, I suppose it was inevitable that I would find someone else eventually.

When Pyke and I stopped seeing each other regularly, at first I just wanted to go out and have fun with my friends, I didn't want to betray the memory of Pyke and the love I had for him, but gradually my friend Pete and I became quite serious.

Pete is quite a story in his own right. He had been in my comparative religion class, one I was taking at the same time I was in McKenna's bio class. Pete was very quiet and reserved. I didn't even notice him for a long time, since he always sat behind and to the left of me. He says he noticed me, though, from the first day. Must be Pyke's predictive theory at work again.

The first time we ever spoke was in a small group discussion; we were talking about faith and certainty, and I, having been influenced strongly by Pyke by this time, was holding forth for the position that it was a moral obligation for all of us not to believe things for which sufficient evidence couldn't be produced. But Pete, very unpretentiously, made a case for the view that there were things beyond our understanding, things like the beauty of trees, and the fact of love, for which there was no rational explanation. He stated that, for him, he accepted that these things were there as evidence of God's love for us. I argued that just because we didn't understand the reasons why those things moved us so powerfully, that they didn't have to represent something supernatural, and that it was likely we would understand them someday, understand them in a predictive way. (You can see how much Pyke had taken over my head.) Pete said that he couldn't believe that, himself; he couldn't imagine a way to produce some equation that would explain why certain pieces of music, for example, sound exciting and good, whereas others affect us negatively or not at all. Then he quoted E. E. Cummings:

> "As long as you and I have lips which are for kissing
> or to sing with,
> Who cares if some oneeyed son of a bitch
> Invents an instrument to measure Spring with?"

Well, that made everybody laugh, and I had to admit the man had a point. We continued our discussions, in class and then outside, becoming closer friends, although there were times when he just didn't come into my thoughts at all; days when I only had time for Pyke. But one evening when Pyke hadn't called for weeks, he did and came over to talk to me for a couple of hours, and made me feel a lot better and less sorry for myself. I kissed him for the first time when he left, and held him for a long time; it felt so good I could hardly stand up. And things began to get serious for us from then on. But I still couldn't believe it, thirteen months later, when I found myself standing up in the little Catholic church in his home town, listening to a priest marry us. And he's not the slightest bit like Pyke, of course, but I love him very much and I want to stay with him and have his babies and grow old with him. There will never be anyone else in my life like Pyke, I realize, and I'm sure that a lot of other people will say the same thing. But Pete is the one man for me, and from now on I'm a one-man woman.

You know, maybe I shouldn't even mention this, I never told it to anyone else before, not even my husband, but I see Pyke in my dreams. It's like we both know he's dead, but it seems perfectly natural that we should meet and sit on my bed and talk about the past. And when I wake up, I'm happier somehow. Maybe at the level I see him at, he and I are just as dead or just as conscious; and in my thoughts, he is as alive as he ever was; and we can be together and just as happy as we were in the best of times when he and I were both really alive and in love. Maybe there's something wrong with my head that a guy who's been dead for several years should mean so much more to me than the living people I see and work with and talk to every day. But there's absolutely no way I can forget.

Well, I'm making no sense, I know. You ought to spend your time talking to people who knew him professionally, knew his skills as a teacher and his abilities as a scholar, or whatever. But thanks for letting me have the chance to reminisce. And I hope you know I'm not lying when I say I'll always love him and my last thoughts on earth will be of him. The most beautiful, the most wise, and the most gentle man I will ever know. Pyke, baby, God rest your lovely soul.

Pyke 1

(In one of Pyke's desk drawers I found a group of six cassette tapes, held together with several rubber bands. A variety of material is on these tapes, but in general through them all runs the theme of "My Days at Cimarron," and I think that for a time Pyke may have been thinking about putting together his own life story. That project did not come to pass, and I will use some of the material from these tapes at appropriate points in the text. None of the selections are dated specifically, and I have no idea when he recorded them, but internal evidence usually allows me to place the events they recount with some confidence into a particular period. The following vignette may have occurred in Pyke's very first semester at Cimarron State, between January and May of 1949.)

In my early days here, I used to show up unannounced in all manner of classes all over the campus. To some degree, I was seeking knowledge, but something made me act in a surreptitious fashion on these excursions. Later, of course, when I had become locally notorious, it became impossible for me to do this. At any rate, I'd sit near the door and take notes very ostentatiously. I never said anything. No one, including the lecturer, who was usually a young graduate T. A., knew who I was. When the bell rang, I'd leave right away. I am quite sure that I fettered the free flow of human knowledge on more than one occasion, but I always thought a lecturer should know how to speak to a hostile or indifferent audience. As a parenthetic example, I started out my career, such as it has been, as a biologist for the state highway department of a state somewhat east of here. Those bridge-and-dam-building bastards did not wish to hear that their destructive activities were going to annihilate a trout stream, or forever to befoul a clean stream. It was my task in life to tell them so. When I would speak to them, either individually or (more usually) to a considerable body of their ilk, I was the recipient of a series of most pointed and inimical questions, often containing remarks of a somewhat personal nature. I recall "bug-and-bunny-loving son of a bitch" to be the kindest of these latter appellations. So I knew a thing or two about speaking to unfriendly gatherings.

Several years ago, before I finally gave up these visits (in addition to one's becoming too well known, it becomes less likely that one will see or hear something exceptional), I chanced, very early in the term, upon a chemistry laboratory class. I came in late, and the students were being instructed in those black arts at the far end of the laboratory. I remained near the door, partly because I was terrified of foul and pestilential vapors ineluctably assailing my delicate mucosae. I really worried to some degree about entering the chemistry building at all, because the feeble odor of unspecified synthetic compounds was omnipresent. I doubted that any of the substances contributing to this odor, which I imagined would be similar to that which would ensue upon the opening of an Egyptian tomb sealed for millennia, could have been beneficial to my metabolism; and I also knew that at least a few molecules of all the toxicants ever synthesized or worked with in this building were still there, roaming the hallways and waiting for an unprotected piece of DNA to attack, and with my luck it would be one of mine, and ten years later I would come down with a particularly noisome affliction.

Although the room was lit only by a few ancient and dusky bulbs, probably of Hungarian origin, I was able to see the lecturer quite clearly. Neither he nor the students noticed me there in the gloom. He was a dwarf, standing on a metal stool in order to reach the blackboard. He was wearing a white lab coat, and it fell below the level of his feet and covered the seat of the stool, making him look like a grotesque dressmaker's dummy come to life. Occasionally he would clamber down the stool like a baboon in order to move it to an unused area of the board. I no longer recall the sense of his remarks, but only the style of their delivery; the childish twitter of the voice, followed by the greasy squeaking of the chalk, in a sort of call-and-response motif. I don't believe I have ever held the attention of my classes as well as that young man did that day.

Later in the term I thought I would check back on the same class, and was surprised to observe that the original lecturer was no longer there. His place had been taken by a brusquely efficient young woman, huge and blonde, with a wholly different style of teaching. I remember my attention, that first instant I looked through the door, being drawn to her eyes; they glinted, metallically blue, hard and unyielding as those darker eyes of the women who fought for Franco. Next I heard her voice, a flat, flannel-mouthed twang slapping at me like a plank. Oh, yes, and also I cannot forget to mention her hair, a cloud of fine, clear gold enriched by silver highlights; rich and full, with long bangs billowing out, cut straight across at eye level, so that she looked as if she was peering intently out from under a warrior's helmet. She stood in the center of the laboratory; she had obtained powerful fluorescent arcs, such as those used to simulate tropical sunlight in northern glasshouses, to illuminate the room; and in that pitiless glare she brandished the implements of chemical transmogrification, waving them like censers toward the far corners of the room. The students, bewitched, hunched over their benches, unthinkingly carrying out the arcane and meaningless tasks set out for them in their sacred cookbook, in the precise fashion laid out for them by their priestess.

My presence in the room soon disturbed the acolyte of alchemy, and she cried out in a great yet injured voice, "May I help you?" It was clear that my intrusion was disruptive of serious matters of a practical nature; the accusing stares of the initiates were growing hotter with each passing millisecond. My sang-froid deserted me entirely. I could only mutter unconvincingly that I was looking for the chemistry storeroom (which, in fact, was some three floors above, and in a wholly different wing of the building) before beating a confused retreat. A few steps down the hall, my face burning, I heard a burst of laughter from the room I had just left. I have not set foot in that building to this day.

Bruce 3

And so it came to pass that I had to meet my first class. A new class, an advanced class, one I had devised all by myself. My title for it was Concepts of Mathematical Biology. I planned to discuss sampling strategies, statistics, significance of data, population variability, matrices - I had it all sketched out, although I hadn't actually written more than a smattering of the lectures. I had decided how to bring the students into classroom participation; I was going to have them work on problems, individually or in groups, right in class. I was going to devote about fifteen minutes of each hour to this, starting with the very first lecture. The students would get credit for these exercises, and I was going to insist that everyone participate in at least three problem-solving sessions. I was actually looking forward to this class and feeling quite proud of myself. Maybe I was cut out for this teaching stuff after all.

The only thing I didn't like was the time of the class, first thing in the morning Monday, Wednesday, and Friday. I always liked to have a free hour at the beginning of the day to relax and think about the way I was going to present the material; I hate the feeling of going into a classroom cold. Also, I think it's cheating the students to improvise a lot of stuff that you haven't thought deeply about. So I would have to change my ways and perhaps become a more early riser.

Anyway, I had a preregistration of twelve students, not bad for a first-time class at the upper division level. Jesus only had twelve, I said to myself. And I had my first lecture, at least, all plotted out, and I was ready to take the class with me on a roller-coaster ride into the realm of fast-paced mathematics. So I put on a long-sleeved checked shirt, and a dark blue knit tie, even though it was supposed to get almost to 90 that day (also, the Dean pressed us to wear ties; he thought they made us more reputable in the eyes of the students). And I was ready. I punched the air with my fist as I left our apartment to drive to the campus. Viola, looking out the bedroom window at me, called "Go get 'em, tiger! Earn your salary!"

I entered the classroom punctually at five minutes to eight; only one student, an Indian woman in a sari and with a red caste mark in the middle of her forehead, was there. She sat in the first row, directly in the center. I called out a cheery good morning to her but she only lowered her eyes, appearing to want to read the cover of her new textbook, with the price sticker from the college bookstore still on the upper right-hand corner. No matter, I thought to myself, and began to spread out my materials on the table top at the front of the classroom. Good, there's a lectern, I thought, and propped my detailed lecture notes for the day on it. This is one problem with my teaching methods, I always have to have everything all written out in advance; I can never trust myself to improvise. I read my lectures, I don't speak them. And yes, I thought, there's even chalk, and lots of it, and all long pieces, no short stubs. Everything just so, just the way I like it.

The students began to drift in in ones and twos; I looked at each and smiled, but they all seemed reserved with me; not many looked back. They were obviously much more comfortable with each other on their side of the classroom, secured in their desks bolted to the floor in that unchanging, subservient, traditional pattern. And they took their assigned seats, not assigned by me but by some deep-seated instinct that each of them had, for nearly all students will always take the same seat in the classroom time after time. And finally the inevitable bell buzzed in the hallway, and I took a deep breath and got my professional teaching career underway.

DEGREES OF FREEDOM

There were only nine students seated in front of me, six men and three women, the women in the front and center and the men farther away, in the corners of the room. All looked impossibly young and unsophisticated; was it possible that I was only five or six years older than some of them? I announced the name of the class and my name in the conventional academic fashion, not calling myself Professor, or Dr. (I could never get used to either, they sounded too pretentious), or even Mr., but plain old Bruce, Cahill. And of course, at this point the embarrassed student who had found himself in the wrong class, the boy seated at the greatest distance from the door, had to repack his briefcase and leave as quickly as possible.

I called the roll for the first and only time in the term, and then gave them a general idea of the subject matter of the class, handed out some mimeographed notes, and then off-handedly asked, "How many of you have had calculus?" I was taken a little aback when only one student, a small, smug-looking young man with a scanty blond beard, seated in the rear of the room, raised his hand. I paused for several seconds before saying quietly, "Oh, really." (I had counted on a little more mathematical sophistication than that.) I went on, "And how many have had analytic geometry?" This time, the first boy and two other boys responded. "Trigonometry?," I said, and this time all the boys and one girl lifted their hands. Finally, with "Algebra?" I got a unanimous response; even the woman in the sari smiled as she was finally able to answer me affirmatively. I wiped my brow in relief that was not entirely mock, but all the while I was thinking that I really hadn't bargained on teaching elementary mathematics to all these students; I had hoped that this class would be able to use the knowledge they already had and put it to work so that they could do some science.

I decided I was going to have to abandon most of the subject matter of my first lecture, which was on regression and the analysis of variance; I was prepared to talk to them about the statistical analysis of how data scatters, and the fitting of equations to data, and how to tell when you can have confidence that observations of dynamic phenomena are really pointing to something significant. But this required some discussions involving calculus. So I threw it out the window, figuratively, and took another deep breath as I cast around in my head for another subject that I could discuss without calculus and without careful notes. This is going to be a short lecture, I thought, especially since the problems I planned for the class to work on today won't be suitable. So I finally decided to talk about correlation and causation, about observations of phenomena that might or might not have something to do with each other.

"Perhaps you have noticed," I said, finally, "that men who wear hats or caps also seem to drive their cars very slowly. Let's try to design an experiment together to test whether this hypothesis is indeed true." I called for some response from the class, and we had a quite spirited discussion at some length on how we could sample the population of automobile drivers accurately. I made the students do almost all of the talking; Pyke would have hated the way I was running things. I was kept active writing down and erasing their ideas from the board. We had a long discussion over the differences in drivers of cars, trucks, and buses; bus drivers, we estimated, would be likely to have to wear a cap as part of a company uniform, and should not be considered. Trucks were probably not driven, on the average, as fast as cars, we further concluded; after all, the speed limit for trucks was 15 mph slower than that for cars in those days. However, students who drove often on the interstate highways disputed this observation. At any rate, after much discussion, we finally decided that only cars should be included in our samples. We defined a car as "a motor vehicle with four wheels, capable of being fully enclosed, whose primary purpose is to carry passengers." I doubt that Webster could have put it better. The class also decided to sample only male drivers, because we guessed that the fraction of hat-wearers among the minority of women drivers would probably be too small to give us an accurate set of data unless we had a prohibitively large sample size. (I tried to impress on them from the beginning that biologists don't have boundless supplies of money or time to perform their experiments. "We don't have the money, so we've got to think," I told them, paraphrasing some physicist of the early days of the 20th century, before physics became a glamour science.) We decided to separate caps and hats, thinking that very different kinds of men wore one or the other. We defined a hat as a head covering with a radially symmetrical brim, and a cap as having either no brim or an asymmetric brim. Yes, we recognized there might be problems with firefighters and football players, but were willing to risk them.

We judged that we should not take data on Sunday mornings, since churchgoers might wear a hat then and not at other times; besides, one young man said, we had to set aside some time to analyze the data. No, to go to church ourselves, said a young woman.

We elected to take the speed data with a concealed radar gun, since it was decided if we tried to follow the drivers in our cars to determine their speed, we might affect their driving. To avoid bias, we chose to station the radar gun operator far enough away so that he could not tell whether the driver was wearing headgear, and have a separate observer with binoculars to pass judgment on that question. I was glad to see that they recognized immediately that an observer can influence the data being measured, and that a simple hypothesis can entail a complex structure of tests.

Finally, we were ready to make up some fictitious data for our little thought experiment. I played the role of the observer with binoculars. I took up either one, two, or three pieces of chalk and concealed them in my hand; then I pointed to each student in turn and asked how fast the imaginary approaching driver was going. When the student gave the speed, I opened my hand and placed the value in blackboard column 1 for hats, 2 for caps, and 3 for no headgear. Naturally this approach gave quite scattered results, especially toward the end of the exercise when some of the class became rather silly and had the hypothetical drivers out in Ferraris or go-carts. Anyway, I collected fifteen numbers, five in each column; I added each column up, divided by five, and the averages came out different; 67.4 mph for drivers with hats, 54.8 for those in caps, and 61.0 for the bareheaded.

"So," I said, "assuming we collected these data legitimately, could we therefore conclude that drivers in hats go faster and those in caps go slower?" No, said the class in unanimity, there are not enough points. "Well," I said, "suppose we had a hundred or a thousand observations, and the same averages, would that be enough?" Now opinions were divided, with some saying that would be sufficient to prove the hypothesis; "How much more could you ask for?," and others not so sure. I goaded these latter students, asking them why they were so difficult to convince; what does it take to get you skeptics to believe something? And eventually, after some but not too much help, they saw the point I was getting at, that the important thing was not so much the average, or mean, but also the range, or scattering, of the data. I introduced them to several concepts for assessing the scatter of data sets, such as the standard error and the standard deviation; I also defined a few elementary bits of statistical jargon, such as "mode," "kurtosis," "goodness of fit," "dispersion," and "degrees of freedom," the last of which sounds quite noble, but means nothing more than the number of pieces of data you have to work with, minus one.

If a group of values was scattered enough, I pointed out, there was really nothing special about their mean value, and certainly nothing significant you could say about that value compared to another set of values with a different mean. But if the range of the data was close enough, then we could begin to have confidence that the mean was representative of the true value of the observations. And if all men with hats whom we observed drove between 65 and 70 miles an hour, and we observed 200 of them; and 200 other men with caps all drove between 52 and 57 miles an hour; then, we could probably say that there was a significant difference.

"Remember this," I said, "when someone tells you that 'science has proved' such-and-such. Always look at the range of the data, whether the hypothesis being tested is that heavy smokers get lung cancer or that Group A of the population has inferior intelligence to Group B. A lot of good science, and also a lot of not-so-good science, is based on observations of just the type we are talking about. And even when the data do fit well, remember that correlation doesn't necessarily imply causation. In other words, even if men in hats do drive more slowly, as we hypothesized in the first place, it is quite another hypothesis to state that the hats caused the men to drive slowly. This is something that's usually much more difficult to assess. We'd have to take men who didn't normally wear hats, put hats on them, and monitor their driving behavior before and after."

"You can see some of the problems," I went on; "but again, a lot of science is based on observations that are probably just as artificial as my example. We may be measuring a response of the personality, whatever that may be, to two quite unrelated things; a basically conservative person may dress conservatively and also drive conservatively. But to prove that statement, my friends, would be a very difficult exercise, given our present knowledge of the human psyche." And at that point, wonder of wonders, the bell rang and my first fifty minutes of professional teaching was over.

Thomas

(Excerpts from a letter sent to Pyke in July 1967 by his brother, Thomas McKenna, a colonel in the US Army stationed at the US Embassy in Saigon, South Vietnam. Col. McKenna, a career military man, entered the army as a second lieutenant directly after graduating from Ohio State in 1953.)

I expected that everyone here would hate me on sight. I expected to be spat at, or cursed in a language I couldn't understand. But instead I feel almost invisible. Only the little kids stare at me. The kids and the whores. God, the whores are sad to see; without a doubt the most beautiful young women I have ever seen, and so many of them! Their lives totally brutalized by Americans, finishing a process the French probably started; or maybe the Chinese, who the hell knows, the country has been in a state of occupation by foreign armies for centuries. Also, I feel so self-conscious, driving through the streets in my Datsun, the only automobile for blocks (although there are a fair number of motor scooters), threading my way through the thousands of bicyclists; but they pay me no heed whatever.

Meanwhile, I see and hear the most fantastically incredible things going on around me in those same streets. I know I can never remember them all, but I'll give you some examples. An old man with an Uncle Ho beard selling snakes, live snakes, from a big black kettle on the street corner. You pick one out, he pulls it out of the kettle and cuts its head off, he wraps it up in newspaper and you take it home for supper, still squirming and bleeding. He leaves the heads in the gutter; I suppose the rats get them after dark. Naked little kids pissing and shitting in the same gutter. School kids, all girls, probably Catholics, dressed in dark green uniforms, looking like girl scouts wearing ARVN caps, holding hands, standing gravely and silently in a queue a block long. A guy carrying a pig's head in his bicycle basket. A black American soldier fucking a Vietnamese woman in a doorway, sitting on a rattan stool, holding her on his lap, trousers pulled down, still wearing his uniform cap and shirt and boots.

It's about a twenty-minute trip from my apartment to work. And then I drive through the gates into the embassy. It's not just a different world, it's a different dimension, a different universe altogether. I hold up my little plastic picture ID card to the guard, who comes halfway out of his cage with the bulletproof glass, mechanically, like the crossing guard on the Lionel train set we had as kids. He's clutching his automatic rifle across his chest in both hands; he squints at the card and at me, he doesn't say a word, just waves me into the compound, not with his hand, because that would mean he'd have to let go of his weapon, but with a jerk of his head. He does this every day. He knows it's me, but he has to do it by the rules. (I wonder what would happen to me if I pasted a picture of a dog's head across my face on the card. Would I get wasted? There's no place to pull off the road, or even to turn around, and there are 20 cars behind me. I think he'd simply take my card away. I'd have no identity at all. I'd be trapped in Saigon forever, roaming those wet hot streets, fighting the rats for snake heads in the gutter.)

So I pull through another gate, past more armed guards in fortified turrets on opposite sides of the road, who are there just in case I somehow got past the first guy. They never move, they look like painted images. I think of the money these guys are earning for doing nothing day after day. In one day they earn more than the peasants in the countryside see in six months. Finally I get to the parking lot in back of my building, which is indistinguishable from the one in any suburban shopping mall back home. Same black asphalt, same yellow diagonal stripes. I could be in Cincinnati, except for the smell; they haven't been able to figure out a way to suppress the stink of the Mekong yet. It's like rotten eggs, rotten fish and unwashed armpits all together. Inside the building, though, I escape even that. The building is air-conditioned, of course. A huge Carrier unit in the basement, whirring away 24 hours a day. Can you imagine where the service would have to come from? Or maybe all the big American corporations have branches in Saigon. Imagine a sales manager in Topeka saying to his (best? worst?) rep, "O.K., Jazzbo, you're off to the Saigon office tomorrow." Anyway, it hasn't broken down yet. It's cool in the summer, and cool in the winter (although the winter isn't much different from the summer here, just not quite as unbearably humid and stinking.)

There's still another guard inside, but he's nowhere near as menacing as the ones outside. He just has a sidearm. And a pot belly; the guards outside are hard and helmeted and humorless. This guard smiles, he's got bad teeth. He never checks ID. There's never anyone here who ain't supposed to be. He sits behind his silly little table and jokes and flirts with the typists. He waves me on down the corridor to the elevator, which takes me to the fifth floor. The elevator has Muzak, for God's sake, the Melachrino Strings playing Jerome Kern and other favorites on an endless tape loop. The same fucking music every day. There is an unbelievable version of Beethoven's Für Elise in which the arranger has stuck in a sort of Argentine tango motif section for two saxophones. It's enough to make me physically ill. I'm getting to know the places where the tape stretches and you hear weird distorted passages. Those are my favorites.

Then I come out of the elevator into the hallway. It's about a hundred and forty feet long, completely empty except for a few fire extinguishers hanging on the walls. The floors are tile and the ceilings are wood, and the walls are made of concrete blocks, painted yellow. The hallway echoes, you can hear anyone walking toward it, like from around the corner, from a long way off.

All the offices are off to one side or the other of this hallway. Some are small, especially those of the brass, but most of them are big rectangular spaces with anywhere from six to twenty people working in them. Mine has twelve. The office has windows, but they're covered up in heavy wire mesh, so nothing looks real when you look outside. Actually, all I can see anyway is the side of another building, and a small parking lot with a few jeeps and trash cans in it. The atmosphere inside the office is completely sterile. There's no one here but Americans, except once a day a native Vietnamese woman comes through and scrubs out the toilets with pine-scented disinfectant. Pine, for Christ's sake, the nearest pine tree is nine thousand miles away. She never speaks, just hums or grunts two notes under her breath, over and over again. Huh-huh, huh-huh. Tonic, dominant, rest, tonic, dominant. Key of G I believe. (G-I, I made a pun. Hot damn.) She uses heavy black brushes that look like they're for cleaning cannon barrels. I wonder whether she has any idea what she is doing. We are so paranoid that while she's here we lower our voices, speak in guarded and ambiguous phrases. Do we really believe she's a VC spy? I think we're in more danger from the fumes of the bowl cleaner. The stuff burns in my throat for a couple of hours after she leaves. And she cleans the goddamn bathrooms every fucking day. You'd think they were used by a herd of camels.

What do I do every day? I correlate reports that come in from the field commanders, vast waves of bullshit, utter lies about how successful our fine units have been in bringing peace and sweet reason to this troubled land. At first I could hardly bring myself to do it, I would read the shit and think about the lieutenant who had to write it, how he had to make things look optimistic even if Charlie snipers had gunned down three of his men the night before and one guy had flipped out and run off into the bush firing his rifle at shadows and hadn't come back, and most of the rest of the men had terminal diarrhea or some nameless jungle fungus.

Later on, I didn't even think of the reports as something that was supposed to have any relationship to reality, I would simply take the data and the numbers on the kill ratios and the pacification encounters initiated this month and how they were 16% higher than last month, and just transcribe them into my summary reports for my region of the country, which is Region 3. And since I don't want to make any waves that will ricochet back to my ass either, I inflate the positive and deflate the negative data by an acceptable factor so things wind up looking 5% rosier. Eventually, all the summary reports from me and my eleven regional coordinator colleagues, the ones in the other offices up and down this long hallway, go upstairs, where a one-star general and his staff collect everything together and put in their lies, and then he passes his monthly report on to the press information officer, who feeds the whole load of crap on to the US media for passing on to you gullible civilians back home.

And why is it necessary for this stream of lies to continue to come forth from our office? I have asked myself this question often. It was answered for me in a staff meeting last month. The one-star general I mentioned, who is my nominal boss, although I only see him about once every six weeks when he's not away from the office glad-handing the other brass, or giving parties for visiting media types in from Hawaii, said it. He informed us that our work of disinformation, or "translated fact," as he called it, was important so that "those with an incorrect view of the war" were not encouraged in their efforts to derail our efforts to defeat the communists. I was stunned to hear such a bald-faced remark at first, but afterwards I saw that it made a crazy sort of sense, given the context of this operation. God, What a mountain of idiocy.

The worst thing about this job though, worse than the lying, is the necessity to do night work. Routinely, we junior staff officers are moved around in our shifts, and one week in every two months I have to work either from 4 pm to midnight or midnight to 8 am. I really don't like driving around Saigon in the middle of the night! The staff is down to a skeleton of its usual size; there's practically nothing to do unless someone on the day shift has something urgent due and leaves me a note to work on it. I try not to sleep, although absolutely no one would care if I did; actually, I'm a little too nervous to sleep, really. Most of the time I just sit in my office and read. Recently I read all of Sartre's *Being and Nothingness* in one week. I don't know that it made a lot of sense, but at least I can say I read it. It's no more incomprehensible than some of the army code books I have to know about on the day shift.

On cooler nights, I even sit outside on the lawn in front of our building. I just take out a few cans of beer and sit out there in the middle of the night. I can watch the lights of the city, see our command posts with the cardboard guard figures (still staring forward just as they do in the daytime), and listen to the sounds of Saigon. Once in a while there is some distant gunfire, but not often.

I have fourteen years in this chickenshit outfit, and I'm looking forward to retirement. One year in Vietnam and then back to the world for three more. The brass hats are already putting pressure on me to re-up, but I'd have to be crazy to keep pounding away at this kind of rat shit. I need to get into a sensible world, like your academic world, where things may be freaky but you're not usually at risk to your life day in and day out. If I can handle the paper-pushers of the Regular Army and the freaked-out Vietnamese civilians, your professors and students ought to be a piece of cake for me. Keep your eyes open for a job in your neck of the woods, although I have a feeling it might be a little too quiet for me there, especially after this zoo.

Pfaff

(A taped interview with James Marshall Pfaff, Dean of the Division of Biology and Agricultural Sciences, who was born in 1913 in Pawnee Springs. He obtained an undergraduate B.A. from Cimarron State in 1935 and a Ph.D. in wildlife management from the state agricultural college in 1939, and came right back to Cimarron State to teach. He worked his way rapidly through the ranks and took his current position in 1950. A tall, slender, rangy western type with a long nose, a deeply cleft jaw, and a prominent Adam's apple, he moves slowly and speaks deliberately. With the appropriate uniform, he would make an exemplary highway patrolman. However, he wears the pinstripes of the administrator; but he always wears them with boots, elaborate cowboy creations in two or three colors of leather.

Dr. Pfaff has other idiosyncratic traits. He is an avid boater, although there is little water in our vicinity. On most weekends he hitches up one of his several powerful craft, which take up much of the space in his back yard, to his Oldsmobile station wagon and drives more than a hundred miles to an impounded lake across the border in the next state to the north. He usually brings his teen-age son or daughter and some of their friends with him on these trips; they love to water-ski. On his vacation, he visits more distant lakes, usually in Arizona, Wyoming, or Texas.

Dr. Pfaff, with his brother Les, also owns a large pig farm about twenty miles west of Pawnee Springs. The farm gate, in heavy wrought iron with gold-tipped vertical bars, is emblazoned with a gold boar's head in heavy relief. Once a year, usually in the early summer right after classes end, he invites the faculty and their families to the farm for a barbecue. He and his children take care of the main course, a whole pig baked on a motor-driven spit over a bed of coals; meanwhile, his wife and sister preside over a trestle table made of ten-foot planks, on which is arrayed a spectacular assortment of spicy and sweet farm-style dishes. His brother, a stocky, taciturn bachelor in sunglasses, battered straw hat, and bib overalls, principally concerns himself with the beer, dispensing it in unceasing streams from two kegs into our plastic steins, the same ones found in the Faculty Club, emblazoned with the Cimarron State seal.

The Pfaff brothers apparently turn a tidy profit from their operation. In addition, they are usually the winners of many of the blue ribbons given out for hogs at the state fair.)

Those years just after the war were so exciting, Bruce. It was like the country was brand new; everyone was enthusiastic, impatient, cheerful, like we had just finished cleaning out a septic tank and were breathing clean, fresh air again. There was a kind of muscular, practically palpable vitality in the atmosphere of society, something we never experienced before in my memory and something we haven't seen since. And there seemed to be no limit to what any of us could achieve, either alone or in groups. So it was a thrilling time to be in academia. The college had a sudden bulge in enrollment because of the GI Bill; the teachers were putting in overtime; it was the first time we'd ever had evening and Saturday classes here. The students were enthusiastic, too; they wanted those degrees so they could rush into the mainstream of postwar American life and recast it. To become successful, that's what they wanted; to get what was good out of life now, no need to forgo any more. And this was the kind of environment that Pyke McKenna came into.

DEGREES OF FREEDOM

I really thought McKenna had the makings of a star, or at least as close to one as we ever had in this instituion. I used to hold my breath when I thought about how blessed we had been to stumble onto him. He had everything going for him. He had been to Ohio State and had actually finished his degree, wonder of wonders in those wartime days, and he had even written up his dissertation and published it as a long paper in the American Midland Naturalist. It came out in 1949, I remember, and I in my files I still have the carbon copy of the manuscript, it must be 100 typed pages, that he gave to us when he arrived for his interviews. Professor Krantzler, his dissertation adviser, was an old friend of mine and had high praise for him, and he'd gone into the service and served his time for the Allied cause. When he interviewed, you could sense how eager he was to plunge into academic work; it was as if it was printed right there on his forehead. He was a striking figure in those days, very thin and intense, if you can imagine Pyke McKenna thin; and his eyes would almost snap as he spoke to you about his work.

He became a brilliant teacher, also; from the beginning, he showed great promise, and after a few years he became almost a beloved figure. That didn't last, of course, but he had an extraordinarily productive start. I thought of him as the embodiment of my theories of higher education. The concern he showed, both in the way he conducted his classes and in the personal discussions we had, that every student be educated to the fullest extent he was capable of, really warmed my heart. I have always said that the survival of our country as a democracy depends on an informed citizenry, and that it is the duty of higher education to produce a leadership caste for the nation. And as far as Cimarron State is capable of carrying out this mission, I think we can be proud of our role. Our division, at least, in my opinion, has many graduates who are mainstays of society and the agricultural and biological professions, both around here and around the world; and McKenna served well in helping to prepare these fine men and women for their obligations to society. At one time, I thought he was my heir apparent; it was my intention, at one time, to make him head of Biology, and then as his skills grew over the years, I thought I would feel ready to give him Divisional responsibility and recommend him for deanship. But of course that never came close to happening.

RICHARD LARSON

I did have some problems with him at the beginning because he always assumed that anyone would be ready to talk about his research and his ideas with him at any time and for any length of time. Now he did have some very interesting ideas, don't get me wrong, but I had just become Dean a year or so after he came, and I was still feeling my way around and was deluged with my administrative duties, so I couldn't always give him the attention he wanted.

In fact, he was the reason I moved Miss Freemartin into the nose gunner position just outside my office; I never had a system of appointments before; everyone knew when I could or could not be bothered. I suppose you know that I am a local product, and have lived in this area all of my life. I know the local people, and I know this institution, having gone here as an undergraduate and only leaving to go away to the state university for my doctorate. So what I am saying is that I felt very relaxed with all the staff here, not just the faculty and the rest of the administrators, but everyone all the way down to the groundskeepers and the freshman class. I never felt the need to systematize my life to that extent. But McKenna was slow to take the hint, so I thought it would be best for all concerned to put matters on a more formal basis. Well, you can imagine, I suppose, how McKenna responded when Miss Freemartin first told him that he would need to make an appointment to see me. I had the door closed and I didn't really hear what transpired, but I gather from what Miss Freemartin told me that hot words, not a few of which were of the unprintable variety, were exchanged! And McKenna was quite cool to me for an unreasonable length of time, years in fact, after that.

But he continued to do his job and do it well, and about as well as anyone we had on the instructional staff, for a long time. However, we no longer had the same kind of professional relationship that we had at the beginning of his time here. And I regretted that, but one thing I have learned as an administrator is that you have to guard your time or you will be chewed up and never be seen again. All of a sudden your presence or your opinions or both are wanted by a variety of people both within and without the state university system, and it takes a colossal amount of time to balance the needs of other people with those of your own and to make a contribution to the future.

DEGREES OF FREEDOM

At any rate, McKenna was the star performer of the department before and after that episode; he always came out on top in the numerical rating system I instituted to measure faculty performance. I think he was given tenure in a shorter time than any other professor we have had. But gradually he began to turn sour. I suppose I should have realized at the time that there were serious flaws in his character - flaws that turned out to be absolutely fatal, first in a professional sense and later, unfortunately, in a literal sense.

His problems stemmed, I am now convinced, from egomania and paranoia. As for egomania, they say all academics are prima donnas, and I suppose no one stays in teaching unless they have a need to perform before an audience, to lay out their life on the line in front of the students; I think every professor thinks they're someone special, that from their years of study they've discovered important things about life, and they want to pass it on, not necessarily the knowledge but the attitude they have toward learning, the joy of discovering new ideas. But most of them stop short of the dictatorial absolutism McKenna had about his thinking. He began to take it as a personal affront if anyone questioned what he was saying.

I've had students come in and say that McKenna nearly destroyed them in introductory courses by his heavy-handed superciliousness that he used in response to their innocent questions. For example, I think you may remember Tammy Dickerson, who finally graduated last year after being an off-and-on student for maybe ten years; she told me that in the introductory course she asked Dr. McKenna, quite innocently and for the purposes of information, or even curiosity, only, what he thought of the possibility that the world could have been created by God. McKenna stopped the class, she said, and stared at her for a long time, and then came down off the podium and descended into the midst of the class, came down as though he were stepping carefully into a manure-filled farmyard, then stopped in front of Tammy and addressed the class, saying, "Students, look carefully at what has happened just now; for you see clearly that representatives of the forces of repression are still about. These people are responsible for thousands of deaths, for endless suffering by innocent people, and for the unnecessary plunging of western civilization into ignorance, for the wastage of countless lives that could have been productive.

This young woman is a perhaps unwitting representative of a long and bloody tradition of philistinism, of an anti-intellectual movement that treats honest inquiry as heresy, as an activity punishable by torture and eventually by burning at the stake. Her question may seem innocent, but it betrays an attitude that says; there are some things that should not be thought about, things that we, the authorities, fear to be known. Let us live by convenient and traditional fictions, for they make us happy and content; it is more important that we live thus than that we know what is true. For the truth will not make us free, it will make us distressed, and negligent in our civic duties, which consist of the following: working all our lives for substandard wages in order that our bosses and their bosses may profit, and laugh at us over their costly after-dinner liqueurs; and voting for the candididates that they, the bosses, deem friendly to their causes; and not rocking the boat when evidence of grave injustice comes to light. Let us have faith that injustice, ignorance, poverty, and suffering are inescapable concomitants of the human condition, and let us live by the faith that nothing will ever improve for us until after we die. For this will make us docile herd animals, willing to follow wherever authority may find it convenient to lead us, whether this be to the breadlines of unemployment, or into the jungles of Vietnam." That was only one example; I think you might have heard about many other such instances.

And these events fed his paranoia, his other problem; he believed that the authorities, or the enemy, or (toward the end) the capitalist conspiracy were trying to disrupt his classes or other aspects of his professional life. He seemed to really believe that his name was on a list somewhere headed "Enemies of the State," and that was why he had so much trouble in his career.

I think I first noticed the decline of his professionalism in his committee work, where before he had always been conscientious and willing to take on big responsibilities - to write the department's five-year plan, to work on the community service policy statement, to take charge of the arrangements for the annual picnic - he did it all and did it well. Then I began to notice his attention wandering in meetings. He'd stretch and yawn loudly, or make sarcastic comments (which may have been funny taken out of context, but we had serious work to do), or he'd mutter things under his breath and hold his head in his hands. It became terribly disruptive. Then he'd volunteer for fewer and fewer assignments, and the ones I gave him to do would show up late or be halfheartedly done. So, to a large degree, he took no part in the growth and the progress of the department; it had to go ahead without him.

I think at the beginning, or at least after he'd been here for a few years, he had formulated, in his mind, a personal vision of the ideal department of biology - one organized on his principles, leading to his goals. But inevitably when you have groups of people who work together, there will be disputes, and you have to reach consensus if you're going to accomplish anything. And I don't know why McKenna was never able to understand that simple lesson. He was unwilling to compromise, and when his judgment was questioned, he'd yell and make personal remarks, and make everybody upset at him; and after a few iterations of this, he started to lose the respect of everyone. Finally, it seemed as if he completely gave up and retreated into himself, permanently.

Then, at that point, he became a vociferous complainer about the way things were decided. We had endless arguments over policy. He was a most articulate opponent, and at times he had points that were well taken, but he used to spoil it all by interjecting personal remarks directed to me. I am a very easy-going person, as I am sure you can attest, but some of the names he called me, I thought, were uncalled-for. More than one of our discussions ended with him stalking out of my office and slamming the door. When he was feeling coherent, though, usually toward the middle of one of our arguments, I asked him to bring up his objections at the scheduled monthly faculty meetings so that everyone on the staff could discuss these issues, but he could never be bothered to speak in such a structured forum. He seemed to prefer to speak through memoranda, addressed sometimes to me and sometimes to everyone on the staff - I am sure you got some of those - but he appeared incapable, by that time, of speaking in other than an insulting and self-righteous tone in his memos, so I doubt that anyone was converted to his point of view. And finally, toward the end, even those stopped coming. He no longer seemed to be a part of the department at all; his life, as far as he was concerned, was outside, out on the campus where he tried to be a sort of Messiah to the students, who would have nothing to do with him; or in the neighborhood taverns, where according to my sources he was spending more and more time.

Also, his professional attitude became more discourteous and remote. I remember one incident in particular, perhaps you were in the audience at the time, when we had an outside speaker, a young microbiologist from the University of Oregon, and McKenna got up after no more than ten minutes and walked out. Slammed the door then, also. I asked him afterwards why he stepped out so soon, and he said to me, "I didn't see how I could trust the man's science when he made so many linguistic solecisms - he couldn't tell the difference between principal and principle, and he thought media was singular. I do think a scientist ought to know how to read and write, at least a little bit, don't you?" And he would never even try to get outside research support. He claimed it was all rigged in Washington, wired, I think was the expression he used, and that only those who were in cahoots with the program administrators ever got funded. He said it didn't matter how good your ideas were, just who you knew. Well, it may have been that way at one time, and it may be coming to that again, but certainly during the late 50s and on through the late 60s there was a lot of money coming down for those who would take the time and effort to apply for it. And certainly at that time many people on this campus were raking it in. But then he would claim that his ideas for research were too unusual, or too advanced, and any reviewer or bureaucrat who looked at them would just be confused at what he was trying to do and he couldn't get a fair hearing. Well, I certainly never saw any evidence of that in any of the research work he did do with the undergraduate students. He didn't even try to publish any of it anywhere at all to my knowledge, never presented it either on or off campus.

I asked him every year if he wanted to give a paper at the state Academy of Science meeting, and he always answered me with some obscenity. I never knew what he had against the Academy; it has a very nice journal, and the annual meeting is very friendly and low-key. Lots of students come. We always try to get some big-name scientist from Texas or California to come in and give the keynote address; once Linus Pauling even came, I think back around 1951. My, that was exciting.

But to get back to McKenna; I was beginning to wonder how we could get rid of him; he was showing up for his teaching assignments but his lectures were becoming more and more incoherent. I heard tapes of some of them, and they were rambling productions which were just as likely to be about sociology, or claptrap metaphysics, as biology. To me they were absolutely unlistenable; I was ashamed that they were coming out of our department. But then that summer, just as I was trying to put together a case for dismissing him, he managed to kill himself. I was shocked, of course, but I'm not ashamed to tell you I also felt a great sense of relief. Well, the department hasn't been the same since he left us, but to me it's a lot smoother running operation. I certainly hope we never have a faculty member like him again, even though it was thrilling to have him around at the beginning. Sometimes, I do miss him; he was one of a kind. Thank God! (Laughter)

Conversation: Education

(During the six years I knew Pyke, we spent some time nearly every day discussing more or less important matters. These discussions took place everywhere we were together; in our offices, our homes, in bars and restaurants, and even [sotto voce] in faculty meetings behind Dean Pfaff's back. I have tried to reconstruct one or two of our conversations for this memoir; naturally, I have had to take great liberties in their arrangement. I have tried to keep pure invention to a minimum, and I fervently hope that whatever I have put down is true to the spirit of Pyke and also to my own beliefs.)

BRUCE: I've just come from teaching my first class, and I must say it was a real experience. I threw away my lecture notes and invented the whole class off-the-cuff; and I think the class even liked it.

PYKE: It doesn't surprise me in the least. In fact, that's usually what happens. The students can tell when you're reading from notes, in the same way we can spot LBJ or Walter Cronkite reading from the Teleprompter. There's something false in the tone of your voice and in the way your eyes move. Why did you do such a drastic thing, by the way?

B: I overestimated the background the students brought to the class. Would you believe only one of them had taken calculus?

P: Of course! You should have asked me first, I'd have filled you in with the straight skinny. Biology is sort of a consolation prize at Cimarron State; the students who have some ability in science and mathematics wind up in the physical sciences or engineering. After all, you can get a decent job after graduation, with some defense contractor, with no problems at all. Opportunities for advancement are unlimited, if you consider a life as a corporate yes-man an advancement. Our biology graduates wind up as sales reps or unemployed. Word gets around.

But we always get the romantics, the "feelies;" the ones who like to get in touch with their feelings, the ones who got all misty-eyed when they read Walden in high-school English, or when they went to see Bambi with their old maid aunts. We'll always get those as students. You know, the ones who love Nature as long as it's either cute or magnificent. They appreciate puppy dogs, baby seals, grizzly bears, whooping cranes, and bald eagles soaring over Mount McKinley; they don't like maggots, bats, spiders, slime molds, the Okefenokee Swamp, caves that aren't paved, or anything dead.

So I suppose you must have been a bit flustered when you realized all your careful plans were down the drain.

B: Man, I was sweatin' bullets up there. My throat got dry and I started to feel faint.

P: That's when you see what you're made of. I'm convinced the greatest teachers are the ones who can take that feeling of chaos, of being on the brink of disaster, and use it to sharpen their performance to the fullest. It must be like being a great athlete, or a singer in a difficult role, or a soldier in the heat of hand-to-hand combat.

B: There must be failures, though; disaster must happen once in a while. I know I don't want to repeat this experience ever again.

P: I suppose so, but what a thrill to pull it off!

B: Are you trying to tell me that's the way you give your lectures?

P: Not for a long time. I've probably given close to five thousand hours worth of class lectures at this institution, and I think I know every way to do it. I've come in with every word I wanted to say written out on a stack of papers, and I've also come in with nothing at all, hung over or otherwise unprepared.

In every case, I finished the class and never ran out of things to say. I don't really think there were ever any disasters.

Sometimes, of course, it goes better than other times. Nowadays, I usually remember roughly what I said in a similar class last year and also five or ten years before, so I don't need to bring in detailed notes. If I prepare at all, I suppose I prepare in my head, in the ten minutes before the bell rings; I try to think about the topics I need to cover and maybe some of the things I want to be sure to remember to mention. But once I get started, it seems as if one sentence calls others into my head, and I wind up improvising in a way throughout the whole lecture.

B: I don't think I could ever do that. I want to have everything planned. I want to cover, in my allotted hour, just what I intended to cover, and get through all the material by the end of the term. I think the students would feel cheated with anything less.

P: Not so. You beginning teachers are all alike. You're so earnest and motivated to serve the students. You'll change, though, we all do. I was exactly like you; I had the same problem. I remember the first class I ever taught here; it was on animal biology, a course for those who'd already had the introductory class. I thought I knew exactly what the students needed. I had a syllabus all down on paper. So many lectures on this group of organisms, so many on the next, going from the most undifferentiated to the most complex, culminating in the last lecture with a great peroration on Man. But it never turned out that way. None of the students could move along the path I'd laid out for them. Some concepts bored them and some puzzled them. This was back in the days when I still felt guilty if the students were confused. Now I know I'm doing my job correctly if at least half of them are. I had to spent much more time than I thought on what I thought was rudimentary, material I thought would certainly have been covered adequately in elementary biology; but either they'd forgotten it or it wasn't properly given to them. I felt guilty that I wasn't presenting material that was as advanced as I thought that they should have been learning, but at least they were undeniably learning something. In fact, not only did I never get to present my great ultimate lecture on the unique phenomena of human biology, I never got to humans at all; in fact, I never even discussed vertebrates! But still, it was a very successful class and the students never complained that they weren't getting their tuition's worth; in fact, more than one came up at the end of the term and told me it was not only the best biology class they'd ever had, but maybe the best class of any kind they'd ever taken.

B: The more I see you work and hear about you, the more I realize that you are one of the most skillful teachers I have ever met. I can't believe you're still here; why haven't you gone somewhere else? Actually, what made you come here in the first place?

P: Why did I come to Cimarron State? Do you think I should have gone to a place like Columbia or Caltech? Those places are for pansies, or maybe I should say African violets. They're hothouses. It takes a real man to survive in this environment.

No, seriously, you feel close to the earth here. This place is mythic; it's the hinge of the continent. We're in the middle of everything; I believe we're the college closest to the geographic center of the United States. Furthermore, amazingly, Pawnee Springs is at the absolute average elevation for the whole country, which is 1,803 feet above sea level! Anyway, it does feel, for whatever reason, like the place where everything began, an Eden. This is the zone where everything is in flux, whichever direction you look. Just think about it: to the east, don't you feel North America wearing away and sinking into the ocean, and to the west can't you sense the forces that created the Rockies still at work, grinding away causing earthquakes in California and geysers in Wyoming?

Even the weather is fierce, it's uncompromising. In the winter, we get blizzards and ten-foot snowdrifts; we could be in the Yukon. In the summer it dries up and gets to 110 above and we might as well be in Hell, or (worse) Las Vegas. We get those absolutely terrifying thunderstorms several times every summer, when the sky turns black and the violet light at ground level takes on an unearthly fluorescent cast; the colors of everything change, especially reds - barns look positively indigo -- and everything becomes still for a minute; you can sense all living things getting ready to hunker down for a big blow. Then the wind starts to sweep in, and the temperature suddenly drops ten degrees, and the first huge raindrops splatter on the ground. Oh, I love it, I really love it.

DEGREES OF FREEDOM

Quite a few tornadoes roar through this area every year, as well. I have never been really close to one, but I saw one on the horizon north of town, just last year, when I was out in the field collecting. The light was just right, illuminating it from the front, so it didn't look like a savage black storm. It was a glorious, rich greyish brown, like the fur on a grizzly bear's back. It didn't look real because it was so far off; it was almost like a painting from the National Geographic. Man, it was one of the most beautiful things I ever saw in my life.

So I can't leave here; I wouldn't want to, anyway. Cimarron State. Cimarron is an interesting word, etymologically; most people just think it's the name of a river, but it's a Spanish word that means, approximately, "wild and free." A wild horse is cimarron, and so is a human recluse that runs away from civilization and lives by himself in the hills. This wild and free place, this Cimarron State College - damn it, I love it here. This is the home of my spirit, and I really think I'd wither away and die if I had to teach in some college that was in the middle of a big city, like the University of Chicago.

Still, I can't deny that big and famous universities have something of a lure about them. They're the big leagues, and every academician would like to see how he'd measure up. The greatest advantage that I would see is that the students would be better. Only on the best campuses would you find a large number of the students who were like we were when we were in school. Here, the vast majority of the students in our classes are mediocre, "mediocre in the extreme," you might say.

B: But of course, we teach in a democracy. We live in a democracy, and we have democratic ideals. All of our citizens have a right to the best education we can give them, don't they? This is what the Dean told me on my first day on the job.

P: True, as far as it goes, but does that mean we have to give every one of our citizens an equally mediocre education?

And, of course, the Dean is far from an authority on education; he's really only a blockhead who blundered into a position of authority. A strangely truncated man, the Dean; his brain seems somehow impaired, don't you think - deficient in some integral design elements? At the very least, you'll agree with me that he doesn't exactly think with a Descartean clarity! He hasn't stuck his head inside a classroom for ten years. He hopes no one will notice.

His ideas on education are nothing but lackluster commonplaces that he trots out once in a while and parrots yet once more. The Chamber of Commerce likes to hear him, the Ladies Garden Club loves him, too. Both of them invite him over and over again to speak to their meetings; he puts it all in the division newsletter, remember? "The speech," I call it, is what he repeatedly presents - the high-sounding call for higher education to provide functionaries to carry out the machinations of the Realm. They've heard it all many times before, but that's what they like about it; it leaves them with a nice warm comfortable traditional feeling; they feel good about themselves that they agree completely with everything that this nice professional education administrator says.

So, contrary to what Pfaff says, we don't want to give everyone identical treatment in any class, even the most elementary. And, of course, we have to realize that not everyone has the right to an advanced degree. There is a place in society for the best, and for the best of the best.

B: I'll be damned, Pyke McKenna is an elitist. I'd never have guessed.

P: You're damn right I am. Tell me, how do you teach your classes? Do you try to stimulate the best students, or do you scale back to the pace of the average student?

B: Give me a break, your lordship, I just started out in this business. At the moment, I think I'd answer by saying that I have an obligation to the taxpayers of the state to give all their children something. In the classroom, I believe I would try to find enough of a middle ground so that nearly everyone in the class would come away with something they could hold onto and maybe even use. But I'd try to say enough that was stimulating so that the brighter students would seek me out after class, or better still, go off on their own to learn more about what interested them. I'd regard that sort of outcome as a success.

P: I used to think exactly as you did, but now I think you're mistaken. I've become an elitist, as you implied. Now, I deliberately frame my lectures so that the average student gets lost; my goal is to puzzle and provoke the few kids in the class who have an intellectual cast of thought, even to offend them, if need be, to get them aroused. I don't want to be popular in any sense. I'm hard-nosed, I have little or no tolerance for sloppy thinking, and I don't want to run a class where everyone leaves the room feeling nice and warm. I think my classes have the highest percentage of dropouts of anyone in the division. But I want it that way; I want to spend the majority of my time dealing with ten percent of the class.

Incidentally, as far as the taxpayers are concerned, they have given me the freedom to teach the way I see fit. (By way of their duly elected representatives, the state commission on higher education of course, who awarded me indefinite tenure by their official action of May 22, 1953.) My point, I suppose, is this; what is the reason to struggle at the difficult enough task of being a professional, a professor, if the bulk of your existence consists of exercises that have the effect of watering down your most deeply held beliefs?

B: Well, I'm not convinced a professor can't be gentle. As we all agree, not everyone in society can be a scholar. But living as we do in a system of government where the people have the ultimate say, or are supposed to have the ultimate say, in what goes on in it, I think it's critically important that the majority of the people understand at least a little bit about what goes on in science, how scientists live, what they do, and how what they do fits into the whole cultural background of the rest of society. I'd like to make people more aware of science. I doubt that very many men and women of any age ever think very much about scientists, or have any kind of curiosity about what they do. And this despite the urgency and necessity of science in everybody's daily life. I really think that should change, must change if we scientists are to continue to be seen as a necessary part of the culture, and to me it seems clear that every practicing scientist has a duty to inform the public about our work and why it's important. I mean, especially biologists have to be cognizant of this. We have to convey the fragility and the diversity of the natural world and why it's important to keep it as intact as we can. But besides, virtually everything people do has a scientific component, and if you're ignorant of the basic principles that govern your whole existence, you might as well be in the stone age, or sleepwalking through life. I really don't see why society, now, doesn't demand some evidence of scientific literacy, the way they do with mathematics and reading. And to me, a lot of classroom teaching, at least of undergraduates, is about that, about conveying fundamental concepts, and increasing the base of scientific literacy of my students. I would feel better if I could teach so that no one would drop out, and at the end the majority of the class would retain an appreciation of the background of my field, rather than having 90% of them gone and grumbling by midterm, with only a few left who wanted to go on professionally in biology.

P: Well, it's an issue that's many-sided. But to me it comes down to honesty with one's self. Maybe there are professionals, educators of a sort, who ought to devote themselves to the kind of basic instruction in the most rudimentary aspects of a subject; but it seems to me that this should not be our job. The students ought to be well past that stage when they come into our classes. We should not have to convert the heathen; we should be instructing them in the minutiae of the priestly rituals.

I mean, why do we bother to call ourselves professors? I have anguished over this for years. I suppose one of the meanings of profess is to pretend; to claim to know something we don't. In some of our classes, many of us follow this definition. I've done it myself, hundreds of times. It is necessary, we say, at times, not to confuse the beginning student with our doubts, for the same reason that when we teach a baby to walk we don't tell him he may be hurt if he falls down. So we make everything a little simpler than it really is.

Then again, we also profess in a different way when we assert that we know or believe something, as in a profession of faith. In our overall role as academics, I think we intrinsically use this definition. We believe that we are a special class of humans, qualified by training or experience to inculcate facts, knowledge, or wisdom to those who listen to us. This seems to me to be an ideal goal for most of us, as when a Christian minister says that he is a man of God. He may be sometimes, but he is human, and has failings. So do those of us who profess to know.

Finally, profess is the root word for professional, which implies a mastery of some difficult skill. We would like to believe this of ourselves, that we are artisans of the truth; but most of us, I think, are still untalented apprentices, forever conscious of imperfection, of clumsiness in the way we perform our duties. After a lecture, most of us have a twinge of guilt over not really having said what we wanted to; we resent it that there are students in our class who did not listen, and we rack our brains for ways to improve our timing and our stage presence. We are like actors who strain to fill the roles given us by the great playwrights; but in our case the lines are not written for us, the play is not divided into acts, and neither we nor the audience may completely understand the language of the drama.

Dworshak

(Larry Dworshak is a sociologist who works for the U. S. Department of Commerce in a small two-story building near the railroad yards in Fort Worth. The office in which he is situated is a large open communal area in which roughly thirty people work. Most of the employees seem to be engaged in briskly transferring substantial accumulations of paper from one part of the room to another using wheeled carts. There is little privacy except for chest-high panels on two sides of his desk, and a continual clatter of typing fills the room.

Dworshak collects data on urban poverty in southeastern and southwestern cities and attempts to project future trends in the area by writing elaborate computer models. He obtained his M.A. degree in sociology from Cimarron State in 1967, having attended our school from September of 1965 to that date. He had graduated as a physics major from the University of Delaware in 1963, but dropped out of college life for two years for, as he puts it, "my Wanderjähre," roaming across the country in a Volkswagen bus, with a constantly changing set of companions, and taking a series of short-term employments when he needed money.

Larry is a bony, dark fellow in his early thirties, prematurely balding, with a rumpled black beard about nine inches in length. His long teeth are discolored and somewhat askew, and he smokes heavily. The day I interviewed him, he was dressed from head to foot in black; a turtleneck sweater, denim slacks, and engineer boots.)

I can't believe this fucking place sometimes, man, Fort Worth and working for Uncle Sugar, I mean, especially after thinking about what an unreal place Cimarron State was when I was there, and probably still is to a great extent. Chicken Shit U, I used to call it. Pawnee Springs seemed like a throwback to Truman's America, with those tree-lined streets and Norman Rockwell back yards full of collie dogs and freckle-faced boys. Although in other parts of town we had a strong conservative religious undercurrent, too, with the Mennonite and Jehovah's Witnesses enclaves, full of somber men and tight-lipped women in black. Yet downtown, in complete contrast, was a group of asshole entrepeneurs in wing-tip shoes, straw hats and double-breasted plaid suits, running the city for their own selfish commercial advantage. When I was there, I think the mayor owned a funeral home and the city council had as its four members a Jesus-freak housewife, a lawyer, a department store executive, and a chicken rancher. Not exactly reflective of the socioeconomic distribution of the population. I think they had the precincts, like, gerrymandered so no academic could win even if every student came out to vote for them, and of course they were so fucking apathetic I doubt if they got a 10% turnout anyway. I could hardly believe my fellow students; it was like the 60s were not happening to them. I mean, like obviously most of them were from rural areas or small towns, but going to college is supposed to expose you to new viewpoints and to show you that the way you and your parents have always thought about things isn't the only way to view the world. But these students were all pathetically eager to get their degrees, so they could go out and get a good job - which around PS meant either being a salesman for some feed grain dealer or an account executive for a slaughterhouse. They seemed to be programmed - to have had some goals, put into their heads by some uncle or whatever when they were ten years old, that had never changed - and they were continuing to carry out this program like they were a fucking bunch of robots. And anything that might cause them to deviate from the prescribed course that the uncle had laid out for them was to be resisted, whether this meant becoming politically active or trying pot for the first time. So the great majority of them were bourgeois apathetics. The townies and council types were prepared to tolerate the college as long as the students, such as the ones I just described, and especially the faculty didn't make any waves, man; as long as they'd keep coming downtown and buying the college pennants and chocolate malts and third-hand convertibles they'd been selling to the college community for as long as Cimarron had been there. What a bummer.

So this is the way things had been like, I guess, for forty years. And all of a sudden here we are in the middle of the Vietnam War, but you sure as hell couldn't tell it from the way people around Pawnee Springs were behaving. Were those headlines in the newspaper just fairy tales, is that why people paid them no attention? I think our local paper - the Gazette, wasn't it? - would just as soon have ignored the whole thing, for fear it might upset people; but luckily that wasn't quite possible.

Even before I came to Cimarron, in '65, I was against the war. I remember how I felt when I heard about the Tonkin Gulf incident in '64; I was down like on Fisherman's Wharf in San Francisco, me and a couple of my buddies, and they let out a big cheer and allowed as how we were finally going to show those North Vietnamese bastards a thing or two. And I could tell, man, that the whole thing was faked; I just knew from the way Johnson announced it that it was a trumped-up incident, sort of a Reichstag fire affair. Conveniently forget that it says in the Constitution that Congress has to declare war. Like blame the Commies and declare a national emergency, and careful democratic scrutiny of the issues be damned. It's a traditional tactic that totalitarian societies use to arouse their citizenry; "our countrymen are, like, in danger and desperate measures are necessary; give us temporary emergency powers to deal with the desperate situation." It worked for Hitler and it worked in '64, and I imagine we'll see it again at intervals throughout our history! LBJ was itching to bomb the North Vietnamese, and we found out later he had his list of targets already drawn up, but even if this had not been the case, this phony "reprisal" of his, seven miles off the coast of North Vietnam, was a pernicious and treacherous misrepresentation. I tried to persuade my friends that this was what was going on, but they wouldn't hear any of it. They weren't used to being lied to by the U. S. government, not yet, though they should have known even then; but I guess they finally like realized, not too long afterwards.

Well, for me, that really galvanized me against the war. I suppose I started to become somewhat of an anti-war freak, one of the first, probably. It was also probably when I started to grow up.

I was a complete hedonist at that time, man; my only standard of ethics was what made me feel the most groovy at any particular instant. But for some time I had been wondering whether I could go on that way for the rest of my life. It seemed as if I owed our society something, strange as that may sound, especially since it looked as if it was about to go astray in a really big way. I must admit that I thought about running away from the system, like so many of my friends had done and would be doing; but when I thought about that realistically, it made no sense. What would I do for the rest of my life in Amsterdam, or Manchester, or even Toronto? I'd always be a foreigner; I'd never fit in. So I was stuck; I'd always be American, and damn it, this is my country, man, and while it's still a free society, I'm going to do what I can to make it see the error of its ways.

Well, once I'd decided that, like in a general way, it was only necessary to work out the details. This is the way I was thinking then; shit, was I naive! I could do most, I decided, by going back to school. Even though our country's perception of intellectuals has always been a disapproving one, I felt there was too much factual material I was still ignorant of for me to make an impact. I had a certain, like, native articulateness, but that was all I had going for me.

I'm not sure why I wound up coming to Cimarron. I'd been through PS on my way to California, but I never spent any significant amount of time here; I remember the college, but I had no particularly favorable impression of it or of this area. I suppose my thinking went this way; I am a bright enough guy, but all my training has been in science. Now I'd like to change fields and work in more of a social science area, and also I want to have a chance to speak out and be heard. If I go into some prestigious Ivy League or Big Ten program, I'll have to work so hard on my academics that I won't have time for public expression of my views. In addition, I'll be, like, a little fish in a big pond. Maybe I'd be most valuable at an institution far away from the hotbeds of radicalism; someplace in the heartland. If I can reach the conservative middle-America farmers and ranchers, maybe I'll really have accomplished something. God damn, I can't believe I ever thought that way, but I sure as hell did!

And finally, there was the matter of money. I don't know if anyone on the board of trustees realizes this, but at Cimarron State there's no such thing as out-of-state tuition. You'll even educate a foreigner from Timbuktu for the same amount of bread as some farm boy from ten miles outside of town. There aren't many academic institutions where that is true any more, especially cheap state-supported ones. So, when all the alternatives were totaled up, there weren't a lot of choices, and I sent in my application and they accepted me right away, although I didn't find out about it for a while because I'd been leading a, like, peripatetic existence for quite a spell, and I'd given a return address where I'd been living for a few weeks; it was a girl's apartment who, by the time the acceptance came through, I hadn't seen for a while, and when she finally got around to forwarding my mail it was a little late to be accepting their offer; but that was no real problem and they were happy to take me on.

So over the mountains I came, and pulled into town from the west in my Microbus, and drove around for a bit, and I had a chill feeling that I'd made a really serious mistake. "Sleepy" is not the word for PS: "comatose" would be more like it. I fought back a sudden urge to keep driving until I got back to Delaware; I remembered what my old man had said the last day he saw me, then, about hoping he'd be lucky enough to die before he ever laid eyes on me again; and that was like a powerful urge to keep me on this side of the Mississippi. So, I, like, matriculated.

At first I signed up for a political science major. But man, was I disappointed in my advisor and in the rest of the teaching staff. A little guy named Wortmann was my first advisor; did you ever know him? He was really a caricature. Tweed jackets with leather patches, white mustache, always puffing on a pipe -- I could hardly believe the guy, here he was two thousand miles from the ivy-covered walls of the fucking Ivy League, acting out a part that no one cared whether he could perform or not. Shit, man, he'd never been east of St. Louis. The only thing that didn't fit his image were his glasses; he had those kind with only a frame on top, the bare lenses just hanging down to his cheeks. They were always twisted; it gave him an incompetent nerdy look. And, intellectually, he really didn't know a fucking thing about government or politics. He'd done his thesis - an M.A. from Nebraska, back in '31 - about self-government in German Catholic immigrant communities in the Dakotas; and he told me, flat out, he was proud of the fact that never even went there, never interviewed one immigrant for his thesis. He got it all out of the literature, he said, and he claimed to be able to read German well, but I think he was lying about that.

Luckily, at a seminar early in the term, I met a young sociologist, Steve Thomson. My man, Doctor Steven J. Steven with a V, Thomson with no P. He and I hit it right off from the beginning. First off, he was a lot younger; he's only three years older than me. He had just got his Ph.D. from Massachusetts, and went right into teaching at Cimarron. We arrived in PS the same day. Politically, he was a really bright and aware guy, and he was a lot of fun besides, very witty, sharp with words, professional and ironic. A clean-cut dude too, tall, lean, rimless glasses like John Lennon, Western shirts, always wore a union button. He belonged to several locals.

Steve was interested in the sociology of poor people, and especially their fate in militaristic societies. He'd done field work among the Indians in the Guatemalan hill country, right after the CIA-sponsored overthrow of the Arbenz government in '54. Incidentally, that is a real-life tragedy, man, that almost no one in this country has ever heard of. Those people in Guatemala are so fucking powerless and oppressed; they've been shot or macheted by the thousands, some of them for the "crime" of arguing with a soldier who's been told to burn their crops. Yet Guatemala is a hell of a lot closer to home than Hungary or the other oppressed Communist countries we bleed our hearts over.

Anyhow, Steve and I would meet for discussions, and drinks, quite regularly at first; the drinks made the discussions easier. Then I started to go over to visit him at his house. He's married to a great-looking redhead from Panama, her name is Micaela; and she has a sister, Consuela Castellana, who lives with them. Consuela is practically a dead ringer for Steve's wife; and we, the sister and I, that is, started to find each other attractive. She spoke almost no English when we met, but as we spent more time together we both picked up each other's languages. I speak a lot of Spanish now, and it's helped me out on this job a lot.

Steve had come to Cimarron to do research on conditions typical of Indian reservations. I told Steve about some of the problems I was having in the Poli Sci department, and he urged me to come over to his shop. Wortmann didn't care at all when I told him; I think he was happy to have one less M. A. to shepherd through. So I became Steve's first graduate student.

He sent me, first of all, to all the libraries within two hundred miles, and also showed me how to get materials from faraway libraries, like that of the University of Illinois, where they got to know me very well, at least by mail. They have great holdings in my field, and they didn't put up a lot of barriers to some out-of-stater borrowing their precious books. A letter on official letterhead, I learned, can get you a long way, even one with the dumb Cimarron Seal with the farmer and the fucking soldier shaking hands.

His idea was that a student should know the literature thoroughly before he set out to do his own research; that way you didn't go rushing off in all directions. Only after I was done with that to his satisfaction, and was able to write a coherent section on the history of my problem, which was matriarchal tendencies among the Plains Indian tribes, was he willing to let me go out and do my field studies.

It was in the library that I ran into Pyke McKenna. I saw a long-haired, middle-aged guy in hiking boots, sitting right on the floor at the end of a bookstack, with his knees drawn up practically to his chin; he was sitting there reading "Black Elk Speaks," which is a book of interviews with the last traditional medicine man of the Oglala Sioux. And I was curious to see anyone at all reading that book, because there's some pretty heavy mystical and anthropological shit coming down from it; and I was even more surprised to see someone I didn't know reading such a book, because I thought I knew everybody from the social sciences who had even a peripheral interest in native American culture. So I stopped and said, "Excuse me, but are you a student of Indian lore?" And he looked up at me with those piercing eyes and said, "No, I am a student of perception, and especially of the ways that non-industrial civilizations look at reality." I must have looked interested, so he went on, holding up the book and shaking it at me. "This man, Black Elk, was a great religious leader; and among his people he would be considered a scientist. He had a great unifying vision of Being. Yes, he happened to be a Plains Indian, and yes, he did take part in what we whites consider to be a massacre, at the Little Big Horn; but he was a great American, as great as Jefferson in his way, and I wish he was here to teach me how to live."

I was pretty impressed. "Hey, I agree with you, man; I also wish he would talk to LBJ."

Pyke laughed, from a sort of sneering expression; it came out as a snort. "That would be an extraordinary meeting. Perhaps the President would make him Secretary of the Interior. It'd be good politics, and he needs a few breaks with the media and also with the rest of us."

We continued our conversation, and I made it a point to find out who he was. It was a rare day when you could find someone on our side in PS. And he was even over 30, haw, haw.

I mentioned him to Steve, who thought he'd heard of him; he got out a file of letters that he'd saved from the PS Gazette, addressing various social issues. And Pyke was in there, several times. I was pretty impressed again when I read them, impressed enough to borrow them from Steve and type copies of them out on my old Underwood. (This was before the days when everyplace had its own photocopy machine; I think we grad students were limited to 20 free pages a month, and the department office had to make the copies for us. I knew they'd look fishy-eyed at me if I brought in subversive stuff like this for my state copying account. Our department head, old "Big Daddy" Starrett, probably would have turned my name in to the FBI.)

When you told me you were coming, I brought them over, just in case you hadn't seen them. These are photocopies. You can have them if you want. Here's one I like a lot, from early '64, pre-Tonkin, remember:

DEGREES OF FREEDOM

"Dear Sir,

"The recent spate of coups and countercoups in South Vietnam does not seem to have provoked the American public. The country is remote and no abundance of our countrymen is there. But the implications of these power struggles seem obvious. The U. S. is being drawn ever deeper into the civil politics of that country. It has been charged that our diplomatic corps and intelligence services are fomenting factional strife, providing assistance and arms to candidates who espouse views that appear advantageous to U. S. interests; this has implicated the U. S. Government in a number of squalid circumstances, including assassination. It behooves all of us as citizens to look away from our confined provincial interests and to consider the global, ethical issues; to what extent does our government, its soldiers and other operatives, have the right to decide for the Vietnamese people what form of government they should have? I doubt that the Johnson administration would abide a pack of rich Asian outlaws who freely roamed our countryside, encouraging and subsidizing our government's most extreme antagonists.

"I urge the residents of Pawnee Springs to take a look at the course we have chosen to pursue in southeast Asia and to ask our elected representatives to curtail our political meddling, before we are caught entirely off-guard and are put into a situation where the bulk of Vietnam's people oppose us. This would be a blow to our global reputation as well as a potential catastrophe for both Vietnamese and Americans.

Yours sincerely, P. G. McKenna"

A few others in the same vein, also; and then look at these, by someone supposedly named "H. G. McHenna;" I was never really sure whether Pyke wrote these or whether someone else did, trying to satirize Pyke's views by presenting their diametric opposites. Here's one:

"Dear Editor,

"From time to time I take time from my busy life to pray for our fighting men in southeast Asia. They are far from home and family, far from their beloved sports teams, and there are no supermarkets or shopping centers out there, far west of Honolulu. We need to show that we support our fighting men at this time in their cause. I was reading the paper the other day with my five-year-old granddaughter, and she saw a picture of soldiers in the paper, and asked me who they were, and I told her it was the Wyoming National Guard. And she said to me, "Grandpa, I love the Wyoming National Guard, and I am going to ask God to bless them when I pray to Him tonight, before I go to bed." Out of the mouths of babes, as they say. I urge everyone in the area to also pray for our fighting men, and to pray for the President (I know every day he thinks of and prays for them, fighting for freedom together), and to pray for the democratic fighting forces of South Vietnam, pray that they will keep their weapons in good condition. I know this will speed the time when our fighting men come home to a grateful and proud America."

(I think that sounds like Pyke, myself.)

About two weeks after I first met him, I called to invite him over to the Arms for a few beers. This would have been in the middle of November, '65. I remember it was a chilly day, around freezing, but the sky was bright and all the trees were bare. Pyke took a minute to recall who I was, but he did then remember quite clearly. He said, "Ah, yes, the one with the pony tail," which I did indeed wear at that time. He was pleased to accept the invitation. I very much wanted him to meet Steve, too.

He came into the Arms, puffing and red-faced, wearing an old blue Navy war surplus peacoat. He looked around and around and finally saw me waving at him and came over and shook my hand and sat down. I introduced him to

Steve, who he hadn't met before. He said he knew almost all the faculty since he'd been there for so long and had served on so many interdepartmental committees. I asked him if he knew Wortmann, and he just looked up at the ceiling, screwed up his eyes, smiled, and scratched his beard; then he slowly said, "Yes," and we all laughed. The three of us were sitting around one of those battered round wooden tables, I'm sure you know what I'm referring to; the ones that look like they've been run over repeatedly by trucks, just this side of the pool tables. Pyke seemed a little uncomfortable, or maybe it was just my imagination; it was a little bit cold in there. We all talked about our work for quite a while, pretending to be interested in each other's specialties. At least I was a scientist by training, in my undergraduate days, and I could respond to some of the things he was saying; his ideas came across as nice, in a way, but a lot of the stuff sounded a little too qualitative for my taste.

Then, as I knew it would, our discussion turned to politics. It was around the middle of our second pitcher of Drewry's. I had made some remark about Johnson; he'd just approved sending in enough more soldiers to boost our troop level to 175,000 men. And this was just after the great blackout in the northeast, and Pyke said, "Yes, he's been trying to turn out the lights on us, but he's going to be surprised; we're going to pull the plug on him. Burn out the light at the end of his tunnel. You know Americans will never stand for all their sons and their neighbor's sons being stationed over there and getting shot at. He can't count on public approbation any more; he's gone over the top, and I think this is the beginning of the end."

Steve thought Pyke was a little early in his judgment; he thought Johnson was such a consummate master of p. r. that it would take a lot longer for the public to see through the deception. I believed that there was such a mass of apathy out there that the Administration could go on manipulating public opinion indefinitely. "Just keep the flag waving and keep raising the Red scare," I said, "that'll keep us amused for five or ten years to come."

Pyke thought we were underestimating the desire of the public for peace. "The voters always go for the peace candidate," he said; "they voted against Goldwater because he scared them. Now that LBJ is starting to sound like him, he's going to lose support; and don't be surprised if it comes fast."

"Maybe you're right," said Steve; "maybe it's time to give the American people a little push. If they had some facts they could understand, they might decide to do the right thing. Why haven't we academicians tried to teach them a few things before this?"

"On this score, there's been a massive failure of the entire American intellectual community," Pyke said, "and it may be too late to repair the damage we've done by our silence; but it seems to me we've got to try. I've sent letters to the newspaper and to Congress, but maybe it's time to try to reach the voters."

Steve called attention to the efforts of faculty and students at the big Eastern and California schools to hold "teach-ins" to try to educate the students and any of the townspeople who cared to listen on what was really going on. "Pyke," he asked, "would something like that have a chance in hell of succeeding here?"

Pyke didn't answer right away. He took a gulp of beer, sighed, and rubbed his beard. "It's hard for me to judge; perhaps a majority of the populace here are down-the-line orthodox flag wavers, maybe even a majority of the students. You'd get bad publicity from the media, that is, those sections of it that would even deign to take notice. We'd need a certain level of support, a dozen or so committed partisans, who would be willing to risk censure. Maybe even someone like yourself, Steve, who would be at hazard because he doesn't have tenure, couldn't take the gamble." Steve waved his hand in deprecation of that view. "At any rate, it would have to be more than just me, or me and a few students. I have a poor reputation around town, and it'd be too easy, I'm afraid, for a group led by me to be dismissed as a band of crazy radicals."

"I think what we need to do," I said, "is to test the waters. Announce the formation of a study group of opponents to our foreign policy, have a public meeting, and see who shows up. Plaster the campus with posters, announce it in our classes, and just see how it goes. Bring out at the meeting the options we could look at trying to do, and see if we can find a nucleus of people to support a teach-in, or protest, or letter-writing campaign, or whatever. If no one is interested, at least there'll still be the three of us."

Steve and Pyke both agreed that it would be worth a try. I volunteered to draw up a poster and Pyke said he'd run off a hundred copies using Biology's copying account. Steve offered to find us a place to have the meeting; it couldn't be in a campus building since we weren't a Registered Student Organization, but he thought the YMCA would go along -- it was only a block away from the Union. So we left the Arms, full of conspiratorial joie de vivre; but it seemed like the beginning of a long journey.

The meeting wasn't as easy to bring about as we thought. First, the YMCA turned us down, saying their rooms were all booked for the rest of the term until after Christmas. I knew for a fact that wasn't true, because I used to hang around down there (they subscribed to a good selection of out-of-town newspapers) and I never saw any type of organized meeting at all going on. Anyhow, we finally managed, by all three of us going down and cajoling the priest, Father Jaroszev, to convince the campus Catholic chapel to let us hold the meeting there. He seemed to worry that we'd all be a bunch of bomb-throwing anarchists, but we assured him that our main concern was educational, and that we merely wanted to make sure that alternative points of view were made available as information to the public.

Then, Steve made what I considered an error in informing the head of Sociology, the aforementioned and redoubtable Starrett, that he was considering some activity in this area. Big Daddy practically blew up at him, saying that it showed a "lack of seriousness" about his responsible state-supported teaching job, and that he didn't see how Steve, as a beginning professor, could find the time to be a social activist and still prepare properly for his professional duties. He practically promised Steve that any sort of bad publicity that might come into the department over the consequences of his political actions would cause Steve to suffer greatly down the line. Well, Steve was really pissed, of course, but he couldn't completely ignore what his overseer said. The result was that Steve didn't think it would be wise for him to be a highly visible figure in the movement; that he would help as much as he could, but at least for now it would have to be behind the scenes.

So that left me and Pyke, and he was adamant that no one would take us seriously if he was seen to be the leader of the group. He refused to be named on the original poster that we put up; and because I wasn't willing to take the heat alone, it was incumbent on me to find a partner to help me organize the meeting. It took me a hell of a long time. Everyone I spoke to who was even a little bit sympathetic to what we were trying to do, faculty as well as students, said they weren't experts and weren't willing to stand up before a group of people and pretend to know more than they did about the situation.

Finally, a week later, I found someone, by blind luck. I was calling a professor at home, a mathematician named Gaylord Mahaffey; but he wasn't home, and I wound up talking to his wife Francine about our predicament. She turned out to be very sympathetic, and amazingly had some experience in southeast Asia! Although a native of Illinois, she spoke French fluently, having studied literature at the Sorbonne, and had been a visitor in Saigon back when it was part of French Indo-China, around 1950. "I always dreamed about going back," she told me, "but then I met Gaylord back in Paris. He's a native Irishman and was on leave from the University of Dublin to take a summer colloquium. We fell crazy in love and the next thing I knew I had moved, from an apartment that overlooked the Seine to one that overlooked the Liffey, and I was married to a strange red-haired man who spoke differential equations and had never heard of Gide." They had come to the U.S. in 1958 and both started teaching at Cimarron, but she had become pregnant and was now caring for their two children; however, she agreed to co-chair the meeting with me and to help out in any way she could. "I owe it to my old friends, who are bound to be suffering terribly in the tragedy of war and repression in that beautiful country."

We agreed to meet the next Friday morning, the day after Thanksgiving, at the Union for coffee and discuss some of the things we might cover. Practically no one was around, since it was a scheduled holiday for classes. When I saw her, my poor heart did a flip; this lady in her late 30s was flat-out beautiful, a lot like Grace Kelly except for dark brown hair with red highlights; and when she took my hand, hers was so soft and warm that it was like making love. It's a good thing Consuela wasn't there; she has a hell of a temper and is ferociously jealous besides. Anyway, Francine took the lead in our discussions; it's just as well, because my tongue seemed to have swelled up in my mouth. She had a big legal pad and sketched everything out very business-like. All I had eyes for, I'm afraid, were her beautiful tits resting lightly on the surface of the paper! "I think I should open the meeting and make a few remarks about the history of Indochina; how there got to be two Vietnams, that sort of thing. Then you can touch on the recent history, the impasse the U.S.A. has gotten itself into. Then, if necessary, someone else can discuss the moral options; or perhaps we could call for discussion from the audience. It should go very well. At the end, we can call for donations, and ask people to sign up for future meetings."

I was pretty excited, for a lot of reasons, at the end of our talk. We tentatively scheduled the meeting for December 1, the next Wednesday.

I called Pyke at his office, and left word with someone who answered the phone from next door (Was it you? No, you weren't here yet, were you? Oh, yes, I think it was you after all) about the time. That evening, he called me at home, asking me if I'd need any help with the publicity. Francine was going to design the posters, so I said that I thought everything was under control. Then he said he'd like to donate some money to get us started, $75, and that he'd also bring something to eat. He'd make his own special jelly-filled doughnuts, he said. And how about coffee, he asked. We'd surely need coffee for the visitors. He said he'd call the priest and see what we could do.

By Monday evening, Francine had brought over the posters to show me; they were beautifully done, on canary-yellow paper. The left half of the design was an outline drawing of an American GI, looking world-weary and smoking a joint. The right half said, in bold type at the top, "VIETNAM: Students and Citizens Against the War." And below, "Informational Meeting and Discussion, 12 Noon Wednesday, Dec. 1, St. Stephen's Church. L. Dworshak and F. Mahaffey, Moderators. All welcome to attend." It looked good to me. There were about a hundred; it wasn't necessary to accept Pyke's generous offer to run them off on Biology's photocopier. Francine said she'd post forty or so around town, in stores and shopping centers, and leave the rest to us to put up around the campus. I put up most of them, but Pyke helped out too; he wasn't in his office when I stopped by, but I left a stack of them on his desk, and on Tuesday, when I walked around the campus, a lot of them were up in places I hadn't put them. It did seem that they got pulled down pretty damn fast.

The day of the meeting, I was strung out. I'd taken mescalin the night before -- my Panamanian friends could always get it, and I was used to it

-- but this time it was rotten stuff. Usually it made me feel free, and let me see and hear the hidden structure of things, but this time it left me feeling cruel and disgusted. Disorganized, was the way I'd sum up what it did to my head. I couldn't wait for it to be over, and fortunately it didn't last too long. Oddly, it didn't affect Consuela that way at all; the only difference was, she took it in pineapple juice and I dissolved mine in Portuguese rosé. She wanted to make love, of course, but I was too wasted to do anything but sleep, so she went home.

Anyway, I woke up that morning around 9; my throat was burning as if I'd inhaled a dozen cigars, and it hurt my head to walk. Every time my foot hit, everything I looked at seemed to light up, bright rings forming around its image.

I breakfasted, such as it was, on strong black coffee and a box of plain yogurt, and headed over to the campus on the bus to try to plan what I was going to say. By a lucky break, I'd written down most of what I wanted to go over the day before, and it probably wasn't going to be too hard, I thought, to cover my territory. Around 11:30, Pyke stopped by, saying he'd give me a ride over to the church. He was wondering what we should do if no one came to the meeting. "If there are only four or five of us in the whole town who oppose the war, what can we do?"

"I wouldn't worry about it, man. There are hundreds, I'm sure, who feel like we do, and thousands more who would if they only got the message. That's what we'll do if no one comes; redouble our efforts to get the gospel out."

"We have to worry. It's a big responsibility, and we're flying right into the face of the System. It has lots of ways to put us down. Look what happened to your friend Steve. I'll bet my ass we won't see him today."

"Hey, Steve's going to help us. He's just got his own priorities. You said yourself it might be a problem with him."

We arrived at ten to twelve. Francine was there, waiting. Unexpectedly, she gave me a big hug (and even a little kiss on the cheek) when she saw me. It really cleared my head! I introduced her to Pyke, who shook hands with her as he eyed her body; he gave me a glance that said, "How'd you pull this one off, sport?"

DEGREES OF FREEDOM

At five to twelve it was looking as though Pyke's gloomy prediction was going to be right; in addition to the three of us there were only the priest and two bored-looking sorority types in evidence, but then the crowd began to pour in. I was amazed. By five past, when Francine opened the meeting, we must have had forty people in attendance. All the chairs were full and people were standing in the back. Though most were students, there were some apparent townies and even a faculty type or two, though Steve wasn't there. Pyke's doughnuts were long gone, as he'd only brought two dozen and I myself had had three already (to build up my strength, I rationalized).

Francine spoke beautifully, putting on a slight trace of a French accent, I thought; and I was even inspired to certain rhetorical flights, going beyond my prepared notes into a discussion of morality in international dealings by powerful nations. I was astounded to see, when I looked down at my watch, that it was twenty to one, and I called for discussions from the floor -- suggestions as to what form our fledgling organization, "SCAW," should take. There was quite a spirited discussion, with a substantial faction calling for it to be an informational society; their idea was that we should meet weekly with a scheduled speaker who would give us a genteel "teach-in," a nice non-threatening academic discussion of the roots of the rebellion. Pyke, however, and several others, made a strong case that we already knew U.S. involvement was immoral, and called for action to protest it.

We weren't ready to resolve the issue that day (most of the audience had to leave for 1:00 appointments), but we agreed to meet again the following Wednesday to debate the issues, and also to make ourselves a formal organization with officers, committees, and by-laws. Father Jaroszev promised that we could meet at this time for as long as we wanted to reserve the room; he also initiated a collection for the organization, passing around a nice circular wooden tray with green felt lining, that turned out to contain a total of $33.69 afterwards. Not bad for a bunch of beginners!

Pyke, Francine, and I took time out for lunch at the Union afterwards. We felt pretty encouraged by the turnout, but as usual at meetings only 10% of the attendees had contributed 90% of the discussion. Francine was very optimistic; she said she felt that this had been a historic occasion, and that a groundswell of anti-war sympathy was about to break out all over the country. Little gatherings like this, she was sure, were being held everywhere, and soon the popular resistance would be too great for the government to resist. It had to be that way, she said; it was so obvious that our policies were unprincipled and malicious that once people took the time to examine them rationally the whole program was bound to collapse.

Pyke, surprisingly, took a decidedly more cynical view. Maybe he'd been listening to Steve and me. "You underestimate the skill that the system has developed to manipulate public opinion. Most of the people in America are unwilling to question authority, especially in foreign matters. It makes them very nervous to "go against the President." The system has always made heroes out of soldiers who obey orders without thinking, and villains out of so-called 'radicals' who want to change accepted behavior. And make no mistake, these policies are nothing new; they're outgrowths of the expansionist and exploitative mentality that's governed our attitudes to vulnerable foreigners since the Mexican War; maybe earlier, back to the Louisiana Purchase and the slave trade."

I tried to take a middle ground; we had to expect opposition, maybe even powerful opposition. We might be threatened, or persecuted, or beaten up. But we had to keep working, someone had to. Eventually, we'd prevail, although it might take many years.

I was right, of course.

Our meetings continued to be held every Wednesday. We tried to be all things to all members. We did have outside speakers who presented us with information - people from the two state universities, even Steve, who gave a talk with a nice neutral title that I forget now; but we also went ahead and tried to change things. Letter-writing campaigns to our representatives in Congress; shit, what a fucking waste of time that was.

And Pyke even got into trouble on that score. He typed a letter, more or less a copy of the one we'd sent to Congress, to the editor of the Pawnee Springs Gazette; he's dead now, but maybe you remember him, a little wizened guy with a frozen half-grin, result of some childhood neurological disorder, name of Buck Flint. Buck came here from Minnesota; no background in journalism, never went to college - just a drifter, I'd call him, but a drifter who was inordinately ambitious. He worked his way up all the way from printer's devil to editor-in-chief, took him about thirty years; but on the way up he learned it all, all the dirt about everybody important in town, probably including the editor whose job he'd taken. So he had a lot of power, based on blackmail, I guess it would be correct to say, even though it doesn't sound very nice. A domineering old fart, he was, who ran his paper like a platoon. He fancied himself a critic, and wrote a book-review column, notable principally for its unregenerate philistinism and its palpable contempt for anything more urbane than Audels' Guide to Repairing Your Buick.

Buck, I guess, examined Pyke's letter with a magnifying glass, or under ultraviolet light or something, and found to his abhorrence that Pyke had dared to write it on paper with the College watermark. Not letterhead, y'understand, just plain white second sheet stuff. So old Buck got real upset, drooling with self-righteousness, and called up President Ogden right away, harangued the poor man on the phone for twenty minutes; complained about irresponsible College faculty using stationery paid for by the state to espouse their radical views. Said he thought McKenna deserved a reprimand. So, naturally, the President got on the phone to Dean Pfaff and asked him to pass the message on to McKenna; and poor Jim Pfaff had to call Pyke and give him the word. You can imagine, I expect, how Pyke responded to that. He flew off the handle, you can be sure, with some choice words for everyone down the line. Then, he wrote a long memo to Ogden with a copy to Pfaff. He calculated the cost the state had incurred, based on the price of paper by the sheet, the fraction of the life of the typewriter ribbon, depreciation of the typewriter and the building during the time it took him to write the letter, even the five minutes of his own time. (He'd used his own envelope and stamp.) He computed that he owed the state $0.37 and enclosed a check for that amount. I don't know that it was ever cashed. I think that he also wrote, then, a rightist letter under an assumed name on the same stationery, and was unsurprised to see that it, unlike his original letter, was published without delay.

What else did we do? Passing out literature at the information table in the Union -- that was mostly preaching to the converted, but gave me a chance to sharpen my argumentative skills with the ROTC and FFA types. Not much of a contest, really! In the spring, at the church, we held a "Vietnam Solidarity Evening," with singers, poetry readers, more-or-less ethnic food (preparation supervised by Francine), and finally, some spontaneous dancing (I don't know what the Father thought of such unseemliness, but he swallowed hard and let it go on). That was a financial success, if nothing else.

The membership became fairly constant at about a dozen supporters, not always the same people, but always roughly the same number in attendance.

Somehow, we found a dynamic leader, a TV repairman of all things, about 22 years old, named Chuck Vieste. A dropout from Cimarron's engineering program. He'd turned up at our second meeting. The guy was unquestionably something special - curly long dark hair, eyes like precious stones, a voice like butterscotch pudding. Although he smiled a bit too much for my taste, he had a native articulateness, forceful and compelling. Like, a real stage presence.

I was very much drawn to him because of our similar backgrounds and preoccupations. Also, I thought he needed help from me. Chuck was quite a speaker, all right, but he had problems with preparation; he wasn't the strongest organizer of facts, but once he had them straight in his mind, he could be off on a fucking tear. I always regretted that we couldn't arrange a debate with anybody from the Establishment. I'd have loved to see him take on Starrett.

Chuck was a strong advocate of action. Once he assumed more and more authority (which we were quite happy to see him exercise), he pushed us into some quite high-profile activities. The most notorious of these, I suppose, was the picketing we did at the armed services recruiting center in downtown Pawnee Springs.

It was late spring of '66 when Chuck broached the idea to us. Things were going badly for the anti-war movement. U.S. troop strength was approaching 300,000; our forces were firing into, and probably invading, Cambodia; and the bombing of the North was becoming fiercer. He convinced us that we were going to have to become more militant in our opposition if it was to mean anything. "Our lives must be put on the line," he said, "just as those of our Vietnamese and Cambodian colleagues are. They need our help." Pyke supported him; "This is the hour for action. We've got to draw people's attention - everyday people, people who shop for groceries, worry about their taxes, and go to church; we've got to get them thinking about the injustice in southeast Asia. We've got to take chances; the situation is desperate." I said, "Yes, but we're not going to get that sympathy if we come on like a bunch of fanatics. We have to be ordinary citizens like them, and the more of us we can get on the scene, and the more ordinary we look, the better we're going to come off." "OK", Chuck said, "but we've still got to do something really theatrical, something that will grab their attention. Take hostages, burn the state flag with napalm, something. For myself, I'll dress up like Lyndon Baines. That'll be a start, anyway. I've already got a mask."

We agreed to picket the recruiting center, a symbol of the military dominance that was taking over American lives. At the center, we'd see how we were received by the personnel there, by the police, and by the media; then we'd decide whether we'd just pass out literature, try to convince people from entering, or actually physically bar the door with our bodies.

It was getting late in the school term, and not many of us pitched in to make posters and to take part in the demonstration. There were only seven of us.

The day of the demonstration began, a humid morning, heavily overcast, with a thunderstorm likely. By about 9:15 everyone had arrived at my house. It was already about 80 degrees and it looked like it was going to be a scorcher, but everyone had heeded my advice and no one was dressed in shorts or had the American flag sewn onto his jeans. We appeared as straight as it was possible for us to look.

We coordinated our arrival so that all three cars pulled up outside the recruiting center at once. Pyke pulled his car into the loading zone, followed by Francine's Volvo and finally my VW. Chuck was already wearing his LBJ mask. The center was open but no one was around outside except for two coarsely dressed men, transients I suspect, one white and one Indian, sitting up against the building, with a bottle in a brown bag resting between them. Both the men were tall, heavy-set individuals with unkempt hair and bloodshot eyes; the Indian's face was smooth, composed, and glossy, but the white man's was cragged, and his rasping breath came from between crooked, carious teeth.

As we approached the Indian followed us only with his eyes, but the other, especially when he saw Chuck, began to lean forward and clutched the bottle to his chest as if he felt threatened.

We started to unload the signs and the pamphlets, causing the white derelict to begin to shout something incomprehensible at us. He sort of half-stood, so that his body was bent forward, while he buried his bottle in his stomach with one hand and forced the other hand against the wall behind him, as if we'd cut him off from some avenue of retreat. He stuck his jaw straight out toward us, and the veins on his neck swelled out like cables. I tried to listen to what he was declaiming, but it sounded as if he was just randomly choosing consonants and vowels and alternating them to form one rapid ceaseless stream of nonsense syllables. All the while, his companion remained seated and stolidly looked ahead at nothing. The white guy kept bellowing, as I thought what an amazing talent it was to maintain that continuous high level of rhetoric but never to utter one cogent word.

The disturbance led one of the recruiters to come to the window; when he saw what we were doing, he came out of the door to watch us. He was a very young guy, no older than twenty-two, maybe five foot three and stocky, in sergeant's dress blues and a blond butch haircut. The first thing he said was to yell out, "Move it along, boys!" and I thought at first he was talking to us; but then I noticed him making shooing motions at the drifters.

They got up and tottered off, the Indian still stolid and the white dude still incoherent, but grumbling now and not raging. The officer then turned his attention to us, watching narrowly; he apparently determined that Pyke, as the oldest, must have been our ringleader; he asked him, "Would you mind telling me what you folks are doing here this morning?" Pyke looked him up and down, and then said very deliberately in his wonderfully contemptuous voice, "We're citizens of the United States, and as you can perhaps see for yourself, we're making a public statement." The officer rubbed the lower half of his face with his right hand, sighed, and asked, "Is it really necessary to do it right here?" Pyke replied, "No, of course not, but it is our choice to gather here on this particular public sidewalk at this time. I am sure you can have no objection, but even if you do, we will remain here as we have every right to." The kid stuck his fists down into the pockets of his uniform jacket, spun around to face the door, and then spun back to confront Pyke. His face had changed to a mask of fury, but he spoke with a clipped and chilly correctness. "OK, Mr. Citizen," he said, "but just be damn sure you don't block my door, or detain any potential enlistees. And don't lean your asses, or your goddamn signs, up against my building, do you hear me, mister?" Pyke, grinning broadly, replied, "Aye, aye, cap'm, sir;" he turned to us, raising his splendid eyebrows, and the officer stamped back into his sanctuary. Pyke said, "We've moved in a little too close to his territory, and he's got to piss on us a little to show us he's top cock around here."

We fanned ourselves out across the side of the building. Chuck stood on the corner, waving at cars and pedestrians as they passed. His mask was really pretty good; he was dressed right, with his big ten-gallon hat and boots, and he was built like LBJ as well, long and lanky; so he really drew stares. He held a sign that read "I love the smell of napalm." I stood next to him with my stack of handouts and tried to engage as many passers-by in conversation as I could. It was pretty frustrating; most people didn't want to talk - said they "didn't have time" - and those who did stop usually turned out to have pretty conservative views. I found that I didn't object as much to the people who'd spit at me or call me obscene names as I did to the ones who'd completely ignore me, walk by as though I wasn't there.

Pyke had the best bit of repartee; some punk in a cut-down '55 Chevy leaned out his window and yelled "Why don't you assholes go back to Russia, where you belong?" Clever, eh? So Pyke bellowed out, "Sure, man, just as soon as you move your asshole to Nazi Germany."

One other ugly incident that took place; one of us, Cindy something, I forget her last name now, was about eight months pregnant; and she stepped out into the street to try to hand some literature to the passenger in a pickup, and just as she reached over the driver gunned it and the truck's rear fender hit her, spun her around, and practically knocked her down. She was OK, but it could have been really bad. The rest of us probably would have crucified the guy if we'd ever got hold of him.

The media, we were surprised to note, did drop by. Not the biggest and oldest television station in town, the one that was owned by Buck Flint's paper; they routinely ignored every vaguely progressive story in the state. But the smaller station, that had just begun broadcasting three years earlier, did send a reporter and camera crew. A young black announcer, female, got out of their van and looked around, asking us, "Who might I interview for a story on our evening newscast? Do you have a spokesman?" Francine, Pyke and I all motioned toward Chuck, but she just rolled her eyes at him and asked, "Anyone else?" So, by default, I agreed to be interviewed. It wasn't painful at all; I thought I came off pretty well. Serious and thoughtful. Of course, that evening they did devote a lot of footage to Chuck and his inflammatory mask and sign, but at least they did pay some attention.

After the TV people left, we got a visit from the sheriff. It burned my ass. Here we were, trying to do what we could to stop needless killings of Americans and Asians, peacefully trying to call attention to the excesses of our military establishment, and we are the ones that get a visit from the law; the cop car comes up with its lights flashing and sirens blazing, and disgorges a huge pig with metal sunglasses and a howitzer strapped across his chest. The very sheriff himself; man, this is serious shit. He saunters up to us and tells us we're within the law as long as we watch our steps. Hey, man, give us a break; we know what we're doing.

Chuck, bless him, chose this moment to pull his stunt. Our buddy, Sergeant Top-cock, has ventured out on the sidewalk to watch the show, to snicker at us as we get our stern lecture on public decency from John Law. Unbeknownst, Chuck sneaks up behind him and grabs him around the shoulder, hugs him like a long-lost pal. He starts shouting through his mask, which gives his voice a muffled and gargling quality; he also tries to put on a Central Texas accent, for which he has no talent whatever, making him sound still more bizarre.

"This here's mah man, ossifer, me an' him's thick as fleas on a blue tick hound. Him an' me go way back. We love the smell o'napalm, an' we love ta burn them gooks, specially the real old ones. Whynchah get a pitcher of us, ossifer, we's the hope a the nation."

DEGREES OF FREEDOM

The little sarge is pissed as hell. He acts like Chuck's a leper, or maybe a rapist; kicks and screams at Chuck to let him go. Chuck's damn strong, though, and it takes him a while to pull loose. Then he stands there, puffing and fuming, his uniform in disarray, and berates the sheriff, saying, "I demand that this man be arrested! He assaulted me! I have a constitutional right to be secure in my person on a public street!" It's a ludicrous scene, a military officer of the U.S. Army whimpering to a beer-bellied sheriff about an alleged attack by a masked eccentric.

The sheriff's pretty cool; he doesn't actually smile, but he pulls the little man aside and talks turkey to him; and the sergeant lifts his chin high and walks back to the door, but then he spoils it all by turning around and announcing to us, "I dropped the charges - this time." Well, all of us break out howling with laughter, but the sheriff lifts up a finger and gives us a cautionary nod. A cool dude, the old sheriff, after all.

So that was about it. We stood around for a few more hours, until it started to drizzle; we packed up our signs, and went home, and watched ourselves on TV - a two-minute story sandwiched between the war news and a fire in Philadelphia. No lives lost or changed, probably no minds even changed, by what we did. But I think we had to do it, to say what was inside of us; we couldn't have done less, and I'm sure none of us regrets it.

The war went on, of course, even as it still does, and all of us went on working against it. Even Steve came out of the closet and worked openly with us. He stayed at Cimarron only long enough to get me through my degree, and then, by "mutual agreement," he left his position and moved on to Cal State - Fullerton, where he's much happier.

Pyke kept up his activism, of course, as you know, all the time right up to his death. I heard that his brother was killed over there, and that might have taken some of the fire out of his belly, but I was gone by then, so I can't really say.

Consuela stayed here, with me, and we got married a month before I graduated. We're still together, just celebrated our fifth anniversary last week. We've got a kid now, a little girl named Isabel, three years old; the smartest and prettiest kid I ever saw. I look down at her sometimes as she sits on my lap and I think; will she and her friends have to go through anything like we did? Because I think this war has poisoned us as a country. We're all crippled from Vietnam, even those of us who never heard a shot.

I think we're in for a generation of cynicism; everybody's going to be looking out for himself. The idea of social justice is going to sound pretty hollow a few years down the line. In fact, I see it now in the way my colleagues and bosses approach their jobs in this agency. Urban poverty doesn't seem real to them; it's not something that they feel, a stabbing pain of hunger in the guts of a kid like my Isabel; it's a name on a door, a box on an organization chart. You get your paycheck and you drive home to your nice comfortable suburban house, and pour yourself a cold drink, watch a couple of insulting shows on television, then go to bed and next day it's another uneventful day shuffling documents.

What can we expect, I suppose. I don't know how much longer I want to stay in this country, anyway. Consuela wants to go back to Panama, because her father's been very ill; and I've been trying to get a job down there. But it's not easy, even in the Zone, where even more than here it seems to be who you know in the hierarchy; of course, in Panama itself, there's almost no hope for any gringo, even if he speaks fluent Spanish, as I do now. I think if things get much worse up here in El Norte, I'm just going to sell everything and move down there. Even if I don't get a good position, we should be able to live pretty well on my savings. And of course, Consuela can work, although she never has; her father's pretty well off, has a string of taxicab fleets all over the country. She's got seven brothers and sisters, though, so we'll never inherit very much of it, especially since she married this rich gringo and doesn't need it. Such is life, man.

Well, Bruce, it was a sad time for the U.S.A., and it still is; but the one thing that made it worthwhile for me was, I saw that many of us still have that urge to be free. It's going to be damn hard to stamp that urge out of us. Maybe it can be done, but I wouldn't want to try. I only wish I understood what it was that made a great free spirit like Pyke McKenna want to give it all up. The guy had talent he hadn't even touched yet; so why, why the hell?

If you find out, man, let me know.

Pyke 2

(This is the longest of the tape recordings Pyke left behind. These reminiscences fill all of one 90-minute tape and part of another.)

After I had been on the staff for several years, I began to feel somewhat comfortable and professional. I would lean back in my chair and think about making a splash in the world of research. I kept having a nagging sensation that I was, in spite of everything, a good scientist. My ideas were as good or better, I was sure, than those being thought by my peers in Cambridge, Massachusetts: Urbana, Illinois: or Palo Alto, California. I was in my mid-thirties, and this was when all the sociological studies showed that scientists tended to be most productive - when a touch of experience and wisdom met up with the vigor and enthusiasm of youth - and that was exactly how I felt.

All I needed was an important unsolved problem to apply my talents to. It was like an itch - something I would keep thinking about over and over again. I'd go to sleep at nights thinking about research ideas; I'd wake up in the middle of the night and write something down, usually gibberish when I looked at it in the daytime. In the morning while I fried eggs, I'd think about insect eggs and what made the female lay them where she did, and how the various reasonable hypotheses could be tested. I read all the important journals in the biological sciences - I subscribed, at considerable personal expense, to the ones our inadequate library didn't have. I thought continually about evolution and the forces that drove it, the constant struggle of plants and animals to survive in the teeth of harsh and constantly changing environments. I marveled at the versatility that living creatures showed in adapting to the challenges posed by their enemies and by unpredictable Nature. There were so many strategies, so many solutions; many had failed, but countless ingenious combinations had been preserved. It seemed superficially chaotic, but I could sense deep order underlying the process. It seemed to me there was some key element missing, some Rosetta Stone just waiting to be deciphered by an ingenious cryptographer.

I ached for intellectual peers to discuss these cosmically important matters with. I was so far removed from serious scholarship in this area. I tried to correspond with the authors of papers I thought had made important contributions, but few of them ever wrote back even once, let alone made a continuing effort to keep in touch. Telephone calls were practically out of the question, with the Dean breathing down our necks to keep the overhead expenses down. (It got to the point where we even had to sign out for a box of chalk.)

I decided I needed personal contacts, and the most efficient way for me to make them was to go to a large national scientific meeting and force myself on these famous or brilliant people. I knew this was the way things got done in big-time science. The idea was something new around Cimarron State, though. The Dean was reluctant to send me to a meeting during the term; I was so invaluable because of my heavy teaching load. Finally, after nearly ten years on the job, I got my chance.

The year was 1958; the American Institute of Biological Sciences was meeting in Kansas City, a place close enough to drive to, and in the late summer before classes started here. The preliminary program looked interesting. I wangled the registration fee out of Pfaff by promising to chair the Community Outreach Committee for the next academic year.

The day before the meeting, I fired up my old '54 Pontiac, newest car I ever had; drove clear across Kansas, crossed the bridge, and got into downtown K.C. Mo. just before it got dark. I located a cheap dive of a hotel that I could afford, on the southern fringes of the downtown area, only a mile's walk from the Muehlenbach Hotel, where the meeting was being held.

You may not know it if you have never been to one, but AIBS meetings are huge affairs; every conceivable kind of biologist goes to them. It's humbling to walk around the places where the scientists gather and realize how much work on so many important topics is being done by people you don't know and can never know. Everyone is stealing glances at everyone else's little paper name tag to see whether the wearer could be anyone with a recognizable name, someone it might be interesting to talk to.

The program is broad, to say the least. It requires approximately sixty closely-spaced pages of small print simply to list the names of the talks and authors. Unless you are a narrow-minded specialist, there are many presentations to attract your attention. And my interest was evolution, one of the most revolutionary ideas that anyone ever had, the broadest concept in all of biology, the great idea that ties together and explains more of the subject matter of the science than any other. So, needless to say, it was difficult to pick just the right papers to sit in on, the ones that might be more likely to lead to a synthetic approach to broad, unexplained and seemingly unrelated data as opposed to an analytic approach to some minor point.

In my stuffy hotel room, undeterred by the varied noises of my fellow patrons - honeymooners, drunks, and high-school day-trippers - I read the program in painstaking detail, putting large black dots beside the titles of the talks I thought I'd be sure to want to attend, and question marks beside others that I might go to if I got the chance. Then my attention fell on an announcement of a day-long symposium, called "Plants and their Predators;" the chairman of the session was Harry Messersmith, an old friend of mine from graduate school. He had been reasonably successful in the academic world, and was already a full professor at the University of Arkansas at Fayetteville. In addition, he had just written a paper in Science which tried to show that plants were far too efficient to have to concern themselves about anything trying to eat them. All they had to worry about, Harry had written, were other plants who would use up the available sunlight or underground root space.

We animals, he said, were just along for the ride. And we should enjoy it, for the world was bountiful enough to support us all and many more of us too.

Not too surprisingly, this was a controversial viewpoint, and Harry had assembled an interesting group of speakers, including, I was happy to see, the principal detractors of his idea. Chief among these was Irving Popovich of the University of California at Davis, a specialist in noctuid moths. Popovich seldom thought about plants except in terms of their suitability as food for his beloved larvae, and was outraged at the suggestion that his beauties were having no effect whatever on their hosts. Recently much of his work had been done on pests of agriculturally important crops grown in the rich farmland in the Central Valley of California, near the Davis campus. "The U. S. Department of Agriculture," he had written, "has not spent millions of dollars on pest control research because of their interest in academic hair-splitting. They are practical, hard-headed men, and their dollars have spoken against the point Dr. Messersmith is trying to make." Many of those dollars, not coincidentally, had gone to fund research that Popovich wanted to do, and he wanted to make sure it kept coming. He and Harry had been engaged in acrimonious public correspondence of this nature in the pages of several prestigious journals for some time.

I was of an open mind on the subject, though I tended to believe that there had to be a reason why different insects were found on different plants, and that some could attack many food plants while others were specialists. There was some evidence that the older belief that all insects had pretty much similar nutritional requirements was not correct, and that it was wrong to believe, as Harry might, that just any old plant would do. I was prepared to believe that predator species could alter the course of evolution by allowing the plants they didn't like to eat to be more successful. But I wasn't sure that this was the case, so I was anxious to hear what these ponderous authorities would have to say as they jousted with one another. So I made a point to sit in on Harry's symposium from the very beginning, which was tomorrow morning at 8:15.

I didn't sleep well, thanks to my immediate neighbors, who I think were a couple of sado-masochistic faggots, beating on each other, laughing, and groaning all night long. I expect they were small-college teachers.

DEGREES OF FREEDOM

After a hasty breakfast of a glutinous, gummy Danish pastry and a Styrofoam cup of bitter coffee to go, I hiked to the Muehlenbach. It was drizzling, but I pulled my raincoat up over my head. I found the room where the symposium was to be held; I was in plenty of time, at least ten minutes early. I grabbed myself a raised doughnut, one of the few not completely covered with sticky frosting, and then I saw Harry at the front of the seminar room. I hadn't seen him for at least ten years, but he looked just the same - round face, snaggly teeth, uncontrollable spiky hair - except for being somewhat better dressed. He was fussing with the slide projector and I didn't want to disturb him, so I took a seat on the aisle just behind him. But he caught sight of me and cried out, "Well, god damn, they'll let anybody in here. Pyke McKenna, you old son-of-abitch, I haven't seen your ass for a crawdad's age. How the fuck have you been?" I told him I wasn't doing too badly, and that I had been reading about him in the gossip columns of Nature and the Annals of the Entomological Society of America, and that I was looking forward to sitting in on his symposium. "Yes," he said, "I really seem to have hit the fan head-on with a bucket of shit. Hard to believe these candy-ass Ivy League and West Coast professors can get so uptight about what a hillbilly from the University of Arkansas has to say. Between you and me, I wish I hadn't gotten started on this subject, because I think herbivorous insects are a very drab and dull group of organisms; but then what can you expect of animals who are constantly surrounded by superabundant food? Anyway, I did get involved in this controversy and here is a serious little symposium to, perhaps, shed some light on the issue. But we should have some lively discussions today. Hope you will contribute a few trenchant remarks, couched in your usual inimical and inimitable fashion."

At this point in the discussion a small, neatly dressed man in a tiny mustache, about fifty, approached us; and Harry introduced me to Irving Popovich. I shook his thin, moist hand and tried to look into his eyes, but he would not return my gaze; he looked rapidly and furtively in all directions as we spoke, twitching the folds of skin under his eyes in a way I had not seen the like of before. He spoke very briskly, as if unaccustomed to the conventions of conversation, clipping off the ends of his sentences and inserting jerky pauses in inappropriate places. If I tried to respond to something he had said, he went on without acknowledging my contributions by so much as a glance of recognition. He had the air of a man with much urgent information to relate, but one who was being followed by tiny, swift, and implacable enemies.

By this time it was getting close to the scheduled opening time for the session so I told Harry and Popovich I'd talk to them later, and took my seat, about ten rows back and on the aisle to the left of the slide projector. Harry made a few quite bland opening remarks, interspersed with non-threatening jokes and smiles, and then introduced the first speaker.

Professor Sir Herbert Harlow-Montague of Oxford University was to give the plenary address for the session. Of course I knew his work, especially his monumental Treatise on the Coprophilous Coleoptera, written around 1949. I wasn't quite sure what he was doing in this symposium, because I wasn't aware that he had worked in this area. The title of his talk was promising, however; "The Reason Beetles Eat the Vegetation They Do."

After Harry's introduction, Sir Herbert slowly arose from his seat in the first row. He was a tall, graceful, magisterial, but almost effeminate gentleman of about fifty-five, with a mane of flowing blond hair. He was wearing a powder-blue double-breasted suit with a large windowpane plaid pattern outlined in thin red stripes, a red-and-white striped tie, and black patent leather shoes. After mincing up the steps to the podium, he slowly unfolded a sheaf of papers, put on a pair of half-frame glasses, stood briefly facing the audience, blinking as if blinded, and then began to speak in a high and pinched voice, saying, "Thank you very much, Dr. ...ah ... Messersmith," reading Harry's name from a card. He spoke with a traditional upper-class Oxbridge lisp and stammer, but what he proceeded to say was decidedly untraditional. He began his talk by presenting a slide showing the development of the families of the Coleoptera, from the most undifferentiated, unspecialized, and presumably primitive types to the most advanced families. Then he showed a series of beautifully prepared slides of common European representatives of a variety of beetle families, some of them photographs, some of them pages from illuminated medieval manuscripts, some of them detailed plates from Victorian treatises on natural history. Finally he showed a beautiful drawing by Dürer of the cockchafer (Melolantha melolantha), a very common beetle of the family Scarabeidae. It was a close relative of his favorites, the dung beetles, those coprophilous Coleoptera on which he'd built his reputation. "This insect," Sir Herbert said, "is abundant throughout Europe; it has common names in every European language; it is found in a variety of ecophysiological habitats from the beaches of the Greek islands to the waterfalls of the Norwegian fjords north of the Arctic circle. It has been recorded on a variety of vegetational types; crop plants, trees, coastal grasses. In years when it is abundant, it can completely strip certain trees of their leaves. It will also burrow into the earth and consume plant roots. In other words, it is a very successful insect, evolutionarily speaking. On the other hand, consider these insects, Meligethes berenbaumii; [a slide showing a group of shiny black beetles on a leaf was shown] it is a member of the relatively advanced family Nitudulidae, the "gloss beetles." Parenthetically, I might note that we were the first to describe this species, which I saw in a quite small vegetable garden in Staffordshire. The owner used horse dung to fertilize her plants, and while searching for scarabeids, I found this particular specimen. Later, the insect turned up in a variety of similar habitats all over Britain; it is not at all uncommon, but it was as though no one else had found it worthy of notice. They are rather small. In any event, its feeding, and that of its conspecifics, is largely restricted to a small group of related plant species, namely the cruciferous plants, and its distribution is quite limited. Recently, we have made the curious discovery that the insect we identified is also found in large numbers on crucifers as well as other plants beside the major English motorways. We asked ourselves the question, what was it about the food sources of these two animals that made it possible for one to be such a generalist, and the other to be so specialized?"

The very question I had asked myself so often in the past dozen or more years! I continued to listen in fascination. Sir Herbert spun out the story in enormous detail. His research associates collected all the plants that Melolantha, the generalist, fed on and performed chemical analyses on them. The same was done with the Melolantha themselves; in these analyses, males were separated from females, and larvae as well as adults of different ages were collected and also analyzed separately. They collected soil and water samples from the collection areas and analyzed them in the same way. Then they collected samples of plants which, although abundant in the areas where Melolantha populations thrived, were not eaten. He showed slide after slide of minutely detailed tables and summary charts on their chemical work, and finally he focused in on the key points of his presentation. Out of all these data, seemingly collected in such a random fashion, a compelling story began to make itself known.

Melolantha appeared to feed only on those plants that had a particular range of ratios of elemental composition; specifically, those plants that had unusually low ratios of calcium to iron. The animals seemingly had a need for iron-rich diets, but it was not the absolute amount of iron they sensed, but rather they appeared to be able to calculate its concentration relative to the much more abundant element, calcium. This finding, I thought, was remarkable enough, suggesting many avenues of research in insect biochemistry, behavior, physiology, and nutrition, but there was an even more remarkable discovery. All the plants that Melolantha consumed grew on soils that contained rather high concentrations of what are known as "transition metals" -- some of which were nutritionally important, but others which were quite toxic. They are a group of similar substances found in a particular area of the periodic chart of the chemical elements -- metals like copper, zinc, mercury, lead, vanadium, and several others. Sometimes they are called "trace metals," or "heavy metals." What Sir Herbert had found was that Melolantha's food plants were apparently not able to concentrate these metals from the soil to the degree that other plants, not eaten by Melolantha, were. In other words, Melolantha, although superficially a generalist feeder, stayed away from plants that had high concentrations of potentially hazardous elements. So not only was this little animal performing, without reagents, glassware, or spectrophotometers, a simultaneous analysis for iron and calcium, but also it was analyzing its diet for most of the other transition metals as well!

Also, the researchers had done, almost parenthetically, a remarkable experiment involving the use of radioactively labeled iron. They grew the plants in a solution containing the isotopic element, so that they took it up normally into their tissues. They then fed the labeled plants to Melolantha and dissected the insect's mouthparts, cutting them into tiny slices which they positioned on photographic film, kept in darkness. After a short period, they developed the film and examined it by microscopy. The film was darkened where the radioactive element had become localized. The exposures clearly showed dark spots with sharp boundaries, located at the ends of the maxillary palps. These structures are used by the insect to chemically test its food before it is ingested. Montague hypothesized that these spots were receptors specific for iron; in other words, the insects were chemically testing their diet using their taste receptors!

Finally, Sir Herbert considered the case of Meligethes. The same approach was used. The data were clear. Meligethes fed on plants that were unusually high in lead concentration. These species of plants had evolved a mechanism for concentrating lead from the soil and for tolerating its toxic effects; they stored it and used it, apparently, to poison their insect enemies. It was very effective, too, except in the case of Meligethes, which had also stumbled onto a method (perhaps the same, perhaps different) for protecting itself from lead poisoning. In the process, the analyses showed that the beetle also developed extremely high concentrations of lead in its body. Incidentally, Montague said, Meligethes itself may be repellent or toxic to its predators; we have attempted to feed it to jackdaws, but they reject the insects even when starved almost to death. We are currently beginning experiments, he said, where we will add varying concentrations of minced Meligethes to an artificial diet and feed that to birds. We hope to observe whether or not there are any toxic effects that result from the ingestion of such a lead-rich diet. Meligethes, he continued, now was able to exploit a food resource that no other insect could; a food resource that may have become very abundant in the past in the absence of insect feeding, so abundant that Meligethes now preferred to feed on it even though other apparently suitable plants were available. "So now," said Sir Herbert, "what are these plants to do? If they increase their internal lead burden, they may kill themselves. If they try to reduce it and increase the concentration of another toxic transition metal, Meligethes may die out but other pest species may take over as predators. Very difficult evolutionary choices may need to be made. It is apparent that beetles and their food plants are engaged in a sort of evolutionary chemical warfare, in which complex strategies of attack and defense are being played out every day. I believe that the study of these interactions will lead to major new understandings of the role that diet has played in the great scenario of evolution. Thank you very much."

I joined in the applause, which was not as enthusiastic as I thought it would be. I looked around the room and saw that several attendees were either drowsing or fiddling with their conference materials. *Chacun à son gout*, I suppose, just as Professor Harlow-Montague had just told us. Sir Herbert answered two or three trivial questions from the audience; I was full of questions of my own but was too excited to articulate them. Here, I thought, was an idea, a great idea to which I could contribute from the very beginning. I had the tools; I knew how to analyze plants for their metal content (I'd done a lot of that work for my dissertation), I knew the local insects and their food plants - I could begin right away!

I was itching to find out from the great man what his ideas were for the immediate future, so I could be sure that I wasn't trespassing into an area that he'd already mapped out. As he was speaking, I felt sure that the domain of the Lepidoptera - moths and butterflies - was the most logical field to move into. There was a tremendous variety of these insects; the larvae of many were abundant and easy to find, and some were not too difficult to grow in the laboratory. I was writing some of these ideas down, and the next speaker was already droning well on into his presentation, when I looked around the room and saw that Sir Herbert had already left.

I thought that perhaps he'd stepped out into the hallway to discuss his work with someone, so I slipped out to look for him. Well, he wasn't there or anywhere in the immediate vicinity, including the mens' room (I'd have recognized his shoes), so I went back to the seminar room, thinking he would probably come back. However, by 10:30 there was still no sign of him. At that point Harry called for a 10-minute break in the proceedings.

During the break, I interrupted Harry, who was in the midst of yet another heated discussion with Popovich, to ask him if he knew where Harlow-Montague had gone. He said he wasn't sure, but that it was possible he was only going to be here for the day and might already be preparing to leave. I explained to Harry that I was interested in talking with him about his research ("Fat chance of that," Popovich interjected, "that man only wants to get drunk and get laid, and not with a woman, either"). Harry said he didn't know where he was staying, but that I could find out at the meeting registration center in the lobby.

So I left the meeting room and walked down two flights of stairs to the registration center, which consisted of three long tables, behind which were sitting six women sorting great stacks of 4 x 6 file cards. When one of these good ladies turned her attention to me (she was an extremely fat young woman, rapidly chewing gum, possessed of hairy arms, a bad complexion and a nearly shaved head) I explained my problem, and she began riffling through one shoe box after another, calling out to her companions for help as she got stuck, and asking me three times what Sir Herbert's last name was. I had to spell it for her twice. She couldn't find him!

Finally, she had a glimmer of insight, producing a snaggle-toothed grin that exposed her cud of Doublemint. "Would he be a late registrant?" she asked. I said I didn't know, that he could be. Then, retrieving an expandable file from beneath the table, she thumbed through a sheaf of pages, one by one (they didn't appear to be in any particular order), and finally stabbed at the top of one of the last of the sheets with her pudgy forefinger, shouting, "Here he is! He's the one, isn't he, sir?" And indeed it was him. There was only one problem. The line on the form labeled "Meeting Address" was blank. I groaned. It seemed as if I had lost him forever.

Then a tiny, older woman down the table, wearing a printed black dress and with her hair in a tight bun, called to me, saying, "He must have been one of the last to register. He might have even registered with me this morning. What does he look like?" I described him (luckily, he was unique), and the clerk said that she remembered him quite clearly. He'd registered that morning, asking if he could pay his fee in pounds: he was wearing a cape, looked a little bit like Count Dracula. She thought there was a good chance that he was staying here, in the Muehlenbach Hotel, since it had been raining this morning and he didn't look as if he'd been out in the rain.

So I thanked the ladies for their help and rushed upstairs to the hotel lobby. The clerk, a slender, nicely dressed young man with a neat goatee and that clerkish habit of never looking at the person speaking to him, spoke slowly to me in a round voice, saying, "Yes, he was registered here, sir, but he checked out this morning about an hour ago. No, sir, he didn't leave a forwarding address or mention any destination. He did ask if he could pay his bill in pounds. We were happy to do so. I assume he was a British gentleman. I'm sorry I can't help you, sir."

So I had finally lost him. No matter, I told myself, I will write to him at his Oxford address. Surely he will help out a struggling American academician who only wants to follow where he, the noble scholar, has shone the beacon of truth. Meanwhile, the best thing I can do is to return to the symposium, enjoy it and the rest of the meeting, work on my own ideas and go ahead with them. This is the most excited I've been about research in my life, I thought to myself.

Back at the meeting room, I sat next to Popovich. He asked me, "You ever find Montague?" I shook my head sadly, saying, "He flew the coop." Popovich snorted and said that it was just as well, that Montague was the most pompous asshole it had ever been his misfortune to meet as well as the most self-centered. "Did you notice," he asked, "how he pretended to stumble over Messersmith's name, as if Harry was too insignificant a character to bother keeping in his mind? That's the way he is with everyone. When I went over to lecture at Oxford, he refused to introduce me as Professor; he told me to my face that he thought most American academics didn't deserve that title. He treated me during my whole visit as if I was some monkey-faced aborigine pretending to be a scholar, and he was stringing me along for his own amusement. He's anti-Semitic, also; I could tell by some of the snide remarks he made when we were at lunch together, something about not being able to vouch for the tableware being Kosher. He might have spoken civilly to you, you being a Celt, but more likely he`d have treated you like a stablehand or a barber. All in all, you're fortunate to have missed him."

Ah well, we shall see about that, I thought to myself. Harry was in the midst of the final presentation of the morning, just before lunch; I had missed most of it because of my wanderings in the bowels of the Muehlenbach. My attention was distracted by Popovich's snorts, perhaps of derision or perhaps reflective of some respiratory disorder, which occurred every twenty seconds or so. He also had another annoying mannerism, that of pulling quickly at his nasal septum with the thumb and forefinger of his right hand just before or after a snort.

After the talk was over, I went up to ask Harry if he wanted to get a bite to eat. "Yes, I would," he said; "there is a Chinese place just down the street, I and several of the speakers are going there. You are of course welcome to come. How about you, Irving?" "Not a chance," Popovich said, "you've got to be crazy to eat Chinese in K. C. A steak is the only thing to munch on here."

So we left him to his red meat and several of us walked four blocks to a vulgarly decorated, red-and-gold restaurant. I no longer remember the name of the place, but the columns outside the main entrance were made up of red dragons twisted around a blue ribbed background which I suppose represented water. I had, for the first and only time in my life, the wonderfully named Chicken Dung Goo, a sort of bitter, woody-flavored dish with a melon and mushroom sauce. I also drank too much gassy, glycerin-tasting beer, poured from squat green wide-mouthed bottles having only Chinese characters and dragons on their labels.

That afternoon, I returned to the symposium. Popovich was the first speaker scheduled, and he presented an attempted rebuttal of Harry's ideas. By this time, I was convinced by Montague's data and my own intuition that Harry was wrong, and there were reciprocal impacts by plants and insects on each other, but the way Popovich chose to respond was almost enough to swing me to Harry's side of the fence. His arguments were clumsily mustered; he went on at length about irrelevant issues and ignored or offhandedly dismissed what I thought would have been strong and cogent evidence. The effects of my lunchtime beer were also making it difficult for me to keep awake, and I was also feeling oddly numb about the lips, perhaps a consequence of the peculiarly spiced Chinese food I had eaten. At the end of his talk, trying to help Popovich out, I asked a question concerning one of his remarks that I thought he could expand on; but he somehow seemed to get the mistaken impression that I was trying to trip him up, and he answered me as if I was one of the enemy and he didn't have to dignify my question with an answer.

The rest of the symposium was essentially irrelevant, except for one paper by a slender young man, about 27 years old I would guess; a new assistant professor at Kansas named Paul Ehrlich, who had just got his Ph. D. in entomology from there. He made a striking figure on the podium; although he was not tall, he had penetrating blue eyes and a deep, opulent voice, with just a trace of an eastern big-city accent. Also, he had a felicitous way with a turn of phrase and an instinctive feel for how to make a presentation impressive. As it turned out, the world would hear much from Ehrlich in the years to come, but I don't have time to go into that here.

The subject of his talk was the coevolution of plants and butterflies. Ehrlich's ideas, which he presented in an off-the-cuff fashion as if he were just making them up on the spot, were similar to those of Montague's; except instead of metal ions, Ehrlich proposed as a possibility that complex carbon-containing (organic) compounds from plants made them unpalatable to some potential predatory butterfly larvae. Then, during evolutionary time, other species could move in who were less susceptible to the organic compounds and become specialists. Although Ehrlich's hypothesis was interesting, it didn't seem to be backed up by data to the impressive extent that Montague's was. However, I was encouraged that others were open to the notion that Lepidoptera could be active agents in an evolutionary struggle mediated by chemical "weapons." After Ehrlich's presentation, there were a number of questions, including a couple of tough ones from Harry. Ehrlich didn't field them very well, in my opinion. It was pretty clear that he had only begun to think about his concepts.

After the symposium ended, I got a chance to talk to him for a few minutes; he didn't think much of Montague's experiments. He said it was too easy to be fooled by contamination from the surroundings, especially in some of the urban areas they were collecting in. "Organic compounds," he went on, "because they are complex naturally occurring products, have the virtue of being specific for the plant that contains them." I said that I was hoping to do some experiments similar to Montague's, except with Lepidopera; he wished me luck, and even said he'd help me with some of the collections if I wanted him to. "If the work goes well," he said, "let me know and I'll invite you over to Lawrence to give a talk on your research."

That evening, I skipped going out for dinner with my associates and new acquaintances and sat in my hotel room with a loaf of french bread, a wedge of cheese, and a six-pack of beer, and sketched out some plans for research on my new-found project. I felt possessed by an enthusiasm that I was unfamiliar with; I knew something about the excitement of scientific discovery, but this was different, a sort of anticipatory thrill, like watching an attractive woman undress in my bedroom; the promise of what might be about to happen was extremely exciting and rewarding to think about.

I covered about a dozen sheets of paper with possible experiments, the methods to be used, and the questions the experiments were designed to answer. In three hours, I planned roughly three lifetime's work. Although some of the experiments looked like they could give answers fairly quickly, there were many problems about the design of the research that I could foresee; and, being a good scientist, I knew that the difficulties I couldn't foresee were going to be more troublesome (as well as more interesting, of course).

I needed some guidance badly, and it looked as if the only person who could give it to me was Montague. Although I didn't want to tip my hand too obviously, I thought I should try to communicate what I planned to do in a general way and get his opinions on some issues. Finally, around midnight, I gave up thinking about it and tried to sleep.

The next morning, I drove back to Pawnee Springs in a sort of daze. My lack of sleep combined with the three cups of coffee I'd had with my breakfast gave me an odd sensation of nervous rootlessness. The day was clear, still, and hot; the blacktop roads were ornamented with mirages, tiny lakes on the road that vanished as I approached. All I could think about were my plans for my research, but I couldn't concentrate; experiments, potential results, techniques, imagined interviews with potential graduate students, all kept popping in and out of my thoughts.

I opened all my windows, and drove swiftly across the steppes, the wind blasting in my ears like a steam whistle. My car was dark green, and the dry heat from the outside world reverberated off its surface and made the interior like an oven. The wind had begun to pick up, also, and dry tumbleweeds were being driven over the fields and across the road in dusty whirlwinds. My eyes were aching as they dried out due to the combination of the wind and the heat, and my neck also ached from being held in a rigid position as I drove.

I began to have more and more extravagant fantasies, mental mirages that were as convincing and also as chimerical as the visual ones appearing on the highway in front of me. First, I pictured a series of elegant papers, written by me and my colleagues (I, naturally, was always listed first), crisply and logically set out, in the world's most prestigious scientific journals. I saw the bound volumes of those journals, on the shelves of the library at Harvard, their edges black with handling and the pages worn where the hands of hundreds of eager scholars had turned to my words. Penciled annotations gently corrected my minor typographical errata. I imagined letters and postcards pouring into our department office from laboratories all over the world, begging for reprints of my work. I imagined the look on Miss Freemartin's face - Miss Freemartin, who would now be my personal amanuensis because I would have so much correspondence - as countless dozens of postcards bearing colorful stamps from Africa and Asia would come in day after day, and I magnanimously would allow her to clip the stamps from the cards so that her little nephew could mount them in his Scott's Beginner Album from Woolworth's.

At that point, my reverie was momentarily interrupted as I nearly ran down a startled antelope that had been standing in a bewildered manner in the right lane of the highway, but I was soon back at it.

I rehearsed my haughty answers to the telephone calls that would clog our switchboard after a garbled account of my research would appear in the Wall Street Journal, possibly with a title something like "Insect Pest Scourge May Be Near End - Obscure Plains Scholar Discovers Secret of Their Appetite Mechanism." Yes, my will would have to be strong for me to fend off the job offers from the world's leading universities, especially after my frequent appearances on the network television news shows. I pictured myself, resplendent in my academic robes, mounting the podium in an oak-lined commons room at one of the ancient Oxford colleges, to be given a medal of the Royal

Society, draped around my neck by none other than Sir Herbert himself. You could bet your ass he'd call me Professor then.

And finally, in a triumphal concluding fantasy, the President of the United States came to my office door in Musgrave Hall, holding his fine Stetson diffidently in front of his chest, eyes dewy and with a crack in his voice, humbly asking me to tour the world's hottest trouble spots as a special envoy for peace, because the forcible voice of my reason could make despots see the folly of their ways and cause the formerly exploited and embattled peasantry to sing in gladness.

Going through matters similar to the above in my mind, over and over again and with little or no systematic thought, I drove for eight hours without stopping, and finally realized only at the outskirts of Pawnee Springs that I was very hungry, stiff, and thirsty; so I stopped at the HoJo for a bowl of soup and a glass or two of beer. I didn't get back to the area of the campus and my apartment until almost 1 AM, and even then, despite everything that had happened in the previous 40 hours, I still couldn't sleep. This time, I kept composing and recomposing letters in my head to Montague, written in different styles and tones that I thought might have more success. Finally, after some more alcohol and a few aspirins to numb my brain stem, I was able to get a few hours of shuteye.

The next day, I found that my subconscious had done its job overnight, and I was able just to sit down and write out a letter in what I thought was just the right mixture of respect and forthrightness. I wrote it down on yellow legal paper and brought it in to the office for Miss Freemartin to type up and send off. My lectures were probably not very inspired that day, as I had these other things on my mind, but no one filed any overt complaints.

I had become more and more convinced that I should work with butterfly larvae. They were abundant, conspicuous, and had well-studied feeding preferences. There were two quite common species I thought would be good initial choices; both were in the family Nymphalidae, the brush-footed butterflies. Many of the larvae of these butterflies build webs around their food plants that are easy to spot from a long way away. The first one I wanted to study was the Red Admiral butterfly, *Vanessa atalanta*; their larvae fed on only a few plants, all in the nettle family Urticaceae. I had seen them often on such plants as the tall stinging nettle, Urtica dioica, wondering how they were able to cope with the toxic secretions of this noxious plant. The other butterfly, the Painted Lady (*Vanessa cardui*), although a close relative of the Red Admiral, fed on many plants; I had seen their larvae mostly on thistles, but the literature reported that they also ate many other plants of several different families, including mallows, beans, sunflowers, and artihokes. These butterflies were not unknown in our part of the state, but I knew many other good collecting sites about 100 miles to the east. Perhaps Ehrlich knew of collecting sites, as well. All I had to do was to collect some of the larvae, so I could perhaps study some of their feeding behavior in the laboratory, and also collect their food plants from the sites where they were feeding, and start doing the metal analyses.

Meanwhile, I had to gear up to stock the lab with the materials I needed for the tests. I had to go back and review my thesis, to do a bit of literature digging, and to make lists of chemicals and equipment I would need. Then would come the hard part; I would have to present Dean Pfaff with a list of needed supplies and he would have to try to find a way to buy them out of the departmental equipment budget. Luckily, the academic year hadn't yet begun, so the department should still have some funds left, and I might be able to get a jump on the rest of the faculty if I put my requests in soon enough. Furthermore, although it was becoming later in the summer, I thought I might be able to collect enough insects and food plants for me to begin some of the research right away and carry on with the rest through the winter. Although I was very nervous about these developments, I was in a continual state of excitement because I finally felt I had found some research worth living for.

Weeks went by and I thought I was making good progress. I had reviewed the literature for metal analysis in plant tissues, and had picked out several metals that I thought would be meaningful to test for and that I could determine at low enough levels by simple, relatively cheap methods. I needed a centrifuge, and had convinced the Dean that we should buy a new one out of instructional funds. The fall term had started by this time, and I had lined up a couple of student research assistants; as always, they thought they could work twenty hours a week, but I knew that once the term started in earnest I would be lucky to get five out of them, so I was prepared to work them hard at the beginning of their tenure and hope that they wouldn't leave just as they were figuring out how to get results in the laboratory.

I still hadn't heard from Oxford, and I wrote a follow-up letter just in case the first one had gone astray. At this point, I had a research meeting with my small staff of principally volunteer help, and sent them off to collect plant and insect material and to get started on their laboratory work. I was prepared to step in and help wherever it would be necessary, and expected to do most of the laboratory analyses myself.

Shortly afterwards, I received an air letter from England, which I tore open eagerly (and as a result garbled a portion of the letter written on the creases of the paper). It was not from Montague but from his secretary; all that it said was that Professor Harlow-Montague thanked me for my interest in his work and that it had not yet appeared in print, but that it was being prepared for publication. No answers to my specific questions, no indication that he would send me a draft of any manuscripts or otherwise let me know about the progress of the work. I began to think that I was going to have to proceed on my own; if I found significant results, of course, professional courtesy would require that I inform Professor Montague of my findings, acknowledge the important role his presentation and data had in the genesis of the idea, tell him I was thinking about publishing them, and asking whether he would like to present some of his data at the same time. But that was a very long way off yet.

So, there was nothing to do but research. My young staff plunged into the task with determination, and within a few weeks we had enough material collected to fill virtually all the department's refrigerator space; we had to store the excess in our own home freezers and refrigerators. There was some grumbling by our colleagues, our roomates and our loved ones, those not involved in our research project, about bales of stinging nettles being placed among their valuable specimens and (still worse) among the edibles; I had to remind the complainers that nettles, when boiled, were said to afford a delicious soup, although I had never quite had the nerve to try it.

This was the easy part of the research. We then proceeded to work up the material by the painstaking techniques outlined in the literature for the analysis of plant tissues for metals. There were some shortcuts that I thought we could take that turned out not to be possible, so that set us back. We had the usual problems with unfamiliar analytical methods. We spent long hours in the late afternoons and evenings rehashing our experimental designs.

Unfortunately, one of the students I had most counted on got cold feet; after about two months, just when he was getting to the point where his work was reliable, he decided he didn't really want to work in science after all, saying he wanted a career that had more to do with people, and left. I saw him on the campus a week or two later, picking up papers with a pointed stick; I didn't speak to him.

The real problems, though, were with the last phase of the research; the metal analyses themselves. I had convinced myself I could do the tests accurately. I added known concentrations of metal ions to the plant material, ashed it down in the furnace, dissolved the ash in acid, and did the titrations or colorimetric tests necessary. My data were good in these types of tests. I trained another person to do the same procedures and had him check my analyses. Usually, the agreement was satisfactory.

However, when we did the tests on "real" plant material, with no external metal added, we never got consistent values. Leaves from the same plant species varied widely in metal content. Even individual leaves from the same plant weren't consistent. And when it came to comparing different species, it was hopeless. I banged my head against the wall for months to try to figure out what was going wrong. Finally, I had to conclude that our data weren't going to give us any answers. I decided to write to Montague again, explaining our problems and asking for advice. It was late winter by this time, so with much less lab work to do my staff was beginning to run out of things to keep them busy; I tried to give them encouragement, but I really hadn't had time to do a lot of planning beyond the initial stages of the project. They were becoming quite disappointed, and frankly so was I.

Not surprisingly, no letters were forthcoming from Montague. I decided to give the project another chance in the upcoming growing season. This time, we would perform the analyses immediately, on the freshest plant material we could obtain. We wouldn't store, freeze or refrigerate anything. I really doubted if this would make any difference, but I was willing to try.

Another problem was that I was running out of money. Pfaff had advanced me $500 to do the research. That was an unheard-of sum in the history of our department, and I had little to show him for it. I knew I couldn't get any more from him on the basis of the findings we had. In addition, I had greatly underestimated the expense it would take to perform the experiments. Most of the cost was in wages. I had to pay some of the students; I couldn't foist a senior thesis project, which cost me nothing, off onto all of them. We only had to pay a minimum of $1 an hour in those days, but even at that low rate most of the money was gone.

We plunged ahead. We collected a new batch of plant material as soon as we could in the spring term, toward the middle of May. Just before that, we had prepared a whole new batch of reagents. I bought a new lamp for the spectrometer out of my own pocket; I didn't want to have it burn out and go begging to Pfaff for another one. This time, also, we were careful to separate leaves of different ages, since I thought that older leaves might perhaps have very different metal contents from newly emerged ones.

We set up the experiments excitedly. We had every hope that things were going to go differently this time. Then the data started to come in, and they were unambiguous; everything came out just the same as it had before. There were no correlations, no trends at all. All of our data was garbage, it was a goddamn load of crap.

Once again I racked my brains. What was different about the way Montague had done his experiments? Geography, certainly. Maybe the enfeebled soils of Europe, washed over dozens of times in the last two thousand years by the gunpowder and the blood and the household scraps and the excrement of conquered and conquering tribes, were so contaminated by trace metals that all their plants were different from ours here in North America, where we had only one group of natives and one wave of conquerors so far. Maybe Ehrlich was right, and Montague's data were ruined by environmental pollution. Or were we to blame, was there some little systematic flaw in the way we set things up so that everything wound up giving random numbers?

I actually considered calling someone from our chemistry department and asking for advice, but I doubted if any of them would have anything useful to say, even if they had deigned to comment on such an applied and unromantic project as this one.

Or was it really a difference in our plants? Couldn't this randomness we were seeing actually be a part of some devilishly clever evolutionary plan - the plants in a population being genetically or developmentally different in unpredictable ways, making it impossible for a predator to know, biochemically, what it was letting itself in for when it took a bite out of one. Maybe the bulk of the plants in the population would be nutritionally all right, but every seventh or tenth one or so would store toxic levels of vanadium or lead or whatever. It couldn't be much more unlikely than that or the toxic effect wouldn't be significant in terms of survival value for the plant.

The more I thought about it, the more I became convinced that such a strategy would actually make a lot of sense if it could actually be carried out; every predator would be playing a potentially fatal game if it tried to feed on that species. Even if they could detect the toxic levels in one leaf or plant, they might gather in increased numbers on the less toxic areas and thus be more easily seen by birds or other organisms that ate them, and thus the strategy would even protect the less toxic members of the population.

I tried to think of ways to test that hypothesis. It seemed to be almost impossible unless we could generate tremendous amounts of data. We would have to pick one metal, probably, and do thousands of analyses on many different populations, and at the same time try to correlate feeding damage to the leaves with metal concentration. Also, since the plants that could concentrate a lot of metal might be genetically different from the rest of the ordinary ones, they might look different, also, or have something about them that would correlate with their metal metabolism and also make them less attractive to predators. So we would need a lot of observational data to cover that possibility.

I went back to all our analyses and tried to see how they distributed themselves, trying to find one set that would show a nice even distribution in which possibly 10% of the samples were much higher than the average value. It was a staggering amount of work. As it finally turned out, there were no sets of data that showed the nice even Gaussian pattern that I would have liked to have seen, with most of the values in the middle and falling nicely to a few very low or very high concentrations. However, there were some that were skewed out so that most of the numbers were low, and then the data tailed off so that there was a significant number of quite high levels. One of these was the set of values for copper. Now this was an interesting metal, because it was absolutely essential for life; every organism had to have some low level of it in order to function biochemically. But copper could also be quite toxic if there was enough of it around, more than the organism needed.

I had also been thinking about the plants we had chosen to study. Possibly, small plants were not the right ones to look at if this within-plant heterogeneity in the leaves was really correct; it might be better to look at trees. They would have branches of all different ages that might have different mechanisms of protection; old branches that had been around for many years might need less protection from herbivores than the newest ones, and thus the young ones might have higher copper concentrations. Branches at the top of the tree would be exposed to greater wind and light stress, but they were also extremely important since the tree probably needed to maximize its height for maximum survivability. Furthermore, leaves on the outside of the tree, which would be most obvious to flying insects or adult insects who might want to deposit their eggs, might need more protection than leaves well back toward the trunk. All in all, it seemed quite reasonable to assume that some mechanisms of differential protection were likely to be present in large trees.

So it was going to be trees, which pretty much limited us to cottonwoods because they were the only ones that grew in substantial numbers in our cold dry environment, and it was going to be copper. One unfortunate feature of this proposed study was that I didn't know much about the predators on cottonwood leaves, and whether there were some insects that specialized on them. I knew there were some net-building caterpillars on them occasionally, and I had noticed aphids in large numbers, but I had never spent very much time trying to key them out or determine whether they were also found on other plants. Thus, that part of the research would also have to be done simultaneously, literally from the ground up, and we more or less had to hope that something interesting would fall out, figuratively speaking.

I actually felt better about this research plan, because I thought that whatever we discovered, it would be useful. No one had done very much on cottonwoods as a food source for insects, so just counting the species and their abundances on the leaves could be a valuable contribution. I could even write such a document up and bury it in the annals of the state academy of science, where Pfaff had been pressuring me to publish for years. And if anything better came out of the data, I could dare to hope that my work might be published in an internationally prestigious multidisciplinary journal like Nature or Science. That would surely be a first for our department. In any case, I was definitely feeling more relaxed; less concerned over whether our findings would be sensational, more ready to take whatever came along.

In a way, it would be nice to be a celebrity, but it would also be quite bothersome. I imagined all over again how annoying it would be to deal with well-meaning suburbanites who would call the department office with their dumb questions on what to do about Japanese beetles jeopardizing the japonica, after reading an article I had written for the Washington Post, or seeing me on Jack Paar's talk show. Not to mention the professional annoyances - being called on to organize meetings, give lectures on "Biological Research Needs for America's Future," sign petitions for saving the Amazon jungles, and serve on Presidential panels to select the recipients of the National Medal of Science. I probably wouldn't like working with the President at all; Eisenhower would be bad enough, but any future President would probably be a real snake-oil salesman by the time I got to be famous enough. And all for honoraria not likely to exceed $25 a day. No, I might be better off in obscurity.

Finally, the following spring rolled around. I had assembled another small staff of volunteers and senior thesis students. I hired a young man to collect the leaves and the insects from the field sites, trained another to help me with the insect identifications, and another to do the chemical workups. This time I even had a graduate student, an earnest young woman named Dorothy Mallory, who wanted some research experience to go with her M.S. in science education, to help me out. She had talked to me several months earlier about my research interests, along with everyone else in the Division, and I was quite surprised when she showed up at my office in early May, asking if I could supervise her research. She started the next day, and I soon found out that she was an indefatigable researcher, putting in long hours, days, evenings, and weekends.

Dorothy was very tall, almost six feet, very thin, very bright, and very serious. My jokes were lost on her, being greeted always only by polite and puzzled smiles. She was a somewhat odd-looking person, though not unattractive. Her arms and legs were extraordinarily long; they were the same length as mine (we measured them; face to face for the arms, and back to back for the legs), and I was about four inches taller. She wore big, round, frameless glasses. Her dark, thick hair was gathered up in impenetrable Teutonic buns over each ear, but a few wispy strands escaped and trailed down the back of her neck. She had small, hard, high breasts, concealed to just the right degree in her neat white blouses. And she always wore long flared skirts, embroidered denim patchwork creations extending to mid-calf; I suppose they did not hinder her strong-willed strides. I never saw her in jeans.

She was interested only in science; I found out from our casual discussions in the laboratory that she had never heard of King Lear, Spinoza, or W. C. Fields. Despite these cultural gaps, I discovered that we worked well together. I had taught her to do the copper analyses, the most boring but most important part of the work. Her performance was exemplary; it was as if she had been born to do the job. She was meticulous; her data books were almost pathologically neat, written in India ink in a minuscule hand, perfectly aligned columns of numbers, each decimal point exactly below the one above; with perfectly centered headings printed in tiny capital letters with serifs.

I can still see her as she was one evening shortly before she graduated and left town; seated on a high metal stool by the spectrophotometer, elbows on the bench, leaning forward over the data book entering the numbers. She was oblivious of my presence; she was humming quietly, one finger of her left hand tapping a slow rhythm on her cheek. Her knees were pressed firmly against the doors of the cabinet, and her feet were held tightly together and locked into the bottom rung of the stool. The main lights in the room were off and her head was lit from behind by a small red gooseneck lamp that she'd set on top of the spectrophotometer. The stray strands of her dark hair formed a halo about her round, madonna-like head. Alas, Dorothy, you who were never my love, where are you now that I need you? I stare into raging winter storms and see your face. Where have you gone and whom are you laughing with tonight?

So, with Dorothy and the others doing yeoman service, the research toddled along that spring and summer; I felt a sort of lazy pleasure in the way it was developing. We had long experience in the project now, we knew more or less what to expect, and although we were turning up nothing immediately arresting, I had the feeling we were assembling data that could be made to tell an interesting story. Our research group met once a week at the beginning, but gradually we became lax and eventually stopped meeting altogether except when one of us came up with a particularly interesting finding, an event that did not happen frequently. Still, we were learning things that no one else had learned, and the erudition that was coming our way brought with it a certain pride. With enough labor to correlate the data, the story would begin to unfold. Unfortunately, no one could really do that except me, and I had many other things on my mind. The summer began to slip away and I had classes to prepare for.

Suddenly, two years to the day from when I had heard Montague's inspiring message in Kansas City, and just when I was becoming quite indifferent to the prospect of never hearing from him, I ran across his name again. I received a printed announcement from the Entomological Society of America concerning their forthcoming meeting, which was to be held in Phoenix that year in mid-December. There, in the list of distinguished scientists who were to give plenary lectures, was the worthy name of Professor Sir Herbert Harlow-Montague! Topic: "Sacred Beetles and Sacred Cows: Reflections on Thirty-five Years of Entomological Research."

Hot damn, I thought to myself, he's not going to get away this time. Phoenix is a damn sight farther away than Kansas City, but I'm going there and nothing will keep him out of my sight. I'll put our data together and collar him and make him sit down and see what there is to see. And then either he'll tell me what we're doing wrong or he'll at least let me see his own data. I won't let him forget me or ignore me this time.

I put in a few late nights as autumn gave way to winter and the meeting approached. I hadn't bothered to write to Oxford again; I was just going to barge in on him and ask him what the hell was going on. Our data were actually showing some trends in the copper analyses, but it looked as if it was going to turn out to be the oldest and the largest leaves, those closest to the ground, that had the highest concentrations; just the opposite of what I would predict if copper was a defensive anti-insect weapon. I really wanted to see what the great man had to say about that.

So finally the time came for the meeting. I didn't bother to register; I couldn't afford it, and besides, I was only going there for one presentation. Nobody ever checked those ridiculous badges anyway. Montague was going to speak on Tuesday, at 11:00, so I left at one o'clock in the afternoon on Monday. I skipped out of my next-to-last class, an anatomy laboratory section; I let Jack babysit for me. That late in the term, it was more or less a question of busy work anyway, both for us and for the students. It was going to be a drive of almost a thousand miles, and I wanted to drive it without any long breaks. There was reportedly some snow on the roads to the southwest, in northern New Mexico, and I wanted to be sure to allow myself plenty of time to get into Phoenix, find a place to park near the meeting hotel, and find the conference room.

My trip began auspiciously, I thought; the Pawnee Springs student FM station was rerunning the Texaco opera broadcast. It was Tito Gobbi in Verdi's Don Carlo from the Met. I had missed the broadcast on Saturday and was delighted by almost every minute of this brilliant performance. For some of the arias, I sang along with the cast, but when Gobbi came on I fell into a respectful silence. I was able to listen for nearly 70 miles but then the music was overwhelmed by static and I turned it off.

As the afternoon wore on I drove through eastern Colorado and up and up into the desert plateau of New Mexico. Americans who only know this area from the movies, or from summer vacations, would find it a very different world in midwinter. First of all, the light that glares so harshly and starkly off the rock outcrops in midsummer becomes muted and pale in December.

Grey clouds stretch from horizon to horizon, choking off the red heat of the sun. The stone formations no longer look like unwelcome intruders in their surroundings, but become innate with it, congenially lit by the filtered yellowish winter light. Their colors, so stark and dramatically contrasted, red, orange, purple in midsummer's glare, retreat to become almost subdued, taking on the greys and browns of decaying leaves. In the foreground, every greasewood and creosote bush and yucca plant takes on a subdued brownish cast; the leaves look furry and blurred, almost like dark snowflakes, not like those harsh waxy green spikes you see in July. The desert is far more self-contained in winter, not an inimical and destructive environment but a place of peace on its own terms.

Light snow covered much of the desert, in patches that showed where the faint sunlight didn't reach, and even clung to some of the vegetation; a few flakes fell occasionally out of the grey afternoon skies, but they always stopped after a few minutes and I gave them no further thought. Practically no one else was on the highway on this bleak afternoon. An occasional trucker coming from the opposite direction gave me a wave or flicked on his lights as a salutation. I continued to drive without incident through the late afternoon, stopping only three times; first for a stretch, next to fill my tank, and finally to swallow a couple of bottles of soda pop, bought from a gas-station vending machine, to keep me awake. I watched the violet sun setting behind the Sangre de Cristo mountains; I had covered nearly 300 miles already and anticipated no great difficulty getting into Phoenix in plenty of time.

What a shared cultural experience we twentieth-century Americans have in the long car trip, I thought to myself. It's a ritual with its own paraphernalia, priesthood, and places of worship. I could imagine a time in the next century, after the petroleum's finally run out, and our descendants sit around in little electronic cottages reminiscing; the old folks telling again about the days when they were children and they all got in the car, with mom and dad in the front, and they set out on a long safari halfway across the continent - all the way to California. And the children of the next century, who have had no way to visit California except by video, look on wide-eyed and try to imagine what it must have been like on such a pilgrimage so far from home; the heat, the noise, the cramped surroundings - man, they must have been made of tough stock in those pioneer days.

I stopped in the little town of Las Vegas for dinner around six-thirty, pulling into a place called the Rancho Verde Steak House, just south of the city. This Las Vegas was a humdrum, gravelly place, without a trace of the glitter of its better-known namesake to the west. The parking lot and the sign for the restaurant were illuminated by a single powerful yellow bulb on a high pole near the street. Five pickup trucks and three battered cars were dispersed around the parking area. At least one of the cars and one of the trucks had badly cracked windshields. The entrance was a low black door with a single tiny window, above a metal sign declaring "Entrance."

I entered to find myself in a brightly-lit one-room cafe in a typical new-West style, trying to evoke the mountain lodges of the last century. It was one of those knotty pine-paneled places with a flagstone floor; most of the floor space was occupied by booths fitted with benches having many coats of heavy varnish. An electric heater stood in a blackened stone fireplace at the end of the room. The place smelled of old grease and old cigarette smoke. There were only six tables, but none were occupied. The tables were not covered with cloths; instead each had four symmetrically placed paper mats bearing a rodeo scene. I noticed from the small print in one corner that the mats came from someplace in Pennsylvania. The tableware was already in place next to the placemats, wrapped up in paper napkins.

Along one wall was a bar fronted with studded green leather; eight male patrons, wearing identical sheepskin jackets, sat in front of it, nursing identical brown bottles of beer. The four patrons on the left end of the bar all wore cowboy hats, and the four on the right wore caps bearing the logos of farm implement manufacturers. One of the customers had brought a radio, had set it down on the middle of the bar, and was listening to country music, bobbing his head back and forth and periodically emitting soft cries of approbation. At the right-hand end of the bar, a hand-lettered cardboard sign taped to a scuffed and dirty door announced "Rest Room's."

Objects related to fishing and hunting hung from the walls; a deer's head (about a 10-point buck), duck decoys, two fly rods, a flintlock rifle, bowie knives, canoe oars, creels, a mounted bass, camouflage caps, and waders all dangled into the dining area.

Since no one came out to seat me, I chose a booth on the wall to the left, the one directly across from the bar. I sat directly underneath the rifle, figuring if anyone jumped me I could at least get in a good swing with the stock before I went down. Everyone had become silent and had turned to look at me when I came in, making it possible to hear a low continual buzzing, due to the resident fly population; but I apparently proved to be relatively uninteresting, and all the gentlemen at the bar soon continued their conversations.

I sat quietly, looking at my fingernails, for several minutes, and finally a hardscrabble-looking woman, perhaps fifty but conceivably much younger, clad in a striped apron, approached me, wiping off her hands on a soiled towel tied at her waist. She said to me, "What can I get for you, sport?" I asked if I could please see a menu. She laughed, saying, "Most of our customers either eat steak or drink beer. You want anything much different?" I said, no, that was fine with me; just a small steak, medium rare, a baked potato, and a large glass of water as well as a bottle of beer.

With that, she left without a word; she didn't write anything down or advise me what I might owe. I was left alone again for some time, to contemplate my fingertips and listen to the conversations of the regulars. As nearly as I could discern, they appeared to be principally concerned with the performance of their cars and farm machinery and the lack of performance manifested by their wives and girl friends.

A much younger woman (she couldn't have been older than nineteen) emerged out of the shadows behind the bar; she, it turned out, was the barkeep; her name appeared to be Agnes. She was attractive in a callow and tawdry way; small, dressed in tight jeans and an absurdly scanty, lacy apron, her light brown hair pulled back in a ponytail held by a wide red rubber band, she was chewing gum noisily in a ribald and agitated manner. She also wore a short-sleeved scoop-necked blue sweater that revealed a significant fraction of her bosom whenever she leaned on her elbows across the bar to talk to a patron, which was often. Her unvarying high-pitched giggle rolled through the room after every off-color remark directed her way by her customers; there were many.

After several minutes more, she ambled out from behind the bar and sauntered toward me. Busying herself with tidying the table nearest my booth, she called, "Jorder sumpin t'drink, sir?" I said, yes, I'd ordered a bottle of beer from the other lady. She replied, "I c'n bring 'at t'ya. Y'want a Bud, or a Miller, or a Coo-oors?" The tone of her question suggested a choice from a menu of erotic services.

I opted for a Miller, and she quickly returned with one, carrying the clear frigid bottle for me, holding it in front of her in both her dainty hands as if it were a talisman of grave religious significance. Only for me, this small and fragile thing, and she was the vestal that I of all men was lucky enough to command at this instant. She leaned gracefully toward me, bending from the waist, and positioned her payload deliberately and delicately in the exact center of my rodeo placemat. She held the upright bottle for a second or two in that position before releasing it. Although my gaze was mostly directed down the front of her sweater, I also saw that the nails on her blunt fingers were neatly cut, straight across, and adorned with pale pink polish. Then she stood up slowly, rubbed her wet hands languidly over her apron, smiled quickly, stuck her pink tongue into the corner of her mouth, gazed into my eyes (my heart was beating like a little snare drum from what I had seen and nearly seen, and from the scent of her perfume), and said, "Y'ditn't wanna glass, did ya?" I managed to choke out that just the bottle would be fine, and she retreated to the bar, her hips swaying suggestively, after collecting thirty-five cents, looking back over her shoulder every few paces to smile at me.

After a further long period (during which two of the cowboy-hatted patrons left, in a hail of boisterous goodbyes, diminishing with their departure the symmetry of the bar), the elder waitress finally emerged from the swinging doors of the kitchen, struggling to bear in only her two hands a large circular plate with my steak (much bigger than I had expected), a smaller oval plate with a foil-wrapped potato, a glass of ice water, and a bottle of Budweiser. After she had discharged the order to the table with a clatter, I explained that the barmaid had already brought me a beer, pointing to the Miller on the table. She paused, then said, loudly, "That bitch!" and strode immediately over to the bar to complain over what was apparently a territorial incursion by Agnes into her rightful domain, that of proper tables and chairs and decent family people. Her animadversion to this behavior made perfectly clear, she returned to my table and said, "You don't mind drinkin' another one, do you? I arreddy opened it." I said that, well, I'd really only wanted one, but I supposed it would be all right. She clapped me on the shoulder and said, "Good for you, I can tell you're a big strong buck who likes to knock back a couple of brews every now and again." Then, as she turned to leave, I said to her, "Miss, just one more thing. I did order a medium rare steak. This one is much too well done and I don't want it."

She paused, looking at me as if I had just announced that I was the Devil and I needed her as a human sacrifice. Her eyes kept getting bigger and rounder. Finally she said, "You want another steak? You want me to take this one back?" It clearly was not something she was accustomed to doing. I said, yes, please, I had after all ordered a medium rare steak and that was not what I had been given.

So, staring at me over her shoulder the whole time as if I might be a menacing ogre somehow having assumed human form, she retreated back to the kitchen with quick, mincing steps, gingerly carrying the plate with my steak on it at arm's length, muttering disbeliefs under her breath. The room had fallen totally silent during the discussion and all the patrons had resumed gawking at me, even interrupting serious drinking for a few moments over the occurrence of such a bizarre phenomenon as this. One obese patron wearing a plastic John Deere cap that was much too small for his great gourd of a head beheld me with a fixed smirk, shook his head at me slowly, and spat on the floor before turning back to his beer. As for me, I took advantage of the quiet to eat a few bites of my potato.

Out through the swinging doors, then, appeared a hulking man, huge and surly and bone-browed like a Neanderthal, dressed in an undershirt from whose several rips, front and back, protruded long tufts of iron-grey hair. Not a cigar stub (as might have been expected), but an unlit pipe, was clamped in his jaws. At his waist was a bloodstained, ragged cloth that may once have been an apron. He carried a cleaver in one hairy hand and in his other was the plate with my steak. A few great strides, not taken with any particular rush but very efficient in the way they covered ground, brought him to the side of my table. An overpowering smell of sweat, mingled with the musky reek of rancid oil, washed over me like a wave when he halted.

I stared up at him from a slightly hunched position, as if to ward off a blow; he was huffing heavily and frowning in a manner to bring forth thunder from the heavens. He said in a deep growl, "You sayin' there's sumpin' wrong with this here piece a meat?" As he spoke I saw, peering out from behind each massive shoulder, my two waitresses, looking abashed and animated at once, as if in anticipation of some grisly but tantalizing spectacle. The scene reminded me of Michelangelo's God, from the Sistine ceiling, drifting toward a powerless Adam, with Eve and the angels crowded behind Him.

I took a deep breath and, speaking slowly and distinctly, said, "The only thing wrong is that it is overcooked. I prefer a medium rare steak. This one is too tough and too dry for my taste." The giant looked down for some time at the meat. His breathing continued to come in rattling gasps. He couldn't seem to comprehend that people could want it cooked any differently; it was as if I had just complained to him about the shape of the moon. "You really don't like it bloody, do you?" he said. I replied that, as a matter of fact, I did prefer some of the natural juices to remain.

He looked at me with a long and disdainful scowl, and finally said, pausing to pant between sentences, "Mister, I don't understand people like you. I been cookin' meat for thirty-two years. It's the only business I ever knew. I like the taste of meat, I eat it every meal. I know a thing or two about meat. A piece of steak like this costs me good money. I think guys like you got problems. I guess what I'm sayin' is I don't know how to cook a piece of steak the way you want it. Maybe you just oughta find some other place to take your business."

Just as I was about to take him up on his offer, a weaving shape appeared in front of my booth. It was one of the gentlemen from the bar. He was a lean, hard, cowhand type, maybe sixty years old, wearing tight jeans, a blue plaid cotton shirt, high boots, and a big grey Stetson. A thin stream of spittle had dried on his jaw. Still clutching an empty bottle of beer by the neck, he said, "This gah givin' yew a hard time, Leon?" The chef replied without looking at him, "Siddown, Smitty, I got no trouble here." Ignoring Leon's advice, Smitty pushed forward, saying to me, "You sunnabitch, what you doin' here muckin' up this fahn place? We don' lahk your kind a trash around here. Look at me, asshole, what y'got ta say for y'se'f?" The chef placed a restraining hand on Smitty's shoulder; it was the hand with the cleaver. Smitty tried to shrug him off and then suddenly lunged for me, twisting and diving across the tabletop, shouting, "Lemme at the piss-ant!" Unfortunately for him, his lurch resulted in the heavy cleaver falling from Leon's hand, and the blade caught him square in the small of the back. I watched in horror as it dropped, stuck in his flesh for a few hundred agonizing milliseconds, and then tumbled to the floor with a clang. Smitty screamed and jerked up suddenly, grabbing at his back with both hands, and spun around to confront the chef. He dropped his bottle; it smashed into splinters on the stones, several feet away, as if thrown. I watched in alarm as dark wet blood spread from the gashed shirt and oozed down past his heavy leather belt to stain the seat of his pants.

There was a moment in tableau as he faced the trio of them, Leon flanked by the two waitresses, all looking at each other in big-eyed terror. Then Smitty said to them in a whimper, "What'n hell'd you do to me? I was jus' tryin' ta he'p out. Jus' tryin' ta be a pal. And what does it get me, you jus' stab me in the back. Well, fuck you, buddy, I got other things t'do." By this time, I had emerged from the booth and had come up behind the wounded man. I had wetted my handkerchief with my ice water and was going to try to slow the flow of blood. As I said, "Let me help you," and tried to pull the shirt up to examine the wound, Smitty whirled around in anger, saying, "Get your fuckin' hands off me, piss-ant!," and struck heavily at my throat with his forearm. I staggered back a couple of steps and stumbled over a chair leg; falling backward, I hit the back of my head on the floor with a thwack. Momentarily stunned, I looked up at my assailant, expecting to see him crouching over me and ready to attack me again where I sat (in a pool of beer, broken glass, and blood); instead, I watched in dread as he staggered sideways, moaned, and clutched at his stomach, looking as if he was going to be sick. His eyes rolled up to the ceiling and his knees buckled. He pitched forward in a faint and was immediately surrounded by Leon and the other customers, who had come rushing from across the room. Leon yelled, "Grace, get some bandages and call a doctor!"

I felt a hand on my shoulder as I was trying to stand. It was Agnes. She spoke very quietly, saying, "I think you'd better leave now." I stood up, brushing myself off as well as I could. Agnes kept a firm hold on my arm. Looking back at the little crowd around Smitty, which was still looking down at him, but silent now, waiting for something to develop, she quickly and quietly led us out of the door and into the parking lot.

Even after we were outside, she continued to hold onto me, and still whispered. She said, "I'm sorry for what happened. We don't usually get people like you in there, people who care about themselves and what they eat." I said to her, "I suppose I should pay for what I did eat." Agnes replied, "Don't be silly. Just get out of here, now. They're gonna want to find somebody to blame in there. Some of those old boys are meaner than badgers; they'd as soon cut you down as say howdy do." She continued to pull at my arm, drawing me toward her. She looked at me imploringly and went on, "Listen, mister, I got a favor t'ast of you. I can't stand it here no more. I gotta get out of this town. Could you help me? I just need to pack a couple bags and I'll go with you, wherever you're goin', just so it's away from here. Really."

I paused before answering; although I felt a certain commisseration toward this trapped girl, knowing a little about how it feels to be young and doomed in a dead place, I said, "No, I can't. I have to leave right now. I've got a long way to go and not much time to get there." She looked up at me, rubbing my arm from elbow to shoulder with both her hands, and said, "I understand. But if you come back through here, give me a call. Here, the number's on this matchbook. I'll write my name inside the cover. I usually work here four to midnight every day 'cept Sunday an' Monday. Today, though, I'm fillin' in for another girl; that's why I was here tonight. I think it was fate, mister, that you come through on my day off an' I was still here anyways. You just give me an hour's notice and I'll be ready to go with you. Understand? I'll go anyplace with you, mister. I can't take it no more."

I put the matchbook in my shirt pocket and left her. She pressed her breasts to my arm at the moment I pulled away, smiling weakly as if to say, "Maybe that will change your mind just a little?" And as I started my engine and moved away across the parking lot, I watched her wave and blow me a kiss, standing in the yellow glowing circle like an ingenue taking her bows.

I was soon out on the highway again, driving westward in a profound blackness broken only rarely by a yard light illuminating a circular segment of some rancher's property. Almost three hours had passed since I pulled into the parking lot of the Rancho Verde. I thought back on what had happened in the restaurant. Already the events were beginning to take on a surreal quality, producing the feeling one has when thinking back on a grisly horror film, full of zombies and psychopathic killers, that one saw and dreaded as a child. The fear and anxiety I had felt in the restaurant had completely faded and was having less effect on me now, it seemed, than the far-off headlights approaching from miles away. The characters of the episode no longer seemed like palpable beings, but more like allegories or mythic constructs. Only Agnes still seemed human to me, and in her case I could still imagine the soft insistence of her bosom, and still smell the faint residuum of her perfume on my arm. Her face was even sharp in my memory, the forms of the shadows of her facial bones still clear as I remembered how they were outlined in the glare of the light. As I reimagined the events of the immediate past, I considered the effect they would have on a listener to whom I might relate them, and I suspected that the principal impact would be one of amused skepticism. If I was ever to tell anyone what had happened, I might have to water down the events into a less colorful but more credible account.

I withdrew the restaurant matchbook from my front pocket and stared at it, rubbing over its shiny surface with my thumb and feeling the silver embossed letters, not quite readable in the dim glow of my dashboard lights, on the kelly green background of the book. I was trying to believe that what had happened to me there was real and not just a fever dream of an overactive academic imagination, longing for corporeal and verifiable events to overwhelm the weak and pallid conjectures of a life spent buried in books. Well, it was certainly real. The people were real, the smells real, the overcooked meat real; the knife wound in the cowboy's back was as consummately genuine as one of these mountains around which I was driving.

Speaking of this, it was beginning to snow more steadily as I moved into the high elevations of the Jemez Range. I had just left the turnoff for Santa Fe behind and was about fifty miles from Albuquerque; from there, it was another 450 miles until I reached Phoenix. I was making good time, I thought, in spite of everything, practically halfway there after eight hours on the road and fourteen more hours left to make the other half of the trip.

I descended into the valley into Albuquerque, the largest city in the state. The lights of the city were clear, sharp, and starry, not haloed by mist. It had stopped snowing once again and I pulled off the highway to seek a grocery store or restaurant that might still be open at this hour, which was now close to 11 p.m. There were no people on the streets, and few other cars; only an occasional large semi, banging through the streets on some commercial errand that might have started in Los Angeles and might end around dawn in Amarillo, kept me company.

I was realizing how hungry I was and how long it had been since I'd eaten anything substantial. The downtown streets were quiet on this chill Monday in mid-December, and I was beginning to doubt that I was going to find anything. Then, just before the Rio Grande bridge, I came to a medium-sized hotel with an attached cafe. As I parked in front of the entrance, my car was bathed in the glow of yellow neon-like tubular lamps that spelled out CAFE, ROOMS, and EAT in repeated blinking messages (mirrored on the hood), and as I stepped out of the car, I saw the skin of my hands glow with a green fluorescence.

Once in the lobby, a musty, dark and empty place faintly lit by two chair-side lamps, I was able to see that there was apparently no one in it, nor the restaurant. Suddenly, a silent-footed bellhop materialized out of nowhere behind me, and asked, "May I be of assistance, sir?" The voice was warm, serene, and cultured - almost certainly trained as an actor's. He was around sixty, with full, greying hair; small-boned and lean-faced, with a gentle smile; and he held his hands together in supplication in front of his chest as he looked up at me. I explained my predicament, and he said, "It will not be a problem, sir. Our restaurant has just this moment closed and I shall be able to bring you some perfectly fresh and acceptable food from the kitchen. It cannot be an elaborate meal, of course; it will be more like a picnic lunch; but I guarantee to you that it will meet your needs."

I assured him that was exactly what I wanted, and he retired to the restaurant as I waited in the lobby, sitting in a dark, straight-backed, meagerly upholstered chair, and watched the desk clerk (a young man in thick-lensed glasses, muttering the names of two-digit numbers) manipulating columns of figures with a lever-operated adding machine, producing an endless ribbon of paper that spilled out onto the carpet.

The bellman returned in short order, bearing a white cardboard box tied up with string. "I believe you may find this satisfactory, sir," he began. "I prepared a ham sandwich and a roast beef sandwich for you - they are on white bread, sir, but it is very good white bread - and I also found two excellent pieces of baked cold chicken, a breast and a drumstick. I have also included two pieces of fruit, an orange and an apple, and even a small dessert, a piece of white cake with orange frosting. In addition, I have included a small bottle of club soda, unfortunately not cold, but I shall bring you a small box of ice forthwith." I began to salivate, but was able to tell him that the ice would not be necessary, and to ask him what I owed him for this unexpectedly thorough service. He looked away briefly, and replied, "I should think two dollars and fifty cents should cover the cost adequately, sir, if that would be satisfactory with you." At that point, I would have been willing to sign over my firstborn if I had one, and quickly handed over three one-dollar bills, thanking him very much and imploring him to keep the excess. I felt very fortunate to have struck such a bargain at this late hour. He smiled very broadly, bowed, waved the bills at me in a gesture of farewell, and said, "I thank you very much, sir, and I bid you a bon voyage and a very pleasant day to come."

I left the lobby and returned to my car, and immediately tore open the parcel to find the very items the bellhop had so succinctly described. Even before starting the engine, I attacked and ravenously devoured the roast beef sandwich - he was right, it was very good white bread, resilient to mastication and with a faintly sour flavor - and also the apple, a mealy but sweet Golden Delicious. I saved the remainder of the food for a late-night snack and for breakfast, started the car, and crossed the river to find myself on Route 66 headed dead west for Arizona.

The night had become even clearer; stars were visible even through my windshield, and the temperature, it seemed, was right around freezing. The air seemed as crisp and pellucid as quartz. In the moonlight, I could see occasional ranches, in front of plateaus where tufts of grass and shrubs dotted the sandy soil. I knew there were mountains in the distance, but I felt rather than saw them. The roads were dry and almost abandoned as I drove rapidly across the floor of the desert, crossing a series of small Indian reservations that were uncannily pitch-dark. Only an occasional adobe hut near the edge of the road, sometimes with a chained-up barking dog, was distinguishable. I imagined strange rituals, in nearly-dead languages, being performed in those darkling huts, lit only by a single candle made from rendered chicken grease. These rituals, I was convinced, would have changed little since the days of the legendary Ancient Ones, who had created a powerful civilization in the middle of this arid wasteland, full of cathedrals and cliffside dwellings, and then inexplicably vanished, as near as we could tell; but something of their culture and indeed, of them, lived on into the present, and it was expressing itself now, I thought, as I drove past. I conjured up old men sitting in a ragged circle, intoning solemn canticles whose words were nearly all devoid of meaning to the chanters. They were, I was sure, undergoing ritual confessions, spiritual cleansings. The rites might involve such things, I imagined, as a concoction made of the dust of the desert mixed with the blood of a freshly killed chicken and powdered rattlesnake scales, heated in a silver cup and drunk by the initiates, while they invoked spirits who might even now be hovering around me, waiting for the call of the faithful to smite the white intruder, to turn his mighty roads into pillars of flame and to cause his obscene cities to melt and to sink without trace into the crevasses of the desert. We shall have our land back, they would say, when our gods are ready to return them, but we must be ready too. Great gods, here we are; we are ready, we shall remain ready always.

After about eighty miles of such driving and such thoughts, I passed into the little town of Grants. The waxing crescent moon had just ascended over the sill of the mountains, casting silver shadows across a panorama of lava beds and dunes. I crossed some railroad tracks at the western edge of town, and then the road began to rise steeply into the highest parts of the Rockies. I had to be very alert, as the road was entirely unlit and only the double yellow line and the moonlight guided me around the sharp bends around red sandstone bluffs, and soon, switchbacks that climbed unrelentingly up and up the sides of the ancient volcanic cones. Again and again I shifted the gears up and down, twisted the wheel sharply left and right, hitting the brakes for especially sharp hairpins. Finally, just after passing through the tiny settlement of Thoreau (ah, Henry David, I said to myself, see what has been wrought in your name; a few metal shacks, a general store, and a tavern, carved out of this magnificent wilderness), I ascended the steepest road of all, spending most of the time shifting back and forth between first and second gears; and after a seemingly interminable climb, the road flattened out into a high alpine meadow and I saw a small brown wooden sign: CONTINENTAL DIVIDE. I felt a sting of exhiliration; I had made it, I and my Pontiac, we climbed the toughest climbs this brittle rind of a continent could throw at us, and here we are at the summit.

A short pullout road, a few hundred yards long, led around the meadow to the right, so I swung off the road and got out for a stretch. My watch read three a. m., straight up; eight hours until I had to be at my destination, and three hundred and thirty miles to go. I turned off the engine of the car and stepped out into the darkness. The odor of pines was intoxicating in the thin, cold air. The stars were bright and close as I had never before seen them. Ah, my America, I thought, this is why the pioneers left the comfortable east behind; a land that holds such beauties is a land worth risking everything for. This is a holy place that blesses even those who have never come here, for they are enriched by its heritage.

Such high-flown sentiments, however, were short-lived. I felt urgency in my bladder, and took a leak onto the Divide, feeling pleasure at the thought that the water molecules produced by my metabolism would percolate through the rocky soil and, centuries later, some of them would find their way into the oceans lapping at either coast of our country. I wondered what the nation would be like then; whether it would be devastated by nuclear disaster and populated only by a few tough-gened savages, or, perhaps worse, in the absence of such a catastrophe, wracked by overpopulation and filled with China-like mobs ransacking the last forests and streams; what it or its daughter republics or monarchies would be called, and whether men and women would still climb these inhospitable peaks to gaze off in all directions to the horizon.

I felt stiff and weary; I needed a brief rest. I had brought my alarm clock, and I set it to go off at four-thirty. There were no more great mountain ranges to conquer from this point on, merely the high arid mesas of Arizona; it was literally all downhill from here. I decided to sleep in the car rather than try to find a soft place, free of scorpions, amongst the boulders.

After a long, last stretch, I returned to the car, drank my bottle of soda and ate my two pieces of chicken; then I rolled the driver's-side window part way down, tossed the bones out into the grass, set the clock on top of the dashboard, curled up in the front seat with my jacket as a pillow, and fell immediately into a dreamless sleep.

After what seemed to be only a few minutes, I was startled awake by what felt like someone moving my body, or pushing heavily on the car. Was someone trying to wake me, I thought? ("Officer, I promise to leave in a little while, I ain't doin' nobody no harm...") No. The car had moved, I felt certain, but everything was silent again. I was completely awake now, my eyes staring uselessly into the blackness. My nostrils caught a slight, wild scent, like old urine or dilute ammonia; this led to my next thought, that I was trapped in the beginnings of an earthquake or a volcanic eruption, and I was smelling the gases being released from below the earth's crust where they had been trapped for millenia. I wondered for an instant what the hell I should do, and felt profoundly paralyzed by my inability to assess the options of such a hopeless situation.

Then I heard a deep rattling grumble; was this the next phase of the cataclysm? No. I saw something or someone move on the hood of my car, felt the car shift again as the thing moved about heavily. The lights of the stars winked out behind his or its massive shape. I was seized by throat-tightening panic; my heart went into an instant frenzy. I dived for the glove compartment, where I had a flashlight. For a moment my fingers trembled too much to press the catch, but I did, and got it out, and pointed it out the window, and flicked it on, revealing ...

A face from hell. An open mouth with long fangs, side whiskers, glowing fluorescent green eyes, and pointed ears ...

A mountain lion. Holy shit, I said to myself, and rolled up my window just as fast as I could. The thing probably ate my chicken leftovers and was checking me out as the main course. I kept the light on it, and it struck the window with a thump of its heavy paw; it let out a screaming snarl at the same time. Then, without a glance back, it turned around and leaped off the hood, disappearing into the trees. The car bounced once or twice on its worn-out shocks and was still.

I lay back on the seat, still holding the flashlight in my lap, directing the beam uselessly up to the roof. I clutched it tenaciously in both hands as if I was afraid the lion would come back and snatch it away in its powerful jaws. God in heaven, I thought, what next? Attacked by a giant, a drunk, a siren, and a ferocious beast; this is a journey to match those of Hercules, Jason, or Odysseus.

After a minute, I sat up. My teeth were still chattering in my shuddering jaw, my heart was thumping, and my throat felt like I had swallowed an icicle. I shone the beam of the flashlight carefully in all directions; no sign of the lion, of course; it was no fool. I was dangerous, willful, and unpredictable, and there was no future for it in hanging around to wait to see what I would do. Curiosity killed the cat, you know, my son; what did the cat want to know, daddy?

I checked my watch; it read 4:10 a. m. Not too bad, an hour's sleep; almost as much as I had bargained on. I stretched myself in the car (no sense taking any risks venturing out into the darkness), yawned deeply, started the engine, turned on the lights, and headed down the mountain for my rendezvous with Montague.

On this side of the Rockies, the mountains seemed different; no longer volcanic cones with relatively smooth sides, these were immense craggy blocks of sandstone that launched themselves from a level tableland strikingly high up into the air, far taller and more sheer than I would have thought possible. Also, on this wetter side of the mountains the forest was much denser, with an understory of aspens and junipers joining the towering pines I had noticed on the eastern slope of the Divide. The valleys here were filled with irregular slabs of shale, not the rounded house-sized boulders I had been seeing.

Shortly after five, I passed through the town of Gallup, a center for sheep ranching and coal mining. I drove slowly through the narrow dark streets, looking for the twists and turns made by Route 66 as it snaked through the city. Although most of the townscape was dark and deserted, I passed a group of shabby-looking men outside a brilliantly lit building, perhaps a tavern. In the center of the group, one, perhaps an Indian, was squatting down and gesturing to the rest. As I came abreast, he stood up and raised both his arms toward me, waist high, palms outward, seemingly in a gesture of benediction; and then, I swept past, leaving the mysterious tableau behind forever.

West of Gallup, it began to snow. The dawn was just beginning to redden the horizon I drove toward, but it was still almost totally dark. Flurries of snowflakes swarmed in my headlights, almost obscuring the edge of the road.

The sky was heavily clouded, and as the sky became lighter I saw bands of violet and grey in the distance as the banks of cloud massed over the mountains near the horizon. Occasionally, the road cut through a hill, revealing brilliantly colored bands of soil; red, yellow, and orange layers that contrasted strangely with the changeless grey of the highway. As the sun began to rise, I began to see isolated sandstone bluffs with extravagant shapes peppering the desert. Farther to the north was a more nearly continuous range of sandstone cliffs whose angular contours had been softened by snowdrifts. I imagined mountain lions in those hills, cousins of the one I had just encountered, watching me speed past in my incomprehensible vehicle, snarling once, and then turning away to go about their day's business.

Descending the mountain, I saw that it had snowed rather heavily on this side of the Divide; high banks of the stuff were piled up on both sides of the highway. Road crews had been through some little while ago, cutting a long slab-sided notch down the road. My tires no longer whined steadily on dry pavement, but moaned and thumped as I crossed patches of packed-down snow.

Immediately after sunrise, I crossed a rocky little stream that came rushing out of the green and piney mountains to make a black streak across the snow. Gathered on the banks was a small herd of mule deer, perhaps seven or eight individuals; some were drinking from the stream and some scratching in the snow to try to find something edible. They were the first animals I had seen since my episode with the lion, and I felt a little more comfortable to be in their presence.

Just before the Arizona line, I climbed a tiered ridge of steep piled-up bluffs; the road was packed with snow and I had to proceed carefully. Near the top, my wheels spun ominously on patches of ice that were difficult to see in the surrounding snow. I slowed the car considerably at the crest of the hill in order to descend; then halfway down the slope, I looked in my mirror and saw, terrifyingly, a hundred yards behind and closing rapidly, a truckload of logs. I saw the driver of the truck clearly; he was a bony, florid-faced man with jug-handle ears, wearing a yellow cap. He swung the truck abruptly into the left lane to pass, leaning on his air horn; I tried to pull my car as far to the right as I could. The truck engine roared and whined as he downshifted to maneuver through the packed-down snow. He swerved back into the right lane, but I saw that he had misjudged the distance; the trailerload swung erratically toward my car. As I watched the huge swaying logs apparently about to broadside my front end, I braked in terror. Unfortunately, at that moment, my wheels were on ice, and the Pontiac swung in an arc toward the trailer; but luckily, its high rear end had sufficient clearance to swing right over the top of my hood, so we didn't collide. But by this time, of course, my car was completely out of control. It described a 180o turn and started to skid backward in the left lane, but then the rear wheels left the pavement and the car bounced to a stop, pointed uphill, its rear tires deep in snow and its left front wheel delicately perched on the pavement. I leaned forward until my forehead was resting on the steering wheel, let out a gasp of relief, and turned off the ignition. I was all right.

In the mirror, I watched in disbelief as the logging truck continued to speed away, indifferent to my plight. I first leaned on the horn, then leaped out of the car and waved, but the driver didn't even slow down.

Well, I had come through this little episode unhurt, and the car was probably undamaged; but it looked as if I was really thoroughly stuck. And in this remote country, there was no way of telling when someone might come by to help. It was not snowing heavily at the moment, but the skies were threatening and I had no idea what was forecast. The nearest town of any size was Gallup, fifteen miles back.

It was now just after 6:30, and unless I got myself back on the road very quickly, my hopes of seeing Montague in Phoenix were shot. I still had nearly 300 miles to go. Maybe, I thought, I can dig myself out. I managed to get the trunk open by scrabbling off the snow with my mittened hands, but I found, as I was afraid I would, I had nothing like a shovel. I disassembled the jack and began to use its square bottom plate to scoop away the snow from my rear wheels.

After about fifteen minutes of excavating, while kneeling in the snow, my legs and feet were chilled, but I had worked up a sweat that was running down my face. The rear wheels looked a bit more exposed, but when I tried to move the car they only spun uselessly against the soft snow. Something for traction, I thought. No, I have no fifty-pound sacks of sand and gravel; what else is there? I wrapped the jack stand in my overcoat, and the rest of the jack in my suit coat, and jammed them as hard as I could in front of the rear wheels. This time, when I stepped on the accelerator, the car made a momentary lurch, but then resumed spinning ineffectively. When I got out to see what had happened, I saw that my overcoat had been thrown back from underneath the right rear tire, which then had continued its useless, frictionless whirling. The jack-suit-coat combination had remained in place, however.

I tried some other combinations, wrapping the stand in both the coats, putting everything under one tire or the other, trying to dig down to gravel, trying to fill in the holes made by the spinning wheels with brush, trying to block against the tires with good-sized stones pried out of the roadbed. But all failed. Finally, I sat sideways on my front seat, gazing helplessly down the empty road and wearing both wet and frayed coats, trying to decide if I should set out walking in one direction or another for help.

Unexpectedly, in the distance coming up the hill toward me, I saw a black pickup truck. Standing up, I jumped up and down and waved frantically; the driver and a passenger, two middle-aged men, saw me and blinked their lights. They drove about twenty yards past me and stopped at a more or less level spot in the uphill lane. Leaving their engine running, they opened their doors and came ambling back.

"Howdy. Looks like y'had a bit of a skid," said one of the two, the driver of the pickup, a man of the range in a black ten-gallon hat and sheepskin vest. His companion, a short, dark, hatless Hispanic, who was smoking a hand-rolled cigarette, said nothing, only tittered anxiously. He had long silky eyelashes and tight black curly hair, and fancy boots in blonde leather.

"Yep, got sideswiped by a truckload of logs. Just missed getting my front end bashed in."

"Damn fools come over here from California t'work here winters, never saw snow before. Lucky you didn't get rear-ended. Guess we'd be scrapin' yuh off the highway then." The Hispanic giggled again and looked me up and down as if he was sizing me up as a dancing partner. He dropped his tobacco into the snow and ground it under his boot, leaving a smooth oval patch.

"Well, I reckon we oughta see if we can get y'on your way. Where yuh headed?"

"Phoenix, hope I can make it by noon. How're the highways west of here?"

"Clears up about twenty mile ahead. This here's the worst spot, right in here. Always is. Still, y'll hafta burn rubber t'make it by then. This is a damn fine car, though, '54 Pontiac, last good year they ever had. It oughta hold together till yuh get there.

"Ruiz, let's see if we can push this here gentleman out. Sir, if y'don't mind, just pull down the hill t'that level stretch, an' wait there until y'see if we make it up the hill. Otherwise, we might need t'have you return the favor."

"I'm most indebted to you good folks; I'd be happy to pay you for your trouble."

"Not a word of it, stranger, just our Christian duty. You'd do the same for us. 'Sides, Ruiz here'd just drink it up, and I need him to put in a day's work. Ready, Ruiz?"

"OK, boss." He could speak after all. I got in the car and started the car; the two Samaritans braced themselves against the drift. I gunned the engine as they thrust manfully against my rear end; Ruiz was looking directly at me, smiling, but the other man looked straight down at the pavement. The car gave a shivering lurch and spun free; I was back on the road.

After watching their truck disappear over the hill, I set off again, crossing the Arizona line to continue my journey, perhaps a bootless one now, but I was determined to finish it. I felt in my bones that I was going to meet with Montague today, and that it was going to be a meeting of destiny.

After a short drive through the Apache reservation, bleak country covered in light snow, with only occasional huts and adobe mission churches to break up the rocky landscape, I turned south onto U. S. Highway 666. The number of the beast, I thought. But it still seemed possible that I could make it with luck and that I might not have to face my own personal apocalypse.

I calculated that I had 275 miles to go, and it was not yet 8:00. The road was clear of snow and I was averaging between 60 and 70. I might actually still make it before his talk ends, I said to myself. Traffic was practically nonexistent. I needed a few lucky breaks, now, after all that had gone wrong; and I was wide awake, actually quite exhilirated to actually be back on the road with a good chance to see my man.

I was surprised at the landscape of northeastern Arizona, which I had not seen before. I had expected a barren and desolate desert, but the terrain was quite diverse. There was some desert to be seen, but it was broken up by mountains, forests, rivers -- even a few lakes. Occasionally, I saw a dude ranch or golf course, but more often irrigated agricultural developments appeared. The irrigation canals stretched straight to the horizon, placid in their concrete banks. "There is something deeply wrong," I muttered to myself, "about 300 acres of roses suddenly appearing in the northern Arizona wilderness." Every few miles, also, there was an abandoned roadside stand with a hand-lettered sign, like as not misspelled, advertising silver or turquoise jewelry. "Authenic Navahoo," one sign announced.

Rarely, an abandoned miner's cabin, walls weathering away and roof long since tumbled in, appeared by the side of the road. They were so wretched and forlorn that I couldn't imagine a grizzled prospector somehow appearing in the scene with his burro; it was clear that such a time had long, long passed.

The sky had cleared and the temperature was comfortable, in the upper 40s. I drove steadily for several hours, without slowing down or stopping to rest, except when I needed gas; then I treated myself to a big Styrofoam cup of coffee and two Danish rolls wrapped in cellophane, to go.

I turned from a southwesterly heading, at the town of Globe, to head straight west on the last ninety-mile leg of the journey. It was a blur of cattle ranches, irrigated fruit groves, and copper mines. The few towns were past almost before I could notice their names.

Suddenly, it seemed, through the light haze, I began to see buildings, quite large ones; and then, almost immediately, the trappings of suburbs, of a modern city, appeared -- gasoline stations, small motels, power lines. Damn, I thought, I'm almost there. I have averaged no less than 65 miles per hour on this leg of the trip; it's 11:35 and Montague is no doubt standing over there somewhere, in the Oasis Hotel, droning through his talk, more than halfway done. And here I come into the outskirts of town. It's going to be a close call.

Mesa, then Tempe, I left behind - stop-and-go traffic all the way. Arizona State University, Phoenix Zoo; no, I'll visit you another time. Five minutes to noon, approaching the center of town. I pulled off to the right-hand curb, into a bus stop, rolled down my window and called to a young man in a coat and tie waiting for the light to change. "Where can I find the Oasis?" I shouted at him, and he replied, " 'Bout ten blocks ahead. Turn right on Central. Just north of downtown."

Thanks, I waved. Damn, I might make it yet. Traffic crawled along, though. Third Street, Second, First - next better be Central - yes, it was. I turned into the right lane and found myself just behind a garbage truck. A stocky Hispanic-looking man in grey overalls and a sweatshirt with a hood was running back and forth with a rusty barrel between the businesses on the sidewalk and the truck, dumping loads of steaming wastes into the rear hopper, and flicking on the motor that shoveled the trash into the dark maggotty innards of the box. I had no way to get past; the left lane was jammed. Finally, I got a momentary break, gunned the engine, and shot past the truck; the driver, a tired-looking black man, gave me a desultory wave. I was momentarily startled by the "whites" of his eyes, which were bright yellow, like a lion's. I wondered whether he was suffering from jaundice or was addicted to some strange drug.

Exactly noon, and there it is. There was no way to miss the Oasis. It looked as if it had escaped, neglected and wounded, from Vegas, stumbled clumsily across the desert, and finally died here in north Phoenix. It consisted of a gleaming white Moorish tower with an onion dome; bricked-in, crenellated archways; and perforated battlements in pink and white stucco. In front, in its own grassy oval, was a huge diamond-shaped sunburst sign up and down which waves of flashing yellow bulbs surged; in the center of the sign was the word Oasis in lavender neon script, surrounded by white bulbs that raced around it in an endless circle. I turned left into the driveway and marvelled at the landscaping. There were some few real plants -- saguaros, large yuccas -- but also an abundance of over-lifesize date palms in glossy plastic, and statuary of camels, Bedouins, and touring minstrels carying exotic stringed instruments. Directly opposite the front entrance, hard by the sign, was a fountain shooting jets of water into space; and in the center of the fountain, incongruously, was a wire sculpture of Atlas holding up the world.

I pulled up to the front door of the place, leaving my car in the no-parking, registration-only zone. My watch said 12:03; if luck was with me, Montague's reminiscences over his past glories in science had gone overtime and I could still catch him. I bounced out of the car and swung the door back to close, I saw that it didn't quite shut and was hanging open about six inches. By this time I was halfway to the door and I didn't retreat to close it all the way; I figured I'd be back soon, one way or another. I approached the guardian of the gate, a black doorman wearing a squalid beefeater uniform; I watched his expression change from a welcoming smile to a puzzled scowl as I rushed past him without a friendly glance or word.

Crashing through the revolving door, I stormed into the lobby, my clothes smelling of stale beer and blood and covered in fine muddy dust; my jacket was soiled and threadbare, and my face was streaked with grime. I could feel the grit in my eyes every time I blinked. The lobby was full of people, entomologists, almost certainly; thin, pale, bespectacled men in out-of-fashion suits, clutching plastic glasses and gesticulating as they conversed about their arcane research with newfound, bored-looking acquaintances. I looked around in a frenzy to find the meeting rooms, and saw an arrow pointing up a short flight of lavender-carpeted stairs to the "Kalahari Ballroom." All the meeting rooms were named after deserts, I noted -- Kalahari, Sahara, Sonora, Mojave, Nubia -- how appropriate for an academic conference.

Shouldering aside a Navajo-looking gentleman maneuvering a long-handled whisk broom, and also a few small, starched dowagers (almost certainly not entomologists), I sprang up the steps two at a time, huffing with the effort. I entered a high-ceilinged foyer, lined with flocked mauve Regency wallpaper and congested with chandeliers, and facing four white-painted and gilded double doors, from which was streaming a throng of biologists. The Kalahari Room! Hot damn, I thought to myself, I fucking well made it. Now to find my professor and put the strong arm on him.

I fought my way into the ballroom, sculling upstream through the crowd like a salmon come home to spawn. As I passed through the double doors, I felt a blast of conditioned air; it was winter-cool outside, and the lobby had been heated to an artificially warm and summerlike condition, but at the same time the meeting room was being artificially cooled back to a winter climate. My eyes bulged and throbbed with the constantly-changing temperatures. The Kalahari was a long, square hall with a vaulted skylight, filled with gold-and-white leatherette chairs in temporary disarray. The ivory walls were covered with deep monochrome blue frescoes, pastoral scenes from an imagined and idyllic Mediterranean with fauns and olive trees and shepherdesses (what Kalahari is this, I asked myself).

And then I saw at the far end of the room, yes, standing in front of the dais, surrounded by admirers and illuminated by a shaft of sunlight (ah, he is a minion of God, I thought) gleaming off his flaxen tresses, looking as beatific and as wanton as a Mannerist cherub; yes, the man I had come all this way to see. I sighed with joy. I can't believe it, I said; I fucking well made it, and there he is, and goddamn it, I'm going to talk to him at last, I can't miss. Damn.

This time, his costume was restrained relative to that he had worn the first time I'd seen him; now, he was wearing a velvety dove-grey suit, bold blue-and-white striped silk shirt, and wide lilac tie. He had just said something that had made his little company laugh, the laughter echoing in the huge hollow room, and he was beaming at them and holding one finger up in the air to silence them and to make another point, when he caught sight of me coming down the center aisle toward him. He stopped smiling at once, and dropped his finger to his chest, where it began rubbing his tie tack nervously. Did I look directly threatening to him, a roughly dressed and obviously unwashed rogue in complete contrast with the elegant gentlemen in pinstripes fencing him in and cutting off his retreat? Or was I merely indecorous, intruding into the civilized milieu he had set up and was luxuriating in?

I stopped well back of the little detachment by the dais, not wanting to interrupt, but it was too late. Everyone had turned to stare right after Montague stopped speaking. He and I kept our eyes fixed on each other for some time, and finally he spoke, saying, "Yes, sir?" to me in a patronizing manner. I said, "My name's Pyke McKenna, and I'm very sorry that I missed your lecture. I've driven more than nine hundred miles to talk to you about some of your past research." Putting on a trace of a sardonic grin and glancing at his admirers, he replied, "Oh, really?" And I went on, "Yes, the work you discussed in Kansas City two summers ago, about food selection by plant-eating beetles. (He looked momentarily confused.) The trace metal work." "Ah, indeed," he said, speaking hastily, "I should be most happy to discuss that with you. Unfortunately, at the moment, I must attend to various other matters -- committee meetings, you know, that sort of thing -- but let us arrange to meet sometime this afternoon. Would it be convenient for us to chat, say, at around three? I should like to meet you in the lobby of the Barrowholt Hotel; that's approximately two streets from here, I believe. Is that all right? There's a good chap. Ta-ra, then."

The group around Montague broke up; he shook many hands, embraced one elderly gentleman, and then strode directly past me without a glance, gazing down at the carpet as if he was expecting to step in something unpleasant.

Well, I thought, there is little else for me to do but wait for him. It is now 12:20 p.m. and he wants to meet at three. I returned to the lobby and bought a newspaper from the desk clerk, who sniffed at me faintly; apparently my appearance was not up to the normal standards of the hotel's guests, even those temporary visitors, only milling about in the lobby, who were so obviously field biologists, with their plaid shirts, heavy beards, and boots. But I was not up to explaining my adventures of the previous day, so I left the lobby without a further word to anyone and returned to my car.

The door was still standing open. The doorman gave me a glare, and turned his back on me, clutching a silver-tipped baton behind his back with both hands as he hummed a march-like melody. I decided I would get something to eat, park my car near the Barrowholt, and wait for Montague to appear. I started the engine; at least my battery had survived intact. I pulled out of the driveway of the Oasis (was it my imagination, or had that doorman given me the bird as I left?), and began to cruise the streets of Phoenix in search of lunch.

First, I thought, I'd better be sure I find the Barrowholt, so I began systematically to cruise around the blocks in the immediate vicinity of the Oasis in ever-widening circles. Eventually, after inquiring directions from two pedestrians who gave me somewhat different but overlapping advisories, I did find it; it was not two blocks away, as Montague had implied, but more like six, across from the bus depot on Monroe Street. Luckily, there was a parking garage next door, so I abandoned my car in it and set out to eat.

A Mexican restaurant a little more than halfway back to the Oasis, on Polk Street, had caught my eye. It had a wonderful wooden sign, multicolored, but dominated by bright yellow, and about twenty feet long, hanging from the facade of the building; at the top was a depiction of the sun, not just a yellow ball but a swirling mass of flames in hot colors, complete with sunspots and corona as if plagiarized from the latest issue of Scientific American. And below the sun was represented a young woman in a long white dress, with swirling black hair, fierce eyes and Indian features; the eddies in her hair paralleled those of the sun. Holding up a black tray which accommodated either the moon or a piece of cratered, circular cheese, she was standing barefoot on a sun-yellow beach, with the ocean in the background, and around her were cherubs, accompanying her as if she were Botticelli's Venus. On the sand of the beach was written in shaky letters as if drawn by a human finger in the sand, Casa del Sol.

I entered the place. Mariachi music was playing and most of the tables were occupied; I saw the band at the back of the room through a fine mist of smoke. Most of the seats appeared to be taken up by fiftyish Latino businessmen sporting sharkskin suits and narrow-gauge mustaches. The hostess spoke to me in Spanish but switched to English when I mangled the phrase "una mesa por uno, por favor". I was led to a small table quite close to the band, but it stopped playing within a minute after I sat down. The audience applauded thunderously, with shouts of "Arriba!" and I joined in the applause, but did not shout.

Within a minute, a gloriously alluring waitress, practically a double for the one on the sign, took my order. I was doing well, as far as being served by attractive women was concerned, on this trip. I ordered two cans of Tecate, two soft chicken tacos, and a vegetable plate.

The service was professional, and fast (how unlike that of the Rancho Verde!), and the food was excellent, rich and spicy-hot but not overwhelmingly so. The proportions were generous, but I was hungry (how long had it been since I had eaten a decent meal, anyway?); I even ordered dessert, a fried ice cream dish (batter-covered vanilla ice cream dropped into deep fat), and it was delectable as well. Groaning and patting my belly, I paid my check and ventured out into the street just as the mariachi group started up again. It was only 1:50, and since I was closer to the Oasis than to the Barrowholt, I thought I would sit in the lobby there and read my newspaper while I waited for my meeting.

Passing through the swinging doors this time, I nodded and smiled at the doorman, but he didn't look me in the eyes and muttered something I couldn't hear. No matter, I thought, I'm not likely to see him ever again after the next few minutes. I sat on a high-backed chair across from the lobby desk, leaned back, and began to read; nothing really new; accounts of the conflict in Laos, and the possible requirement for intervention by U.S. troops if the new right-wing government couldn't maintain power.

After a few minutes, I was astonished to hear a familiar British accent just behind me, the voice saying in its familiar stammer, "I'd like my b-bill, please; I need to check out, and I also need a t-taxi right away." What the fuck was this? Is he trying to run out on me again, after I told him I'd driven a thousand miles to talk to him? I wasn't about to let this happen. The son of a bitch.

I dropped my paper on the floor, spun out of my chair, and sprinted to the desk in three paces, coming up just behind his left shoulder. "Excuse me," I said, tapping him on that shoulder, "but don't we have an appointment to talk about your research?" He started and looked back at me with bulging eyes. For a long time, he said nothing, just stared. Finally, he nodded slowly and said, "Yes, Mr. McKenzie, I'm extremely sorry, I quite forgot. Allow me a moment to check out and then I shall sit with you right here, in the lobby. Please forgive me for my lapse of memory."

I walked backward from him, keeping watch. Feeling my way to a round-backed chair in front of an impossibly low table, I chose a position between the cashier's desk and the exit. I was ready at a moment to sprint and bring him down with a flying tackle if he should choose to make a break for it; but he didn't, merely finished his business and shuffled slowly over to where I was waiting. He held his cashmere overcoat in a bundle, like a little girl's muff, with both hands. He looked like a guilty child whose mother had told him to explain what had happened to the dozen cookies she had left on the kitchen table.

As he sat down clumsily in the chair opposite me, he emitted a world-weary sigh, saying "I need a drink. Would you care for one, Mr. McKenzie?" No thank you, I replied, and the name's McKenna. "Ah, of course," he replied, "Excuse me one moment. Will you watch my greatcoat?" And he was off again, to the barroom across the hall. Well, I thought to myself, if he skips out on me now I've at least got this garment; it must be worth at least $300. But he came directly back, carrying what looked like a triple Scotch. He picked out the ice cubes with palpable distaste and flicked them into a potted plant. He then licked his long fingers, each one separately. Then, after taking a deep swallow, he set his drink on the table, lit up a French cigarette, and exhaled a long drag through his nostrils. "Now then," he finally said, "exactly what aspect of my work was it you wished to discuss?"

I explained how his Kansas City talk had inspired me, and how our early results had been confusing, and then mentioned our later ideas and some details of the recent data we had obtained. I asked what he thought of our work and how it related to his; why he thought it was that our results were so different. I expressed regret that he had never published his findings; I told him I thought the world of science needed to hear about his excellent and innovative work.

He sighed again. "Mr. McKenna," he said, "you clearly have no conception of my professional life. I serve on too many committees and boards and review panels for me to keep track of. Both Oxford and the Nation have expressed a continuing need for my services, for what I suppose are my talents. As you see, I also have international commitments. Such research as I am able to conduct is now done in my name by surrogates; I regret to tell you that I haven't peered through a microscope at my beloved scarabeids for several years. Needless to say, it is difficult to attend to one's responsibilities to write and publish; it is one of the most time-consuming obligations one has."

"Yes," I said, "but you have all those beautiful data. Surely the collection and analysis of the data that told such a compelling story was the hard part. Weren't you driven to get that information out as soon as you could?"

"Ah, Mr. McKenna," he went on, "again you misunderstand. It is regrettable that at times one's enthusiasm for creative work is overmatched by the bondage of time. Especially when dealing with postgraduates and their bewildering idiosyncracies, one tends to oversimplify the course that research takes, to extrapolate too readily from a preliminary report to the final appearance of the work in print. I have always, I am afraid, been too ready to agree to future presentations of our research, reckoning on an orderly progress of work that is unfortunately too rare in science. In the instance you refer to, I learned only a few days in advance of my presentation that my student had, I regret very much to say, fabricated some of the data. The results he'd given me in tables of data were nowhere to be found in his laboratory notes. Perhaps I was partially responsible, for I had become dismayed a few months earlier by the slow progress of the man's work and had - how do you Americans say it? - blown my stack at him."

I could hardly believe what he was admitting to me. "Are you saying," I responded angrily, "that you deliberately reported findings you knew to be false? Fabricated data? Lies?"

"Ah, Mr. McKenna," he replied, "such harsh words. And please, not so loud. You need to consider my position at that time. I had to leave for the U. S. in two days. I had committed my time to give that presentation. My expenses were being paid. I was going to meet with many distinguished biologists. The talk was only a small part of my visit. I had as yet no idea of the extent of the fraud. I had called in my student, my flim-flam man, and told him of what my suspicions were. He became very indignant, but he had no explanation for the discrepancies I pointed out. He denied any possibility of dishonesty. What was I to do? There was no absolute proof, and I saw no way to present my talk without the data he had said he'd collected. I didn't feel quite honorable, but I had no choice. After I returned to Oxford, I discovered the student had fled, taking his notebooks with him; so I have to believe now that everything had been falsified. I am sorry that I had to present --what do you Americans say? - a load of crap, but I felt at the time there was no other way out of the situation."

I was stunned. "I wrote you letters," I said, "three of them, and never got a response. I was excited by the findings you presented. All I wanted was to follow where you had led. Instead, because of your deceitfulness, I wasted more than two years of my life following a mirage. Would it have been too much for you to tell me then, at the time I wrote those letters, what you have told me now?"

"Ah, Mr. McKenna," he said, "I regret more than you can know how the whole situation developed. I felt deeply betrayed by that young man. I, too, was very excited about the way the work seemed to be moving. After the affair was over, I felt unclean, raped. I only wanted to forget everything about it. I shunted all inquiries, such as yours, aside. I thought that at some later time it would be right to make a clean breast of the affair and to answer letters such as yours, but it always seemed as if something more pressing would come up and I didn't find the time. Eventually, it all died down. In fact, you are the first person I've admitted all the facts of the situation to. Incidentally, I hope you will not find it necessary to disseminate this information. I am an old man, Mr. McKenna, please let me bask in those of my scientific achievements that have been worthwhile; I don't want to be remembered for a scandal. You are a young man; you have many productive years ahead of you. I advise you to forget this episode and get on with your life as a scientist."

He looked away from me. I saw that his eyes were filling with tears. "Mr. McKenna," he said in a breaking voice, "wherever your career may lead you in the future, don't ever let yourself become too well-known. It's a curse; it's not worth it. Your time is taken up by strangers you don't like, but you put up with it because of the favors these strangers might be able to do for you. And most of the time, the favors never materialize. You are in the position of a naive prostitute who gives herself to men who promise her great material rewards. And nothing happens except a temporary thrill, the vicarious excitement that comes from experiencing someone else's ecstasies. This is my problem, Mr. McKenna; I'm dead inside, I have only my past, and the only thing I'm good for any more is to give someone else a tingle, because I still remember a few of my old whore's tricks. It's not much to look forward to, I assure you, Mr. McKenna."

He stood up, awkwardly, leaving his drink glass behind on the table. I tried to rise, also, but he put his hand firmly on my shoulder and pressed me back down into my chair. "I must leave now," he said. "I know now a bit more of what has taken place as a result of my misdeed, the one I so casually entered into. I can only hope that more time hasn't been lost because of what I have done. I assure you, Mr. McKenna, that I have learned a painful but valuable lesson, and I hope that because of it, you have learned something, too, and won't be tempted to repeat some of the same errors that I led myself into. Goodbye, sir; and I trust that if we ever meet again, you will have been able to absolve this old man, and will have achieved far more on your own than you could ever have done by following in the footsteps, the footsteps made by the feet of clay, of others. Goodbye, now."

Finally, reluctantly, I thought, he withdrew his hand from my shoulder; it brushed my hair as he receded toward the lobby door. (A taxicab, I saw, was waiting.) His last look in my direction as it drove away was an imploring gaze, but all I could give him in response was an expressionless glare.

I sat in my chair, unmoving, for perhaps two minutes. I had jammed my hands down into my pockets and I sat stiffly, with my legs stuck straight out. Well, damn, I thought to myself. McKenna's screwed up again. And I had to drive a thousand miles all by myself through mud, rain, snow, fog, and sleet, and through myriad terrors of the road, to find out. And now I have no choice but to drive the same thousand miles back again. Well, damn. I know a bit now about how Sisyphus must have felt, early in his career as a puppet of the gods. Gods, if you be out there, I thought to myself, what have I done to deserve this kind of treatment at your hands? Don't answer that, gods, I just remembered some of the things I've done that I should feel guilty for. Well, will this be it? Have you had your fun now? A really hearty celestial guffaw at my expense? You sadistic bastards, I'll bet there's more of the same to come.

I suddenly realized how utterly tired I was. I thought, I need that drink now, Professor Montague; may I charge it to your room tab? Ah, just my luck, he's halfway to Greenland by now. Well, I can always drink what he left behind. Like hell, the guy's probably got every venereal disease that's ever been described and a few personal strains besides. Maybe I'd better wash my hair and my shoulder now before the spirochetes crawl into my brain. Shit, I'll just buy my own triple scotch and poison them from the inside.

I went into the bar, muttering to myself, and ordered not a scotch but a bourbon and soda. The barkeep was a man this time, a small, delicate-featured young fellow with dark slicked-down curls, sad eyes, and a wisp of a smile. As I sipped my drink, he busied himself polishing glasses with a terry towel. Looking at me in the mirror and correctly identifying me as a biologist, he asked me without turning around, "In for the convention?" His voice was surprisingly deep. I answered in the affirmative, but volunteered no further information. He asked me what insects I specialized in and I answered "English stink bugs." That quieted him down and I was able to return to my drink.

A patron to my right, an unshaven, lantern-jawed man of about sixty wearing faded green coveralls and a woolen cap, asked me if I had a match. I started to say that I hadn't, but then I remembered the Rancho Verde matchbook, and handed this over. He lit his cigarette from deep within his cupped hands, in the practiced gesture of one who regularly smoked outdoors in stiff winds, and handed it back to me with a concupiscent grin.

I read the cover of the book again, then opened it up to see the name written there in girlish penmanship. I realized this was the first time I'd looked at what she had written. Agnes Garcia, it said; somehow I hadn't expected a Spanish name. And below that, her phone number, and then a tiny heart and a word written in minuscule block capitals; ANYTIME. I sighed deeply, put the matchbook in my breast pocket, drained my glass, and walked out.

On the way back to the garage I was in a foul mood, kicking debris on the sidewalk and glaring at old ladies. Better than the other way around, I thought to myself. I really wondered at how foolish I had been to drive all the way here on the merest hunch. I hadn't even called to make sure that the program of the meeting was still the same. "To depend so much on faith is unbecoming for a good scientist", I said to myself aloud, drawing a perplexed stare from a small boy.

I got into the car, paid the attendant, and started the long drive back. At least, it was a beautiful day. The palm trees lining the boulevards were still green, and the sky was cloudless. It seemed that it was going to take much less time to make the return trip than it had to come into town; I noticed the landmarks I'd seen coming in receding back at a much faster apparent pace. The retirement villages that had been artificially hacked out of the desert a few years ago were beginning to show the signs of wear. Their "giant half-acre" lots were beginning to crowd in on one another, and the houses on the lots were as likely to be Cape Cod or Colonial models as something with a Spanish influence. In twenty years, I predicted to myself, they'll be indistinguishable from the suburbs of Cleveland.

I was quite a bit more relaxed, for one thing, on this return trip; and I had no deadlines that I had to make. I just had to get back to Pawnee Springs in the next few days; Jack wasn't expecting me to get back in time to meet the Wednesday class, which was tomorrow, and that was the last one of the term. My first final exam was not until next Monday morning, and I already had that done; all I had to do was show up and proctor it. Actually, despite what I'd gone through with Montague, and an apparent total waste of time, I felt rather good; it was as if some great responsibility had been taken from me, and I was free again to do whatever I wished.

    I decided to go back a slightly different way. Coming into Phoenix, I has approached directly from the east on U. S. Highway 60. To return, I elected to leave Phoenix to the northeast, taking State Highway 87. During the afternoon, I drove through the Tonto National Forest, a scenic and mountainous area with very few trees, despite its name. The winter desert struck me again with its magnificence. The colors of the mountains seemed even brighter in the winter sun than they did in summer. Driving through the town of Payson, I noticed a low stucco building labeled "Opera House;" it was a two-story structure with ornate grillwork of the kind you'd see in the French Quarter of New Orleans, gas lamps, and beautiful red doors with a leather-like texture. I wondered what operas had been put on there in the past, and what clientele sat and listened to the difficult, foreign music - were there impatient cowpokes who shot up the place if they didn't approve of the singing? And were there any operas scheduled now? I noticed elaborate posters on the facade, but I couldn't tell if they were calling attention to current attractions or were only records of historic productions.

    North of Payson, some semblance of forest did seem to develop, with stands of magnificent ponderosa pines beginning to dominate the surroundings. The road ran high along an escarpment, providing magnificent vistas of rolling mountains to the north. I stopped in the town of Winslow for dinner, eating at a restaurant with a French name, "L'Etoile des Rochers;" despite its name, the menu featured American and Chinese entrees. I ate a rather good sweet-and-sour shrimp, the sauce neither too gummy nor too sweet. That night, I slept as soundly as I had for weeks, in a soft bed with real feather pillows and a mattress that smelled of pine needles, in a motel called the Clear Creek Inn.

    The next morning, after a heavy breakfast of hard-cooked eggs and thick slabs of bacon, I continued my drive back toward home. The landscape began to break up into a hybrid melange of desert and forest. Almost bare hills, perhaps volcanic in origin, appeared in the distance; they were topped with occasional paloverde trees, with tiny green leaves shimmering in the sun. The foreground still showed occasional rocky, forested vistas of scrubby pines, aspens, and mesquite, although patches of desert were more common, with brittlebush, chollas, and prickly pear cactuses the dominant vegetation. At higher elevations, especially where a stream coursed down, was disclosed a mix of small trees such as ironwoods and cat's-claw acacias.

Near the New Mexico line I rejoined Route 66 and began to retrace my steps back home. The snow reappeared, and at around 10:30 in the morning, I climbed the same hill where I'd had my skid; the dent in the snowdrift looked exactly the same as it had when I left it. The sense of deja vu was so strong that as I went over the hilltop, I half-expected to see my friends in their black pickup, pulled over by the side of the road waiting for me; but of course they were nowhere to be seen.

How different things look in different lights, and how much experience can change one's perspective of life. At the time I passed by here last, I was filled with the dread of not making it to Phoenix in time to see my professor. Now I had seen him, and what I had hoped would be a life-changing visit had turned out to be worth nothing. I'd have been better off to stay at home and cultivate my own garden, to plunge ahead with my own little research project heedless of what its results might have done for my reputation among the Montagues of the world; just do what comes to hand, and if nothing much comes of it don't worry about it, I should have said to myself. That was what I was thinking now. I was driving through this beautiful country in the daylight, seeing in full-hued color what I'd missed in the middle of the night before, and revelling in it. How much better it is to travel this way, without anxiety, merely letting the glory of the world soak into your being. I resolved to change my life.

I crossed the continental divide again, waving in the direction the lion had gone (just in case he was watching), and stopped in Grants for lunch. I ate at a place called the Ice Cave Grill, a busy mom-and-pop luncheonette; a pleasant enough place, with many small tables crowded close together; fresh white cloths topped each table. Most of the customers were apparently ranchers and miners. Through the large front window I saw, across the street, a quite beautiful old stone mission church, a plain white plaster facade with square windows cut through the thick walls. Heavy roofbeams stuck out of the walls into the street at two levels. On the roof was a bell cupola topped by a plain wooden cross. In front of the church, though, was a jarring modern note, a Pepsi-Cola machine.

Several soda drinkers, Hispanic boys and girls in their teens, were leaning on the machine, laughing and joking. As I emerged from the restaurant, one of the boys gave me a curious look and raised his hands to the sides of his head, forefingers extended like horns. All his companions snickered. I didn't have the least notion what he was trying to convey about me, but I shrugged and went on my way.

That afternoon, I continued to retrace my path, seeing now so clearly in the sunshine what had been hidden from my straining eyes such a short time ago. No longer was I anxious and sluggish; I felt as if I had passed through a painful and mysterious rite of passage and had become, in some real sense, a man. The car sped along as if it were suspended in air, and the rush of the wind was like the sighing of goddesses in my ears. The beauty of the landscape thrilled me; rock towers writhing out of the sand like massive heads piercing the surface of the soil; herds of goats, cattle, and sheep, tended by immemorial Indians riding bareback on flaming Palominos; and great lava flows, dark and congealed like the dried blood of murdered deities. I relinquished the dash-and-crash attitude of my earlier trip along these same roads, and took plenty of time to stop, stretch, and walk around the landscape. In the late afternoon, I navigated down from the mountains into the tree-filled bottomlands of the Rio Grande, through Albuquerque, its streets now teeming with Christmas shoppers, and continued on to Santa Fe. Coming into the old town from the south on U. S. 85, I crossed a narrow bridge over the Santa Fe River and found a place to stay; a small hotel, the Mountainair, on Otero Street, just behind the hospital.

By earlier standards, those of two days ago, I had covered hardly any distance on today's drive; only a little over four hundred miles. But I felt profoundly exhausted, as if I had walked for many miles over rough ground.

It's finally catching up with me, I thought. I lay on my springy bed, fully clothed except for my boots.

Before I sleep, I thought, maybe there's something I should do. I reached into my shirt pocket and pulled out the green matchbook again. It was showing signs of wear, the crisp right-angled corners weathering down into arcs, and the shiny green cover beginning to lose its sparkle and become limp. But inside, Agnes's name and phone number were still clear, their acutely transcribed characters still dispatching a distinct message to my brain. "Anytime," the message said, and I had to decide whether to act.

What did she want from me, really, and could I realistically give it to her? I knew so little about her. Should I try to find out, to get to know her better? Would she really want to see me again, to get in my car and drive off with me? I'm only eighty miles away; I could be with her in less than two hours. Should I really offer to help her, take her away from the madhouse in which she was trapped? And would it be any better for her in Pawnee Springs, or anywhere else she would go? Was she really the kind of person I could influence to live a better life? Was I being presumptuous to think I knew what such a life should be for her? Or was I just being seduced by the thought of her hard young body, pressed against mine so invitingly, in the last moment we spent together that long-ago night, two days ago now, or was it three?

Oh, what the fuck, I thought to myself, and before I could think better of it I dialed the number.

"Hello? Rancho Verde?" She pronounced it to rhyme with birdy. My God, it was her. She answered on the first ring.

"Agnes? This is Pyke McKenna. I met you Monday night. I'm the guy your boss threw out because I didn't like the way he cooked my steak, remember?"

"Oh, yeah, I do remember now." She was laughing, covering the mouthpiece with her hand to muffle the sound.

"Listen, how are things with you? Have things quieted down any?"

"Yeah, I guess so."

"How's the cowboy, the one who got hurt? I hope he's OK."

"Yeah, Smitty, he was in again last night arreddy. He's just the same as ever, in fact, he's here again right now, raisin' hell. Y'wanna talk to him?"

"God, no, Agnes. Listen, I just wanted to know how you are too. Remember, what you said to me in the parking lot. Just before I drove away."

"Uh -- I'm not sure I remember what you mean -- "

"You remember, about wanting to get away. To go somewhere, anywhere, away from that place."

"Oh, yeah, I remember now. Say, listen, I might have sorta changed my mind about that. Uh, I can't really talk right now, but I met this guy, see. He's about my age. Uh, I sorta want to hang around for a while, y'know, see how things work out. I'm sorry, y'understand? Hey, great talkin' to y'again, but I gotta get back t'work. Listen, stop in anytime, OK? 'Bye now."

And the receiver buzzed in my ear. Man, I felt ridiculous. But did I do the right thing? I think so. Under different circumstances, I thought, I'd do it again. If I get the chance, I will do it for someone else. Male, female, good-looking, unbecoming, I promise. Life is too short to live in a condition which is not free; this is what I believe. Yes, I will try to be of service.

I threw the matchbox into the wastebasket, took off my clothes, and went to sleep. I dreamed of impossible birds, shining silver finches with ribbons in their scarlet beaks, pulling me in a golden cart down Kearney Street as my friends all stood alongside cheering. And Agnes was there among them, showering me with glittering confetti and blowing me kisses, as she stood wearing a tight strapless kelly-green silken gown under a spotlight in front of Old Main; somehow, she had become the President of Cimarron State, and she was there to greet me on my return from some voyage of triumph.

I woke early Thursday, and drove through the remaining 350 miles of sugar beets, sagebrush, and grama grass, back to Pawnee Springs. Although I must have driven past the Rancho Verde, in truth I did not notice it. I was back by five, and watched the sun turning the hills to russet as I entered town; and that evening, to the sound of carolers from the Lutheran church singing outside my window, I burrowed into my blankets, yawned once, and slept like a babe in arms.

Yolanda

(The saga of Yolanda Scott represents to me an example of how satisfying hard detective work can be when it works out. In an folder containing some of Pyke's early class notes, I found a folded sheet of paper with the word Yolanda written over and over again in different colored inks and styles of writing; also on the page was a large red heart, pierced by a black arrow, with drops of blood falling from it. I asked everyone who knew Pyke in the early days whether they had ever heard of anyone by that name, but no one had. Later, in one of Pyke's boxes marked "Letters," I found an undated one-page note in large, loopy handwriting; "Pyke: Meet me at the stage door after the recital. I have something for you. Love, Yo."

I wondered whether this Yo, who was presumably Yolanda, might have had something to do with the music or English departments, so I called the heads of those units. Professor Irons of the English department responded that of course he remembered "the famous Yolanda Scott," said that she had been an instructor in English as well as in dance here in the 50s, but that she had left to pursue a career in ballet in New York. He told me that she had published several poems in "little magazines" with a national reputation, and also had contributed poetry and short fiction to our own campus literary magazine, Foothills. I looked in the back issues of this journal in the college library, and did find several items published during the period 1953-57; but in addition, a short, atmospheric belles lettres piece, entitled Fort Tryon Park: Sunrise, appeared in 1968. The tag line of this piece identified her as a "founding member of the Dance Theatre of Harlem."

Next I tried the Manhattan and boroughs phone books, but the only Y. Scott listed, in Queens, turned out to be a man named Yancey, who was unhappy about being interrupted and told me so using colorful language. After that, I looked in the Herald Tribune and New York Times annual indexes, and found a story on the Harlem dance company in the issue of the Times for Sunday, November 16, 1969, in which she was identified as the associate director of the company and the principal danseuse in a work entitled Suprematist Composition: White on White. I tried several times to call the DTH to speak to her, if she was still there, but I could never get past the first person who answered the phone. She told me that it was "Theater policy" not to relay telephone messages to members of the company. I suppose she thought I was just another stage door Johnny. My letters were returned, stamped "Not at this address."

So I seemed to be at an impasse when, a month or two later, I noticed that the Dance Theatre was going to be in Denver on tour. I never have been particularly interested in ballet, but I was determined to find this woman somehow. I called the number given in the advertisement for ordering tickets by phone; I didn't order any tickets, but explained what I was up to to the young man at the other end. He was very sympathetic, and told me if he could find anything out from the promotional information they had, he would send it to me. I was surprised to find, three days later, a fat envelope from him in my campus mail box, full of all sorts of glossy brochures about the DTH, and with a nicely typed letter summarizing some of the information and suggesting some people it might be useful to contact. So thank you, Daniel Cassidy, for your help; and thanks to you, Marissa Stanley, Assistant Artistic Director of the Dance Theatre of Harlem, for telling me that Yolanda Scott had left the company to start her own troupe in San Francisco; and finally, heartfelt thanks to Miss Scott herself for taking time from her busy entrepreneurial schedule to write and to telephone me, giving me the following information.)

DEGREES OF FREEDOM

He wrote me a letter, saying that he had seen my dancing and admired my artistry very much. This would have been in 1953, the first year I came to Cimarron; my mother, who lives in Omaha, had seen an advertisement for the position I eventually took. They wanted an instructor in dance and in gymnastics, and although I had no training at all in athletics, I thought I could handle the job anyway. I was a brand-new MFA from Columbia, 24 years old and ready to take on the world. And then when I got there, they were very flexible about what I could do, so I wound up teaching dance and assisting in the English department. They found someone else for the gymnastics duties, I surmise.

One of the first things I wanted to do was to choreograph something simple but beautiful for myself and my students. I was surprised to find so many young girls with native grace and a willingness to work hard and to accept direction from someone like me, who was unlike anyone they'd ever met before. (There were no blacks at all in the rural counties most of them were from, and the few black residents in Pawnee Springs weren't, I'm afraid, exactly the type to hang around the campus.) At any rate, I made a setting of Vaughan Williams's Fantasia on a Theme of Thomas Tallis for eight dancers, and we performed that, all dressed in white tulle, and also some folk dances from Africa and eastern Europe, and I did a solo number from Giselle. A real mixed bag of dancing; not exactly a model of formalism in concert programming. However, I thought it came out really well, and I was very proud of my girls and I told them so.

Although I don't usually notice the audience when I perform, I know this one was quite small; not that I expected very much interest at the beginning of my work there. So you can imagine my surprise, about a week later, to get a nice hand-written letter, on College letterhead, from a biology professor. He had been in the audience, he said, in the ninth row, and had been very moved by the depth of my artistic convictions. He said he was not an expert in ballet, but that my presentation had made him eager to learn much more. He hoped that he was not being too forward to ask to meet me and to seek my recommendations for material he might read on the subject. He gave me his campus address and telephone number if I would be so kind to call or write him, or he would call me in a few days.

Well, I had to laugh at his letter; it seemed so earnest and naive. I imagined him at the time to be about 65, someone stuck down in Pawnee Springs all his life, never having given the outside world a thought, and now seeing it for the first time and hoping it was not too late to take some of it in. But I was curious to speak to the gentleman, so I called him that day. He answered on the first ring. I fantasized that he'd been sitting there all day waiting for me to call. I introduced myself and he became very excited. I could tell from his voice that he was much younger than 65. I thanked him for his refreshing letter (that was the word I used, I remember), and he thanked me for a thrilling evening. The man always did have a way with flattering words. He asked me when and where we could meet and talk; I said, "How about right away, at the Union? I'll buy you a cup of coffee." He eagerly agreed to that, and said, "I expect I'll recognize you even without your leotards." I asked, "And how will I know you?" He replied, "I'll be the tallest and most eager-looking white guy there, with the biggest smile."

I walked over to the Union. I congratulated myself on my looks; I was bound to make a good impression on this man from that standpoint alone; and who knew, maybe we would be able to be friends. Although my work was going well, according to my colleagues, I sometimes felt very lonely and would just like to go off with real friends and have fun, and not worry about what kind of professional impression I was leaving someone with, or what I had to finish up tomorrow.

My hair was pulled back tightly along the sides of my head and gathered in a bun at the back. I was wearing a short black dress, about knee length (that was very short by the standards of the day), fairly high heels, and a long coral necklace that swung down to my waist. Again, things like that were practically unheard-of at the time.

I walked down the steps to the coffee shop, and saw him immediately. He wasn't at all like I had anticipated; he was tall, long-necked and lanky, was wearing a long-sleeved pinstriped shirt with the top button undone and the sleeves rolled up exactly twice, to a point just below the elbow; a navy blue knit tie, no jacket, and his hair cut quite short. His arms were long, and his big bony hands were stuck into his pockets; he was indeed smiling, what my mamma would have called a shit-eatin' grin, and he was leaning up against the wall with his legs crossed at the ankles. He said hello, and extended his hand for me to shake (also very unusual behavior for a man meeting a woman at that time), and asked me to come in and sit down.

We both smiled at each other for a long time; neither of us could think of anything to say, apparently. I was trying not to laugh, because I thought we made an odd-looking couple; a black girl from the big city, dressed to kill, and an ungainly rural Midwestern farm boy grown up, pretending to be a responsible adult. Finally he said, "You look even taller now than you did on the stage, Miss Scott ... may I call you Yolanda?" I replied, "You may call me by my first name, but it is pronounced Yo-lahn-dah, with soft A's, if you please." He apologized, with a laugh, and said, "You have a beautiful name; it sounds like a warm breeze blowing over a tropical island. Mine, on the other hand, sounds like a chunk of meat. At least it's impossible to mispronounce my name, although almost no one ever spells it right. It's Pyke with a Y. My father picked it out; I have no idea why he chose such an unconventional name. It isn't a family name, or a historic name, or a place name, and I have never seen it anywhere else.

"But enough of such taxonomic chit-chat. I am a biologist here at Cimarron State, as I mentioned in my letter. I am a teacher and a scientist, although I doubt if a particle physicist would give me the benefit of that latter categorization. Perhaps I am actually more nearly a historian, a natural historian. I look at nature as it is now and I see the past, not just the human past, but life's past, all the way back to the first warm little ponds where life first originated.

"I love to think about science and I love to practice science, but science is not enough for me. I also need the exciting confusion and the electric thrills that art can offer, and I seek these out to give my soul a jump-start on days when my scientific battery is weak. There are many times when it is hard to find the boost I need. I might listen to the opera, or read French Symbolist poetry, but that may not be right. At least the evening I went to your performance, I was ready for just the kind of galvanic uplift you provided. Afterwards, I was almost numb. I went home and lay on my bed and relived the things I'd seen and heard. I was fascinated with the way you had performed, so gracefully and expressively; it was as if you could make your body speak, in a language that had no words, but by your gestures you could convey messages between your emotions and ours, directly, simply, unequivocally. I have certainly seen dancing before, but it never hit home to me in that way."

Well, he finally came to the end of that long speech. Nobody ever gave me that kind of a spiel before. I was wondering if he'd memorized it or if it just came out that way. Certainly he never referred to any notes; he was looking at me the whole time. I'm used to being stared at, because I know what makes me look good and I use it, but his gaze was different. Most men keep flipping their eyes up and down from your face to your body, but his eyes locked into mine and wouldn't let go. I didn't feel as if he was challenging me with this stare; he was perfectly relaxed.

Anyway, I finally got to give him my own speech. It was a variant of one I'd used in other contexts, but somehow his virtuoso performance made me want to outdo myself. I thanked him for his kind words, and told him that I was still learning my trade, but that my goal was just what he had grasped. (As I spoke to him, he inclined his head slightly to the left, as if he were a cocker spaniel desperately trying to understand what its owner was saying.)

"I would like to dance so clearly," I said, "that there would be no room for doubt in the audience's mind as to what I intended. I would like to dance a charging rhinoceros, so realistically that everyone in the hall would run for the exits in terror."

His eyes opened wide at that, and I think he actually whispered "Wow." I went on, saying, "But I think to portray concrete objects is beyond my art. What I want to portray is emotion, human emotion stripped bare. So maybe I can't convince the audience that I actually am the rhinoceros, or a roaring lioness, but maybe just for a flickering instant I can speak to them by my movements so that they feel the same wonder and fear that the actual lion or rhinoceros would call up in them. That, to me, would be success."

He said, "You have really opened my eyes. I suppose I knew there was real passion in art, but until now I haven't been able to experience it directly. On the printed page everything is vicarious; you feel Emma Bovary's desire, but you don't see it. In painting and sculpture, everything is also distanced; there is no motion. The defiant scream of Goya's condemned revolutionaries is eternal, so it loses some of its force after a time. And the passion of music is abstract, more so than words.

"But the passion of dance, as you have explained it to me, is immediate, concrete, and personal. It's like the passion of biology, where the flame of life is always all around; just to go into a forest or to look at a drop of swamp water is to feel the thrill of the struggle; the effort to keep breathing, or break through the implacable soil, or to wriggle out of a rotifer's grasp."

I did say it, out loud. "Wow," I said, "are all biologists like you? I never heard anybody talk like that about science. I always thought scientists were old, cold, analytical, and devoid of all passion for anything other than their slide rules."

"Unfortunately," he said, "there are too many of us who have the characteristics you describe. Devoted to the collection of facts, they lose sight of reality. Data, for them, has a grim fascination; they love a neat-looking graph with nice tight points. Their goal is to make observations that agree with those of previous workers; they become quite nervous if they actually have to think of something new."

"Miss Scott," he said then, raising his eyebrows after looking at his watch, "I really need to go; I have a class next hour. But I have enjoyed this conversation more than you can know. I would like to invite you to continue our discussion when we both have more time. Would you like to come to my office, say sometime late tomorrow afternoon? You can see how I live, professionally speaking, and we can talk together, and then maybe go out for a drink." I agreed to that, and we took our leave; he shook my hand again, holding it for a few more seconds than I think he would have ordinarily done, and left the cafeteria, looking back at me over his shoulder, smiling, as he did, until he almost ran over a small coed.

Well, I thought as he went out the door, I surely have never come across anyone like this man. Such a way he has of formulating his conversational responses. It must be spontaneous because he couldn't have known what we were going to say to each other. And he's cute, too. What if he is white (sorry, mamma), I don't care about that, some of my best friends are ofays and I don't care if my sister does marry one. Besides, I don't even have a sister, and my only brother Gilman is living with a white chick in the Village, and mamma doesn't like it but she's still speaking to my brother. In fact, she sends him money every month, more than she ever did for me, not that I ever asked her, or could ask. So, Professor McKenna, watch out; I'm ready to get to know you damn well, if you'll have me, and if you don't want me maybe I'll make you want me. Oo-wee, am I ready for this!

I went over to his office the next day around four. It was in a musty old building that smelled like something had died in it two years ago and had never been found. The elevator wasn't working so I had to walk all the way up to the fourth floor.

I found his office right away. When I peered in he was in a swivel chair and had his back turned to the door, and his feet up on a low file cabinet, and was talking on the phone in a loud voice about some matter involving, I think he was saying, sampling. He was wearing a blue cotton work shirt, tan chino pants, and heavy boots. I sneaked in and sat in a wood straight-back chair just behind him, trying to be as quiet as I could. The conversation continued for some time. The other person was doing most of the talking. Once in a while he would say, "Uh-huh," or break out in a great laugh.

Finally, he spun himself around and saw me there; I was smiling broadly, and I gave him a tiny wave with my fingertips. He opened his mouth wide and whispered "hello" to me in a stage whisper, and then said to his phone partner, "I'll call you back later; I'm late for a meeting," and hung up. He stood up, looked down at me, took my hand and kissed it, and said, "How wonderful to see you. I'm glad you found the place. This is where I spend as little time as possible; I hate being hemmed in, and I despise the telephone. I've been out-of-doors most of this morning, out in the mud and dirt, collecting insect larvae; that's why I'm dressed this way. These are my work clothes, like your leotards and slippers. Will you join me in a cup of espresso?"

I said that I'd be delighted, and expressed surprise that his office was so small and dismal; it had only a tiny window. He replied that surely I understood about departmental politics; he had been there only a short while, and no one owed him very many favors yet.

As he bustled about with the espresso things, I looked around his office. In some ways, it looked like I'd have imagined a scientist's lair would look. He had his desk, covered with papers in disarray, some of them in piles just about to fall over, held down with big bones or skulls that I guess he was using as paperweights. On a low table in the corner was a microscope; a little light bulb was shining underneath it, and a little wooden box of glass slides stood beside it. He had a great many books, many of them big, old, and leather-bound.

But his walls were decorated with beautiful works of art - no charts of the internal organs or periodic tables of the elements for him; it looked like most of it was primitive or folk art from the Americas.

The largest object he had was a sort of painting made of lengths of yarn glued down on a wooden panel. It represented a serpent, with its tail in its mouth, coiled around a small cactus. There was a sun and some purple mountains in the background. I stood up to look at it more closely. He called to me from across the room, "That's a Huichol yarn painting from western Mexico. The Indians take lengths of yarn and press them down into molten beeswax that's coated onto plywood, and arrange them into a traditional design. I love that one very much; I bought it in a small village south of Tucson last year. It's a representation of one of their principal deities, a snake god who symbolizes the eternal return of time. The cactus is a sacred peyote. The Indians think of it as a god, because when it's eaten they see visions of heaven. Have you ever heard of it before?" "No", I said. "The painting is very beautiful." "Yes," he went on, "and the painting comes directly from their religious tradition. Art for them is not something pretty, something to decorate a wall, the way heathens like me have used it; it's a direct line of communication with the deities that govern all aspects of their lives. To them, art is a sort of sacred medium of exchange, a gift to the gods that will help to bring them what they want. And peyote is a key piece of their religious beliefs; when they eat it, it shows them the true reality at the heart of things. So I am told, at least, I've never had any, although I might try it if some was offered to me."

He set the espresso pot on a little hot plate with a big black knob in the center of the front panel, turned on the heat, and sat back down in his big chair, leaning back with his arms behind his head. Sweat stained the underarms of his blue shirt.

"So this is how I live," he declared. "Is this anything like your professional life -- do you have an office and a lot of moldy books?" I told him that I had an office, also small and windowless; right now it was in the gymnasium, but I was hoping that space would become available in the English department. I kept my books at home, where I also prepared such formal classroom material as I had to be responsible for. Like him, I spent little time in my office; it was near to large rooms where I could exercise my body and work on dance routines for my classes. I mainly needed it for the telephone; luckily, I shared it with another instructor who was there much more often than I was and didn't mind taking my messages.

"It's lucky I decided to write you rather than call," he said. "Actually, I'm a rather shy person and it took me some time even to get up the courage to approach you that way! But I'm glad that I did." "Yes," I responded, "you seem to be a quite interesting person, nothing at all like I imagined scientists to be."

"Well, we are all kinds," he said. "Just like artists, I imagine, or anyone else. Some of us are totally bourgeois, interested in our investments and our lawn furnishings. Others are petty, self-centered, and vicious. Still others have great personal charm and no talent whatever. Sound familiar?"

"Yes, but there must be something different about you all. What is it that makes you go into this profession?"

"Some do it because it beats working at manual labor. Others lust for fame; they want to be the next Pasteur, or Einstein, and to be an object of adulation. I went into it because I had to; I couldn't imagine a life that wasn't filled with the joy of studying living things. To me, that keeps me going - much as, I expect, you would hate a life that had no beauty in it, where you had to spend all your time scrabbling for food."

He gazed at me with a dreamy smile. "I love things that are wild," he said, "things untainted by commerce or improvement. My greatest joy, I think, is to climb high cliffs where no one has been for years, on a clear warm day, and just to lie up there quietly by myself and look off into the empty skies. Then, I believe, one can feel a little bit of what it is like to fit into the system of nature, and not worry so much about being a mortal animal. Have you ever known such feelings?"

I had to laugh. "No, I'm afraid I'm a girl from the big city. It really makes me a little nervous when I'm away from a crowd of people!" He shook his head, disbelieving. "No, really," I went on, "out on the street where I'm from, if you're by yourself you're vulnerable. It's better to stay in the herd. Aren't there some animals like that?"

"I think there probably are. It's useless to try to imagine how animals envision themselves, but I'd guess that reindeer, maybe, animals that migrate in big herds, are always aware of a multitude of companions. They probably associate the smells and sounds of the herd with their own well-being, and might become panicky if they were separated out." He paused for a moment and scratched his cheek. "I'm not sure whether humans or their ancestors were ever like that. I'd guess that our behavior is a little more complicated - that we've always done some things in isolation, and others in social groups. Thank you for making me think about that, by the way. It's good to talk with someone who stretches your imagination!" He took my hand and shook it heartily, and smiled into my eyes. "I'd like to take you to the wilds sometime, because I'm sure you'd love the experience. And I'd also like to go to a big city with you, someplace you know well and could show me around in. I'd like for us to explore new possibilities together."

He said it so seriously, as if he was making a proposal of marriage. "It sounds interesting to me," I said. "Take me to one of your wilderness redoubts, and if we get a chance I'll show you around New York. That's my favorite wild place."

That's how we got started. We tentatively agreed to take a trip over to Muspell County, where there were some interesting cliffs, he said. That Saturday, shortly after dawn on that late October morning, he came over to my apartment building; I was waiting for him in the hallway. He pulled up in a little red pickup truck that must have belonged to the college, although the seal on the door was battered almost to the point of unrecognition. He was wearing a crushed leather Australian bush hat, tan chambray shirt, and cloth work gloves. I probably wasn't properly dressed in my flat penny loafers, black wool stirrup pants, and scarf; but he didn't say anything.

The sky was an enamelled blue, with only a few cool billowy clouds, as we aimed the truck southeast toward Muspell County. I really hadn't imagined the variety of landscapes we had to choose from in our area; like most city dwellers, my concept of the countryside was a pastiche drawn from childhood books -- picturesque, gingerbready farmhouses, scarlet barns, windmills, and smiling animals happily serving their master, Farmer Brown, who with his white-haired, rosy-cheeked wife presides over the whole warm and happy band. But the reality of the area south of Pawnee Springs was much larger than this. Out of the sweep of the measureless prairie morning rose long-shadowed moonscapes of rock, formations that resembled castles of giants surrounded by their armies, all frozen in position as if in wait for a time when, by moonlight, they could descend on the unsuspecting townsfolk up the road. Occasionally, we would see a lonely farmhouse in the shade of a solitary guardian tree, an ancient cottonwood. Often, a few cattle would be placidly lying near such a tree, and once we detected a living human soul; a huge, black-bearded giant of a man, seated on a rocker in the dancing fire of the morning sunlight, holding a long rifle across his lap.

After almost an hour's drive we reached the cliff Pyke wanted us to climb. "I call this 'Grandfather' because it's so much older and craggier than anything else around here." It was roughly the shape and color of a round loaf of bread, and it lay a few hundred yards off the road. Pyke rolled the truck onto the shoulder of the road, and we got out and set off toward it. He was carrying a woven reed basket, covered with a cloth, that I assumed contained our lunch.

We climbed a low hill for a better look at Grandfather. It was impressive in the silence; the only sound we heard, except for the wind, was an occasional chirping call as we flushed a meadowlark. As we walked, I felt tiny stinging sensations, that I noticed were caused by seeds of grasses, shaped like tiny lances, that caught in my trouser leg.

After climbing a few stepped ridges, we came right up against a sheer cliff, a slab of stone that ascended up for two hundred feet. "Now what?," I asked, nervously. "There's sort of a trail," he said, taking me by the hand and leading me around the left side of the crag, where I saw a foot-wide ledge that headed up at about a 30o angle. "Man," I said, "you expect me to follow this all the way to the top?" He said, "Don't worry, it gets better. Just hang onto me and watch where you put your feet."

I don't know how we ever got up that thing. He was carrying the basket the whole time, and dragging me along behind; he bounced up the trail like he was a goat. Hugging Grandfather's ridged stone wall with my right arm, I clutched Pyke's hand for dear life with my left. My shins and thighs ached from the unrelieved climbing. And I thought I was in shape! I tried like hell not to look down, but once in a while I did. He'd lied to me; it never got better.

I thought every step was going to be my last; but somehow, we made it. Once we were actually on top, it wasn't bad at all. In fact, he was right, it was beautiful.

Out of the basket, at the top, he pulled a coarse green blanket and spread it out near the edge of a sheer drop; then he lay on his stomach, stretched out, put his chin on his arms, sighed, and stared off into the distance. "Come on," he said, "this is great." I sat on the blanket, too, but not too close to the edge, because it made me nervous. I looked at the view, but I also looked at him; his thighs and buttocks, wrapped tightly in his jeans, looked strong, tough, and sexy. I ached to touch them and have him touch me.

We must have been up there for three or four hours; at times, I thought he was sleeping, but instead, he was intently staring, taking the whole landscape in at once. Periodically, he would say to me, quietly, something like "Red-tailed hawk," and I would strain to pick out the bird from the surroundings. Sometimes I could, but more often I wasn't able to find what he was pointing out to me.

Well into afternoon, I asked him if he was getting hungry. "Oh, I'm sorry," he said, "I completely forgot. I brought some sandwiches." He extracted from the basket a battered knapsack containing some bologna sandwiches on white bread; somehow, up there, they tasted good.

Later, a few clouds came up, and with them a rather cold wind from the northwest. "I suppose we'd better head back," he said. "I hope you enjoyed yourself. Not very exciting, I suppose."

"Oh, it's very beautiful here. Very peaceful. I think I see what you mean about seeing how we fit into the world. Maybe I should come out and dance here in the wilderness sometime; I think it might be a great experience."

"I'd like that, and I'd like to be with you when you do it, if you can tolerate a spectator."

He threw himself back on the blanket and gazed straight up into the sky, and then stretched out both arms and both legs full length, until they pointed to each corner. It reminded me of Leonardo's Vitruvian man, measuring out his circle in the exactitude of his fingers and toes. "God, I love this place," he said. "You may not believe this, but I've spent all night up here. Actually, just after sunset's my favorite time; you never know what's going to happen to the sky. It depends so much on the exact atmospheric conditions. Sometimes, especially when there's a full moon, the sky turns a deep, deep indigo that's just a hair's-breadth away from black, and the aspect of silvery wisps of cloud seen against this velvet backdrop is stupendous, a miracle of beauty.

"Later, in the middle of the night, I hear the tiny scuffling of small animals, mice, probably, going about their business in what seems to me to be total darkness. Yet, to them, the night is full of tiny sounds and scents that must give them a richness of sensation that's beyond anything we can know. But I'm pretty sure they have no conception of their surroundings; they must live their whole lives up here on the top of the mesa, oblivious of these great twenty-mile vistas in every direction. If one of them walks walk up to the edge of the cliff and falls down, the others can't know what happened; it must be just the way it seems to us when someone we know dies in a terrible accident at a tragically young age."

He shrugged, then, sat up, rolled up the blanket and stuffed it roughly into his basket. "Well, we'd better head down. Don't try to go too fast."

Descent was more harrowing than going up. For one thing, you couldn't help looking down. Also, my feet kept slipping on the loose stones, and if Pyke hadn't been in front of me, I think I might have fallen. As it was, my feet and, again, my shins ached annoyingly when we reached the bottom.

In the truck, I invited Pyke to come over for dinner. He acted more than a little surprised, wanted to go back for a shower and change of clothes first; but I assured him that wasn't necessary. So, grudgingly, it seemed, he agreed.

We walked up three flights of stairs to my apartment, and I opened the door and ushered him in. Man, was he ever nervous! He looked all around, inspected everything hanging on the wall, every book on the shelves, as if he worried that he might have to pass an important examination on the contents of the room. Finally, he sat himself down in my big leather chair, sitting gingerly, as if he expected to sit on a pin, or maybe as if arthritis was bothering him. He leaned back stiffly with his legs thrust straight out and his hands clasped behind his neck. I pulled up a corduroy pillow and sat in front of him on the floor, facing him, with my legs pulled underneath me.

He kept wiping his brow with his big plaid handkerchief. I didn't ask him if he was too warm, because I thought I knew what was on his mind. He was trying hard not to look at me, but he kept glancing at my legs and breasts. I wanted him, too, but I knew I had to go easy. The man was skittish, like a wild colt. I wasn't sure whether I should offer him a drink or a joint (probably not, I told myself). I wound up offering him a Coke, which he accepted eagerly.

When I left for the kitchen to make something for us to eat, he insisted on following me. Oh, well, as long as he's in here with me, I thought, I'll give him something to do. Taking him by the arm, I adopted the tone of a head chef. "Chop these mushrooms and onions, my boy," I ordered. "We're going to make something curried." He had no idea what I meant, but I guided him step-by-step through the simple dish. He'd never even made plain boiled rice before. And then, he made a green salad; at least he knew that much. I gave him a kiss on the cheek as a reward.

At the end of dinner, we returned to our former positions, he in the chair and I on the floor. He did, however, seem to be a little bit more relaxed, so I decided to make a move. I leaned forward, set my chin on his knee, and put one hand on the outside of each of his thighs. "I think this has been an important day for me," I said. "I did some things that were new for me, and had my eyes opened with someone I hope can be a good friend."

"I hope so, too; I've never been so excited about a friendship before. You're so cultivated, and friendly, and attractive; I've never met anyone at all like you before."

"I feel the same about you. I think we can be very close. I feel good about today and tonight, very comfortable and relaxed with you, as if we've known each other a long time."

He didn't say anything for a long time, but then looked into my eyes and shot out his hand awkwardly to touch my neck. "I want to be close to you, Yolanda. I don't know what lies in store for us, but I want to tell you now, if you promise you won't be angry at me -- I'd be honored to be your lover." When he said that, I lunged out of my sitting position, swung my legs up like a Russian dancer, and sat on his lap, straddling him, squeezing his legs with mine. He was surprised, to put it mildly, and grabbed me by the waist to keep us from falling over backwards. I brought my face up next to his and pushed our noses together; then, I leaned back slightly and said, "You silly, silly man. It's not a question of anyone's honor; it's pure biology. You, of all people, ought to know that." And I slowly brought my lips up to his, and we created a soft, slow, writhing kiss that set off bells in my head and made his breath come in ragged gasps. His hands slowly drifted up to my breasts, gliding up as if they were floating in water, and as we kissed he simultaneously touched both my nipples with his thumbs. Electric thrills raced down my belly, and I wriggled deeper into his arms.

"Wow," I said, "are all biologists like you? If so, I'd sure like to meet a few more." He laughed and kissed me again, a kiss I felt surging down all the way to my toes, then drew back and said, "You silly girl; you of all people should know. Biology has nothing to do with it. This is pure art. I'm an individualistic craftsman, with my own creative style."

He kissed me again, longer and harder this time, with his tongue plunging deep into my mouth like a stubby, hysterical fish; and when I caught my breath, I said hoarsely, "I'd like to show you my bed," and he didn't reply, just started kissing me again and then stood up from the chair, lifting me into the air, holding me around the thighs so that my chin rested on top of his head. I held onto his ears for dear life.

I didn't have to tell him where the bedroom was; I suppose he'd seen it out of the corner of his eye when he was reconnoitering earlier. We fell onto the mattress, with him on top of me. I pressed his head into my breasts and twined my legs around his, as he writhed and twisted in a swimming motion, like a larger fish, maybe a shark, struggling to bring our mouths together again. Two thuds on the floor told me he'd removed his shoes, and then he was kneeling over me, looking down into my face.

"I'd like to loosen your clothing, now, Miss, if you don't object."

"Oh, please, Professor, I've been hoping you'd have time to examine me today."

When he unhooked my bra, exposing my breasts, he let out a whistling moan and his face looked as if he was in agony; he drew his head close to me, and as he kissed each nipple, very delicately, I saw stars behind my closed eyelids.

Then it was my turn. I pulled his shirttail out of his trousers, and started unbuttoning, revealing his beautiful thick pale shoulders and the carpet of dark ringlets on his chest. It was almost too much for me to endure, and I reached out and wrestled him down so that I was on top of him and grabbed him by the head and rubbed my chest all over his. Then I sat up, and we each, trembling with expectation, unzipped our own pants and pulled them down. For a moment, we looked at one another's bodies, touching each other delicately on the arms and shoulders; then, helpless to hold back any longer, squirming, moaning, and biting my lower lip, I settled my pussy slowly, lingeringly, down on his hammer handle of a dick. And then, like soft gentle animals, his arms moved, practically unbidden, along my thighs to their final resting place on my hipbones. His hands clasped me indulgently, and I felt my body lifted and lowered, languidly, as if I was floating in heavy waves. I looked down at his face as if from a great height; his tight-shut eyes inside their lids rolled up and down, mad and mindless as bound birds. A few minutes later, shuddering and bouncing, we came with a deep groan pouring up as from our very bones, almost simultaneously; and we melted together into a heap, sated and exhilarated with one another.

"Oh, baby, I don't know about you," he said, "but I've never felt anything like that before; never."

"Hey, boy, you not bad yousef, fo' a beginner."

"I love the way we look together. Your skin is so rich and russet-brown. See how my hands glow against your body."

"Thank my mamma for that. My daddy was half-white."

"Have you ever -- you know -- with a white guy before?"

"No, my man, I've just this moment lost my virginity with your kind. And you?"

He laughed. "Hell, I'm practically a virgin with all races. Usually, when I've done it before, I've been too goddamn drunk to feel anything."

I rolled off him, finally, and held him close to me, kissing the hollows of his neck. We lay pressed together, holding each other, not saying much. After about twenty minutes I was feeling aroused again so I reached down and got my hand on his cock. I started massaging it slowly, making him breathe heavily. When it was erect, I held it by the end and maneuvered it back and forth, and whispered in his ear, "Ding, dong, ball; pussy wants it all."

This time he rolled over on top of me and fucked me again, as I lay tensed underneath and took everything he could throw at me. I closed my eyes tight and caressed him lightly all over with the tips of my fingers; his body was a delight of different textures, soft and furry in some spots, gristly and muscular elsewhere. His ass felt like polished metal, like wrought brass. He was like a pile-driver, a machine for producing joy! His dick slipped in and out in a cadence that drove me into deepening rapture; every thrust ratcheted me up a little closer to that consummate euphoria I longed for so much. And when it came this time, I felt like I was being wheeled through mists, cascading beyond exhilaration toward a warm darkness of tranquility. I heard myself crying out, heard it as if it was coming from someone else a long distance away. It was like a deep dream, like that of anaesthesia; and it took me some time, maybe a minute, to wake up and find Pyke clutching my shoulders tensely, almost hurting me. His breath steamed in my ears.

"Hey, brother, you're really some talent for this stuff." I grabbed at his wrists, raising him up so he could look in my face.

"I love you," he said, calmly. Each word was like an individual firecracker exploding inside my ears.

"Hey, baby, you don't have to say that. You can be cool with me."

"I know. But I do. I know."

"OK. But you're makin' me a little nervous, understand?"

"Oh, darling, I'm sorry, but I have to say what I feel. I need to tell you."

"OK, I got the message. Thanks, baby. You want to get up for a while, maybe have a drink?"

He rolled over and sat up, looking away from me. "I hate to do this, but I've got to go home. I've got a pile of work to finish that's due Monday. Could I see you for a while, maybe around noon? We could have lunch, maybe. My treat. Wherever you'd like to go."

I watched him out my bedroom window as he left in the van; I rested my chin on the lintel of the window and pressed my bare breasts against the cool glass. He was something special, all right.

Obviously, we started seeing each other regularly. He was sensational in bed, but it was amazing what he didn't know about. Oral sex was a complete novelty to him, for example. The first time I took his dick in my mouth, he laughed nervously and said, "Isn't this a felony?" But he was a fast learner.

I taught him most of what he knew about food, and absolutely everything about drugs. For all his brave talk about peyote, he was jumpy as hell about even blowing grass. He wouldn't even try it the first two times he saw me with a joint; said he was afraid it'd make him nauseous, like tobacco did; or that he'd become dependent on an "unnecessary" substance. But after he saw what it did for me, especially when we made love, he gave it a go. It took him a couple of tries, but he learned to get high, all right; and after that, it seemed like there was no way to keep him off the stuff. He became a real fanatic, practically a religious convert.

This was, actually, the main problem I had with the man. He went overboard on things, just go right off the deep end and to hell with everything. For example, the business about being in love with me. Hey, I liked being with him a lot. He was a great friend and an exceptional lover. But I needed my freedom. I wasn't about to dedicate my life to anyone but me.

Practically right away, he started to talk about getting married, but I told him straight out it wasn't ever going to be possible. "You're an idiot, you know," I said to him, "We can't even get a hotel room, let alone an apartment or a house. I'm not sure it's even legal for us to be man and wife in this state." So he started to rave about leaving the state, even leaving the country -- going to Sweden, or somewhere more tolerant. I just could not believe, sometimes, the ludicrous things the man would say. "Sweden? Sweden? You gotta be kiddin'. I don't know about you, man, but I can't stand the motherfucking Swedes they got around here. I sure as shit don't want to live in a whole country full of the bastards."

Well, those conversations never got us very far, and we dropped them. I could never stay upset with him for very long, even though it seemed at times as if he really wasn't listening to me. My philosophy was to have as much as we could together for as long as we could, and then let go when we had to. He grudgingly went along with it, though he never stopped dreaming his ridiculous dreams about some ideal of eternal happiness we could have together, somehow, somewhere.

I went home for Christmas that year, to Omaha, I mean, to visit my mamma. We had a long heart-to-heart talk about me and Pyke, and my mamma was a little bit upset with me. She told me my brother Gilman's live-in white girlfriend had just broken up with him, left him to run away to Florida with some slick night-club pianist; they'd broken into his apartment and taken almost everything he had. Didn't even leave a note to say goodbye. Mama wanted him to press charges, but he didn't want to; he was feeling guilty, feeling that the whole thing was all his fault somehow. I called him up, discussed his problems and mine with him. He had to laugh when I told him about my white beau. "Watch out, sister; those people speak another language. I never understood what my girl was trying to tell me until it was too late."

Well, as much as I tried to tell myself those things weren't about to happen with me and Pyke, I suppose I must have had some little reservoir of mistrust; and maybe subconsciously, I tried to put a little distance into our relationship.

It was pretty difficult since neither one of us had anyone else we wanted to be with, for very much of the time. And we still had that great lovemaking, always; but I was getting sort of tired of the need to keep it all hidden. At that time it was almost unheard of for people of different races to show any affection toward each other; I certainly have a lot of sympathy with gay people, today, who have to deal with the same kind of problems the two of us had. We didn't dare walk hand in hand, or God forbid, kiss each other. As it was, although we were careful, people (including educated people you'd think would know better) would look at us very strangely, and mutter to themselves or even make thoughtless or insulting remarks aloud. When that happened, Pyke would get furious; but I managed to convince him to keep cool, that nothing was going to be gained through savagery.

But we kept it going. It was good for both of us; we learned things from each other we'd never have encountered otherwise. I think I'm a better artist because of what he taught me. I might not have helped him in his science, but I think I changed him, too, quite a lot.

After a couple of years, both of us seemed to come to an impasse. We were doing the same things, over and over again, with each other; and I was stuck in my job. It was obvious I was never cut out to be a traditional scholar and produce long disquisitions on ambiguities. I liked teaching, especially when I could combine it with performing, and the dance program liked my work; but I ran into trouble with the English department.

In the first place, since I was only being paid half-time by them, I wasn't part of the daily ebb and flow of their politics. Although some people on the staff approved of my contributions, there weren't enough of them to make much of a difference. The stories and poems I wrote for the campus literary quarterly apparently didn't carry much weight, although I thought they were pretty good; I wasn't ashamed of them. I hardly ever went to their faculty meetings, and when I was named to their committees I wasn't exactly the most diligent performer. I really didn't feel like one of the gang, was my problem. So, to make a long story short, they terminated my appointment after three years. They gave me all of three months notice.

I knew when I opened the little manila envelope that it was the end of my career at Cimarron. There was no way I could make it on half my salary, and there was no way any other department could pick up the slack, nor was there any other way to bring in that money, such as by being a cocktail waitress at the Holiday Inn at nights. I was finished.

Pyke was devastated when I told him. He suggested that I file suit for wrongful dismissal, but I already knew that would get me nowhere. Besides, what would I do if I won? I certainly didn't want to hang around English like a fifth wheel, and I'd never win enough in damages to make it worthwhile.

Then Pyke suggested I move in with him to save money. Like I said, the man was berserk! Obviously, such an arrangement would have lasted a week, at most - until his landlord found out he had a black tenant and threw us both out, or, more likely, until one of us murdered the other.

I told him we weren't getting anywhere with these discussions, and I asked him to leave me alone for a few days, not to call or see me. I felt a need to think for myself.

Naturally, I called my mamma. And just as naturally, she told me to come home; but that also would have been a senseless move. I needed to obtain some independence from everyone in my life, and start my career over in a place where I'd have some flexibility. Yes, without a doubt, the place for me was New York.

I didn't call Gilman, but I sent him a letter; and the dear boy said in return that I could stay with him while I looked for work. He still had this big place and no one to share it with. We'd really enjoy ourselves, he was sure. I decided then and there to do it.

I didn't tell Pyke right away. We kept seeing each other, but not very often; I was preoccupied, trying to make plans as well as I could, and he didn't want to make things worse by pressuring me. But finally, one evening when I was over at his apartment having dinner, everything came out in the open.

It was in the middle of November, and I was going to leave at Christmas. He had to know and I couldn't put it off any more. We had just finished eating Louisiana shrimp and rice and drinking a lot of white wine and I was sitting on the floor, leaning back against his legs while he sat in his recliner. He'd built a fire in the grate, and it was snowing lightly outside. He was softly stroking the top of my head with two fingers, smoothing down the hair on either side of my part.

When I told him I was going to leave, he stopped a caress in mid-stroke, gasped audibly, and stood up suddenly. I fell back, bumping my head against the chair, and watched as he took two or three heavy steps toward the fireplace. He looked like he'd been clubbed. Then he collapsed to his knees, looked into the flames for a moment or two, and buried his head in his hands. He started sobbing, and I came up behind him to hug him. "Oh, God, Yolanda, I love you so much," he blubbered. "All I needed was to have you here with me, and now everything's gone to hell."

"Oh, Pyke, it isn't going to be so bad. We'll have some more good times, just you and me, and we'll say goodbye before it has a chance to go bad. This way we'll have great times to remember forever. You know we'll never forget each other."

"Darling, I tried so hard to be right for you. You're the best person that ever came along in my life."

"Hey, my man, you too. You're my lifelong friend, no matter what."

"Oh, God, I just wish it didn't have to end this way. Please say it doesn't have to end."

"Pyke, it isn't the end at all. We're here with each other at the beginning of our lives. I don't know about you, but mine started the day I met you in the Union."

"Right, lady, I'd wasted my time for those thirty years and then I had three good, productive ones. Sounds a lot like Jesus."

"Except he was a master and I'm a mistress."

"Yolanda, I won't hear that stuff from you. I love you, damn it, and you're the master of the way I think, and feel, from now on."

He stopped crying, and sighed loudly as if he was finally coming to terms with reality. "Will you write to me? I promise I'll write at least once a week. I'm a really good correspondent."

"I look forward to your letters, baby, and you know you've got a standing invitation to visit. I owe you one for taking me to the top of Grandfather."

"God, that was an embarrassing day for me. I thought I'd made a really huge mistake. Some first date! I didn't even know what to say to you, and I was so flustered I wound up saying nothing for hours."

"You haven't forgotten what happened afterwards, have you?"

He started laughing his huge laughs, and grabbed me around the shoulders and pinned me to the floor. "I think you'll notice that I haven't!"

So before I left, starting then, we had an absolute whirlwind of sex. We made love almost every day, buried under the blankets in the midwinter chill.

Finally, the day came for me to leave. He drove me down to the bus station, where I was going to hop a Greyhound for Omaha and visit my mother for a day or so before I flew off to New York for good. He was strangely calm and silent in the car, and also while sitting in the terminal with me waiting for my bus to be called.

"Don't ever forget me, Yolanda," he said suddenly. "I need to be sure someone will remember me, all their life."

"Oh, you foolish man, you must know by now that my last thoughts on earth will be of you; I'm going to die with your name on my freezing lips."

The bus for Omaha was announced. We stood up, and he said, "I love you." And, for the first time, I said, "I love you, Pyke, and I always will." So he took me in his arms, right there in the public bus station, and kissed me as he had the first time; and it was as if all the disapproving people in those tawdry surroundings fell away, and there was nothing left in the world but him and me in some immense darkness. But then I had to pull free, and stumbled up the steps of the bus and found a seat near the window so I could see him; and I watched for as long as I could, watched his burning eyes watching me as I glided away.

Yes, we wrote for a time, but I no longer have his letters. It seemed at some point that they were no longer meaningful for the person I had become. I had kept one picture of us, but now I will bequeath it to you. I hope it will help you to remember what he was, and to understand what I once was for him. Also, I hope that loving me was a force for good, overall, in his life; because he showed me, for the first time, the necessity of a balance of intellect and passion in a creative spirit.

DEGREES OF FREEDOM

I am glad that you were able to know Pyke and to appreciate his unique qualities. I am sure that for you, as well as for me and many other people, Pyke McKenna will always live in your heart.

Anonymous

(An unsigned and undated letter from Pyke's "miscellaneous correspondence" file.)

    we Know what your doing and we Dont like it. Why ca'nt you stand Up, for america and what We are trieing to do for the world. my Brother died in vietnam thanks to your Kind. my Friends and I have our eye on you. One time you will look around and it will be us. Do'nt worry Pal we will get ours.

Lecture 1

(Excerpts of a lecture given to McKenna's Biology 103 class, "An Introduction to Biological Science," on Friday, October 17, 1969. From a tape recording.)

This area where we are now seated has changed radically in the last hundred years, but there are still landmarks here we could recognize if we were to go back in time. For example, this hill where the campus is situated is still essentially the same hill that has been standing here for probably about a hundred thousand years. "Old as the hills," people will say, and compared to us they are indeed old. However, if we were to go back still farther in time, time so great that to us they are beyond understanding in any substantive sense, we would find things changed very much indeed.

For example, a hundred million years ago this area was the middle of an ocean, or at least of a large inland sea. It was not the first; seas have come and gone like temporary puddles in the midst of this huge land mass of North America, while the land around it has not been at rest, either, but wheels and thrashes about as if it is made up of the bodies of great beached whales. Mountain ranges are thrown up and erode away; the sea rushes in and rushes out again; and this happens over and over, on a scale of time that we are powerless to imagine. This particular ocean I just spoke of had been created perhaps fifty million years earlier, when it rained without stopping for a hundred thousand years at a time. Imagine what that must have been like, nothing but heavy clouds, thunder, lightning, and rain every day, forever, with no chance of the weather breaking. Think of that the next time you feel like complaining about a week of drizzles, or 100 degree temperatures! On the banks of this ocean, giant reptiles swam; and over the bays and shallows, pterodactyls and birds with teeth flew and dived and fished. And there were smaller animals, too, lizards no larger than mice; but we know less about them. The bigger animals always seem to be so much more interesting! For example, teeth of sharks are found quite commonly around here, but the one everyone remembers is the one, nine inches long, found in 1939 sticking out of a cliff only twenty miles from here, over in Muspell County.

But then the seas slowly drained, as the mighty Rocky Mountains were thrust up and literally tilted the land in this area so that the oceans were poured off to the east, just like milk sluicing off the edge of a table, into the Gulf of Mexico. Afterwards, as nearly as we can tell, we then had maybe thirty million years of calm. Heavy forests must have developed, forests of great tree ferns and conifers covering the landscape for as far as one could see if anyone had been there to see it.

And then, much later, say about ten million years ago, giant volcanic eruptions blackened the sky for weeks, raining down ash much worse than that of Pompeii, although there were no human beings here to see it. (Inaudible) If we dig down a few yards into the earth under this spot, we would find that same ash layer, ranging from ten to twenty feet in depth. Paleontologists who have dug into this sooty soil have found well-preserved bones of camels, and mastodons, and saber-toothed cats, and rhinoceroses, who died horribly on the spot as the ash choked and buried them. Wild horses, also, not at all like the ones left behind by the Spanish conquistadors, but small ones, barely a foot high. Imagine herds of those little creatures, the tracks made by their delicate hooves in the dust, and their tiny whickering sounding more like the calls of birds than those of horses. And there are perfectly preserved fossil insects, too, the images of their bodies beautifully perpetuated in that hardened ash; you can see almost every wing vein and scale, shining out of the stone in exactly the way they shone in the sun in those long-ago days before the tragedy.

And then, quite recently really, within the last two hundred thousand years, came the great glaciers; there were several waves of them that we know of, and there will probably be a few more in the relatively near future. Only one of them has got as far south as here - so far, anyway. Those great walls of ice, what it must have been like to see them on the horizon thirty thousand years ago, crushing the earth flat with their enormous weight. Won't it be exhilarating to see the next one coming over the ridge and smashing the football stadium flat, grinding those bricks into pink powder! (Scattered laughter) Huge rivers were dammed by those glaciers of the past and had to go around them; for example, the Missouri River used to flow into Canada!

And even within the past few hundred years, the native wildlife of this area was in astonishing abundance. A quotation: This is the finest country and the most beautiful land in the world; the prairies are like seas, and filled with wild animals in such quantities as to surpass the imagination. End of quotation. So said Etienne Veniard de Bourgmont, one of the first Europeans to visit this area, around 1717.

And now, so short a time after this sentence was written, Homo sapiens is unmistakably and unfortunately the dominant life form on these prairies. He builds towns, roads, irrigation ditches, he strip-mines coal and drills holes into the earth's crust for oil, and burns the wood, coal, and oil to change the atmosphere. And everywhere the other mammals who used to dominate this area are in retreat. Herds of bison used to extend from one horizon to another, and now all we have left are a few pathetic stragglers, maybe three hundred animals all told, carefully managed so that tourists can show them to their kids and tell them lies about the brave pioneers in the frontier days. The last mountain lion in our state was shot in 1900. The grizzly bear was gone even earlier, in about 1850. The wolves are all gone, all shot or poisoned decades ago.

So here we are. Mankind bestrides the cosmos. But let me tell you a secret, mankind will not last. We shall certainly become extinct. Over 99% of all animal species that ever lived are now extinct, and we are too complex to survive much longer. Even if we don't kill ourselves with nuclear bombs, the pressure of our ever-growing population is going to foul our environment. I don't know whether it will be water pollution, air pollution, famine, or some sort of plague that wipes us out, but we are on our last legs as a species. I guarantee it.

It is not a tragedy of enormous proportions yet, although it could be if it takes us a long time to go and we find ourselves bringing a lot of other species along with us in our death throes. We've already wiped out so much of the wildness of the world, as I already told you, that it's nowhere near as diverse a place as it was. We have become a horrific force, an agent of extinction as powerful as any that this old globe has seen for the past billion years. Somehow, in the process of becoming "civilized," we became separated from the rest of the biosphere; we started to think of ourselves as different from the rest of creation, somehow "better" and "dominant;" because we were able to destroy whole ecosystems, we did so, carrying out the Biblical injunction to fill the earth and exhaust it, for God has made it for our use, so it says in Western society's dominant myth. And we're in the late stages of the process of destroying some of the last wildernesses on earth, and with them their noble populations of rare and exotic animals and plants. But this also happened in other great extinctions, when the climate changed radically; although many species, including some of the most dominant forms, were exterminated, those species that were adaptable enough to survive pulled through, evolved, and gave rise to the creatures we see around us today. But those extinct creatures, such as the dinosaurs, that have left us, did not inhabit another world; they are our cousins, just a slightly different solution to the problem of assembling a large and complex system that can live, metabolize, and reproduce. And there will be many, many more solutions to this problem after we are gone, each of them imperfect but each something Nature will find worth trying for a while.

Take a look at this graph, showing the rate of increase of human numbers since 1800. And now look at this graph, showing the typical course of increase and decline of a bacterial culture, in a medium that is rich in nutrients and in which predators are absent. Look how well they fit. Notice that the bacterial population increases logarithmically until a point is reached where the medium won't sustain the rate of increase any longer, and then it goes immediately into a logarithmic death phase. I guarantee to you that that is what is in store for us. But is this an unmitigated disaster? No. We have only been a species for a million or two years. The thin film of life has been unbroken on the surface of this planet for more than a thousand times as long as that. The film will continue; life will spread back again into areas where mankind can no longer live. Other forms will develop after we are gone; we are only transients, temporary visitors who will leave no effect on the continuum of life.

This is the glory of life, students, don't you see? Life is going on with us, as it went on before us and will go on into the unimaginable future after we are gone. Glory with me, students. See the flow of life as I have, glory in the miracle that is here among us; that we exist at all, that evolution has thrown up a conscious animal, capable of perceiving its own wonders. Glory at the sight of this miracle of life, the most miraculous phenomenon we know.

And now the bell is about to ring, so I shall release you from the classroom; all I ask is that you stop for a moment, out there in the world, to consider the wonder of life, the extraordinary achievements of biology at work in the world. Take a look at an ant on the sidewalk, and instead of crushing it consider what a wonderful and powerful mechanism it is, and how it and us and all of our fellow living creatures have transformed the globe from a hideous miasma of choking gas to the lovely blue heaven that it is. For this is the true heaven, students; this earth of ours, this earth that we live in in our time. Go forth now, fellow students, and try to live wisely in it.

Bruce 4

It took me between two and three years to get things shaken down and really feel at home as a small college professor. I hadn't really realized the difference in atmosphere between big, research-oriented campuses and a place like this. At a big school the faculty are nearly all hard-driving and aggressive individualists, trying to outmuscle each other on the frontiers of scholarship. They're always on the make for new discoveries, new money, and prestige. As a result, they are quite similar in terms of personality. They are managerial in their approach to their profession, manipulating their subordinates for maximal benefit to themselves. Much of their time is spent in cajolery. Among themselves, they affect a sort of urbane insolence in speech and manner. They are absolutely incapable of any sort of cooperative activity, due to the two personality traits that constitute the principal motivational factors of their behavior, namely greed and suspicion.

Those who can't succeed in that kind of professional atmosphere are kicked out, although some drop out; some of them end up in places like Cimarron. Here, they tend to behave like minor league imitations of the big-school majordomos, although some of them do go into administrative positions, and if that happens all bets are off. These types constitute one class of professors, but by no means are they a majority. I think our majority is made up of gentler souls, people who really like teaching; men and women who decided in high school, perhaps under the influence of a really gifted instructor, to make it their life's work. These are the ones who came willingly to small colleges like Cimarron, and stay here happily. They couldn't care less about making scholarly discoveries out on the frontiers of their professions; they are quite content to report and interpret the findings of the pioneers.

We also have our dead wood, as the bigger schools do, but whereas in research it is usually quite easy to calculate when a professor becomes unproductive merely by counting the reduced number of articles produced, in teaching-based colleges it is much more difficult. None of us has time to regularly attend the lectures given by our colleagues and to assess their content and delivery relative to what they were five years ago. It comes out, first, more as a sense that things are going awry, a look about a colleague's eyes at the end of the day that tells you somehow that the excitement is going out of teaching. And then you overhear a casual remark made by one student to another in the hallway, and then other hints begin to come out in conversation. It is a matter of great concern. For in the large universities the success of failure of our associates does not touch us personally, since as individual researchers we are responsible only for our own reputations, but in small colleges the faculty pull together. The teaching load is like an urgent burden that is pulled by all, like a barge being drawn through the Erie Canal by means of ropes tied to mules on the banks. And when one mule falters the rest feel it immediately as an additional stress, a need to make up what has been lost. A small school is thus a socialistic institution by its very nature, and the large university with its emphasis on making it big through entrepeneurship and exploitation is fundamentally capitalistic.

The attitude of the administration of our school toward research was ambivalent. On one hand, they understood that research brought in dollars from the outside world; that was the main thing they liked about it. To them, the prestige of research and its role in the education of the students was secondary, although to the faculty these aspects, as well as the sheer joy of discovering something new, were paramount. The administration also relished the sending out of press releases to the local media whenever someone on the faculty had something interesting to report. Our division was under great pressure to keep up a constant flow of news, since we incorporated not only the biology department but also agriculture; and the college's higher-ups recognized that the farmers and ranchers were our biggest supporters and strongest political allies with the state government, and needed to have their positive impression of the college constantly reinforced.

On the other hand, the administrators constantly worried that the public was going to get the idea that the faculty was a bunch of lazy good-for-nothings, using their sinecure jobs to fool around with visionary ivory-tower concepts. Thus, our work habits had to be constantly monitored and quantified, and reported to the public and its representatives, so that we would be perceived as earning our pay. The division was always particularly worried about our contact time with the students; the number of hours per week we spent in some form of teaching. The college had devised elaborate algorithms to compute this number. Every one of us had to keep data on a form, the monthly "CHR" (Contact Hour Report) on the number of students enrolled in our classes, whether they were lab or lecture sections, and the number of hours we spent outside of class in private or group discussions with students. Time spent on research did not enter into this computation. This form had to be turned in monthly. From it, using arcane formulae, the department calculated our contact hours for the month (using a generous factor for preparation time for lab and lecture classes.) It was important that our MCT, or mean contact time, not decrease for three straight months, or the division would be in trouble. Also, it was essential that the division's annual MCT for any year should not be lower than that of the previous year. In years when the enrollment was surging, this was no problem, but if the number of students, for one reason or another, was static or decreased over the previous year, the pressure would be on. So what would occasionally happen would be that a few days after the CHR forms were turned in, the Dean would be on the phone with us, telling us that our MCT needed to be increased, and weren't there some discussion hours that we'd forgotten to report? Or weren't there more students in a group discussion than we'd remembered? Anything that could be used to raise the MCT. So usually, we'd go along with this. Every division of the college had to play these stupid games, and after a few years of iteration the numbers became simply absurd, but no one dared to broach the subject to anyone who mattered, so the result was that all of us routinely lied about our time spent with students. It became more and more ridiculous, until some genius of an associate dean decided that since over the years academic subjects had become more and more complicated, it was taking us professors much more time to keep up with our subjects and prepare our lectures and course outlines, and therefore the multipliers that had been used for lecture and laboratory preparation time needed to be increased by 30%, thus decreasing the outlandish contact time figures to something more reasonable. So the new factors were duly approved without much fanfare, and after a few months of getting used to the new system, we all learned a new set of lies to use until such time as the next rolling adjustment would be made.

So, after two or three years of teaching, my life was beginning to become somewhat more systematized. I actually found, once in a while, time to think.

Before I started teaching all kinds of subjects, I thought the burden of having to prepare to teach something I didn't know well would be impossible; but I learned the secret of college teaching. This is it, the only one there is. The professor learns along with the students! As long as the instructor is able to keep up with most of the students, which shouldn't be too hard since he's normally brighter than they are, it isn't really necessary to have the whole class spelled out in advance, or to be an authority. You only need to be one lecture ahead; and you become an authority. The only problem is, it does take time. It was much more demanding than being a student. For the first year and a half, I had little time or energy for home life or recreation. I'm pretty sure Viola didn't bargain on hardly ever getting a chance to see me or talk to me, night after night, for months.

At first, we argued. She was offended at the amount of time it took me to get my work done, and her criticisms of these tendencies also expanded to other features of my personality. "I thought you'd married me, not your job." "I work, too, but I try to find time for something else in my life, namely you and our home." "Why do I have to suffer for the sake of your career? I don't bring my job home with me." "The other professors don't seem to disregard their families to the extent you do." "Why does everything always have to be perfect? Can't you accept something less than infallibility? God, I see why the popes and the saints weren't married." And, finally, "You comb your hair before you go to bed," she shouted, "how can any human being do such a thing?"

Then, after a long period when it seemed that these discussions were no longer anything other than repetitive formulas, we separated into a pair of sullen individualists, married in name only. She bought her own alarm clock, got up before me and had breakfast without me, and left without saying goodbye. In the evenings, she always came home earlier than me. Although we used to share the cooking, she now refused to let me do any of it; when I came home, there was always something on the stove or on the table for me, although most of the time she had already eaten. She began to spend evenings out, up to four a week, at night school classes put on by the local park commission. She became, for brief periods, expert in macrame, Spanish conversation, and automobile maintenance; but then she would move on to another topic, and never again referred to her earlier enthusiasms. Late in the evening, often, after one of her classes, she would come home with a couple of beers tinting her breath, a result of, she claimed, the girls in the course going out for a quick one or two before heading home.

Our nights were the only time we really shared; in the darkness, our bodies came together as often as they had earlier, but we spent less time before and after, talking and hugging. She tended to turn away from me and drop off to sleep directly, and she didn't always remember to kiss me good night and tell me that she loved me. Once in a while, it seemed that she was sobbing quietly, but when I asked her whether anything was the matter she told me to leave her alone, it was private.

I was disturbed by these events, but I hoped that it was only temporary; I told her that it would be, and that as soon as things settled down, we'd be able to spend much more time together again.

So time passed, and as usual, things didn't turn out the way I expected. After a few years devoted entirely to undergraduate teaching, I began to miss the excitement of research, and I began casting around for a problem to put my mind to. Pyke and I had many discussions about our research ideas, but we had fundamental differences in approach. My perspective was mathematical and exact; I wanted to study quantitative, measurable phenomena that were reproducible and from which one could generalize and make predictions to other, related problems. The ideal of biology to me was exemplified by Mendel, who carefully kept track of every one of his pea plants, and from the detailed records of their progeny was able to erect a complex hypothesis that became essential for the understanding of heredity.

This strategy Pyke found confining. He wanted to let his free imagination flow, to seek out the unusual problem that had defied solution, to live with it for a while, and to solve it in a moment of insight. I think he would have liked to have done an experiment he told me about; investigators released moths in a room with a bat and followed the bat around with a high-speed movie camera. When the films were played back in slow motion, it was discovered that the bat didn't catch an insect directly in its jaws, as everyone had always assumed, but "batted" it toward its mouth with its wings and caught it on the rebound!

To tell the truth, I never was greatly impressed with Pyke as a researcher; I thought he was, to put it baldly, too scatterbrained to take on a difficult and important unsolved problem and to expend the sustained mental energy required to bring it to a satisfactory, publishable conclusion. He would throw himself furiously into some piece of work and then either abandon it when he ran into difficulties or fail to fill in the gaps in the story once the first easy conclusions had been reached. Furthermore, he would never admit that he had given up on a project, but always try to convince a questioner that it was still ongoing and he was going to put some more time in on it shortly. It must have infuriated the Dean.

I would like to give a specific example of how our attitudes toward performing research differed. Both Pyke and I spent a fair amount of time thinking about birds and their behavior; but Pyke was drawn to study the problem in what I would characterize as a romantic way, whereas I tried a more systematic approach. Pyke, first of all, loved to watch great hawks soaring across the prairie skies, and he would drive around the countryside for many miles to observe them. He would have done this, I think, even if he hadn't been a scientist; something about their effortless soaring spoke deeply to him, evoked something mystical in his persona. Since he was an evolutionist, however, he was always thinking about closely related organisms diverging to form new species; and in the case of the hawks, he thought he had discovered a ready-made problem. There are two relatively common broad-winged hawks, Buteos, in our area; the rough-legged hawk, *Buteo lagopus*, and the ferruginous hawk, *Buteo regalis*. The rough-leg was around only in the winter, but *regalis* could be found year-round. Furthermore, the ferruginous hawk occurs in two color variants, a dark form and a pale form. Pyke wanted to see whether the color varieties were going to develop into new species someday, and in order to do this he said he was going to learn if their habits were different. This required keeping careful notes on the behavior of both forms, and comparing them, where possible, to the corresponding tendencies of the rough-leg - either drawn from the literature, which was quite small, or directly observed. It seemed like an excellent idea, and one that might have paid off handsomely. Pyke plunged into the task; or rather, he saw it as a continuing project, one which had occupied him, off and on, for a decade. For as long as I knew him, on occasional weekends, he would roar off into the wild country west and south of Pawnee Springs, where the hawks could be found. I never accompanied him on such jaunts, but I heard about them from students, usually female, that he'd drag along. The hawks ranged over huge territories, so it might take him a long time to locate one of his specimens, even if he knew the general area where they might be. He couldn't identify individuals, so he never really knew whether the hawk he was observing was one he'd seen before; and it wouldn't have occurred to him to try to band them. He would try to locate their nests and when successful would clamber up stony canyon walls to see the adults and young. Once in a while, he'd proclaim, he was dive-bombed by the adults and only missed serious injury by pure luck. All the while, he was furiously scribbling his impressions in his field notebooks; he had quite a collection of these. At the time, I never could see any rhyme nor reason in the way they were kept, and now that I have studied them in more detail, my initial opinion has been confirmed. For example, there are no columns or tables of data, or any attempt to systematize the observations he made. They are more in the style of a 19th-century naturalist's journal, recounting the vague sensations taken in during a stroll in the woods. Also, he might take three or four pages of notes about hawks, and then a page on spiders; the next page might just as well display a sketch of a squirrel, or exhibit a clipping from the newspaper on the subject of caterpillars. Infuriatingly, also, none of the notes was ever dated, so there would have been no way to see whether any differences he may have observed might have had a seasonal component.

Perhaps I am being unduly harsh on Pyke's methods; maybe he didn't need to write everything down painstakingly; possibly, his memory was reliable enough to have reconstructed the important features of what he saw, if only he'd ever gotten around to doing it. But, realistically, when all is said and done, all of Pyke's work on hawks is now worthless, both as it stands and as a potential resource for future students of the problem.

My own interest in birds came partly from discussions with Pyke, partly from having to teach about them in physiology and anatomy classes, and partly from my own mathematical predilections. I was interested in them because the population was made up of a large number of individuals that could presumably act independently -"free as a bird" we say, after all - but beyond question this was not really the case, and their freedom of action was constrained and ultimately governed by powerful forces outside of them. Perhaps I thus saw in birds a microcosmic example of our own human predicament. At any rate, I became fascinated by the problems of their behavior, and particularly of bird migration; what drove some species to repeat, year after year, the same never-changing patterns of movement across great distances? I would have liked to model migration mathematically; to take a cluster of points that represented every individual brown thrasher, for example, and monitor the movement of the individual points in the cluster over time, and see whether given a knowledge of external stimuli that the birds responded to would allow you to predict how the mass of points would behave and where it would go.

Amazingly, by pure good fortune, I was able to do some work on such a problem. I remember the beginning of my involvement so well; in mid-November of 1965, the division scheduled an invited seminar given by Professor Willard Schofield from Rice University in Houston. He is a skinny guy from California, who smiles all the time, displaying teeth like piano keys; wears ties with animals on them, the bigger the pattern the better (the day I first saw him, it was a cream-colored tie with blue giraffes -- you could see from the last row); and has fine, uncombed blond hair like Andy Warhol's.

Willard is about my age, but unlike me, he'd been extremely successful in research; his field was the emerging field of ethology -- the study of animal behavior. His talk was at 9 in the morning of the 17th, so I didn't get a chance to speak to him beforehand, and I wasn't really prepared for what happened afterward.

The subject of his seminar was the social behavior of crows. In the wintertime, as we all know, crows become very gregarious, forming huge flocks that roost in the same place night after night and scatter to feed during the daytime. Willard looked at the details of this behavior by using tiny radio transmitters; using mist nets, he and his students trapped hundreds of crows at a time and tagged about fifty of them with transmitters set to transmit on slightly different frequencies, so the location of individual birds could be monitored. By setting up detectors quite close to the roosts, a considerable amount of fine detail about their social structure could be obtained. The research produced some fascinating discoveries. First of all, when the individual birds were observed in the daytime, it was found that those crows that were "highest" in the social hierarchy - the pecking order, as it were - also were those who roosted highest in the trees at night. In addition, crows are creatures of habit; not only do they assume almost the same position in the roost night after night, but also their foraging territories are rather well-defined. Even though they may feed many miles from the roost, they often go in small groups to only a few of the many possible areas where they might gather. Furthermore, they fly in almost the same paths to these locations. " 'As the crow flies,'" Willard said, "turns out to mean both more and less in reality than it does in anecdote."

I was able to have lunch with Willard. We ate at the Faculty Club, a group of about eight or so of us biology faculty, together with the Dean, who magnanimously paid the check. I sat next to the visiting expert, and we began to discuss my ideas about mathematical modeling of migration; he became very excited. He said that he'd been thinking about exactly the same thing, but he didn't know anyone with the background and interest to work on the problem. He asked, "Are you interested in cranes?" It turned out that he and a group from the University of Montana wanted to do an extensive study of the migration of sandhill cranes, *Grus canadensis,* those magnificent long-legged wading birds that migrate through the central United States from their winter homes on the Mexican coasts. The idea was to use the results of the study as a starting point for the study of whooping cranes, *Grus americana,* an endangered species that was closely related and that migrated every year from the Texas Gulf coast to northern Alberta. The Montana group wanted eventually to try to imprint captive whooping crane fledglings on sandhill parental surrogates, and let them try to migrate together. This might allow the whoopers to expand their territory. "Sandhills migrate very fast," Willard told me. "They leave their winter habitat in late February, and within two or three months they're all the way to the Northwest Territories and Alaska - some of them are, anyway. They've got to average at least fifty miles a day to get that far. Others stop off around here and stay the summer. Then, in August, the northern populations start to head back; they're coming through Texas in October; and by early December, they're back again. Nobody knows why some go farther than others, whether they mostly fly at night or during the day, or whether they're the same birds every year. They're quite long-lived, and it should be possible to follow individuals for several years. We've been writing a proposal to the National Science Foundation to do this work, but we're really understaffed, especially around here; we could use a group of collaborators to help out in the field, tracking the birds we tag with transmitters. But even more, we could use a person on the project with some mathematical modeling experience, to take the data we generate and make some sense out of it. If you'd be interested, I'd be happy to have you work with us."

So I had been given a serendipitous opportunity to join a team of well-known scholars and also to contribute something substantive to their work. I jumped at the chance. Two weeks later, I attended a project meeting in Colorado Springs. During this meeting, which lasted three days, we hammered out a four-year multidisciplinary proposal (involving seven principal investigators from three colleges) that came in at just under a million dollars! We weren't too optimistic that this would go through, but we decided what the hell, let's take the chance. I was in for $35,000 a year, which would have been an unheard-of sum of money for our department; it was roughly equal to all the rest of the support that the whole biology faculty brought in every year.

The Dean was really excited. "This is what I brought you in here for, Bruce. If this comes through, I'll really be vindicated. Some of the old-timers in our department were a little bit uncomfortable when I made you an offer of employment, but this will make believers out of them."

My wife was pretty unhappy, as I might have expected, when I told her the news. Just when I had been able to take an occasional evening or part of a weekend off, now this came along. "I suppose you'll be running all over North America, for months at a time, with your jet set colleagues - chasing those stupid clumsy birds," was about all she ever had to say.

Two months later I got a call from Willard. "How wild have your wildest dreams been, Bruce? Get ready for this. The NSF loves our proposal, but they're not ready to spend all the money we want; they don't see how they can free up more than $600,000 for three years. However, on their own they contacted the U.S. Fish and Wildlife Service, and it seems they love it even more. They want us to come to Washington and to meet with some of their own people, who are considering a similar project. And - get this - Fish and Wildlife wants to discuss the possibility of a contract with us, at about the same amount of money - but for FIVE years!"

No whooping crane could ever have whooped louder than I did at that moment.

There was just enough time to begin working on the project. Now that we had a reasonable expectation that money would be forthcoming, we had to begin right away. It was already mid-January and the birds would be leaving Mexico momentarily. We had to get to the winter grounds and tag some of them so that we could monitor their movements across the continent. I went to the Dean and he gave me special dispensation to curtail my teaching for the rest of the term; I said a hasty farewell to my wife; and within days, I found myself on the Mexican Gulf Coast, driving air boats and wading around the marshy waters near the Tamaulipas coast, rounding up cranes with a team of researchers.

In order to approach the birds at all, we had to maneuver around at night, taking our air boats out to a staging point and then row the rest of the way to their roosts in almost total darkness; finally, when we thought we were almost on top of them, we'd turn on red lamps to zero in. We had to use stun-guns, including some that had infrared viewers, to get close enough to mount the radios. The trouble was, no one had ever tried to immobilize sandhill cranes before, and the first doses we used were far too high; we must have killed about eight of them before we figured out how to do it. Anyway, we overcame that problem, and in two weeks of work we managed to attach about a hundred transmitters. Then, some of us, including me, flew directly from Tampico to Washington to meet with the Fish and Wildlife beaureaucrats. I had forgotten to pack a suit and tie, and thus was the only one at our meeting in fieldwork clothes; but I don't think it really bothered anyone, except possibly a waiter at a French restaurant where we went for a working lunch. He sniffed at me, but brought me my truite au bleu and a bottle of Macon Blanc anyway.

At the end of the meeting, it seemed that we had made a good impression, and the project was tentatively approved. Funding was to begin in April, at a level to be determined; NSF was going to be supporting us beginning July 1. We all shook hands and prepared for a happy working relationship.

After three exciting weeks, I was back in Pawnee Springs, trying to get back into my teaching and to prepare for the upcoming research as well. I felt that I was really a pivotal figure on the project, and I didn't see how it could have been approved without me or someone like me. This was a good feeling I'd never had before as a scientist. It seemed that I was constantly on the phone to Willard and the Montana people, planning experiments and methods to evaluate data.

At home, however, Viola seemed more and more aloof. As I worked at my desk in the living room, or made even more telephone calls, she'd go upstairs to our bedroom and read, or watch television on a little nine-inch set she'd bought "to keep herself company while I was away." By the time I came up, she was usually asleep. I suppose I couldn't blame her; I'd been pretty self-contained lately.

DEGREES OF FREEDOM

I suppose I wasn't really convinced I was actually going to be paid to do this research until the money actually arrived. Miss Freemartin got the call from the business office at 9:50 on Wednesday morning, March 2. She came sprinting down the hall to where I was teaching my physiology lecture section; the NSF, she told me breathlessly, had authorized a quarterly payment of $8,230 into my account. I felt a leap of the heart. This was totally unexpected. It turned out that NSF had another project that had fallen through, and were able to move ours up by four months! It could just as well have been a million bucks, the way I felt.

Later that day I got a call from Brad Judson, a Rice student who was a member of the Tampico observation team. The birds had been behaving restlessly for several days, and that morning a flock of several hundred had taken off and had headed north along the coast toward the United States. At least seven of them were wearing our transmitters, and they were coming in loud and clear, both to the chase group off the coast and the land-based team. They were all staying pretty close together; Brad gave me the coordinates and frequencies where the various signals had been picked up. I wrote down the data and painstakingly read all of the numbers back to Brad. It looked as if it was going to work, and that we could actually pick up individual birds and monitor their locations.

We didn't know much about the details of this migration, and in particular, it wasn't known whether all the cranes in the area where we'd done the tagging would leave at about the same time, or whether some would remain behind. In addition, we had no idea where members of a flock would go once they started to turn inland. Sandhill cranes are found over the whole western two-thirds of North America, and in principle the ones we tagged could go anywhere in the entire range; but it seemed likely that the ones in our wintering grounds would remain in a flyway that went roughly down the middle of the country. We hoped they'd stick together pretty well; it would simplify the logistics for the field teams that would have to follow them. The transmitters weren't particularly powerful, since they were so light; this meant we'd need to be within three miles or so to pick up reliable signals. It was also desirable, for best accuracy, that two observers should get headings on the same signal.

If a flock of tagged birds didn't stick together and behave fairly predictably, it could be a hell of a mess to run around three states trying to find them.

This was basically our assignment, as it stood right now. Our tracking area was everywhere from the Red River on the Oklahoma-Texas border all the way up to the 43rd parallel, on the Nebraska-South Dakota border. South of that, the Rice teams were principally responsible for chasing the cranes, and the Montana group took over from there on.

Anyhow, this was the beginning; the first of many calls I as data coordinator for the project would be getting from all over the continent. I sat back in my chair, feeling pretty content with my lot. At last I'm a real scientist and practically have a reputation, I thought.

In the afternoon, Pyke dropped by to congratulate me. He brought a bottle of Dom Perignon, the first French champagne I had ever had, cooled in a galvanized pail from the lab using the lab's ice. We drank it, though, not from 100-ml beakers but from real flute glasses, the kind they have in Viennese operas. Where Pyke found them I'll never know.

"How nice of you, pal, it isn't even your project. I should be buying this for you."

"Hey, Bruce, no sweat. You can spring for the next one when your first published paper on the project comes out. Got one written yet?"

"No, just outlined. First data just came in, hot off the phone line. Here it is, right here; the ink's hardly dry."

"So the birds are on their way, eh?"

"Yep, just left this morning. A little late, by historic standards."

Pyke, who had been standing up, sat on my floor, leaning back against the door jamb. "I'm a little jealous of your good luck. Sometimes I think the gods of research are against me. I never stumbled into a paying proposition the way you have."

"I agree it was blind luck, and it'll probably never happen again. I expect this project will last a year or two, and then it'll be your turn, or someone else's, to get lucky."

He pulled at his beard with both hands. "Yes, in research, continuous good fortune only seems to smile on those with direct connections to power in Washington. These days, that means the Pentagon. If anybody wanted to work on new jellied gasoline formulations, or nerve toxins, he'd be rolling in dough. We scientists who only want to understand nature get a bad name." He stood slowly up, poured himself the last of the champagne, and drank it off with one gulp. "Enjoy it while it lasts, friend, and for your sake I hope it lasts forever. Anything's better than having the Dean on your ass all the time."

"Thanks a lot, Pyke; I appreciate this. And I will reciprocate as soon as I can."

He walked out, head down, retracing his steps toward his office like a man looking for a large bill he'd lost.

I went home a little early; the buzz I'd got from Pyke's champagne, combined with the emotional high of getting the money and the news from the field, made it impossible for me to concentrate on my work in my office. I was interested to see how Vi would take the news.

Surprisingly, she was already home, and in bed, when I got back. She was wearing a bed jacket and a green flimsy nightgown I'd given her for our first anniversary, and was reading McCall's. When I came through the bedroom door, she jumped up and hugged me, pushed me against the wall and kissed me hard, forcing her tongue insistently into the back recesses of my mouth. "Oh, darling, I missed you so much! I came home early - told them I wasn't feeling well."

My knees felt weak. "What a surprise, but what a nice one! Listen, Vi, I feel like celebrating. How about you? I got my research money and the cranes are on their way. It looks like I'm about to get my career off the ground in a big way."

"Darling, I'm really happy for you. But now, I want to celebrate right here. Celebrate me, baby, we've been celebrate for too long."

So we fell into bed and rejoiced for an hour. I'd never known her to be so excited; her hands roamed all over my body, her fingers penetrating recesses they'd never been in before. "Oh, baby, I love you so much." She, who was usually so quiet in bed, now uttered up a continual gush of little yips and moans, and when she came it was with a laughing scream that rattled the windows. Holy mackerel, I asked myself, is this the nice little girl I married?

And when, a minute or so later, I had my own climax, she slid down my body, took my penis in her mouth (another first for her!) and sucked it lovingly, lapping off all the juices we'd stirred up and moaning with pleasure as if she was tasting delicious wild honey from the alpine meadows.

In the middle of that night, I was sleeping soundly after a big Chinese dinner when the phone rang. It was Brad. "Sorry to wake you, Bruce, but it's the cranes. They migrate at night! We couldn't believe it. They rest for about an hour around dusk, and then they're back in the air again. Not only that, but another group left the coast just about an hour ago, so they even begin their journey when it's dark. We've got great monitoring data on both groups. I'll call you at your office tomorrow morning around 9, if that's OK with you. Sorry to wake you."

Viola was incensed by the call. "Is this going to be a regular occurrence? Because if it is, buster, you can get your own bed. Damn it, I need my beauty sleep." I told her I thought this was the only time it would happen, that we'd just discovered something no one knew before. What I didn't tell her was that this probably meant there'd be some all-nighters for me in a month or so, chasing invisible birds across the prairie in the middle of the night.

The next few days were a flurry of developments. Data were coming in too fast for me to handle them. In order for me to teach my classes, I had to hire a temporary assistant, a senior boy who had just graduated in January and hadn't yet found a job and left town, to sit in my office all day to take the calls and transcribe the data onto long, multi-columned sheets. I stopped in every few hours to see how things were going and to try to keep things organized. I'd already hired three other assistants, M. S. students in biology and education who were going to man the tracking gear and drive the vehicles once the birds came into our area, so I had to meet with them to go over the strategies we would use when the time came.

At least four separate flocks had left with at least one individual in them wearing one of our transmitters. The first of these had already reached the U. S. border and was temporarily parked on both sides of the Rio Grande. This was the flock that was being followed most closely and had the best positional data, because they could be followed both by land and sea; and we hoped they would fly inland in such a way that the team could keep following them in two sets of vehicles. The project only had one powerful van-based antenna that could work at any distance, which meant that the other sighting crew almost had to be within seeing distance of the birds. This made it difficult to run back and forth to check up on the other flocks that had left later, and therefore we had only scattered data on them. But it was all important, because we had no idea how many flocks we'd lose sight of once they started fanning out over the whole continent.

Keeping track of the data was so complicated that I had to start working very late. I was also plotting the positions of the flocks on Geological Survey maps, and these took up so much room I had to commandeer the whole hallway outside my office, fill it with folding tables, and spread maps out over them. I was like a madman racing back and forth between the tables, with a mouthful of multicolored pins and tags, looking for tiny numbers on the maps with a magnifying glass and a little flashlight. It was very exciting, though, to be able to draw lines between the pins, representing the birds' progress. Also, I was noticing a distinct trend; all the flocks had started slowly, covering a relatively short distance per day, but now they were picking up steam, as if they were getting into the swing of migration. Now they covered more than twice as much ground each day than they had in the beginning.

I came home around ten or eleven every evening, proud of my day's work but exhausted. I ate very little. Viola always left me something but I wasn't always up to eating it at such a late hour, especially since she'd usually already gone to sleep. She was adopting a new regimen, seemingly, that required her to get more rest than before; she said her boss had changed her job assignment to include more physically demanding tasks, and that she had to run around a lot more at work. Thus, the promise of a new and exciting sex life for us, revealed on that one afternoon a short time back, had been delayed at least for now.

We had good fortune with the migratory pattern of the first flock. It had flown up the Texas coast as far as Port Lavaca, and then swung inland to follow the Navidad and Colorado River basins into central Texas. The path of the birds looked like it was going to follow a beeline for the Oklahoma border and hit it somewhere between Vernon and Wichita Falls. Unfortunately, it looked as if we'd lost all the other flocks. They'd all turned inland at different places, and as nearly as we could determine they were all somewhere west of the first one, possibly headed toward New Mexico and Utah.

I figured we had less than a week to get ready for our drive to the Red River valley. We spent a lot of time outfitting our campus wagon and van with the two-way radios and electronic equipment we needed, the various recorders, scanners, and antennas, and we were ready to go out on a test drive in the countryside.

Early one Sunday morning, we all met at the biology building. Two of my assistants left in the station wagon carrying a transmitter, of the kind the birds were wearing, mounted on a little bracket in the rear window. I had told them to drive around in the rural areas outside town for an hour, taking back roads and changing directions often; I gave them a ten-minute head start. The other two students and I were to follow in the van, trying to track them as well as we could. We were to meet back here at a predetermined time and compare notes; if we had done well, or even if we hadn't done well, we would have another practice chase later that day, with the pairs of students switching roles.

It proved to be more difficult than I had thought. We drove around aimlessly for some time, following spurious weak signals that faded out rapidly. We never did find out what those were; theories ranged from aircraft radios to reflections off the stratosphere. But, after almost three-quarters of an hour, we homed onto their signal by blind chance; Jim Bristow, the student operating the scanner in the rear of the van, let out a yelp when the signal hit his headphones, and the recorder in the front seat showed a clear spike. Larry Stacy, the student manning the antenna, was able after a few tries to get a good strong heading, and within a few minutes we were able to follow them without serious problems. As long as they were traveling in a straight line we were absolutely OK, but when they veered off in a different direction things were a little confusing for a short time, especially once when they pulled a U-turn and went off 180 degrees from where they had been going. But we followed them successfully, and I think they were a little bit surprised when we pulled up right behind them in the parking lot.

So, after a few more runs, everyone became pretty familiar with the equipment and we felt we were ready for the cranes. Everyone on the project knew we might have to leave at a moment's notice, even in the middle of the night. The Dean and Viola knew this too, though they both grumbled.

At this point in the project, we had a bit of a setback. A period of rain set in, and it caused some problems. First of all, the cranes didn't seem to want to fly directly north in the rain; they did fly around, but aimlessly, a few miles here and a few miles there. Two or three times, it looked as if the Rice team had lost them altogether; but luckily the flock always turned up.

A second problem was that the rain appeared to short out the birds' transmitters; not all of them, and the ones that were affected weren't necesssarily out all the time, but it was a headache. Finally, though, we got a sunny spell, and it seemed to affect the birds so that they wanted to redouble their efforts, as if to make up for lost time; and, once again late at night, Brad gave me a call and told me that the cranes were near Mineral Wells, west of Fort Worth, and were headed for the border, which was about 70 miles away. "The way they're moving, they'll reach the Red River by about mid-afternoon. I think you ought to head down this way. I'm going to stay here, because I have to head back to Houston; but call me around noon, and wherever you are I'll direct you to wherever our boys have gone at that moment. So far, the transmitters are holding out, for the most part. Good luck. I've enjoyed working with you."

I had to call the rest of my guys and tell them I'd be meeting them around 6:00. We had a 350-mile drive ahead of us. Some of them answered on the first ring, but others slept soundly and were difficult to arouse. It took me about half an hour to finish talking to all four of them. In the middle of my calls, Viola got up and left and went into the living room to escape the disturbance. We slept apart for the rest of that night. When I left, a few hours later, I kissed her goodbye, but she responded only with an angry shrug.

The day was crystal-sharp and sunny; visibility was virtually unrestricted. The horizon was as sharp as an inked line. I rode in the back of the van, while Jim and Larry shared the driving chores; I busied myself with tests of the electronic gear. I opened the porthole window on the sidewall, and inhaled the exhilarating air of spring as it rushed past. The brown dead meadow of winter was just beginning to be overtaken by the mint-colored shoots of this year's grasses.

Around noon, we reached the Red River at the little town of Davidson, Oklahoma. I called Brad, who was in Fort Worth, from the pay phone in a tiny Texaco station where we'd stopped to gas up. When he located us on the map, he became very excited. "You're in absolutely perfect position! Our guys called me 30 minutes ago; they'd just crossed the river north of Wichita Falls. They're in Oklahoma now, following the birds west along the Red River Valley. You can't be any more than 15 miles from them. I'll radio Fred now and tell them your position. You stay put, and you should be seeing them any minute."

When I told the students, they all got out and stood around, sometimes looking east down Highway 70, where our colleagues should be coming, and sometimes scanning the sky to see if they could find the cranes.

And then, I saw the flock. A cry, "There they are!" burst from my throat. I felt mist come into my eyes as I watched a grand, elegant promenade of silent-winged birds rowing through the atmosphere. There were perhaps eighty, strung out in a great ragged V like geese, but the V was not clean and well-disciplined, like that of the smaller birds; it bellied and surged, billowing back and forth like a great wave. The individual cranes stood out as if they were Chinese characters, each communicating one thought in an ever-changing message of freedom to us earthbound souls. And then came their voices, low bugling hoots, solemn and wild as the howls of wolves.

I stared, fascinated and worshipful, for several minutes. I was oblivious to science; at that moment, I could not have cared less for numbers, and mathematical models, and data reduction. I was observing nature, yes, but I was a part of it; my consciousness was an essential feature of this scene. I imagined that my impressions were the same as those our forebears in late Pleistocene Europe must have felt when confronted with a flock of a related species. From my high school days, I also remembered what I had read in Aldo Leopold's *Sand County Almanac*; that our appreciation of nature begins with what is pretty, and then our understanding proceeds through higher levels of beauty until, when confronted with something as ineffable as the flight of cranes, the whole system collapses and, unable to use words, we are reduced (or expanded) to mysticism. Words are flawed children of man, I thought, but cranes are an exaltation of God's spirit.

I awoke from this reverie to feel Larry poking me in the shoulder. "They're here, Dr. Cahill!" "Yes," I first dreamily responded, but then realized he was referring to our colleagues, who had just pulled up in two vans. After handshaking all around, we decided we'd better not waste time; we had data to collect. One of the vans would go back to Houston now, and the other would follow us for an hour or so to make sure we weren't having problems; then it, too, would leave us and we would be on our own, tracking birds through the vast wilderness of the West, going we knew not where, following them as surely as if they were puppeteers pulling the strings of our limbs.

Our tracking went off without a hitch; the birds headed straight west, along the river valley; when it split at the junction of the Red and Tierra Blanca rivers, they turned unhesitatingly up the Red. "Just like they're reading the map," Jim said. It was not always easy to follow the flock when they headed off to where no roads went; but luckily, we moved much faster than they did, and as long as we didn't get lost in a quagmire at the end of some country road (as our partners once did), we never lost them for very long. It was encouraging to observe how predictable their paths were. From their heading and speed, we could calculate very closely where they were likely to be in an hour or two. The only worrisome thing we noted was that we were being led to the west, ever farther away from where our home base was; we had hoped that our flock would carry us into regions from which we could run back and forth to our campus, if we needed equipment or a replacement piece of electronic gear. But instead, we were being conducted straight into the wilds of the Texas Panhandle. All we could hope was that they wouldn't keep heading west, cross the Rockies, and leave us stranded 1800 miles from home!

In order to break for dinner, three of us in the van left the birds behind ten miles east of Shamrock, Texas. Computations based on triangulation suggested that they would fly right past us. We left our colleagues in the station wagon to man the monitors to make sure we didn't lose the flock. In the diner in Shamrock, while waiting for our orders, I decided to call Viola. It was a mistake.

"I thought I explained to you that I couldn't be sure where this was going to take us. We can't count on the birds to fly us right into Pawnee Springs. In fact, it's looking less and less likely every hour."

"So, what does this mean? How long is this going to go on? Can I count on seeing you in a week -- a month -- two months?"

"It depends a lot on which direction they fly. I'd say ten days would be a good guess. Maybe a couple less, maybe a little more."

"Well, I never expected to be left alone like this. I feel like you've abandoned me. Don't you think I have needs? I love you."

"I love you, darling, but I can't stop now. I'm in the middle of my work. I'll be back soon and then we can be together for a long time. I miss you, darling." But at the end of my speech I found I was talking into a dead phone.

Back in the van, we tuned in to the approximate transmitter frequencies we'd been using and found the birds. At first, we congratulated ourselves on the accuracy of our estimates; but then, we noticed that the frequencies weren't exactly the same as they had been before. I scratched my head. What the hell was going on -- had our receiver suddenly screwed up?

Then, I got a call from our companions. I asked them for their location, and they said they'd spent the whole time sitting in exactly the same place as we'd left them. The cranes had come down to the ground and were feeding in a bog a few hundred yards away; they suggested we trade places with them, so they could get dinner.

I suddenly realized what was happening. "We can't! We've picked up another flock! It's one of the ones that was lost before. All of a sudden, we've got two flocks to follow!"

I wasn't sure what to do. If only one team followed each flock, the data would be poorer and there'd be a greater risk of losing them both; but I was reluctant to abandon the rediscovered birds. Yet, if the two flights followed independent routes, we could get farther and farther apart.

I made the decision. The wagon was to proceed into Shamrock, but couldn't stop for dinner; they would have to get along with a meal of sandwiches and sodas bought in a grocery. They would then return to their original position and commence observing their birds. Meanwhile, we would pursue the new flock, which seemed to be heading straight north. In a couple of hours, before we got too far apart for radio communication, we'd check our positions again. If the cranes we'd been following all along hadn't moved, or if they went off in a different direction from these new ones, we'd abandon the second flock and return to our originals. Otherwise, we'd try to track the two groups independently for as long as we could.

Dusk was approaching, and I was apprehensive. We'd never tried to track at night before, but we had to do it; we couldn't let them get away from us. Sleeping in shifts was all we could do, and it was more difficult now that our two teams had been separated; a mistake by one person, which was not such a big deal before, could wipe out the whole project. Since I was too nervous to sleep, I directed Larry into the back to take the first nap.

Our birds were winging languidly north. They were rather easy to follow; they meandered back and forth across the highway, never straying more than two or three miles away to the east or west. It was almost as if they were using it, rather than a river or mountain range, as a guide for their travels.

In about forty-five minutes, we got a call from the wagon. "Our birds just left! They're headed straight north -- I think they're right behind yours. We're just north of Wheeler. What's your position?"

"Approaching the Canadian River. We're no more than twenty miles ahead of you."

"Right. We'll keep in touch."

And then, as we passed through the town of Canadian, and descended the rolling hills into the river valley, our birds pivoted around in a great spiral and landed in a squalling horde on the sandflats; and, a little over an hour later, they were joined in the same spot by the other birds from our original flock.

I couldn't believe it. This was an amazing coincidence, or it was something more than coincidence; but how could these birds have found each other after flying separately for weeks?

Well, however it had happened, we were very happy at the fortunate way things had turned out. We were together again, and had much more data to collect. And, surprisingly, the birds spent the whole night at the Canadian, which meant all of us got a good chance to rest.

The next day, at sunrise, the whole massive assembly, now numbering close to two hundred birds, rose with a great ululation from the vaporous river bed, circled the area once with a majestic spiraling gesture, and winged off to the north. Their flight plan seemed to admit of no nonsense today. They followed a virtually straight path, veering slightly to the east of true north. Crossing the Oklahoma border at about noon, they continued without stopping, soaring over the Beaver and Cimarron river valleys; and only when they entered Kansas did they stop, in a pasture with a large enclosed pond south of Meade.

We spoke to the property owner, an elderly farmer named Charles Grandridge who had been watching "santhills" for decades; he told us that they stopped at his pond every year. This was about an average year, he said in a quavering voice, in terms of numbers of birds; on rare occasions, though, he'd seen ten times as many as this. In fact, he said, he wrote it down in a log book whenever he noticed them. He produced this book (or rather these books, with well over a thousand pages of notes going back more than 20 years) for us, and it was a gold mine! This man not only watched cranes, he counted them and made notes on their behavior; and every day's entry contained barometric, wind, and temperature information. I realized that these data, together with our own observations and those of others, if we could find them, might be used to help produce a working hypothesis or maybe even a predictive theory of *Grus* migration. Luckily, Mr. Grandridge agreed to let us photocopy his notes. He and I drove in his ancient truck all the way to Dodge City, where a puzzled drugstore owner watched us feed nickels into his copy machine all morning. Larry drove over around noon to pick me up, and I took my leave of Mr. Grandridge, me and my stack of pages, and we promised to keep in touch.

The cranes took only three days to cross Kansas, stopping for various lengths of time in river valleys and reservoirs to rest and feed. They were staying together, and we were doing remarkably well at following them, in my estimation. Of the fifteen individuals from these two flocks that we had originally fitted with transmitters in Mexico, we were still able to follow eight; we had no idea whether the rest had died, left the company, or contracted a power failure in their radio collars.

Late one afternoon, in a phone booth on the main street of the little town of Alma, Nebraska, I called my contact man in Montana, Professor Chase Wallburton. Our cranes had just crossed the Nebraska border an hour or so earlier, and had settled down into a good-sized basin behind a dam on the Republican River.

Chase answered his phone in a booming voice; he was a robust, rustic man of sixty who'd spent his entire academic career at Montana (although he'd been born in Delaware County, Pennsylvania), having turned down opportunities to teach or join the administration of a dozen other colleges all over the country. He claimed that once he left the mountains, he started to feel nervous. With his older brother Francis, a similarly rough and ready chap, he'd written a fascinating book on grizzly bears, based on their close observations of the animals in the remote wilderness, that had gone to the best-seller lists and stayed there for several months. I felt privileged to know both of them, and I never knew either of them to do anything in a subtle way; they made their opinions clear, and by God, if you didn't agree with them you were in for an argument. But neither of them was close-minded, and loved to learn new things about nature. Chase had agreed to work on our project, although it was a bit tame for his taste, because he wanted to bring in some money to his department so that he could later buy himself some time in northern Alaska observing polar bears. There was a book contract in the works, and Francis was up there now laying the groundwork for their work.

"Yes, Chase," I said into the phone, "It's Bruce Cahill from Cimarron State, and I'm calling from southern Nebraska to tell you we've got some mighty nervous *Grus canadensis* on our hands. In a few days we're going to want to turn them over to you."

"The hell you say, Bruce. The little bastards really been coverin' the ground, have they?"

"Damn right. They even go for it in the middle of the night. Raises hell with a man's sack time."

"I know what you're sayin', pal, especially when you're on the road without a little woman to snug up to. Or did you bring one along?"

"Afraid not. Listen, Chase, the birds are doing eighty miles a day, sometimes more. I have a feeling they're going to head for those big reservoirs on the Missouri River, up in South Dakota. That'd be almost straight north of here, and they've been sticking pretty close to north on the compass for several days now. How long do you think it'd take you to get down somewhere around there from Missoula?"

"Well, as you know, Bruce, we're going to do things a little different from you. We're going to do most of our tracking in a plane. It's all fitted up and ready to go, so we could get to Rapid City in four or five hours. But my instinct tells me to wait before we leave. I don't know if you can trust them big-assed birds to act rationally. They don't call 'em bird-brains for nothin'. Tell you what, you keep chasin' them little bastards until they get a bit closer to where you have to leave 'em, and call me again then. Gimme eight hours notice, and I guarantee you we'll be down and ready to take over."

Some guys have real style, I thought to myself. He never mentioned anything about an aircraft before. It must have belonged to one of his old Main Line buddies, out to spend the spring and summer out in the wild west. (Anything past Cleveland.) But I had to hand it to Chase, he wasn't afraid to improvise. I just hope he knew what he was doing and didn't scare our birds into heading back to Mexico to get away from him.

The next day, our cranes surprised us again; they split into three groups, very unequal in size. About 140 headed off to the northwest, following the Republican River and then cutting over to the Platte. In about four days, they made it to the Nebraska sandhills, their namesakes, which are absolutely covered with little glacial pothole ponds. They stayed there for a little more than a day and then headed off directly to the north; it was this group that Wallburton followed in his plane, some of them all the way to the Arctic. Although none of the transmitters survived the whole journey, it didn't appear to matter to Chase's boys; they seemed to have great luck finding the flock from the air.

The second group of twenty or so birds scattered in all directions and took up residence in the immediate vicinity of the southern Nebraska reservoir where we'd left them; a last group of about thirty birds continued on a northerly course. They did continue all the way to the lakes created by the big earth fill dams in South Dakota. Larry and I followed them that far, and then unfortunately lost them; they flew north across the reservoir, and by the time we could find a road that crossed it, they had vanished. Of course, we couldn't have followed them much farther anyway, due to a combination of our own commitments back at Cimarron and the gradual loss of transmitter power that we'd been noticing. It was sad to give up after losing track of them; the letdown really left us despondent. It was like leaving a group of old friends and not being able to say goodbye to them.

And thus it was that we returned to Pawnee Springs. The project had just begun, of course. Parts of it are continuing to this day, although I no longer have as central a role as I did then. I'm co-author of six papers that came out of the work, and I wrote one on my own, together with Mr. Grandridge, on the historical record of crane migrations in southern Kansas. Somehow I'm proudest of that paper, even though the general theory of migration didn't come out of it, the way I'd hoped. I'm still working on that. Damn, I'm starting to sound like Pyke McKenna.

The money that those projects brought in was very helpful to my professional development. I shepherded a total of nine students to M. S. degrees; I got all those publications on my record; I worked up a new graduate class on the subject, and enticed Willard up every year to give a few lectures; and I was promoted to Associate Professor in 1968. Not bad, four years, for a guy straight out of grad school; fastest anybody'd done it in our division since Pyke.

I think I grew up a lot doing that work. It's rare to be able to plunge right into a big project as I did, cold, and to be successful. I contributed a lot, and was recognized by some outstanding scientists for the excellence of my contributions; that gave me a lot of self-confidence that I needed. I found out that I was able to work on important projects, sharing the work load with my collaborators and still being free to design my own work. And some of the glory came my way, too.

It made up for some of the losses I sustained in my personal life. Viola felt very neglected, I think, and our marriage was never the same afterwards. She and I became more free, in a sense, to go our own ways; but this produced a great deal of pain and misunderstanding on many occasions. So who said life was a bed of roses? Anyhow, we continued to love each other, and I think we still do, although we no longer say it to one another. I still think of her at Christmas, and on our birthdays and our various anniversaries, those days when we did special things together for the first time. Viola, darling, you were more beautiful than those cranes, and when you migrated to the north, I lost the best friend I ever had. Think of me too, in the middle of those dark nights, when you hear the whispers of migrating birds; my spirit is calling to you. I love you.

Messersmith

(A letter from Dr. Harry Messersmith, a Ph.D. student in the Department of Botany at Ohio State while Pyke was there, currently professor of ecology and systematics at the University of Washington in Seattle.)

I will try to cast my mind back over the years. It will be quite difficult to give a well-rounded picture of what Pyke McKenna was like in graduate school, first of all because I didn't really know him that well. He worked for Krantzler and I was in old man Donovan's group, so we were at opposite ends of the hall. In addition, he was specializing in research on plant nutrition and physiology, and I was more involved in systematics, specifically the taxonomy of ferns, so I spent most of my time squinting at dried specimens through a dissecting microscope, while he was hauling buckets of water through the greenhouse.

One thing we did have in common, though, is that we both worked very hard, putting in very long hours in evenings and on weekends for our research. So he and I were often the only ones there and naturally would tend to swap a few greetings, and after a while it became almost a private joke to see who had left the latest the previous night or spent the most time there on New Year's Day.

RICHARD LARSON

We came from totally different backgrounds. I am from the deep South, born and raised in Lafayette, Louisiana, the son of a restaurant owner; and McKenna was from the rural Midwest, a farming background, I believe. I was stubby and overweight (still am) and he was rangy and tall. Pyke was from OSU's undergraduate school, so all that he did after graduation was to move upstairs. I went to LSU as an undergraduate; Donovan, my future research director, gave a series of lectures there on lichens, mosses, and ferns, that I found very interesting, and he invited me to study with him at Ohio State as a Ph.D. candidate.

So I became a real outsider. I came into Columbus on the train, early one August Saturday afternoon, with no place to live, no car, and not knowing a soul in town. I tried to call Donovan and he wasn't at home. I was really disoriented for the first time, sitting there in the station with my trunk and my two suitcases. I started to wonder whether I hadn't made a really serious mistake. Finally, I began to realize that I was really on my own. I made a decision; I hired a taxi for the afternoon to cart me around, and by six o'clock I had a place to live; by eight o'clock, I had found a bar near the campus; and by ten o'clock, I had a girlfriend for the evening. I began to think these Yankee towns weren't so bad after all.

I think no Southerners are ever prepared for the fierceness of winter in the North; I had never been farther north than Nashville, and that was in July. By the middle of October, I determined that my apartment had no insulation at all. I would wake up in the morning, seeing my breath in front of my face. Little drifts of snow would form inside my bedroom where it blew through the crevices in the window. I'd turned the heat on, all right, but the landlord like as not had forgotten to fill the boiler. Damn, what a way to live.

Everything was so different in Columbus; the food, for example. No grits, no fish, no Cajun food; the dried red beans I was able to find were like library paste. And in those days, there was not even any thought of spicy hot food; the Midwestern diet was totally bland, meat cooked until it fell off the bone, boiled potatoes and overcooked vegetables and no rice dishes except for rice pudding. I had to have Tabasco sauce sent to me Parcel Post. Not that I ever had that much time to cook; I spent so much time at the lab that I ate most of my meals at the student center; that institutional, steam-table fare found in colleges everywhere. And Pyke was usually there too, slurping that pale-tasting food up as he sat by himself, wrapped up in some article or book related to his work. When I did cook for some friends, once in a while I'd have Pyke over. He'd say he liked my cooking a lot, but he didn't eat a hell of a lot of it; of course, I did make it damn hot for northern tastes.

Actually, I recall now, Pyke lived fairly close to where I did for a time, just after I arrived in the fall of 1946. He had already been there for a while; I think he was one of the first to enter after the war was over. We lived just north and west of the campus, on a street called Kenny Road, or maybe it was Kenny Boulevard; he lived about a half-mile further away than I did.

Before I went in to the lab in the mornings, I used to stop off in a little restaurant that had the odd name of Mimi's Well, for a cup of coffee and a roll; and once in a while they had fresh oranges that they squeezed by hand for juice. That was great. Pyke tended to stop in on those days, also (they'd put a big hand-lettered banner out facing the street announcing their great orange bonanza), and we would sometimes sit together and talk for a bit. In the evenings, the place changed its personality completely; it became a typical Greenwich Village coffeehouse. For a long time they had a resident jazz trio, alto sax, piano, and drums. They played quite sophisticated stuff for those days; I suppose it was some form of bop. Anyway, it was quite popular among a certain set; all the artsy-fartsy types would sit around for hours and argue existential philosophy and try to achieve new levels of insight. It was pretty heavy going for biologists, and Pyke and I weren't around very much except in the mornings.

Frankly, I didn't find his company particularly stimulating! He seemed to be mainly interested in the weather, in local sports, and in his research, roughly in that order. He seemed like a real typecast Midwesterner to me; long gangly legs, plaid shirts, big Adam's-apple, sucking on toothpicks, and saying things like "Yup, sure is" and "Holy gosh!"

I actually think he spent more time at his work than even I did, and his research always seemed to yield productive results. Consequently, even though he used to take part of the summers off to work as a biologist for the Ohio highway department, he was able to finish up much sooner than I did.

He and a few of his friends, including me, had quite a bash to celebrate his departure. I wouldn't be surprised if they still talk about it in our old department. My head still hurts when I think about it, and none of us was even drinking anything except beer, except toward the end when some of us stumbled onto a small cache of harder stuff; we made a big mistake when we started to go through that. But I'm getting ahead of myself. The party was held in the apartment of a girl we both knew, a fellow graduate student named Wanda who, up to that time, I had thought was going out with a chemistry major with whom I'd seen her quite often. But he wasn't at her place that night, and she surprisingly spent most of the evening sitting on Pyke's lap, kissing him over and over again. They'd only stop to drink a beer or dance a slow number, clinging together and pressing their hands on each other's fannies. She was much shorter than he was, but similarly muscular and rangy, with slightly bowed legs and slim, simian arms. They made quite a couple.

The rest of us spent the evening drinking and singing; we had an impromptu competition to see who could devise the most apropos and scurrilous words to the song "Goodnight, Irene," which was popular then. I don't remember any of the versions any more, but I do remember some of them seeming screamingly funny at the time. I guess you had to be there.

Toward 2:00 I think most of the guests started to wander off. I was not among them, though, for I had fallen asleep at, I estimate, about a half-hour before that time in Wanda's bathtub, clutching a bottle of lime-flavored vodka. This was the stuff I referred to earlier, that caused one of the grave errors of my drinking career. To put it bluntly, it caused me to pass out in that selfsame bathroom, where I fell down and gashed my upper lip on something unforgiving, like maybe the corner of the sink. Luckily, I suppose, I was literally feeling no pain at that time and was able to crawl off into the bathtub before I could do more serious injury to myself. To ensure privacy, I had pulled the shower curtain so no one could see me. I woke up, probably around 6, with an agonizing headache combined with a terrible stiff neck and my aforementioned cut, which had bled freely down onto my white shirt. No one else seemed to be around so I decided I'd better try to go home and get some bandages and aspirin, or just to sleep it off in my own bed.

All the lights were off in the place and I was trying to grope my way to the front door to let myself out, but I couldn't seem to find the way. My hand fell by chance on a light switch and I snapped it on, hoping to be able to see the door. I did, but only after seeing a strange tableau on the living-room floor. Pyke and Wanda had pulled all the cushions and pillows off the couch and chairs and were lying naked and asleep in the clutter; Wanda's legs were draped over Pyke's chest. Their clothing was scattered to all corners of the room. I distinctly remember a brassiere hanging from the arm of a light fixture and a man's shoe hooked over a doorknob.

My turning on the light disturbed Pyke, and he put his hand over his eyes with a groan and rolled over on his stomach, but he didn't fully wake up, and neither did Wanda. I was really embarrassed, snapped the light out right away, and tried to tiptoe throught the darkness toward where I had seen the door, but I slipped on something silky and fell down with a thud. This time Pyke did seem to wake up, and he said "What the hell?" into the darkness, but by this time I was going out the door and I don't think either of them ever knew exactly what had happened.

I saw Wanda at the lab after that, but I never raised the subject with her. Pyke had left the following day and I didn't see him again until about ten years later, at a meeting we both attended in Kansas City.

I remember very little about that meeting; I remember that I chaired a symposium on a subject that several of us had stirred some controversy on; I remember that Pyke came to some of the sessions; but I don't remember talking with him very much. It seemed that he was somewhat shy, perhaps feeling diffident about the fact that he, a small-college biologist, was in there with all the world-famous speakers who were scheduled to give presentations in that symposium. Anyhow, I don't recall him going out with us all that week, and, in fact, I don't remember seeing him around much at all except on that first day when he came, I suppose, to hear me speak.

And that, I am afraid, was the last time I ever saw him. I was sorry to hear of his death, and I am sorry that I can't help you out with anything more interesting about Pyke McKenna. If there was a scholarship fund, or something similar, established in his name, please let me know because I'd like to make a contribution to it. I hope your memoir goes well, and I would like very much to have a copy when it comes out, if that would be possible.

McNamara

(A letter from Robert S. McNamara, Secretary of Defense.)

ear Mr. McKenna:

I deeply regret to inform you that your brother, Lt. Col. Thomas M. McKenna, was killed in action on Jan. 31, 1968, at approximately 0300 that morning, in Saigon, South Vietnam. Col. McKenna was one of a number of American citizens who died in a surprise attack on the Embassy of the United States. Please accept my deep personal sympathy for this tragic event. A representative of the U. S. Armed Services will be contacting you shortly with regard to your wishes for funeral arrangements and other matters. Since the death occurred in a designated combat zone, the U. S. Government will pay all funeral expenses.

Viola

(This is part of a long letter my ex-wife wrote to me just before Pyke died.)

I still remember the day you came home to me with beer on your breath and an ecstatic expression on your face, and how you were so excited over having met this fascinating man. We even made love, which you had been too busy to do since we had moved to Pawnee Springs. And I remember the first time I ever saw Pyke, when he came over for dinner just before classes started. I wanted to make bouillabaisse, which I had just read about that week in the Denver Sunday paper, and this seemed like a good excuse. Although there wasn't that much fresh fish around town, I located some catfish that looked pretty good, and I bought the shrimp frozen and the clams in a can. I was fairly well satisfied with it, considering. Then I let Pyke into the house while you were upstairs in the bathroom; he was about 15 minutes early. He had brought exotic flowers, those huge purple lilies; he must have stolen them from the greenhouse in the department, I don't believe any florist for five hundred miles around had anything like that in stock. He smiled and blushed like a boy as he handed them to me. And as the evening went on we both were quite carried away by Pyke's style and manner. He was such a charming man, I thought, so witty and elegant in conversation, so cultured. And he really appreciated my cooking; I could tell that he was knowledgeable about food by the questions he asked, how had I steamed the fish fillets, was there anise in the dessert, etc. So when I went to bed that evening, having had too much wine, I couldn't sleep. I always had a problem with new and attractive men in my life, even then when we'd only been married a short time. When I met one my imagination would run riot, and I imagined a lot of things that evening about Pyke. I wanted to make love to you and close my eyes tightly and pretend it was him, but unfortunately you'd had even more to drink than me and were snoring away, so I had to do it to myself which I was never very good at. It took me forever and I thought sure you were going to wake up when I was in the middle of it. So I maybe had three hours sleep, and then you were up bright and early with one of your Saturday Evening Posts sticking me in the back, and I just couldn't do it with you; I was hung over and hardly able to move. But you were a good sport about it as you always seemed to be.

Still, I was pretty surprised after classes began and I started to be alone all day, before I went back to work, when Pyke called me up. The first thing he said to me on the phone was, "Mrs. Cahill, my dear, you have won my heart with fish chowder and I am your slave. You temptress, you knew we prairie boys can't resist properly prepared *fruits de mer*." I didn't know what to say, he sounded so serious; I suppose I giggled a lot. He had the most erotic voice, so deep and dark. Then he said, "I would like to share with you another delightful sort of foodstuff, a recipe that I invented myself. I just happen to have an extra jar of *Mammillaria* jelly, and I would like to give it to you." I asked him to repeat what he'd said, because it sounded like he was talking about mammaries. That made him laugh, and he said, "No, no, *Mammillaria*, the common pincushion cactus that grows around here, one of the many sticky, stinging, or spiny prairie plants that make it nearly impossible to walk around the hills in your bare feet. In the early spring it blossoms, a yellow flower almost as big across as the rest of the plant is; it lasts only a day, and then a beautiful red, berry-like fruit develops. If you can get to it before the birds and insects do, it has a delightful fresh flavor. And I have devised a way to capture this flavor in preserves. I won't tell you all my secrets, but one of the ingredients is chopped lemon rind. I guarantee you will never be able to buy this in a store;

the plant doesn't exactly lend itself to mass cultivation. May I come over now and drop off a jar?"

I told him I was reluctant to have him stop over right then, that the house was in a mess and you were at work, et cetera, but he said that was stuff and nonsense, that he would only stay for a few minutes, and besides, he had a lab to teach that afternoon; so I said it would be all right. He must have been in a phone booth a few blocks away, because in about two minutes he was at the door with his little jar. It was no bigger than a baby food jar and may actually have been one, but the label was gone and in its place was a glued-on, hand-drawn label on glossy paper; with a picture of a peacock, all colored in with bright enamel-like spots of shiny paint, and gothic lettering that said "Ye Gelatine Incroyable, Das Gelee Unico, Fabrique McKenna, Marco Non Registrada." Pyke was grinning and seemed very excited. He insisted that I try some that minute. He'd even brought the proper crackers, he said, and drew out a from his knapsack a little package of those flat, unsalted English water biscuits with the browned edges. So I spread a little of the stuff on one and ate it in two bites. It certainly was different, I'd say that for it. It was partly like a very astringent fruit jelly, like persimmon; and partly it had a sort of musty flavor, like raw mushrooms; and there was even a little hint of fishiness, more a smell than a taste, like the salty sulphury odor you get on the beach in Michigan in the summer with the gulls flying around. He asked me if I liked it, and I said it was very interesting but that I needed time to think about it and acquire a taste. Then he said, "I'm sure you will. I'm counting on you to help me make more next spring. We can go out to the west and comb the flat-topped hills, and find twice as much as I ever found before. We'll be a great team, you and I." Then he excused himself, saying "Try some more later; I'm sure it'll grow on you."

Well, I didn't think much more about it after he left, but then I started to feel dizzy and weak, like I had to lie down. When I closed my eyes on the bed, first of all the bed felt like it was moving across the room and up the wall like a pendulum. That scared me and the feeling didn't stop when I opened my eyes. Then I started to see things, not really visions, not at first, but like an intensification of the patterns and textures of what was already there. The shadows and spots on the walls and the ceiling started to form themselves into swirling images of flowers, or the faces of strange animals, and they would dissolve into each other and move away across the surface, drift off and be replaced by other bizarre images in a way that was marvelous and frightening at the same time. And when I chanced to look at my own hand, it was as though I could see it as it was now, and at the same time it was smaller and softer like a little girl's, and also it was gnarled and bony and covered with brown spots, like an old woman's. And this was all at the same time, not like three shifting or superimposed pictures, but like seeing the same thing from three different angles, as if your eyes were not fixed in your head but were sending signals back to your brain from places around the room. And if I closed my eyes, I would see the patterns that I guess are always there on your eyelids, but much more noticeable and dramatic; great maroon shapes like drapery that would unfurl into liquid banners in deep hot reds and dark oranges, spangled by points of pure gold light that would come and go like electric sparks.

You may not believe this, but while this was all happening to me, I didn't make the connection between those feelings and Pyke's jelly. Maybe I'm just naive, but I hadn't thought a great deal about mind-altering drugs, and in fact I didn't even know that you could eat something and have it affect you. I thought you had to smoke it, like marijuana, or inject it, like heroin. Gradually, though, something filtered through my consciousness; he had done this to me.

I suppose I should have been furious at Pyke drugging me without my consent, but all I could do at the time was lie there and let it happen. It was like my body just had a film to unroll that I had to watch until it ran out. The feelings I had would change rapidly, so I would go from feeling nauseous, as if I was being smothered by something slimy, to pure exhilaration, as if I was soaring among cool clouds in the sunlight.

One remarkable vision I had was of a shimmering castle, but a castle made entirely of cloudy plastic, something like Tupperware, as though some eccentric billionaire housewife had bought hundreds of every kind of container and had them assembled into this; and as I watched, the glowing light from within it gradually reddened, and the whole thing slowly softened and the towers collapsed, fell over and settled into an undifferentiated mass that gradually melted into a dark and slippery heap, steaming and bubbling away. Then out of the center of this greasy sludge, there emerged a giant glittering beetle, like a scarab, whose body seemed to be made of gold and ebony. Although it had come out of the filth, it looked glossy and immaculate, as though it had been burnished to a high sheen with soft and precious fabrics. It poised itself on top of the foul mass and then rose slowly into the air, beating its giant wings and making a deep humming sound. Then it began to fly toward me, unhurriedly and premeditatedly, like a big kite that someone was reeling in from the skies. I was not afraid of the thing at all, only fascinated to see what was going to happen. And finally, when it was about three feet from the end of my nose, it stopped and hovered. I could see that it was as big as I was, and the humming it made filled my head so that I couldn't think or move. But it seemed as though the humming was being modulated somehow, so that out of the hum there would occasionally appear words, words phrased in a very mechanical and synthetic tonality, as if some robot was speaking. The words didn't make a whole lot of sense to me; some were merely nonsense syllables, and others that I remember were "all," "purify," "heart," "abandoned," and "time." Then, the words stopped being formed, and the beetle continued to hover in front of me, as if it were waiting for an answer; but I didn't know what I should do, and I only smiled; and finally, as I watched, it slowly rose up, very high in the air above me, heeled over and banked like a plane, and shot off, too fast for me to follow; and I was left behind, confused, and back in our bedroom again.

The absolute worst thing that happened was toward the end of the whole episode, when my vision went through a series of shifts from normal full-color into a gradual fade to a sort of sepia, and finally went completely out and I could only see things in black and white. When that happened, I was sure I was going to die. But I closed my eyes, and turned over and moaned into the pillow for a while, and when I opened my eyes, I could see normally again.

Finally, after what seemed like days, I began to feel that I had a little control over my own being. So I stood up (it took a tremendous effort) and walked out to the kitchen. It was like wading through deep molasses. Sweat was pouring off my forehead. I found the jar, and by thinking about it very hard, I was able to throw it away in the garbage, burying it under the potato peelings and old newspapers so you wouldn't find it. Then, I was somehow back in bed and you were shaking me, asking if something was wrong. You looked very worried. I told you I wasn't feeling well at all and didn't want any dinner and would you mind letting me rest and making yourself something. All of which was very true, I just wanted to be left alone to sleep off this horrible feeling I had which was making my brain feel like a lump of Swiss cheese.

The next morning I was finally more or less back to feeling like myself. I even managed to kiss you goodbye and joke about possibly having eaten something weird, maybe a combination of cold chicken and moldy pickles. After you left, I was building myself up to a fine fury; I wanted to tell that McKenna asshole that he'd practically killed me and I was thinking about pressing charges. Assault, something. But how could I reach him? He had no telephone. I didn't want to waste my time and go over to where he lived, because I had no idea if he'd be around, and I knew also he wouldn't be over at the campus at this hour. Besides, I might run into you and I didn't want to lie about what I was doing. So I compromised on a letter. If I could get it out that morning, I figured, he would probably get it tomorrow. So I wrote an angry note, two pages long, typed, single spaced, not threatening but he would surely get the message, and, I thought, think twice before trying to poison someone else. But after the mailman took it, the phone rang not two minutes later and you know who it was. He asked me how I was and I started to splutter. I called him a lot of foul names and told him what had happened. And the bastard didn't even say he was sorry. He started to blame me; said that he'd given his jelly to many other people and all it ever did was to cause a slight buzz in the head, or a slight numbness in the lips. He accused me of having irrational anxiety when I was confronted by food that hadn't come in a sanitized package from the supermarket. He said that there was nothing in the stuff that could cause me any harm, it was all a natural high. Nothing chemical like LSD. Finally, all I could do was start yelling. I never wanted him to come near me again, I said; he could shove his natural highs up his ass; he should be locked up. I don't know how much of it he heard, because when I stopped shouting for a minute all I could hear was the humming of the line; he'd hung up.

President Ogden

(Dr. Trevor Selby Ogden has been president of Cimarron State since 1956. Although scheduled for retirement this year, he has agreed to stay on while a search for his successor is continuing. He obtained his Ed.D. from the University of Connecticut in 1932, taught mathematics and was an administrator in the public high schools of Valhalla, N.Y. until 1949, and came to Cimarron State to head the mathematics department in 1950. After a two-year stint as dean of students, he was appointed president when the former president, one Lamar W. Wilmot, resigned to "pursue opportunities in the aerospace industry" in Texas. Dr. Ogden is a small, serious, somewhat paunchy man who wears a black eye patch. He is small-featured, pale, nervous, and energetic. He nearly always dresses conservatively in black suits, white shirt and red and black [or green and black] striped ties. On the job, he is a hard-nosed professional who is not given to nonsense. I have heard even Dean Pfaff stammer and struggle for words when Dr. Ogden is on the phone. However, outside his office he can be flamboyant; I have seen him late at night, in evening dress, a cape, and a broadbrimmed, floppy hat, looking like Aristide Bruant in Toulouse-Lautrec›s painting, striding across the campus arm-in-arm with a strikingly tall, blond, Nordic-looking woman in a white gown, who I am sure was not his wife. The image was so out of character for our campus that I would not have been greatly surprised to see her leading a jaguar on a leash.

RICHARD LARSON

His office is in the center of the clock tower of Old Main, with a panoramic view of the campus. The visitor, after being granted permission to enter it by his secretary (a small dark woman named Mrs. Mullen), ascends a short, steep, darkened flight of stairs to see the president himself standing above, sanctified in a halo of light formed by an arched doorway. I was fortunate to see this busy man in his dramatic sanctuary on an errand of what must have seemed to him of trifling importance. He agreed to a brief interview after several refusals.)

I tried to know all the faculty when I became president. If I'd had the time, I would have liked to meet all the students as well. I spent a great deal of time arranging meetings with every division of the college. I asked every dean and department head to arrange a time when every member of his department or division could attend a meeting with me. I kept careful records of all these meetings. Professor McKenna did not attend the original meeting I had with the biology faculty, and he did not attend either of the two subsequent meetings I arranged for those who could not visit with me at the first round of meetings. I sent out memos and I asked my secretary of the time, Mrs. Huggins, to call those who did not respond to them. She did not get through to Professor McKenna. I think he was the only one, certainly there were no more than one or two others at the most, whom I had absolutely no luck in getting through to. Accordingly, I didn't exactly get off on the right foot where he was concerned. Of course, I knew about him, both the good and the bad, through discussions with people on the faculty over the years, and through his escapades as reported in the newspaper, and through those odd letters he wrote to the editor of the paper, letters in which you could never quite tell for sure if he was being serious or satirical. Those letters practically filled the file we had on him. You look a trifle shocked, didn't you know we have a media file on every member of the faculty? There's nothing secret about it; we just think that it's important for us to know the image the college projects in the public press. So every time there's an article on one of our staff in the newspaper, or if he writes a letter to the editor, or runs for public office, we clip it out and file it. If they appear on the radio or TV, there's also a note on their appearance in the file, also. Of course, we never use the information in any derogatory sense, but we just feel we ought to have it in case anyone asks questions about some staff member. Not that I mean we divulge the material in the files to just anyone. Usually, what happens is that someone will call and ask about whether some professor or other would be a suitable lecturer for the graduating class of a nearby high school, or the garden club, or an athletic banquet; and we can use the material in the file, which after all has already appeared in the public press, so that the person calling can make an objective judgment. Anyway, McKenna had a particularly substantial file because of all the public comment he had drawn and that he had made on his own. But I don't think I ever met him personally until that scandal with the son of the trustee, Virgil Fincher from Totterboro, I think that happened before your time.

As it happened, Fincher's son, a boy of eighteen, Bob or Bud or some such name, was in Professor McKenna's introductory biology class; and being an ambitious youth he took copious notes, writing down exactly what the instructor said. It seems Professor McKenna spent a lot of his time in that class on sexuality, whether of molds or mosses or macaques, or people for that matter, and he apparently did not stand on ceremony when it came to the proper naming of certain activities and organs that have perfectly good Latin polysyllabic descriptors. He tended to use the short and simple nouns and verbs that the students already knew. I should reassure you that I am a great believer in academic freedom, but you must remember the time in which this incident took place, we had only shortly before this rid ourselves of some of the more extreme excesses of such as Senator Joseph McCarthy, but there was still a lot of it going around. The fires took a long time to smolder themselves out here in the back woods. So academic freedom, yes, but academic freedom tempered to the reality of the times, to the wisdom of the times. But to return to the boy Fincher and his father. The boy wrote down everything, even to the drawings Professor McKenna made on the blackboard. I understand that Professor McKenna spent a great deal of time on these drawings, with different colored chalks and shadings and perspectives; and you know already, I believe, that he was an individual of some artistic gifts. Thus, even when we allow for some loss of realism in the translation by the boy of Professor McKenna's multicolored drawing, using a number 1 lead pencil, to the blue-lined, spiral-bound paper of his notebook, and also allow that his father may have lacked some considerable degree of appreciation for the sophisticated fundamental biological principles that I imagine Professor McKenna was trying to get across, I think we can understand the outrage that Mr. Fincher felt when he saw his son's drawing and the words that had been used to label it staring up at him from his coffee table.

So, not knowing anything about any of this yet, I came into my office Monday to find one of those beige "while-you-were-out" slips saying that Mr. Fincher had called before 8 a.m. I was to call him at a local number given on the slip. The last trustees meeting had only been on the previous Wednesday so I had no idea what could have come up. I made the call and found that he had come to town (having left Totterboro, as it turned out, only an hour or two after he had first seen the drawing his son had made), and had driven the 200 or so miles through a driving rain, and arrived at the Howard Johnson's Motor Lodge on the east side of town at just before midnight. He wouldn't tell me what was on his mind, just said it was a matter of the utmost urgency that affected the future of Cimarron as an accredited institution of learning. He wanted to discuss the matter with me before he approached the other trustees. He also said that he didn't want to travel to the campus, because he had a valuable document and he didn't want to risk dropping it in a mud puddle. So he hoped I wouldn't mind if I came over to the motel as soon as possible. It wouldn't take long, he said, and he was sure that I would be able to reach a joint decision with him that would assure that the future of Cimarron would be bright. So I cancelled or postponed several important meetings that were on the agenda for the morning, and got in my own personal car, yes, my famous straight-eight Packard (since it was too early for the vehicle service to be open), and drove myself to Howard Johnson's. I had really hoped that Fincher would have met me in the lobby, but he was nowhere in sight. I was able to call him in his room, however, and he asked me to come up right away. He said he'd ordered a pot of coffee so I wouldn't have to delay any further. So I went up and Fincher was in his pajamas, looking an absolute mess; I'm sure he hadn't slept the previous night, his eyes looked like road maps of New Jersey. The room was littered with crumpled paper and there were two empty Jack Daniel's bottles on the dresser. He got right to the point; he said, "Dr. Ogden, you have a maniac on your payroll. He's worse than a burglar or a rapist, because he's violating our children's minds. He's opening up those innocent minds and pouring filth into them. He's breeding a generation of depraved, antisocial maniacs just like himself. I want you to look at this picture that my son copied off your blackboard - paid for with public funds - after that monster smeared his vile pornography all over it. My baby boy, whose tiny pink nose I was so happy to wipe only a very few short years ago. When I think of my tax money going toward keeping that man alive, I feel an attack of mayhem coming on. I feel like kicking his ass until his nose bleeds." He handed me a glossy print of the page from the boy's notebook; how he'd managed to get this work done on a Sunday, I don't know.

I was speechless, not so much out of outrage over Professor McKenna's tactics, but at the gall of this man to drag me clear across town to show me this vulgar little sketch. So this is what was going to bring down the college? This was going to corrupt our children, in an age when sexually related obscenities were openly spoken on the stage in New York City, and it was only a matter of time until full nudity and simulated sexual intercourse were going to be performed there, and whores in West German bistros were infecting our GIs with venereal diseases we didn't even have names for yet? And we were already becoming deeply involved in Southeast Asia and the sordid politics and sociology of that hellhole, and anyone with half a brain could see what was going to happen there. But this was Pawnee Springs, I had to remind myself, and I had a job of public relations to do. This is where I earn my money, I said to myself. "Mr. Fincher," I said, "I agree that this drawing is in very poor taste. I understand your anger that young people are being exposed to material such as this under the guise of science education. I intend to return to my office at once, and call the teacher who perpetrated this travesty into my office today, and tell him that we do not believe that teaching using this sort of material meets the standards that the public expects to see upheld at Cimarron State College. I will demand that he write a letter of apology to you and that he immediately prepare a report for me on the ways he intends to change his syllabus in order to preclude the possibility of anything like this ever happening again. But,

Mr. Fincher, let us leave it at that. Let us not give this man the satisfaction of publicity. In these times those who rage against our civilized social institutions the loudest are those who are looked up to as heroes by the young. We do not at the moment have any Allen Ginsbergs or Jack Kerouacs at Cimarron. Let us not create them through unwise actions of our own."

    Mr. Fincher said that was not enough for him, he wanted to see Professor McKenna discharged from his job at Cimarron and blacklisted from ever working in the profession again. I had to remind him that Professor McKenna was a duly tenured member of the faculty, and had a distinguished record of service to our institution for many years. As such, he had certain rights and privileges related to that long service. He had signed a loyalty oath, as required by state law, as had every public employee. And since he had not openly advocated the overthrow of the United States government or the government of our state by force or violence, and since he showed up for all of his scheduled classes, delivered all his lectures, and performed all of his other college duties, and had not made a public nuisance of himself through felonious crime, drunkenness, disturbance of the peace, or other forms of moral turpitude, and since he had been duly promoted by the judgment of his colleagues and the administration of the college to the academic rank of associate professor, he could not be summarily discharged. There would have to be a public hearing which the press would sensationalize as it has always done, there would be national attention from teacher's and professor's organizations, the college would get a black eye for its attempts to discharge a tenured professor over his unpopular teaching methods, and, worst of all, the very students we were trying to protect from men like McKenna would become attracted to him because he would wrap himself in the martyr's mantle. No, Fincher, I said, we perhaps should use more subtle methods; pressures to punish McKenna in non-public ways. It could all be done quietly, within the hierarchical structure of the college. It would be possible to make it clear to him that he will not have a bright future at our institution unless he mends his ways. It would be conceivable to withhold honors that would normally come with time to one with as much service time as he has. Limit salary increases, or not give them at all. Increase his teaching responsibilities, rather than remove him from the classroom. Perhaps this is what he wants in the first place. It could be done very subtly, so that even McKenna himself would not be sure what was done to him."

Fincher was not happy. It seemed to him as though McKenna deserved more bad things to happen to him than I was willing to initiate. He said that he would wait for a week at most to see what I was going to do, and then, if he was not satisfied, he would call some other trustees; and he would see if they couldn't come up with a solution that would be satisfactory.

You understand that on this campus the president of the college doesn't have the job security that you professors do. We give it up when we go entirely into administration. We serve at the whim of the trustees, and ultimately the state legislature, and we can be fired not only from the presidency but from the campus. In fact, the governor of the state has a line-item veto on each administrator's salary. We have the same degree of job security, or perhaps even less, than the football coach does. We can go back to teaching in a tenured position only by resigning, and even then the trustees have to go along with it.

After I left Fincher I knew I had another hard job to do. I had to talk to McKenna that day, I had to get the word across to him that the natives were restless, and I had to try to get him to tone down his classroom act for at least a while. The first problem was getting hold of the man. He didn't even have a telephone where he lived, and he wasn't in his office, and no one at the department had seen him. I sent Mrs. Huggins clear across the campus to his office to tape a message to his door, and I left messages for him to call me with everyone I thought might come into contact with him. I was almost desperate enough to go over and wait for him outside his 3:00 class when it was over, when I got a phone call from him around 2:45. I explained the situation to him as well as I could, and he agreed to meet me at my office after his class. He finally showed up about 4:30, just as Mrs. Huggins was leaving, which was all right with me because she was a fine secretary but an incurable eavesdropper and gossip. I was a little bit surprised by his appearance, even with what I had heard about him. He was wearing bib overalls, none too clean, a T-shirt, bright red with some sort of motto that I couldn't read, and heavy work boots. And frankly, he stank, mostly of sweat but also of some chemical which I presume was formaldehyde; I expect he had been handling preserved specimens for his class.

I started our meeting by saying that he and I could possibly both be in trouble because of some ill-considered things that he had done in the classroom. He asked me exactly what I meant by that and I explained what had taken place with Fincher that morning. Then he just blew up, and said, "Fincher! Of course! Bradley Fincher, that little shit-kicking son of a bitch, I gave him a D on the midterm and the little prick deserved to fail, and he came in and told me I had to give him a chance to take it again. He said that he had no real excuses, just that he hadn't known quite what to expect on the examination, but that he couldn't fall down like that in his family's eyes; and I told him that he had no right to be reconsidered. He'd had the same chances every other member of the class had, and he'd just have to take the consequences. So he looked at me like a whipped calf, and said that he was very sorry I felt that way and he hoped I would change my mind. I told him there was no chance of that; that it was a matter of principles I'd had since I started teaching, principles of democracy, fairness, and decency. He backed out of my office, saying again that he was sorry I felt that way. Very sorry, he repeated again, with just a flicker of a sadistic smile. So that's what the servile little mother-fucker has tried to do."

I explained to McKenna that Fincher's father was a trustee of the state university system, and that he was very upset. I handed him a copy of the drawing I'd sketched from Fincher's photograph, and asked him if he'd produced anything like this in his class. He stared at it for a long time, as if he were trying to reconstruct the true original from the diluted, three-times-handed-down version, and finally put it down slowly and said that, yes, he had produced such a drawing, but you had to understand what he was up against in lecturing to the freshmen; that virtually all they cared about was getting drunk and getting laid. "If you are going to get across to them the wonderful mystery of life," he said, "you have to hit them between the eyes with a board. I would never teach an advanced biology class like this. I am taking the risk that in this class of 120 teen-agers there may be one or two that can be lifted out of the morass of their adolescent lives and set on the path of understanding, of correct and moral living. I never know who is out there. I speak to them about sex because biology is about evolution, and evolution works through sexual shuffling of the genetic material. And to teach them about sex, I use concepts they understand." But surely, I said to him, you can be a little more subtle and avoid using language that might get you thrown in jail as a public nuisance? His response to that was, "Subtlety in this context means dissembling. In every other respect we praise forthrightness and economy of words. For this subject we believe that the less said directly, the better. We couch our discussions of sexuality in Victorian obscurity. We are like the Oxford English Dictionary, which defines masturbation, self-abuse and self-pollution in terms of one another. Sex is this century's heliocentric theory; I could be Galileo and you could be an inquisitor showing me the instruments of torture. I can not hide behind the skirts of such subtlety; no matter what you may think, Professor, people are still fucking."

I responded that it was not a question of what I thought; "This man has political and financial power, and he is extremely upset at what has happened. He is articulate in a down-home sort of way, and is quite capable of convincing the other trustees to reduce our funding, to discharge administrators of the college such as myself who are sympathetic to academic freedom. He wanted to have you discharged, but I assured him that was out of the question. Still, this episode will have serious repercussions for the whole program of this institution if nothing is done about it. Every faculty member may suffer for years to come unless we can convince Fincher and his cronies that their children are not in danger. How can we get out of this mess? What do you think we should do?"

He said, "It is really not my problem. All I have done is to teach, by the best means I can come up with, important facts about life on the earth. In my view, if anyone disputes my methods, let him discuss them with me and perhaps, if his arguments are strong, I will choose to modify my approach. Fincher has not chosen to do this. He has gone behind my back, impugned my motives, and threatened my livelihood. By rights, I should feel vengeful. However, I shall attempt to educate the man, although the odds of success are small, probably small beyond calculation. Rest assured, Mr. President, I will not embarrass the college or endanger its financial status. I will send him a written statement of my position, not an argumentative or polemical one, but rather a mild and pedagogic one. If you wish, I shall submit it to you for vetting; all I ask is that, in return, you send me copies of any correspondence from your office."

I agreed with what McKenna proposed, but I urged him to proceed with haste. We needed, I said, to have a coordinated response that stated our point of view strongly and succinctly, but more important still was the need to do so at once. The longer we left Fincher to stew, the more likely it was that he might take precipitate action on his own. So he agreed to work on his letter that evening and would give it to me in the morning.

For once, McKenna was as good as his word. The next day when I came in, just before 8, I saw several sheets of lined composition book paper stuck in the crack of my door. I still have these pages, although I had Mrs. Huggins type a letter up from them, without change. I will let you read them if you like. (the letter follows:)

> Dear Mr. Fincher:
>
> I have recently met with President Ogden of our college, who informed me of some concerns you expressed to him related to my teaching. I am sorry to hear of your opinion, based on a drawing made by your son which appears to be a very approximate copy of one which I used to illustrate basic facts of some reproductive processes, that I should be relieved of my position at Cimarron State College. I wish that you had come to me with your concerns, because I am sure that I could have made clear to you that your misgivings related to my classroom performance are without foundation.
>
> I have taught a variety of classes in the department of biology in our institution for more than thirteen years. I care passionately about my subject; I believe it is one of the areas of human knowledge in which understanding is absolutely essential to civilized existence. I have devoted my professional life to conveying the

basic facts and concepts of biology to the future leaders of society, our college-educated youth.

Biology is a complex group of related disciplines, touching fundamental life-and-death issues that concern every living person. The ideas of conception, birth, growth, metabolism, development, maturity, reproduction, disease, aging, and death underlie the subject matter of the science. It may surprise you to learn that serious teachers of biology are almost monastically and single-mindedly devoted to advancing their craft. I spend hours polishing each fifty-minute lecture, trying to discover just the right mode of expression to convey the maximum understanding possible to the students in the minimum amount of time. I am still learning my trade. After delivering more than three thousand lectures to students of widely varying backgrounds and degrees of understanding, I have never been really satisfied with my performance. I have tried many approaches, and will continue to experiment in order to find a style that works. The drawing to which you objected is an experiment in method, an attempt to teach important material about an important area of biology, sexual reproduction. Biology is driven by the evolutionary struggle for existence, and for nearly all types of organisms, success in individual existence leads directly to the passing on of the successful individual's genes to future generations. Thus sex is supremely important. Unfortunately, it is a topic that we humans, at least in this country, have recently almost stopped discussing. As a result, a child learns about it through hearsay, legend, and misinformation. I believe it is essential that this trend be reversed. I am attempting, in my classes, to convey information on sexual processes, including human sexuality, in an accurate and interesting manner. Whether my approach is succeeding is difficult to determine. I have been gratified recently to note that many of the students to whom I have taught beginning biology, the course your son is currently taking, have been quite successful in some of the more advanced courses offered in our department, and some of them have even gone on to advanced study or have taken jobs in the profession. I would be happy to give you the names and addresses of some of these former students if you would like to use their information in an unbiased assessment of my teaching. I also urge you to talk with my supervisor, Dean Pfaff, about my performance in the classroom in the past and present.

In other words, Mr. Fincher, I am asking that you not judge my teaching ability too hastily. I will be the first to admit that my endeavours require improvement, and that some areas of biology, such as sex, disease, and death, may not be comfortable topics for all listeners. But I am convinced that all of us need to confront these difficult concepts and to understand them as well as we can in order to live full and civilized lives. I would be happy to discuss further any of the items treated in this letter with you, and hope that you and I can arrange to talk together at a mutually convenient time.

Sincerely, P. G. McKenna, Ph.D.

I wrote a cover letter to Fincher, just a paragraph or two, relating my discussions with McKenna, and sent the letters off. I wasn't expecting that I had heard the last of it, but Fincher never said anything else to me on the subject. He only served for about a year and a half longer on the board, and then he returned to his farming and other business interests; we very seldom met or spoke to each other after he left the board. Whether McKenna's letter changed his mind, or whether he just decided it wasn't worth any more effort, I shall never know. Nor will I ever know whether he had a meeting with McKenna. Fincher died last year, at almost the same time McKenna did. His son, Brad or Bud, came into a great deal of money; his father didn't have all his assets in land, the way some farmers do. The son stopped by my office to visit me recently, looking like a very slick and successful businessman in his new pin-striped suit, and he turned over a check that his father's will directed be paid to Cimarron State. It is a sum of money that will fund a small annual award to the faculty member found by an independent panel to have done the most outstanding job in teaching subjects related to business or agriculture. It's too bad McKenna never had a chance to win that award in the days when he was still an outstanding educator, but maybe old man Fincher had him in the back of his mind.

Oh, by the way, I looked up the son's grade for McKenna's class that year. He withdrew with a failing grade, about a week or two after all these events took place. He then repeated the class the following year, with a different instructor, and came through with a D. I think McKenna might have been right about the man's character; he certainly didn't impress me, ten years later, as the sort of fellow I'd want to ride the river with. I'll never forget the patronizing look he gave me as he handed over the check; it was the sort of expression an Olympic hurdler might have as he awarded a medal to the winner of a wheelchair marathon.

At any rate, that episode was essentially all the contact I ever had with Professor McKenna. I wish I had been able to know him better, under less trying circumstances. He certainly seemed to be one of a kind. I am sure that he was an inspiration to many of the people he worked with, at least at one time. When I heard of his suicide, I felt a deep sense of loss, even though I knew him so slightly; I hope that I wasn't one of the people who made his life intolerable.

Good luck on your book. It seems like a daunting task and I trust it won't become your life's work. You seem like a promising young scientist and I hope your future years at this institution will be productive.

Lecture 2

(Excerpted from a tape recording of a lecture given by Pyke in Biology 102 [An Introduction to Biological Sciences], on Wednesday, April 12, 1967.)

There has been a flood. Your neighbors, their home destroyed, are sitting on what was once their lawn, some weeping and some stunned. They are wet and shivering. How many of you could deny them help?

Move your frame of reference. Tragedy is everywhere. Are not all men our brothers? The tragedy of existence is chronic. The tragedy of living is no less debilitating for being continual. We are all dying in the trenches. Our supply lines are too long. We are suffering from shortages of everything we really need, and all that we have enough of is worthless.

The only social imperative is the imperative to help your fellow sufferers in life. This is the sole social duty. We can never be too busy to solace the ill, the hungry, the depressed, and the exploited. Would you not help extricate a child from a burning house because you had an appointment?

We become brutalized beyond caring. The sheer numbers of us oppress. Reading our magazines, we flick past the picture of the big-bellied, fly-blown, brown-skinned child from Upper Volta. As Tolstoy says, there are many such.

Ellen

(Ellen Gould joined our faculty in 1967. Her degree, in veterinary pathology, is from the University of Pennsylvania. She is a dark-haired woman of medium height, big-eyed, big-bosomed, and with an aggressive and expressive mouth. She wears gold-rimmed half-framed granny glasses which give her a droll but somehow calculating look. She smokes rather heavily, which is unusual for a biologist, especially a young one. She has a solid intellect, but those who do not know her well are sometimes surprised by her laugh, which is totally unrestrained and covers several octaves in pitch. This laugh can be heard coming from down the hall from a long way off, and it sometimes interrupts serious discussions with strangers, although those of us who are her colleagues have become used to it by now, just as we no longer are startled by the diesel horn, used to warn of approaching tornadoes, that is tested at 10:30 every Monday.)

I think that Pyke McKenna was in love with me for as long as we knew each other. He never said so as such, and he never tried to do anything overtly sexual with me; he respected my privacy. I think he could never really figure out how I lived. I'm a very gregarious person; I have a lot of close friends, and I hate to be alone, so there's always someone living at my house, sometimes several people. I have a lot of room. I'm not sure he really understood how a number of people of different sexes could live together under the same roof for a long time and not necessarily be having orgies. Anyway, I could tell that he was strongly attracted to me, but I could tell that he wasn't the type who could live communally, like I do, and I didn't think I wanted to change the way I lived for his sake.

We had some good times, just the two of us, though. He said to me he knew only two other completely fascinating people in the world, two men, and that one was in Milan and the other one was at MIT, so that neither one was of much immediate use. He said he loved every minute he could spend with me and that he would feel the same way whether I smoked cigars, was fat, unattractive, or male. And since none of these things applied to me he called that an extra bonus. I don't know, I always thought I had a few more pounds than I could use, but it didn't seem to bother him.

He used to come to my office to ask me questions about invertebrates. To get material for his classes, he'd say. He claimed to be weak on them, not to understand the details of their life histories. And I suppose I did know more about some things than he did. I am a specialist on animal and human pathogens, like the malaria parasite, that have intermediate hosts. Some of them do have fascinating and almost incredible life cycles, and the things I used to tell Pyke would make him laugh so loud in that wonderful bellowing laugh of his. He seemed almost childish sometimes; anything that had anything to do with reproduction or sex would really catch his interest, and he would take some remark that had relevance only for protozoa and try to stretch it to fit some sexual experience he'd had with one of his legions of lovers. At least he tried to convince me that he'd had legions of lovers; and I suppose there were many by the usual standards. I think he used to strain to try to embarrass me, but I didn't bite very often.

Yes, as you know, he lived in a top-floor walkup in a not-very-nice part of town. I remember the address, 1008 Nekahoma Avenue. The house was a cubical wood-frame box covered with that tarpaper with fake brick designs on it; the owner must have liked it because he had used three different colors of it. Pyke liked the fact that it was cheap and that he could walk to the campus. I think there was nothing above the ceiling except a tar-covered roof; it would get pitifully hot in there in the summer. Pyke never would spring for an air conditioner, saying they were unnatural and made his throat hurt, and that whenever he went outside, he'd start coughing. It can't be good for you, he'd say. He certainly didn't feel that way about electric fans, though; he'd taken one of those enormous attic fans and bolted it across the window so it'd blow out. He'd turn the thing on and generate a gale-force wind inside that little apartment. The noise was insupportable; I have no idea how that man could sleep in there, but perhaps he didn't require all that much sleep.

Yes, the first time I saw his place, he invited me up after work for a glass of wine. I think we had known each other for more than a year before he took that step. We walked from the campus to his apartment building; it wasn't far at all. We climbed the creaking stairs to the third floor. He went first in order to point out the broken stairs or the ones where the shabby carpeting was loose. It was not obvious that the landlord had ever cleaned anywhere; the walls were decked out in a mixture of graffiti, spiderwebs, and plain old dirt. At one spot, there was a lipstick spot where someone had apparently kissed the wall. She really must have been drunk.

He opened his door with a flourish, bowing low as he did so, saying, "If you will do me such honor, madame." The door hadn't been locked. You had to go into and through the kitchen, I remember, to get to the living room with its big window and the fan practically blocking the view of the parking lot. I was surprised to see how clean the place was; I suppose I was expecting the traditional middle-aged-bachelor squalor of the popular imagination.

I sat down in one of those old-fashioned overstuffed high-backed mohair chairs with crocheted doilies ("antimacassars," he called them, an old-fashioned word that I remember my grandmother using) on the arms and back, while he puttered around in the kitchen with the wine things. He brought everything out to the living room on a teak tray, including two unmatched glasses; a short, heavy, purplish tumbler for him, and a generously large, engraved, stemmed crystal flute glass for me. He pulled the bottle out of its pewter ice bucket to show me the label before he poured it for me, very elegantly, wrapping the bottle in a towel and the whole bit. I don't know where he found the stuff; our local liquor store only had three kinds as far as I know, Mad Dog for the students, Ripple for the railroad bums and winos, and

Concord Blackberry for the little old ladies who drank it only at Christmas. And Denver was probably the closest place you could find anything else. But this was a bottle of good French Chablis, *appellation controlée* and *mis en bouteille* written right there on the label in purple ink together with a line drawing of the estate. It was delicious, clean, flinty, honest, about five different tastes as you held it in your mouth and finally swallowed it. I really appreciated that from him. Coming from upstate New York, my parents drank the local product, mostly, but they had a certain liking for the non-foxy California variety, and once in a while they'd drink real French champagne, so I wasn't exactly naive when it came to these products.

Well, I suppose I was somewhat nervous as I finished my glass or two, wondering what would be coming next, as I'd heard about Pyke's reputation from everyone, both directly from the secretarial and clerical staff and by innuendo from the faculty. But he just sat there smiling at me for a long time, making me feel uncomfortable. Then I asked him what he was thinking about, and he said he was trying to decide what composer I reminded him of and he had just decided it was Brahms; "Not the grandiose Brahms of the symphonies," he said, "but the private Brahms of the piano, cello, and clarinet sonatas." And with that he got up, and without another word took down a record and put it on his ratty-looking turntable, and handed me the jacket, which was one of those floppy European ones; the record turned out to be French, and of the two clarinet sonatas. I forget the artists, Gervaise somethingor-other was the clarinetist. It was very nice, especially the slow movement which was quite songful and lyrical.

Pyke didn't say anything the whole time the music was playing, and if I tried to make conversation he would shush me with a wave. When it was all over he sat silently on the floor, holding his hands over his eyes, like he was in a trance. The record kept playing in the run-out groove. I thought perhaps he was asleep, so I said "Pyke?" to him, quite softly. He answered, immediately, "Would you please put the record away for me?," still sitting with his eyes covered. I put the record back in his jacket and went to sit on the floor next to him. I thought then he might be ill. When I touched his hand, he took mine in his, and uncovered his face. I saw that he had been weeping. He said, "I'm sorry, but as I was listening to that gorgeous music, with you here beside me, I was overcome with a feeling of loss. The wickedness of time, and how little of it we have, and how joy and beauty must come to an end. I was weeping not so much for myself, but for us; you and I, and all of us around the world, waiting and hoping that suffering and agony will hold off for just a little while longer. Forgive me, I know a host isn't supposed to act this way."

I didn't know how I should respond, but what I did was to put my arms around his neck and just held him close to me. And he continued to sob for a while, and gradually calmed himself. Then he stood up, and took a few deep breaths and went into the bathroom and blew his nose loud and long, and finally came out. His face was all blotched and red and his eyes looked like they were bruised, but he was smiling. And he said, "You know, you're all right; you're a very decent human being. I'm glad you came home with me. I needed someone to cry with. My life has been a wreck, but I feel a little better about the future now. Would you mind staying around for a while longer? I'd like to make us something to eat."

So I did, and I helped him improvise a sort of omelet that we made in one of his big black cast iron pans, with mushrooms and green pepper and muenster cheese and all sorts of spices I'd never heard of; and we had rice, which he made yellow with turmeric, something I hadn't seen done before. And we finished the wine, and were happy with each other, even went so far as to clean up the kitchen before retiring to the living room, then laughing and gossiping until about midnight, when I gave him a big hug and said to him "You're a good man, Charlie Brown," and I walked back to the campus and drove home.

After that, I thought he and I were going to become much closer friends. After all, we'd been through about as emotional a scene I imagine it's possible to have without having an orgasm or getting physically injured. So I was surprised when I didn't see Pyke for several days. I left notes and even a store-bought friendship card (something I don't think I'd ever done before; it was one of those cutesy sentimental cards with dressed-up kittycats on it, something I figured he might get a laugh from) in his mailbox, but no response.

Finally, several days later, about ten minutes before I was supposed to leave for my 2:00 class, he called me in my office. He seemed a little reluctant to talk to me, said he would like to meet after 5 "to clear a few things up." Naturally, after that I was in no mood for teaching, all fluttery and nervous over what he was going to say to me, and my teaching was pitifully poor, the sort of lecture when you are so ashamed at your inarticulateness and just want to stop in the middle and say, "Let's all go home and start this over again next time." And for the rest of the afternoon, thank goodness there were no committee meetings or appointments with earnest, breathless graduating seniors to come in for heart-to-hearts about their delicate and portentous futures. I sat in my office with the door almost closed, chain-smoking, trying to catch up on my reading of journal articles; but of course my mind kept wandering. I looked at my watch every thirty seconds or so, probably, and I kept jumping every time I heard a little noise in the hallway. Anyway, it got to be past 5:00, and all the secretaries and administrative people were gone, and of course there were no students. The only person left in the building, to my knowledge, was Mr. Kapachek, the little Czechoslovakian janitor; I could hear him coughing and spitting and cursing under his breath every once in a while. I was sure Pyke had forgotten about our meeting or that something else had come up, when, about 5:20, there was a soft little tap on my door. I hadn't heard anyone approaching, but all of a sudden there he was, peering around the door and looking very conspiratorial, saying in a whisper, "May I come in?" and immediately zipping inside before I had a chance to breathe out, and quickly closing the door.

He pulled out one of my beat-up gunmetal grey straight chairs, swung it around and sat on it backwards; he crossed his arms and leaned forward, resting his chin on his arms and his arms on the chair back, and let out a huge whistling sigh. He looked like he'd just escaped from a pursuing mob out for his blood.

I said to him, "So how've you been, stranger?" And he just sat there looking at me for a while, then wiped his mouth firmly with both hands, sighed again, and said, "I need to apologize." I was just about to say there was nothing for him to apologize for, but he held up his hand and quickly said, "No; you need to hear what I have to say. I have used you and you haven't even known it, although I'm sure you've been very confused. I needed help from you, but

I wouldn't tell you why until it was too late, and then everything surged out in a rush and things got out of hand.

"The situation is that I have felt a great deal of personal stress lately, connected with a whole series of problems, culminating with the death of my brother in Vietnam. He died in the Tet offensive, a stupid waste of a good man's life. When that took place, I felt a confused mixture of grief, fear, and hate wash over me that made me sick at heart, sick of life and all its ugliness. I hated society for having been so greedy and lazy as to allow the situation to develop which made my brother's death and the death of tens of thousands of other Asians and Americans inevitable. I wanted to die, but I also wanted to kill; to exterminate the generals, the industrialists, the politicians, and all the sick bourgeois war profiteers who have tolerated and encouraged this situation. Never have I felt such naked repugnance. I sat in the darkness of my bedroom in the middle of the night, weeping in my fury, crying for myself and cursing my enemies.

"I kept this up for two days. I could not eat; once in a while I would pour two inches of bourbon into a jelly glass and drink it down in four or five gulps, feeling the fire of it, searing my throat and heating my belly. Finally, somehow, I burned the hate out of my spirit, and I slept for fourteen hours, and woke up feeling like the shell of a building in which there has been a great conflagration.

"I came to work, then, and the people around me appeared like ghosts or automatons; they would move toward me, they would speak to me, but I sensed no conviction in their mechanical performances, no meaning in their facile utterances. I responded, if at all, in an equally mechanical fashion, and I saw out of the corner of my eyes their brows mechanically and quizzically raised. As I walked about, it felt as if I was not moving through air, but some fluid that was a little more substantial and dense. It was a conscious effort to swing my arms as I walked; I just wanted to lie down and give up.

"Then I saw you halfway down the hallway, and you waved to me, and I felt the radiance of your smile, a gift from you across the space between us to me, and it was as if my humanity was being restored. As I stood next to you, and you put your arm around my waist, I sensed a breathtaking surge of the life force flowing into me, as if your fingertips were a high-pressure hose full of it. My voice could not be stopped; it said, 'I haven't seen you for so long, and I wanted to ask you if you'd like to stop over at my house after work for a drink.' And you looked up at me like a pixie, said, 'Sure. Why not?' and that was it, and I felt so happy that you wanted to be with me. I couldn't stop smiling. My luck was finally changing."

He stopped talking, finally, and looked over my head and out the window. After a minute, I said, "So far, I haven't heard one scintilla you need to apologize for. I wanted to be with you, you know."

He held up his hand again. "I'm not sure you understand. My brother was dead, and part of me wanted to forget that he was gone. I seized on you as a way to forget. I'm afraid that it didn't have to be you, it could have been anyone who'd shown any interest or compassion at the moment. So, somehow, I was pretending to treat you as someone special, even though you weren't, not really. Not at that particular moment. This is what I apologize for; I was treating you as a thing, a diversion that would help me forget my anguish. No more than some cheap bagatelle of a joke. I hate myself for feeling that way, because you are more to me than that. I want you to know that. In the future, I promise that I will treat you as a person, a valued colleague, and not as an entertainment - a way to forget my troubles."

"Well, I accept your apology; obviously it's something you believe strongly, but I must tell you I certainly don't feel used. I'm actually honored that I could be of some assistance to you in a time of emotional stress. Actually, I had a lot of fun at your house, and I hope you'll invite me over again. I like to be with you."

"Professor Gould, I salute you. You can't know how relieved you've made me feel! Someday, maybe I can do something nice for you."

I got up from my chair, walked over to him, and embraced him. I gave him a kiss, right in the middle of the forehead. I said, "Professor McKenna, you have and you will. You've been honest with me, and you've been a friend, and you've made me feel happy. I don't know what more a person can ask."

He said, "I'm going to be brave enough to ask one more favor of you; something difficult; something that may not be possible. I'd like you to try to understand me. It's not something I'd ask anyone lightly; it's only those that

I especially want to be close to that I ask this favor of. It isn't easy; it requires hard study and long contemplation, because I'm not a simple personality. I have deep-seated problems.

"Obviously, we both have only a limited amount of time; we're both busy people. But if you're willing to take the challenge, I'll be very grateful to you. In return, I'll promise to be a willing listener to your problems. I realize this is a serious commitment; everyone has complicated difficulties in their lives. We live in interesting times. But that evening we spent together was good for me, and I'm willing to try to continue the process, to work on the premise that it wasn't some fluke."

He stood up from the chair then, saying, "I'm sorry if I worried you. I promise to behave more appropriately in the future. Thank you for listening to my problems."

I embraced him again, and told him that he could count on me. Then, he left, closing my door carefully and firmly.

I lit a cigarette. Wow, I thought, he really does have difficulties, but maybe we can work together and help each other out. I'm not exactly a well-adjusted individual myself. I'm lonely, and I'm not getting any younger. I have a great dread of being old and alone, with no one to love me; childless and unmarried and helpless in some nursing home. I wonder if he has any of those fears, too, and what we can do to combat them.

So what happened after that? I think you can guess. Nothing. Oh, he stopped over in my office now and then, as he had before; but it was as if our meeting had never happened; I'd never kissed him, and he'd never told me how special I was to him. He must have been embarrassed at how much he'd admitted to me.

So, we remained on friendly terms, but nothing else ever happened; nothing substantive. I was really disappointed, because I really thought we could have been close. He was the kind of person I thought was a kindred spirit. But, for one reason or another, it never happened. And the next thing I knew, practically, he was dead. Two years gone past just like nothing; like we never meant anything to each other, after all, and then one of us dies. What a waste. I really never understood it at all. He came to me, and poured out his soul, and I was receptive, and then nothing happened. What good does it do? Life can be so wasteful at times. Pyke McKenna, I wanted to help. I feel guilt that I couldn't help more. It sounds like a philosophy of life. Help me, o Lord, to help those that I wish I could do more for. Bruce, help me to understand.

Pyke 3

(The only sheets of paper found in a manila folder labeled FUTURE PROJECTS in Pyke's file cabinet. The date at the top of the first page is July 9, 1962, but the entries are in various colors of pen and pencil and appear to have been added at several times over the years.)

A. BOOKS:

1. A history of necrophilia; tentative title, "But Think of the Money I Save."

2. A study of the parallels between Darwinism and Impressionism: decline of received wisdom of the Academies in the mid-19th C. The current accessibility and popularity of these paintings have clouded the impact that these works had on the history of art, but they changed our outlook on the world as surely and as irreversibly as the scientific revolutions led by Newton and Darwin. Ask the Guggenheim!

3. Magic and Science. How mankind has sought to unlock Nature's mysteries over the centuries. First by invoking

gods, now by employing the powerful new formulas of physics and chemistry. Show that the underlying mental states for each process are the same. Magical evocation of power through artistic representation of the essence of an object; Renaissance artists interested in accurate description, of every hair of a rabbit (Dürer e. g.) Music as the "voice of the spirit" (New Guinea tribes). Where did magic and science diverge?

4. A science fiction novel ("Country of Darkness" ?) describing the condition of mankind after a plague which renders nearly everyone almost totally blind. The book begins with an aged narrator telling the youth about the old days when the day people were dominant. The horrors that result when society collapses must be described graphically. Complete destruction of transportation, food distribution, electricity; massive starvation, deaths from exposure. Surviving humanity is transformed into practically a different species, with their remaining senses heightened to such a degree that they can distinguish different plants at a great distance by their odors, and different people by the sounds of their breathing. A wonderful new spirit of community develops. The few remaining visual individuals employ huge armies of the blind to protect themselves. Sight as a metaphor for money. The blind finally prevail, overcoming the sighted (whom they call "light-suckers") with the help of their disenchanted mercenaries, in climactic final battles in the middle of the night.

5. A children's book on prejudice, snappy title, something along the lines of "Dr. Seuss's Hate Book."

6. Taxonomy of mythical animals (and deities?) Are there very many legendary invertebrates? Spiders, I suppose; the Kraken (possibly a type of octopus)?

7. A "Lexicon of Invective." Useful for writers of letters to newspaper and scientific journal editors, etc. Need lists of words, especially obsolescent forms deserving of revitalization (such as "rabbit-sucker" = cheat). Nouns: For types of people, lists of synonyms for; barbarian, bigot, bum, charlatan, cheat, coward, criminal, drunk, enemy, failure, fool, geriatric, glutton, hack, heretic, homosexual, madman, snob. For things, synonyms for inferior: works of art, literature, music, science; articles of commerce (houses, automobiles, other mechanical objects, foods, drinks, medicines, clothing); cities, localities; and spoken presentations. Adjectives: for people, synonyms for; arrogant, blind, childish, deceptive, evil, ignorant, lazy, perverted, servile, ungenerous, vain. For things: synonyms for bland, boring, cloying, contemptible, disorderly, false, meaningless, ostentatious, sloppy, ugly, worthless.

   Include useful stock sentences of contempt: "sir/madam, you are not fit to carry guts to a bear." A multilingual section; how to express contempt in eight languages. The equivalent of "I shit in your mother's milk" in Japanese, Serbo-Croatian, etc. (perhaps deserves consideration as a second volume.)

8. "Hard Times and Soft Money," a history of research in America's Universities and colleges.

B. MAGAZINE AND JOURNAL ARTICLES:

1. "Tales of the Old Wives," humorous survey of some of the myths the common people have believed in (and still do believe, to a large extent).

2. "Things Fall Apart." A windy survey of the ineluctability of change. Bring in Yeats, Li Po, Darwin, the Buddha, enzyme kinetics. The impermanence of things. Mere anarchy is loosed upon us.

3. An article on existential despair, for a primarily-women's magazine, maybe Redbook or McCall's. Write it under an assumed female name with a phony doctorate. Perhaps an anagram of my own name? Penny Kemack, Anne P. McKyke (ha, ha), Panky Meneck. Phony case histories designed to appeal to the sentimental readership of these publications, but at least to get them thinking about reality. Analogies between despair and chronic diseases exacerbated by age.

4. The civil rights of the dead. A much neglected majority. Although some have been elected to office, none have been allowed to serve. Their corruption is probably no greater than that of many living politicians. In some districts, dead are active voters, but their interests are never discussed. Consider their wretched "living" quarters, for example - cold, damp, and unlit. Perhaps they should complain more; march on city hall, etc.

5. "A few thousand words on verbosity" for the Writer's Digest? Bombastic utterances as a form of pollution. "Take eloquence and wring its neck" -- Verlaine.

Spud

(Elton "Spud" Gates attended Cimarron State in the late 50s. He is a local farm boy, who grew up about ten miles from the campus. A big-boned, freckle-faced redhead with a ready smile and laugh, he looks and acts now much as he did then. As soon as he is introduced, he takes your hand in both of his, pumps it vigorously, and immediately puts his arm around your shoulders as though you two are the oldest of friends. Although he worked for a time for Pyke McKenna, he is best known as perhaps the greatest football player the Cimarron State Bears ever had. He did not graduate from CSC; he dropped out in the middle of the last semester of his senior year. He was an outstanding running back and still holds most of our career, season, and single-game rushing records.

He is also the only State player ever selected in the National Football League annual collegiate player draft; he was taken in the eighth round in the 1960 draft by the Pittsburgh Steelers, went to training camp that summer, and made the team. Although most of his playing time came on "special teams" - those expendable or inexperienced players who sacrifice their bodies on punts and kickoffs - he did get to handle the ball in one late-season game. On a snowy field in Cleveland, he caught a screen pass for an eighteenyard gain, was blocked out of bounds, stumbled over the Browns bench, and suffered a severe knee injury that ended his career.

RICHARD LARSON

I interviewed him in a small town in eastern Oregon where he is now a dealer in John Deere farm implements and Ford cars and trucks.)

I'm really glad I went to CSC; I had a scholarship offer from Arizona State but I didn't want to move that far from home. I like our climate better, and I made some great friends and had some great times. I think I got a little better publicity by playing on our team rather than in some bigger program. Anyway, I did get a chance to play pro ball, and that was what I wanted.

I really impressed the Steelers in camp. I dropped out of school, temporarily, I figured at the time, and started working out. By the time I showed up, I was really musclebound. My speed wasn't the greatest, but I was the best in camp on the bench press. I made those big defensive linemen's eyes pop with my lifts. They had to make room for me somewhere, even though if they'd had to cut one more guy it would have been me.

Our first game was against the Giants, and I got to get in on the very first play. We had to kick off to them. I was standing just behind the 40-yard line, jumping up and down, trying not to be nervous, and looking at the enemy, mean-looking dudes, most of them black, in their dark blue uniforms. Man, they looked like giants, a hell of a lot more impressive than they did on TV. The crowd was howling like a pack of wolves; they were really pumped up for the home team. My assignment was to run straight for the left goalpost, as fast as I could, until I saw the receiver catch the ball, and then I was to angle toward him. So all of us ran up on the ball, yelling like Chinese pirates, and I ran right past this guy on the return team, or thought I had. He'd actually just stepped to one side, and quicker than I or the referee could see it, he blocked me real hard and fast on my blind side. I would call it a clip, but there were no flags. I wound up rolling almost out of bounds, and I sat up and watched the Giant with the ball running right past where I should have been. Luckily, someone behind me got to him at about the Giants 35-yard line.

So that wasn't a terribly great beginning for my NFL career. However, I learned a few tricks and by the end of the season I was doing my job really well and was something of a leader on our unit. And then I had to go out and get hurt in the last game. Anyway, I worked really hard, didn't make a lot of money, and didn't exactly get to the hall of fame, but I had a good time and made some good friends and maybe that's all that matters.

I was sorry to hear in your letter that Dr. McKenna had died; I really haven't kept in touch and it was a real shock. He was really like a favorite uncle to me while I was there. He taught me a lot about science when I was working in the lab for him. I had no idea how scientists spent their days, probably hardly anyone does. I thought they were all these old guys who just spent all their time at their desks writing equations until they came up with a great idea and then they became famous. But actually it's a lot of hard work, just grinding away at something day after day and when it doesn't work, change something and grind away some more. And then, when something does work, you have to try it again just to be sure it wasn't some fluke; and just as often as not it was, and you can never repeat it again. It's a really hard and frustrating life, and I don't see how you scientists can put up with it year after year. I suppose the rare exciting successes make it all worth while. I couldn't live that way, anyway.

But I had a good time during the few months when I did fool around with science, under Dr. McKenna's direction. I can still see the notice he'd put up on the Murchison Hall bulletin board; "Biology Assistant, 8-16 hours/week, must not fear heights." I may have been the only one who applied, but anyway, he put me to work.

When he interviewed me, he told me that it was imperative that we understand plants and animals better than we did. He said our understanding of the bottom of the ocean was good compared to what we knew about the way trees, for example, grew and functioned. He told me that in terms of weight, and maybe in other respects too, trees were the most important living things. He thought they were practically sacred, and we needed to know them much better. They were difficult for botanists to work with, because they liked small plants that they could grow by the hundreds in a greenhouse and generate lots of data. But we couldn't do that with trees. So we had to go to them.

For my project, I had to go out and measure cottonwood leaves, thousands of them. I'd climb those big old trees as high as I could, and crawl out on limbs as much as fifty feet above the ground with my little ruler and measure their lengths and widths. I had my ruler, tweezers, notebook, labeling tape, a marking pen, and two pencils on long strings tied around my neck so they couldn't fall. They were forever getting tangled up in the branches, so I tried to figure out ways to carry them differently; what worked best was a loose sweatshirt that I could tuck everything into. I used different colored strings so I could remember which was which, but I kept forgetting. You have other things on your mind when you're swaying in a 20-mile-an-hour wind twenty feet off the ground, trying to hold one leaf still. I was quite a sight. I really took stupid chances, but I only fell once and that was from a low height, only about eight feet. I just got a sprain that went away after a day.

Dr. McKenna really didn't help matters much because he used to come out and watch. First I thought he just wanted to see me when I fell, but then I figured out that he was really concerned about me; I think he wasn't sure that his research idea was such a good one after all, being so dangerous, and wanted to make sure I was OK. But he could never just say that, he had to come out and make small talk and jokes when I was hanging by a thread up there. He would also say that he just happened to stop by, was just in the neighborhood, you might say; just happened to want to collect some frogs or mushrooms or whatever. But he'd always sidle over to my tree and chit-chat about one thing or another as I was swaying in the breeze. It's kind of hard to chat when you've got something in your mouth all the time, either a ruler or a pencil or something.

Then, also, he really admired my car; I had one of the first Corvette convertibles ever seen in our part of the world; it was bright orange, which made it unmistakable, and I drove it fast over those back roads. I think he admired my devil-may-care attitude and the skill I had in driving. He'd try to wangle a ride from me, which I was happy to give him. Being up in those trees for a long time gave me the creeps, if you really want to know. So I'd climb down, put the top down and drive about 110 out on the Interstate, and he'd just put his head back and give the rebel yell. Not that you could really hear him very well over the roar of my glass-pack mufflers. I never let him drive, though; there was a rumor that he was accident-prone. So that would be a nice break, an hour or so off in the middle of the day. Then I'd go back to work up in the trees again and he'd toddle back to the campus in his little blue Fiat.

The other part of my job was to take notes on insect damage and try to catch the caterpillars that were eating the leaves and put them in little jars that I carried up there in my ammo belt. Incidentally, he used to get mad at me for screwing down the caps on those jars so tightly that he couldn't get them open. He had to use pliers and a vise, and he broke some of the jars that way. I guess I was just didn't know how strong I was. And then I had to write on those tiny labels in India ink to note down where I'd collected them. That was a really hard part for me because my hands were so big and clumsy. At least I didn't have to identify the insects; he did that, or maybe he had some other student do it, I forget now. He wanted to teach me how to do it but I could never get the hang of it. Besides, it gave me the willies manipulating those dead bodies under the microscope. So I stuck with the field collecting and data gathering. And then when I'd finished with one group of three trees I'd drive to another population twenty miles away and do the same thing with three more, and so on. And then I'd be back out there the next week to make the measurements again.

So after working all day I'd bring everything back to Dr. McKenna's office. I usually worked almost until sunset, but he was almost always there, ready to talk about what I'd done and make plans for next week's experiments. And quite often he'd want to go out for a bite to eat or to get a beer. Usually we'd wind up at the Arms with a pitcher and one of those greasy sandwiches they specialized in. Dr. McKenna was a big, strong guy, and he'd once in a while try to take me on in arm wrestling. He was pretty good, too, but I always beat him. He tried hard, and he wasn't above trickery; he'd try to make me laugh, but that never worked. And once he had Sarah, the waitress, put an ice cube down the back of my shirt; but that just made me mad at the time. We had a good laugh afterward, though.

Then finally, in the late summer, I had to collect leaves from all the trees so he could analyze them for whatever chemicals they had in them. So instead of jars I had dozens of plastic bags tied all around my waist. I must have been quite a sight then too.

The last thing he wanted me to do was to grind up the leaves and extract them with different liquids, acids I think it was, but I could be wrong after all these years. So I was to make up a sort of soup of chopped-up leaves, using the blender, and put the soup in these big plastic tubes and spin them around in the centrifuge so I could pour off the liquid. But I was in a hurry to get to practice, because it was that time of the year by then, and I guess I wasn't listening to him too closely. Instead of putting the tubes across from each other, I put them next to each other, and when I turned the centrifuge on it started to make an awful whining noise, and started to walk across the bench the way a washing machine does, except faster. I couldn't believe the thing could do that, as heavy as it was. I tried to unplug it, but I pulled the wrong plug out of that tangle of wires he had in his lab, and then I lunged for it, as if it had been a running back; but I missed, and finally the machine tumbled off the top of the bench, bounced once on the sill, and then fell right out the third floor window. I suppose the thing was really top-heavy. Luckily, the window was open so there was no broken glass, just a ripped screen, and there was nothing down on the ground except shrubs.

I thought Dr. McKenna was going to kill me, but all he did was laugh and say that he hoped this wasn't the way I planned to do all the samples. I was amazed to find out that once we put a new cord on the unit, it worked just as good as new. But I quit the job just after that; I couldn't be on the team and work for him too.

So I really lost track of Dr. McKenna after that. Although I do remember one time, just after the season ended and just before I quit school, I saw him on the campus, out on the mall, sitting on one of those concrete benches, leaning forward, reading something. He was sitting with a girl but I couldn't tell if they were together or if they just happened to be sitting in the same place. She was looking at him but he was just reading. She was very good-looking, wearing a buckskin vest and tight Levis and boots; she had her legs pulled up so they were under her chin, and she had her mouth open and her tongue was sort of licking her knees as she sat there. To tell the truth, I noticed her first, but then I saw Dr. McKenna sitting there and I sort of gave him a tap on the shoulder as I went by. I said hello to him but he just sort of looked up in my direction, and I don't know if he didn't see me or if he'd already forgotten who I was, but he only sort of grunted. The girl gave me quite a look, though, but

I was late for a class so I had to move on without speaking to them. Anyway, that was the last time I saw him.

I don't know what ever came of all that work I did for him, but I hope he found out something interesting from it all. He was a really neat guy and I wish I'd heard about him dying; I'd have driven to his funeral all the way from here to pay my last respects. It was suicide, you say? Well, I'm glad I don't know what brought it on. Life can be a real pain in the ass at times, but it's a shame a guy like him had to be the one who couldn't hack it.

Bruce 5

The winter before Pyke died, the winter of 1969-70. None of us who lived through that one, and there were some who did not, will ever forget it. The preceding autumn had been dry and cool, and the winter started out quite benignly; there was a trivial and picturesque snow just before Thanksgiving, but then the weather warmed and we had two and a half weeks of brilliant, cloudless days. However, on the ninth of December, a killer cold front stampeded down out of the Yukon, bringing a heavy blizzard with it. After that, it was katy-bar-the-door; the temperature immediately plunged to twenty below and we had a string of below-zero days, fourteen, I believe. When the temperature did finally warm up, it brought more and more snow.

January I remember as one remembers a long debilitating illness, one day after another of driving, freezing winds, drifting snow, tingling cheeks that soon started to hurt, and struggles to get from one place to another whether by car or by walking, that left everyone exhausted. That sickness of despair, leavened by just enough hope to drive us through another day, got worse and worse as the days of January passed, until the end of the month where we got a temporary respite in the form of a solitary clear, warm day with a high of 45, and all the college boys dashed out of town with their girls, riding in convertibles with the tops down.

February featured clear, cold days that warmed to just below freezing - just warm enough to melt a little snow on the streets before it froze again to glare ice; and at the end of the month was another great blizzard, worse than the December one, that left twenty-three inches of snow on top of the fifteen that were already on the ground, and drifts higher than a man in open areas; that broke power lines and left nearly everyone in Pawnee Springs without electricity for at least four days. During that prodigious storm, the atmosphere was charged with some sort of uncanny electricity; green flashes appeared in the sky.

That was the real killer, the blizzard that took the old-timers away when they tried to warm themselves with their gas stoves, suffocating themselves with carbon monoxide. They were the ones who were too proud to join the rest of us in the fieldhouse, our rows of sleeping bags spread in ranks across the basketball floor, while great generator-powered electric fans roared all night long, blowing the warmth of gasoline-fired heaters around the arena.

And it all started with the first great blizzard of December 9. I remember that day quite clearly. It started calmly enough, a damp grey Tuesday of no particular distinction, and that afternoon I was scheduled to teach a comparative anatomy laboratory in the basement of Murchison. The lab started at 1:00 and ran until 4:00. When I went downstairs, it was cloudy outside but not cold; it was just above freezing and there was a slight breeze from the northwest. There were a lot of manipulations to perform for that class, and accordingly I didn't come upstairs until 3; and since there were no windows in the lab, I had no idea what had been happening outdoors. Miss Freemartin had left a note by the coffee maker, saying that she had left early, at 2:15, since a snow of one to two feet had been forecast and she wanted to make sure she made it home. The Dean was also gone, and in fact the whole place looked deserted.

I looked out the window and saw the storm. Although the wind was blowing in heavy gusts, the snow was not coming down in eddying clouds of flakes, but rather in heavy, clotted aggregates that fell almost vertically and clung to what they struck. Although the storm was less than an hour old, the sidewalks, the automobiles, the tree branches - everything - was already buried to a depth of at least five inches. The snow was pasted in sheets to the northwest sides of buildings and trees. People were shuffling through it as fast as they could, averting their faces from the scathing wind and the pasty blobs of snow. The heads of those who had not had the foresight to wear headgear were coated in thick white mats of it.

I decided I had better cut my class short, so I went back downstairs and told the students to finish up what they were doing as quickly as possible and then leave, which of course they were more than glad to do. Within fifteen minutes the last person had left. I shut off the lights and ran back up to the department office, where I thought I'd try to call Viola and tell her I was going to try to come home. Yes, I would say, you can send out a search party if I don't get there in an hour. But she wasn't at the insurance company; no one was; the phone rang on and on. Of course, they would all have been sent home also. When I called our home number, again there was no answer. I found that a little surprising, but rationalized that she might be in the shower, or out shoveling the driveway in case I was coming home soon.

I got my coat and gloves and lunged out of the building into the parking lot. It had become much colder, I noticed, even when one took the wind into account. I felt my nose and my forehead starting to turn red even within the first minute I was outdoors. The first snow that had fallen must have melted and refrozen, since the layer next to the ground was one of almost solid ice. My Ford was one of the last vehicles still in the lot, sitting by itself, like a distant igloo on wheels, halfway toward the fieldhouse. The heavy snow stuck to my shoes and soaked through to my feet even before I got to the car.

OK, here goes nothing, I said; I opened my driver's-side door and slid into the front seat, which resembled a dimly lit ice cave, since snow covered all the windows. I started the engine and set the heater to blow blasts of warm air onto the windshield, then reached into the back seat for my handy broom-cum-scraper, and did what I could to clean the windows, chipping off the hard ice next to the glass and shoveling off the wet snow; there was no way I could keep the fast-falling clots from accumulating, I just had to rely on the heater to melt them from the front window at least. Well, I thought, this is about a six-minute drive on dry streets; it'll be interesting to see how long it takes under these conditions.

I set off at a low but constant speed. The driving snow that filled the air all around, as well as the gouts of it that settled on my windows and slowly melted, had the effect of constricting my world into a tiny, hazy volume -- a habitat that was scarcely larger than the distance my arms could reach. The first thing I had to do was to descend the hill from the campus down to the highway that led to the western suburbs where we lived. Luckily, the administration already had men out with shovels and tractors, clearing and sanding this very drive, even as the snow continued to fall. So that, at least, was no problem, as long as I drove slowly enough to keep the car from slipping at the bottom of the hill and sliding out into the intersection. Then I had to turn left at the bottom of the hill onto the highway. Luckily, there was little traffic and I was able to accelerate smoothly out into the proper lane and keep moving. There had been no time for snow removal equipment to get out yet, but the vehicles that had gone down the busier streets had left deep double ruts almost down to the pavement. This was good in that I didn't have to force the car wheels to smash through snow that might ensnare them, but bad because as new snow fell into the ruts, thick layers of ice formed at the bottoms. When I had to stop, I could feel the wheels spin against this ice as I pressed down on the accelerator, and I prayed I wouldn't go into a skid that would leave me fetched up against the side of a parked car or stuck on a sidewalk.

The deep snow left all sounds curiously muffled; all I could hear was the thump of my wipers, my own breathing, and the rattling chains of oncoming cars. As usual, I hadn't put mine on yet; I hated the sounds they made on dry pavement, and I always waited until after the first heavy snowfall to put them on. Maybe next year I'll change my ways, I said this year as I did every year.

My first real problem came when I had to cross the bridge over the river and also the adjacent rail yards. A long ramp carried the roadway up to the main span, and this ramp was jammed with cars. Someone near the top of the ramp had stalled and couldn't get his car under way again; I saw two men attempting to push this car up the last fifty feet or so, lurching and occasionally falling as they lost purchase in the snow. Meanwhile, at least ten cars were stopped on the slope in front of me; it remained to be seen how many of these were going to suffer the same fate. As I waited, I watched oncoming cars descending the ramp; the drivers were not really in full control of these cars, which skidded to the left and right on the slippery incline; the drivers ineffectually jerked their steering wheels back and forth and just as ineffectually hit the brakes. But somehow, they all managed to bobsled their way to the bottom of the ramp without sideswiping any of us.

Finally, the stalled car made it to the top of the bridge, and it was time for the rest of us to try. I dropped into low gear and prepared to gun it as soon as I saw any sign of movement in front of me. The cars ahead were slewing from side to side, but they seemed to be making headway. As long as one of them isn't foolish enough to brake, we should make it, I thought. Here goes; keep the foot on the accelerator and steer in the direction of the skid. The Ford engine roared; the wheels headed left, I steered to the right; the tires caught some comparatively dry pavement and I was under control for a short while. The car directly in front of me spun out to the left; I caught sight of the frightened eyes of the driver, a young man with a beard, but he fought the car back onto the track at the last second before I would have hit, spattering sleet from the roadway across my windshield as he skidded. Man, I thought, it's like the state fair but with real cars. Finally, after a last whining wheel spin at the top of the ramp, I was on the bridge. I let out a whistling sigh and prepared myself for the descent at the other end.

All right, I said, let's take this slow and easy. I stopped at the head of the down ramp, put the car in low, and controlled my speed with the brake. I let it out just enough to allow the car to move forward in a slow skid. Let's hope I can keep this under control, I thought. I tried to keep several car lengths between me and the car ahead, but the driver behind me was right on my tail. "It doesn't pay to be in a hurry, pal," I said aloud. But we all made it, and we all went off on our separate journeys.

I pulled off the highway onto the less traveled residential streets. The snow was coming down even faster now, and these streets didn't have the same system of ruts that the highway had. Usually only one or two cars had traveled down these streets. There were stop signs at a few intersections on the way to my house, covered up with the sticky snow. I sailed right past these without really even slowing down. I didn't intend to stop unless I absolutely had to. Luckily there was almost no traffic.

I did skid once, about six blocks from my house; going around a fairly sharp bend, I was turning the wheel and braking at the same time. A real no-no, I should have known better. The car kept sliding and wound up in the left lane of traffic, its nose pointed at an angle toward the far curb. Luckily, I was able to get out of it by gunning in reverse and then plowing forward in low, spinning back into the proper lane quite neatly.

Finally, I headed down my street and saw my house. Our mailbox was heaped high with a cap of snow. I checked my watch; only twenty-four minutes on the road, a mere three hundred percent increase over the normal travel time for this same trip. Viola had made it back. Her car was in the driveway, completely covered with snow, and no sign of tire tracks behind it. Good, I thought to myself, she got home early and shouldn't have had any trouble. I pulled in behind her as far as I could (our driveway sloped upward and I couldn't make it all the way, but at least I was off the street). I let go of the wheel and turned off the engine. My hands were cramped and stiff from clutching the steering wheel so tightly.

I stomped up to the door and turned the knob; I was surprised to find it was locked. Come on, Viola, I said, nobody's going to bust in on you in this blizzard. I let myself into the house, slammed the door, and stamped the snow off on the mat. The furnace had been running, and stopped the moment I stepped inside. I felt a surge of relief to be in a familiar, warm place -- the sensation you feel when you have finally completed an unpleasant, time-consuming, wearying task and lie down between warm blankets. But at the same time I began to feel a sense of unease. The house was so quiet, and no lights were on. Usually you can hear a person you live with doing something, making some noise even in a remote corner of the house, but this time there was nothing. What the hell. "Viola?" I called. No answer, no sound at all. Where was she? "Hey, Vi?"

Something is wrong, I thought, she's not here and she didn't even eat lunch; the kitchen was spotless. Maybe she's at a neighbor's? That would be ridiculous, we can't stand any of them. I pulled off my wet shoes, and stepped in my stockinged feet through the kitchen and into the dining room. I kept looking in all directions; is she hiding somewhere and getting ready to leap out and scare me? This is not like her.

A piece of paper was lying right in the middle of the dining room table. It was folded in thirds, as if someone had decided to put it in an envelope but then thought better of it. Viola's silver fountain pen, the one her father had given her for her high school graduation, was lying right beside it with the cap off. Oh, no, I thought, I don't like the looks of this.

I put both hands on the page and flattened it out against the table, trying to put off the moment of reading it. Finally, I picked up the note and read it, and read it over and over with my eyes. My paralyzed mind tried to find some sense in what the marks on the paper were saying;

"Darling,

Art and I left Pawnee Springs around noon. We're not coming back. We are probably going to Chicago. He and I are in love; I love you, too, please believe me, but I can see more and more clearly that I am not right for you. I can never compete with your work. I'm sorry it didn't work out for us. Art and I have been falling in love since I first met him, and I have been unfaithful to you with him for a long time, and now I think it is time I told you the whole truth. I'm sorry to do this to you so close to Christmastime, but I'm tired of living this awful lie and I really can't go on with it one day longer. Don't try to find us; I'll call you in a few days. Please don't worry about me. Everything will be fine, better for all of us this way. I only took a few things and only stuff that was mine, not ours. You can keep my car. Take care of yourself.

Love, Vi"

Finally I couldn't read it any more. I closed my mouth to find it was dry from having hung open for all these minutes. My eyes were dry, though, too. So I sat heavily down in the recliner in the living room, holding the note in one hand, and let the other hang down to the floor, and watched the snow fall and fall and fall.

Arthur Forelli, my wife's immediate supervisor, was a man of forty, older than me; but he was a man with glossy black hair in coils, and eyebrows like a maiden's, and a wit that was easygoing but caustic, sparing no one, least of all himself; a lean-faced man, a sharp dresser in dark hopsack suits with pastel belts and ties, fitted shirts and glove-soft shoes; and with teeth as white as bleached bones. Arthur Forelli, good Christ, of all men to do this to me, a man who had brought over a bottle of good Chianti and drunk it with us only a week ago, so full of life and laughter; of course he was laughing, the bastard, knowing he was going to snatch my wife away from me and fuck her for the rest of my life. And the worst thing was she was watching him and me the whole time, knowing it was going to happen and concealing it from me.

The snow continued to fall. I felt a deep lethargy, a helplessness as if the juices of my body had been drained away and left behind a skinful of dried-out meat, a moribund creature with only the shape of a man, a being that could still move slowly in response to external stimuli but no longer had any volition. What the hell am I going to do now, that being said to me.

Finally, I turned on the radio and learned that the blizzard was general throughout the western halves of the central plains states; the cold front had come straight down the east face of the Rockies and stalled right over us, and the snow was going to continue to build up for at least another 12 hours. Residents were advised to stay in their homes and only to travel in the direst emergencies.

Well, this was not one of those. I wasn't about to go chasing those two, that was for damn sure. What a pair of creeps. How long had they been scheming and plotting this move, I wondered. I had absolutely no idea this was about to happen; Viola had been distant and quiet lately, certainly, but not significantly more so than in the previous couple of years. Why hadn't she told me that something was going wrong? What cowardice to do it to me like this, leaving what amounted to a memo for me to read and not even giving me the decency of a phone call. What a little shit.

DEGREES OF FREEDOM

I really don't remember what I did for the rest of that night; I had a few drinks, maybe more than a few, and I suppose I made myself something to eat, and at one point I lay down on the bed; but I got little or no sleep. I discovered that jealous hate makes you feel very sick. I couldn't stop imagining what they had done together many times already and what they were probably doing at this moment; they were probably in some cheapjack motel with paintings of lake sunsets and sailboats on the walls, with a chenille spread the color of dried blood shrouding the squeaking bed. I could imagine Viola from the back as she squatted over him and rubbed her belly against his, squirming and groaning in carnal delight while he dug his manicured nails into her flesh. They had probably pried the mirror off the dresser and had it propped up next to the bed, had turned on all the lights in the place, and were watching themselves fuck, craning their necks to see his cock sliding in and out of her and to watch him suck her tits as she flopped them down into his mouth for him to bite with his perfect teeth.

Ugh, the thought of that man's little finger with its death's-head ring stuck up my wife's delicate asshole, of his semen (I bet it was the color of snot, full of greenish lumps) spattered inside and outside her sumptuous cunt, made me want to vomit. I fantasized bursting into their motel room and opening fire on the two of them; it would only take one shot with a big enough gun, right through the back of whoever was on top.

I must have slept, finally, for a time; but morning overwhelmed the room, jarring me out of sleep with a contemptuous glare. My eyes gradually cleared as I squinted, over and over, opening my mouth wide as I did. I swung my legs indecisively over the edge of the bed, stood up hesitantly, lurched to the window with its pulled-back blue corduroy curtains, and looked outdoors to discover that the snowing had stopped; the sky was clear and china blue. I decided that I may as well get up.

Over a cup of hot coffee (how do you make just half a pot, I had asked myself in a daze, staring stupidly at the percolator for a minute or so), I sat in silence, glaring at the walls of the empty house that now seemed so huge. What the hell am I going to do now, I asked for the two hundredth time.

The phone rang, and it was Pyke. He sounded bright and cheerful; "How are things on your end of town, got any snow?" he asked. "I didn't have any trouble getting home, and I even have my electricity on," he continued, "which is more than the people a block away can say. A big tree limb came down and massacred the power lines." "Well, I don't have those kinds of trouble," I answered. "What would you guys like to do today?" he asked. "I happen to have both snowshoes and cross-country skis here, two pairs of the shoes and two of the skis, if you two would like to go for a hike in the country. You both can use whatever you'd like. I've got lots of poles, too. I was just out on the highway and it's pretty clear, so if we can only make it out of our own immediate neighborhoods, I think we can get out and have some fun in the snow. What do you say?"

"Well, Pyke," I said after a pause, "It would sound good at most times, but I don't think I'm up to it today. I came home yesterday to find out that my wife had run away from me, run off with a man from her office. So I'm not sure I'd make such good company at the moment."

"Run off." He made it a statement, not a question. There was a long silence on the line. "Stay right there," he said, "I'm going to come right over. Don't go away. I need to be with you at this hour." And he hung up before I could tell him I'd rather be alone.

Oh, well, I thought, maybe it'll be a diversion for a while, keep me from feeling sick and miserable for a little bit longer. If it only makes him feel better, I suppose it's still all right with me.

I made myself a couple of pieces of toast, realizing I hadn't had anything to eat yet that morning. I looked at them for a long time, watching the butter melt and run into the holes of the bread, then looked at the unbuttered side and watched it leaking through. What a marvel, I thought, nature still performs its inexorable feats; the physical laws of thermodynamics and gravity have not been repealed, even on this of all days. Who knows, maybe somewhere people are even laughing and happy, even on this day of wrath, this awesome day when Viola Cahill has torn the fabric of our lives and is somewhere hundreds of miles away from me, where I can't see or touch her and have no idea what she's doing or feeling.

Wilfully, I took a bite of the toast; it felt like a piece of burlap in my mouth, and tasted like dust, but I saw the perfect semicircle that had been made in it by my teeth; it was almost inconceivable to me that I could make my body function this way, that I could will it to perform such a destructive act upon an innocent object that was not myself. I was even able to chew, and, even more amazingly, to swallow this inexpressibly strange, semisolid mass; and even before the food entered my stomach, my mindless digestive enzymes were carrying out the tasks that they had been shaped to do by hundreds of millions of years of evolution; swarming around the starch molecules of the toast, some were busily hydrolyzing them to much smaller glucose units, and others were catabolizing the glucose with equal diligence, converting it to metabolic energy that would keep me moving and breathing for a little while longer. I could no more have stopped or regulated these processes than I could have walked on water. What the hell am I going to do.

Just then, Pyke pulled up. Not in his car, as I thought he would have come, but on his god-damn skis! An absurd fur hat, resembling a red furry wig, was on his head. He slid past the window, saluting me with his poles, and skidded around to the back door. I had to laugh. The crazy s.o.b. I opened the back door and in he came, skis and all, playing a fanfare with his buzzing lips. His eyes were gaping and his cheeks were tight and red, like Santa Claus's. He stepped out of the skis, doffed his hat with a bow, and then came up and gave me a big bear hug, saying, "How the hell are you, man? I just played the brass fanfare from the Berlioz Requiem for you, but remember, it doesn't come at the part where the damned are being plunged into hell, but where the wonderful trumpet, *tuba mirum*, gathers all before the throne of heaven. And here we are, in the midst of this natural wonder of a snowfall, just before the winter solstice when Nature lays the groundwork for the renewal of all things. At such a time we should all rejoice at the glory God has made. We have plenty of time for eternal rest."

"Thanks for coming over," I said. "I'm not sure I'm up to being a congenial comrade today, though. I'm not actually feeling very well."

"I'm afraid that I know that sick feeling," he replied, "the one where you want to cry because your loved one has left, but you can't because you're too angry at what she's done. And that's interrupted by the thought that maybe she'll change her mind, that it was all some terrible mistake, and that at any minute she'll be coming back through the door. Then that hope fades and you start to feel that you're glad she's gone, because if she's dumb enough to take off with the first slick bozo that says hello to her, she really couldn't have been trusted much longer anyway. 'Let her go, let her go, God bless her,' you sing, 'wherever she may be; she may search this wide world over, but she'll never find a sweet man like me.' "

"So the hope and the dread come and go," he went on, " washing across you over and over again, and you start to blame yourself for some little moment of inattention that might have triggered the whole thing sixteen months ago, and then you run over all the faults in her personality that make you glad, for a moment, that she's gone; you feel like you can be objective about your life at last; and then you think about how nice it was to reach over in the middle of the night and grab her by the soft warm tit and have her turn over and start moaning and kissing you. Am I right there, boss, am I right?"

"You got it on the nose, pal, or on the nipple or whatever," I said, "but what the hell am I supposed to do in the meantime? I don't feel like sleeping, eating, working, staying in, going out, killing myself, playing the piano, or listening to the radio - all I've been doing is sitting here staring off into space. I think I'll go nuts if this goes on much longer."

"I'm afraid I can't give you any advice, Bruce. If your experience is anything like ones I've had, it will probably take at least two months before you start to feel a little bit like yourself. You'll have days when you feel really good, free and easy and happy, and then the next day will be absolutely terrible. Little things will start bothering you - things that you'd never even notice, like an old lady driving slowly down the street; you'll feel a surge of loathing sweep over you, and you'll pull around her car with a screech of your tires, give her the finger, and shout, 'Move it, you goddam jackass!' and the poor thing might die of heart failure right then. But you won't even care because you'll feel better for a moment, at least until you reflect on what you did later."

I told him he seemed to know a lot about this for a single man, and he went on, "You don't have to be married to a woman to love her deeply. Single couples can experience tremendous emotions too, you know - maybe you remember? - ranging from rapture all the way to poisonous malice. Oh, the ups and downs do go on and on, and finally it seems that the love that has held the couple together becomes severed, like a piece of metal that's bent back and forth over and over; and something irreversible happens, and then nothing either of you can do or say will help to make things go back to the way they were. Love is really not permanent, you find; it's not forever; it's not a static condition, it's a living process, and when it comes to a stop, it's over. It's really over; it's like some cataclysmic geological phenomenon, an earthquake that thrusts against two pieces of land that used to be contiguous and sets them far apart. But eventually, it ends. The violent emotions you suffer, eventually smolder and die down. And after a year or so, it's all burned out of you, and you can get back to being yourself again. And you know, when something does end, even something you care about - like one of the classes you teach - don't you feel a sense of relief, of exhiliration, almost?"

"No, my friend, not about this. No way in hell. But I didn't realize all this had happened to you. I never heard you speak of anything like this."

"Man," he said, "it's happened to just about everybody. No one in our society wants to put their naked emotions out on the line to other people - especially men, who are prisoners of a social ethos that makes them feel guilty if they admit to feeling out of control, and especially when it brings back all the hurt you felt back then. Actually, it happens more than once to most people, most people I've talked to, anyway. I myself have surrendered my heart more than once, and known the great exaltation that comes of it, and I've known the heartbreak that follows; and I've asked myself if the panicky excitement of the first stages is worth suffering the agony of the loss of love when it comes. Sometimes, I think to myself that my need to be in love with someone must be pathological. But, at least for me it still is worth it. And I actually feel some envy for you now, because I am reasonably sure that down the road there's another glorious lover out there for you. You won't ever forget your wife, but she'll be only part of your life, not the whole thing. And who can say that isn't healthier in the long run?"

"Well, I'd like to believe you," I said, "but right at the moment I feel as if life has left me far behind. I feel old, used, and rejected. Damn it, I loved that woman so much; I was looking forward to spending a snowy night with her, cuddling under our eiderdown, and then sitting around today together in our seedy old robes, just being warm and companionable. And instead I sit here feeling like my guts have been ripped out, trying to behave sociably with you and not bust out crying. Big strong guys don't do that, right, podner?"

"That's right, comrade, we don't. I don't know if we should, but we don't. And as a result we have to do other things. Drink until we almost fall down, punch the wall, and yell real loud. Good substitutes, eh? But right now I'm starting to feel stuffy in here, and I'd like to go for a walk around your neighborhood. Would you come with me?'

He had an imploring look in his eyes. I thought, is this part of some kind of therapy he's trying to feed me, or does he really have a surpassing interest in my surroundings? But I really was too far gone to ask, or to care one way or another how I was spending my time. So we left, stomping off through the chill and deserted streets. It had become significantly colder, and a smoke-colored sky had descended on the town like a pall. No one had yet shoveled a sidewalk, but enough cars had passed through that there was a fairly clear path in the street. It still required considerable exertion to push through the deep snow; after ten minutes, even though I was wearing a relatively light jacket, I was sweating.

As we walked, Pyke asked me many questions about my neighbors - their houses, occupations, and idiosyncracies. I was amazed at how little I knew about the people I lived among. Pyke said he knew almost everyone in his neighborhood; they'd gather for block parties, meet at the local pub, or just talk together as they sat on their porches. I wished I lived in such a neighborhood; now that my wife was gone, I felt really out of place in suburbia, where everyone seemed to be part of a couple.

I asked Pyke if he had ever wanted to be married, and he didn't answer at first; he raised his eyes slightly, looking up at the clouds, and pressed his lips together and sighed. Then he stopped, turned halfway to me, and said, "There were times. More than once. But I'm not sure what happened; things went wrong somewhere along the line. No woman has wanted to risk it all for the likes of me. I don't know whether I'm perceived as unstable, or unreliable, or fickle - maybe I am all of those things in some ways - but I always thought I was capable of the deepest kinds of love, of caring for another person more than for myself. It's always seemed as if the women I've cared for the most - the brightest, the most beautiful and graceful - were those who were the most skittish about being tied down, especially with me. So here I am, still single and free; 'free as a bird' as they say. And it's starting to look as if I'm going to stay that way."

We walked for three or four blocks and finally reached the park, a little place of no more than an acre or two, with swings and slides for the kids and an open space where they and their families could run and play. We stopped for a rest; our breathing made little nebulas in the air. It was windless and silent with that peculiar stillness of snow-covered places. Pyke swung his arms around and around in broad vertical circles, and banged his mittened hands together to maintain a good rate of circulation. He said it'd been years since he'd done things like sliding, that he'd almost forgotten what it felt like; and at that he stamped his way up the ladder of the largest slide, a ten-foot-tall snow-covered aluminum triangle. He balanced on the handrails with his arms and swung his legs forward, sat down in the snow that had settled in a foot-deep mound at the top of the slope, and came down. I think he'd forgotten about the ice that formed at the beginning of yesterday's storm and had also coated the metal ramp; he came down uncontrollably fast, despite the deep coating of snow. He fell backward first, his head bouncing off the board with a clang; and by the time he was able to sit up, he'd reached the bottom, and, thrown off balance in the other direction, pitched forward with a yell, face-first into a hillock of snow.

For some reason, I found this insupportably funny, especially when he got up on his knees and looked up at me, his face white as a pie-in-the-face comic's, ringed with red hair and with a dark open mouth incongruously smiling in the middle. He stood up magisterially and brushed himself off with grave dignity, like Oliver Hardy after he had fallen in the whitewash, and I kept snickering, pointing at him and standing bent over in stomach-clutching mirth.

Suddenly he was after me with a double handful of snow, saying, "What's so goddam funny, you little turd?," but laughing pandemonically himself. He launched his cumbersome missile at my head from a distance of a yard, but I ducked it. He was on the dead run, though, and shoved me down, and was on top of me. Before he could smother me completely, though, I squirmed away, and had almost stood completely up when he hit me in the rump with a smartly thrown projectile. Needless to say, I couldn't let this pass unanswered, and we let fly at each other for a minute or so with a fusillade of frozen missiles; finally, he charged me, grabbed me by the waist, yelled "Death to you, Fascist tyrant!" and threw me down again. We struggled and tussled in the snow for another minute or so, until we were tired and all laughed out. Besides, we saw that we were being stared at by a stout, mustachioed man in a knee-length tartan coat and Russian cap; he was leading a tiny dog dressed in sweater and boots. The man and dog were lashed together by a heavy chain that probably would have restrained a buffalo. Pyke stood up, pulled me after him by the hand, and we brushed each other off. "I think we might be scaring the dog," he said, and I responded, "Or his master."

We walked back to my house, not saying much. We were both wet, weary, and cold. Inside, I asked Pyke to stay for lunch, but he begged off, saying that he had some class work to do; he expected that we would probably have classes tomorrow, but almost no one would come. Still, there were the pre-holiday examinations coming up next week that we would have to work on and he'd better get to them.

He stood in my doorway, a dark shape backlit by the low sun. "Listen to me, man," he said, "I know you're going to be in for some hard times in the next few months. I've been through it, man, and I want to help you if I can. You're the best friend I have in this town. I knew the first day we met that we were kindred souls. I don't have a brother any more, but you feel like one to me; and I want you to know that I'm going to be there for you. So I'm going home now, but don't you dare put off calling me if you need any help, or even if you just feel like talking to somebody. OK?"

I said, "Thanks, Pyke. You're an all-right guy. Thanks for stopping by, and thanks for the encouragement. I'll keep in touch. So long, now."

And he was gone and I was alone again in the quiet house. I stripped off my wet things and had a long shower, using much more hot water than I would normally have done; it was my house now and I'll be damned, I thought, if I'll do anything other than exactly what I want to, from now on. "To hell with wives and all other forms of live-in womankind," I said aloud as the needle streams of water spouted through my hair. Then, stepping out of the shower, I found I didn't have a towel at hand. I was almost ready to call out for Viola, but I checked myself in time, and walked dripping and naked back into our bedroom. I grabbed two towels out of the closet, wiped my body down with one and wrapped the other one around my head. Just the way she used to do, I thought.

I lay down on the bed and put my head on one pillow, then grabbed the other one, lay it on top of me, and squeezed it tightly. Damn, it still smells like her; I wonder how long that will last. Then, angrily, I pulled the case off and stuffed it into the bottom of the laundry bag, underneath my dirty socks and wet trousers. The bimbo, I thought, what's she doing now? Probably sharing a cigarette with him, she who never used to smoke until recently, who probably started to cover up the smell of him, the chimney, on her; lying in bed after lunch and after a good fuck, talking earnestly about their future together. May they set fire to the bedroom.

Pyke 4

(A cassette recording, one of the six from his desk, probably made by Pyke under the circumstances he describes.)

It is roughly, I should judge, 11 P. M. I am lying on my bed, the old soft mattress and the squeaky box spring. My blanket is lying on the floor. The room is stuffy, even with my exhaust fan on its high speed; the night air is humid and smells of mildew. My neighbors are out for the evening, and will probably not return until well after midnight, when they will doubtless make noisy love and then begin to quarrel, both activities which will keep me awake; at around three, spent, they and I will fall into spasmodic sleep.

I have been lying here for the past hour, after having eaten a bowl of black bean soup from a can and drunk three glasses of cheap red wine from a jug with a label like an Italian tablecloth. I am quite naked, having even removed my watch. I have been reading a book on ants and bees, a new book by Ed Wilson, but I have reached that stage where the words are taken in by the eyes but not by the mind, and after several half-hearted attempts to reread the last few paragraphs about social insect hierarchies, I drop the book on the floor and close my eyes. I place one of my hands over my two eyes and feel them throbbing, the muscles squeezing and releasing them. They feel like two trapped animals feebly protesting their long confinement.

My other hand I place on my groin; I adjust my penis so that it lies at full length on my scrotum. I stroke it briefly so that it expands, but just enough to lie in place, neither rising up to point out the ceiling nor falling flaccidly to one side. I keep my hand in position so that my fingers curl gently around underneath and I can feel the difference between what my fingers detect, the fine sparse hairs on my balls, and what my thumb notes, the coarser texture of my upper pubic hairs. At first touch, my scrotum shrinks slightly away, like a marine animal responding to a change in water pressure, but then it swells back again. Between my first two fingers I feel the smoothness of my cock; its texture is curiously botanical, as though it were one of those yellow Mexican peppers you sometimes see in the supermarket. I also feel the slight lumpiness caused by the vein running down one side; if I lie very still, I can feel its tiny throbbing in response to my beating heart.

As I lie here, I have the soles of my feet pressed together so that my knees are pointing apart toward the walls of my bedroom. I try not to be thinking of anything, just feeling the warmth under one hand and in the other. I feel very relaxed and alive, but at the same time I think that if I could die without pain at this moment I would. I feel that this creature in this odd position is the real me, the real McKenna. I want to be buried in this position, I want to have my body laid out like this for my funeral, so that my friends can say goodbye to me as I really am.

I begin to let my mind wander over the details of my past, the many experiences I have had that have been insulting or frightening, and the rare occasions when I have known joy. I often do this at such times as this, letting my mind drift off in a reverie of days gone by, but a reverie which is often of travesties and failures, though mingled with pleasant fantasies.

I think back as far as I can in my childhood, and I clearly remember my earliest memory, my father laughing as my mother bounces on his lap; I watch them, quietly peering through the bars of my crib. I am sucking my thumb and stroking the satin border of my worn yellow blanket. I don't think they know I am awake and watching, and that knowledge confuses and thrills me.

They are in our bedroom, lit from my right by a flickering lantern; I can smell the buttery odor of the burning kerosene. My mother's back is toward me. They are partially undressed, sitting on a green leatherette chair without arms. The stuffing is coming out from one corner of the seat. I see my father's arms wrapped around my mother's pale and spotted back; his sunburnt hands grip her shoulders like the black claws of a raptor. Her black hair is particularly fascinating to watch; it billows out as if in slow motion as she falls from the apogee of her ascent, and then it drops rapidly back down to her bare shoulders. Then she rolls off my father's lap onto the bed, spreading her legs wide and stretching supplicating arms up to him. And then, suddenly, the light goes out and the show is over, and unwillingly I drop off to sleep.

And a few years later, I recall my father driving very fast in our old pickup over the washboardy hills of southeastern Ohio, with me sitting beside him, he guns the engine at the top of the hill so that I lurch upwards in my seat as if I'm at the top of a roller-coaster. He and I both shout "whee!" and laugh. That night I have a terrifying dream, that the truck has gone into the ditch and that he and I are trapped on top of it by wild hogs, thousands of them, snorting and writhing for as far as the eye can see; and my father slips off the top, and falls into the mass of hogs who fall on him, slavering. He screams, but only once.

And when I was about thirteen, I remember one late summer day, lying on my back with my head propped against the utility pole in our back yard, maybe a year after the REA brought electricity to our farm. Squinting up into the clear skies, I saw as far up as I could see, soaring in tight circles, about twenty white birds. I expect they were gulls. I wasn't able to hear anything, only to observe those silvery specks moving in and out of the limit of my vision, the sun flashing off their wings, surrounded by the deep blue of the afternoon. They wheeled above me in a kind of pavane, formal and majestic; they appeared to have amalgamated themselves into a super-organism, a colony of insubstantial beings driven by a single mighty thought; to hover above the mean and dismal earth, the zone of death, and to exalt it with their nobility.

As I continued to watch, I felt my self being transcended, made timeless, lifted up to join the birds. My body shrank until it was only an eye, an eye and a pair of wings, ever-aware, swirling in eddies of limitless scope, following an invisible beacon through a labyrinth of freedom. This wizardry held me in its thrall for what may have been minutes, or hours, but my mother broke the spell by shouting for me to come in for supper.

And then I remember the girl I first kissed, after a church youth group meeting, I think we were both fifteen. Her name was Janice Callisher and her father was a deacon of the church. I am quite sure we belonged to the Methodist church then, although my father did tend to switch denominations quite regularly, over any real or imagined slight tendered him by the hierarchy. He was uncomfortable as a Methodist, given his strong Anglican background, but the Church of England was not one of the stronger ecclesiastical organizations of rural Ohio. A Methodist is nothing more than a Baptist with shoes, he never tired of saying.

At any rate, it was late in the school year, about the middle of May. I was the president and she was the secretary of the group. She didn't go to my high school and the only time I got to see her was at church functions. She was a tall and gangly girl. Her bosom had developed more rapidly than her hips and legs, and her hair was cut very short, so that she looked boylike, but only from behind. I thought she was the most sexy creature that ever had walked. We were idly strolling in the warm darkness behind the church; I had, with feigned casualness, placed my hand on her back, just below her shoulder blades. She was wearing a white blouse, and I remember the way her brassiere felt through its thin fabric; my fingers were actually on the very fastener itself, one above and one below, almost in a position to snap it open and to spill her glorious breasts out of their dungeon and into the open air of freedom. And I remember how my breath was coming fast, my heart was pounding like a steam hammer, and my eyelids wouldn't stop twitching, and how I hoped that she wouldn't tear my hand away and start screaming, for I still believed then the contemporary lie that girls were a different form of life, finer and more delicate than us (coarse males, who only wanted to ejaculate into whatever handy hole we could find, be it a vagina or a hollow hickory log).

And I still don't know if she tripped me or if we stumbled into that pile of leaves by the snow fence, but I remember that first her hot cheek was pressing mine, and suddenly her lips were seeking my mouth and sucking at my tongue and her own tongue was plunging into the deepest recesses of my mandibles.

And her right leg was forced down between mine, sliding rhythmically back and forth over my groin until I thought I was going to have to scream out. Yes, Janice, wherever you are, look at me now, lying here thirty years later, I can still get it up just thinking about that incident.

And then she stuggled out of my grasp and jumped up, saying, "I hope you don't think I'm terrible," and ran around the church into the light, and leaped into her mother's waiting car and sped away while I ran futilely behind, calling out for her not to leave me, saying, "I think you're wonderful!" But she would never kiss me again after that, and shortly afterward dropped out of our youth program, and I heard from someone a few months later that she'd run off with an army officer, an Eskimo as it turned out, and was living with him at a military base up in New Hampshire.

And finally, my parents.

My mother is still fresh in my mind after such a long time, dying when I was still just a little boy. How to begin to describe her? She was beautiful, gentle, but frail. In the barren and purposeless world, she was like a tiny animal trapped in a cage with its ravenous enemies, or like a lost butterfly in the middle of six lanes of rush-hour traffic. I loved her incoherently. When she would embrace me as hard as she could, I could feel her thin forearms trembling with the effort, and the bones in her hands seemed as feeble and brittle as a chicken's wings.

She was always ill, had been since her own childhood. One disease followed another, scarlet fever, phlebitis in her feet, jaundice, unknown fevers and indispositions, including the one that left her unable to raise one arm for six weeks, the one the doctor said was neurasthenia. Her skin was pale and translucent, especially on her face, where I could see the straw-colored blood shuddering in her dilated veins. Ah, mama, when you slept your breathing was so shallow and quiescent that more than once I thought you had died right there in your bed, or under the torn old quilt on the couch.

She practically died, I was told, after she gave birth to me; her dainty body was wracked by septicemia. In those pre-antibiotic days, the doctors and nurses were helpless. Shaking their heads slowly, they spoke in whispers about the tragedy of this case. So young and so beautiful, and with her new infant that she was so looking forward to having; what a calamity. They sent us home, only God could help my mama now, it's all in His hands. My father carried her in from the ambulance. She was trembling like a baby bird in his sturdy arms, hardly able to hold on around his neck; and he lay her so tenderly into their bed, and covered her with warm quilts and blankets, and caressed her wan face with his fingertips and kissed her forehead. She lay in that bed in delirium for weeks. He watched her nightmares come and go as she followed them with wide-open and visionless eyes. My father prayed over her unceasingly; and gradually, she came back from it. How exhilarating those first signs must have been, the feeble glimmer of lucidity coming back into her eyes and the return of her will -being able to lift her hand and move it to where she wanted it to be, to speak a wish for a sip of water or a cool cloth on her forehead.

But for all that physical fragility, how strong her character was, and how happy she seemed. She never once complained about the bad luck that kept bringing her new forms of suffering. Her emotions were close to the surface, like a baby's; she could go from crying to laughing in an instant. And while her tears were subdued and private, her laughter was rich, various, and infectious; it burst out of her like curtains of floodwater coursing over the lip of a dam. And her great joy was to let others join in her laughing, to share her interior reserves of mirth. And she never understood that it was impolite to laugh at one's own jokes; the idea would never occur to her. So prodigiously witty was she that she could reduce herself and me to helplessness with those jokes; again and again, my laughter would become so uncontrollable that it was as if someone pitiless had been tickling me under the arms. And while I loved these episodes, something in me also dreaded them; I knew that when it was over I was going to be absolutely drained and spent, that my stomach would be hurting and I'd have a headache. Oh, mama, the time you improvised those limericks, about people that were meeting grotesque deaths in appallingly ridiculous circumstances, how I was reduced to a mass of screaming giggles. I had to beg her to stop, mama, stop; I can't take it any more, mama, please.

But after my brother was born, then it seemed that she became totally introspective, as if she was carrying on a dialogue within herself between her existence and her death. It was all a mistake, to begin with. The doctor had told her in no uncertain terms that she was not to consider the bearing of another child. Not only had she almost died giving birth to me, but I was thin and ill as an infant. It was my mama's milk, the doctor had said; it's no good, too watery, look how undernourished your baby is, not nice and fat like Mrs. Fuller's down the block. You have to switch him to the bottle, and if God forbid you have another one, it must be given the bottle from the beginning. But by far the best thing would be that you not get pregnant again. Yet something went wrong; I suppose the douches didn't work, those tiny bags of effervescent powder I found in her dresser drawer, stuck back way in the back under the second-best underwear. Her baby was in there, and she wouldn't have wanted to abort it even if she could have. And she loved the baby so much. It practically drove us crazy, she was so careful with what she'd let herself do. She couldn't get excited, she said, and she needed her rest, and she couldn't drink coffee or go to the movies or wash heavy loads of clothes. And somehow, it looked as if everything was going to work out all right, until in her sixth month she tripped on the steps, coming in from outside, and hit her belly; and a little blood came from the womb, and she said she didn't feel the baby move after that. She did not cry, but she behaved as if she had been stunned into a spiritual paralysis, and became convinced that the child would be born dead, or deformed in some horrible way. She took to her bed and almost refused to move for the last three months, developing awful bedsores and a hoarse cough that wouldn't go away. She couldn't sleep, and lost weight, and her eyes started to sink back into her bony face; she looked terrible. And finally, Tommy was born and he was all right; and when they came back from the hospital, I saw that she was crying with joy, and later she held the baby for hour after hour in her lap and over her trembling shoulders, crooning to him in tuneless lullabies like the voice of the wind.

Shortly afterwards, we noticed that her personality started to dissipate, as if it had been sucked inside her at the same time Tommy came out. No longer came the laughs and the jokes; her expression was puzzled and unchanging, all day long. She wouldn't hear what we would say to her until we literally went up and shook her to attention. Even when she was holding Tommy and he was crying, it was as if she was caressing him only mechanically, and her eyes were somewhere far away watching something else, something deeply interesting that had hypnotized her as a cobra is said to mesmerize its prey.

Then she lost her physical strength too, and the weakness of her final illness left her, not a shell of her former self, because a shell retains some form and structure and shows something of what had inhabited it; she was more like a scrap, like a piece of waste fabric that had been cut away and was about to be trampled under the feet of the burly factory seamstresses as the final whistle blew for their shift. My father took her to the hospital in a Yellow Cab; she, dressed in her old nightgown and scuffs and wrapped in a shawl, swayed down the sidewalk taking tiny steps as he held her up, clamping her shoulders in his powerful forearms; she continued to look confounded and confused, as always, throughout the whole thing. Finally, he picked her up bodily and set her on the back seat as the small, dark driver watched in fascination.

And she died in that hospital not long afterwards; I was home from school and sitting on the brown leather footstool that Grandma had sent us, playing with the cat, when my father came home looking grey and old. I ran up to hug him around the waist, and he was stiff in the legs and soggy in the body like a sack of wet rags on stilts. He put his hands on my shoulders and pushed me away and looked into my face with eyes that were rheumy and bloodless as a dog's. He licked his lips and swallowed and said, "She's gone, son. God took mama away at last." And I felt something drain away inside me, and I said to him, "Oh, daddy, what will we do now?," because I was thinking of my baby brother, and then I couldn't hear what my father was saying to me because I was crying too hard, because something had crumbled inside my spirit and undammed a torrent of tears. And he picked me up in his strong arms and carried me to the couch and we sat and wept together, man to man, until we were both cried out.

It was the only time I saw the man in tears, although he was capable of being moved by beautiful things as well as sadness. Although he tried to be a farmer, and to have a farmer's stoic perspective on tragedy and poverty, he was too intelligent to remain stolid in the face of stupidity; and he raged against injustice and the callous unconcern of the moneyed castes all his life, raged while he was sober and raged while consumed in alcoholic depression, as he was all too often in his later years.

Somehow, though, he mistrusted the orthodox procedures of learning about things; he could never understand why my nose was always in a book when I was a kid. "You got one of those storybooks again?" he'd always say. They were always "storybooks" whether they were fiction or poetry or were about something like natural history. And I'd never be quite sure whether he was just joking or whether I was supposed to feel guilty about doing so much reading. Well, I never stopped, obviously, and I always loved and revered my father although I could never quite fathom him.

But still, I (and, I think he, also) recovered from my mother's death, and grew up pretty well without her. My father's death was something else as far as I was concerned. I still don't quite understand this. I was over forty when he died - old enough, you'd think, for a mature man to be able to deal with the fact of an old man's passing. And I was not there trying to take care of him all the time, as he and I had to do with mama - he was in a nursing home not too far away; I had earned enough money to engage the assistance of professionals to make his last days more comfortable. And when I made my weekly visits over there on Saturdays, he seemed chipper enough. He was never an out-and-out laugher, like mama had been; I suppose he was the sort you would call dour, although he had a sardonic and bitter humor that he usually turned to politicians, religious figures, his own doctors and nurses, and other such sanctimonious personalities.

His death was sudden, not like mama's lingering farewell. The home called me at my office on a Wednesday afternoon, a cold grey day in early November, to tell me he'd had a massive stroke that morning. I remember snatching the phone receiver away from my ear and looking at it reproachfully at arm's length, as if someone I was talking to had called me a vile name. And the sinking feeling I felt afterwards was not the same as that one that came over me thirty years earlier; it was a chill that was about knowing I was finally alone. There was no one I could turn to now. The man who pioneered in my life, who helped clear underbrush out of the way of my journey and who pointed out some of the pitfalls and ambushes on the way, was dead, bushwhacked by an assassin's invisible bullet, a sudden physiological missile hurtling into the cardiovascular system. And there was no point man left for me anymore; it was all up to me to face the enemy on my own.

At the funeral, I was the only one of our family there; Tom was in the Phillipines, exactly halfway around the world, and in 1962 it still took too long to make the journey back in time for the funeral. He was on the way, probably about to land in L. A., when I threw the first shovelful of soil on daddy's coffin.

Both of them long dead now, their bones unmemorialized in a forgotten cemetery just outside of a little Ohio town; no one they knew will ever visit their graves again. Neither of their sons left any offspring to carry on their genes; all of their love and passion and the toil they expended to keep our family going has come to virtually nothing. The younger son stupidly dead, a death as absurd as theirs, as absurd as all human deaths. The older son still alive for now.

I am probably the last living person that has any memories of them; when I lose consciousness for the last time, they will be more extinct than the giant ground sloths of the Eocene. "More," not "as," because those ancient megatherians are still thought of every day by a few ultraspecialist scholars, scattered about the world, who sit around and daydream about what their life histories must have been like, what color their excrement was and what they looked like while they were mating. And I think that very soon I will also be dead, and there will never again be another being in the history of the universe who will know and feel exactly what I have, and the memory of me will flicker out in one after another of the dying brains of those who knew me. But rather than terror this brings me a certain satisfaction. For a time after I die, my friends will say to each other, he is gone; but what a man he was, we shall not see his like again. And this has been said about countless corpses, and it has always been true.

And still they keep popping up, these rare individuals, as rare as humanity and as common, popping out of the womb and growing up just a little bit different from every other rare individual. And what a truism it is, but how delightful. And it makes death not only necessary but something hopeful. So I continue to lie on the bed, in the same position, breathing as slowly as I can, hoping to fall asleep this way. And if I die let me be found this way, and let my friends say, he was a strange person; look at him in death, a hand on his balls and a hand across his eyes, surely no one in history has ever done this before. And let them laugh at this, a laugh tempered with a touch of dread as they imagine the embarrassing positions that they may be discovered in as life leaves them, and let them take my mouldering body (in a coarse sack in the back of a pickup truck) to the empty rugged hills and put it in a shallow grave. Let none look on my bones again, but let me be remembered in the hearts of a few for a few more years, and I will ask for nothing else. Except - please put no plastic gardenias on my grave, guys. And now let me sleep and let me leave this recording for my testament, my friends, my sweetest princes and princesses, I love you and may your days be warm and your nights peaceful for as long as they may last. Adieu.

Conversation: The End

(I did not know it at the time, but the following conversation with Pyke was to be my last. At the close of the summer term, I turned in my final grades to Miss Freemartin and prepared to take a few days off. It was Friday morning, July 17, 1970. I planned to fly to Padre Island, on the Texas coast, and not to think about my job for a while. I stopped by Pyke's office to say goodbye to him.)

B: Well, old man, that seems to be it for another school year. I don't know about you, but I'm getting the hell out of this joint and heading south.

P: I think I'll stick around here for a while. There are some things I need to think about, and I can do it best when there are absolutely no other people around.

B: Oh, and what sort of things would those be?

P: Oh, nothing life-or-death, I suppose, nothing cosmically important, just a few decisions I need to make about the way I live and how I can organize my existence better. I don't have much time left on the planet, and I think I should decide what my priorities should be from here on out.

B: Wow, that sounds important. Heavy stuff, man, as they say these days. Are you sure you're ready for this? It sounds like a major task of reorganization. I don't want to come back here and find the contents of your file cabinets all spread up and down the hallway; your junk might make a barrier so I can't get into my office.

P: Oh, no, it won't be anything like that. I just have to spend some time about thinking what it is that makes for a decent life. I don't know if you've ever felt anything like this, but I've been thinking that I've been malingering in my existence, especially my life as a teacher; I feel as if I've been drawing my pay without performing my duties in the way I should. I don't want to be an intellectual or moral deadbeat; I want to leave something behind that will be worthwhile. Nothing spectacular, just something that people will think about years from now and say, that was his, and he was good at it, wasn't he?

For example, take a look at this basket of mine. This one, here, on the shelf; I've filled it full of things to read someday. Let me dump them out here, so that I can show it to you. This basket is one of the most important objects in my life. It belonged to my father's grandmother. She made it, by hand, out of willow twigs that she collected on her meanderings around the bogs in County Antrim, where she lived. She knew all the plants, the ones you could use for herbal remedies and the ones that had roots that were good to eat. She had twelve children, nine of whom lived, and my father's father was the youngest. The basket was probably made when my father was a little boy, probably around 1895; but it might be much older. She gave it to him, anyway, just before he left for America. It was the last time he saw her; she was over eighty then, and she died the year I was born.

My dad told me how he'd help her gather the stems in the spring of the year, when they were still tender and flexible, so she could boil them in a huge black pot on the peat-fired stove to get the bark to where it'd slip off easily. She'd snatch them out of the boiling water and slip her thumbnail down the vines, while they were still hot, and peel off the bark.

So look at this thing; it's about twenty inches long, ten deep, and ten wide. She weaved the whole basket just by twisting those boiled vines, of different sizes, all around one another. She probably made the frame first, out of heavier stems, and then braided in these rib pieces you see here, and then twisted the lightest stems back and forth to make the rest of the basket. All woven by hand. Nothing artificial at all. Someone shellacked it at one time, probably my dad, but that's it. Look at the handles; there are two of them. See how stout and rigid they are. Look how they fold down perfectly over the ends of the basket; look at how they come to the same spot, perfectly symmetrical, on both ends. And then look at the pattern made by the thinner vines, how they are knitted so close together. It's incredibly sturdy, it's perfect. Hold it in your hands and squeeze it; feel how solid it is. You could almost carry water in the thing without it spilling out, even now. A wonderful piece of folk craftsmanship, of folk art, you might say; but it's more than that, it's a perfect piece of utilitarian skill; it's something that was necessary, and it was made without any thought of fame or recognition, just a thing that was done because it had to be, done to last, to be as good as it could be. And don't forget it's nearly eighty years old, this basket, or maybe even more; it's had hard use to a degree we can't even guess at anymore, it's probably been used to carry potatoes, store dirty cloth diapers, lug firewood, God knows what else. I've had it for twenty-five years. Most of that time, it's been stored in damp basements, stuffed in the corners of closets, thrown into the trunks of cars as I moved from one place to another. And nothing could faze it, I'm sure it looks the same now as the day it was made.

It's only been recently that I've taken a good look at the thing. I look at it and I try to face up to what it represents. What have I ever done in all my life that's anywhere near as good as this object? Who will remember what I have done, the way I look at this basket and remember my great-grandmother, someone I never even saw, but someone I have the greatest respect for?

[Pause] I want you to have this basket, Bruce. I want it to go to someone who will keep it forever, look at it often, and appreciate it, and use it as a touchstone for the rest of his life. Take it, it's yours.

B: I couldn't, Pyke! It's your family heirloom, something that belongs to you in the same way that your skin and eyes do. Don't be ridiculous. It's yours; don't do this to me.

P: No, I've had my fill of it. It's served its purpose for me. It's something I love, but I really want you to have it. Just keep it where I can come and visit it when I want; keep it in your office for now. Hold onto it for me, please, Bruce; but I want you to have it, I want to be sure that you get it from my hands, here and now.

B: Well, I don't really like the sound of this, but if you insist I shall give it a place of honor on my shelf. And I won't think of it as mine, I'll just hold on to it until you decide to take it back. I think you're just having a brief spell of disillusion. I know you by now, pal; you'll be back, and when you are, just take it back. It is yours, but I'll hold onto it for now.

P: Oh, no, buddy, it's yours now. Thank you for your help. This is more important to me than you can know.

B: Hey, whatever you want, friend. Anything I can do to give you a hand. You're really a decent guy, you know, every once in a while.

P: There are too many nice men in this world; the graveyards are full of them.

B: Aha, a note of self-pity. I recognize those, pal. Especially those that come at the end of the academic year; when you realize it's only over for a short period, and pretty soon the fresh young faces will be coming in again, endlessly, eagerly waiting for you to tell them things that will change their lives. And after a while, it's hard to face up to them, and you long to tell them to go back home before it's too late, to tell the students that no one can teach them anything unless they prepare the way for it by becoming excited, by almost feeling erotically aroused by the subject matter.

P: Goethe said we only learn from those we love. But you're wrong, Bruce, about me I mean, because although I know the feeling you describe, this one is somehow different. I've been feeling that I'm getting ever closer to death, speeding up on it, and I feel the end of my life hiding around the corner like an assassin. I'm starting to wonder what the point is of staying alive; I'm trying to weigh the merits of living versus dying.

For the first time, suicide seems to me to be a real option. If I'm never going to be able to produce something like my great-grandmother's basket, I may as well step aside and let someone else try. Incidentally, if you are going to kill yourself, make sure you do it right. Suicide is still against the law in this state. I checked it out. It's not a misdemeanor, it's a civil offense with a possible sentence of one-to-ten, and a fine to boot. At least it's not as bad as it was in England, where it was once a capital crime. People who failed in an attempt to do themselves in were lovingly returned to health in order that they could be hanged.

Anyway, to get back to the problem of living a decent life. How ought we to live? My great-grandmother's basket has helped to teach me some of the virtues of frontier and mountain living - toughness, self-sufficiency, life without money, without endless needs; satisfaction, true satisfaction, with what one has; almost a Buddhist ethic. But heaven knows we can't all live that way in our society. Maybe none of us can. How do we set out to live a decent life with the minimum amount of compromise? That's what's been eating at me for the past year or so.

The problem is that life is basically an unsportsmanlike contest. You feel as if you are playing a complicated game, like chess, but with hundreds of levels of play, against an unknown opponent who knows all the rules and can maneuver you into positions where you think you may be gaining a temporary advantage, but which are really traps. The opponent's goal is; never give the opponent anything he wants. "Anything you really want will be denied to you;" that, I think, is as good a one-sentence philosophy of life as I have heard.

So what are the options? You can give up completely and allow yourself to be passively manipulated by the System, or Fate, or whatever you want to call it; or you can continue to struggle against the unfair odds; or you can try to withdraw from the game. You can say, as the Buddha did, that wanting is the whole problem. If you cease to strive after material goals, or the perceived need to feel good, then, he says, your happiness will increase. It's like that equation that's in Paul Samuelson's economics textbook: happiness equals resources divided by desire. If desire goes to zero, happiness becomes infinite.

So far I have tried two of the three options, withdrawing, giving up, and struggling, that is. I tried the Buddha's option for a long time. I lived very simply and devoted myself to my work and my spiritual development. I didn't buy expensive clothes or cars or furniture; I owned only the books that were absolutely necessary for me. I tried, at times, to be celibate or not to eat much, but I could never succeed at such endeavours; I was trapped in my body. My corporeal needs would become overwhelming and blot out all the other goals from view, and I would have to fall off the wagon; but those episodes would bring me such joy that finally, after several years of struggle, I came to the painful conclusion that the Buddha was wrong. His theory looks beautiful in practice, but it just doesn't work as a practical guide for daily life. I think that in this century the Buddha might have become one of those Chinese-American physicists who spend their lives in mathematical meditations upon great theories of Being, trying to account for the complexities of the universe by considering it to be formed by some mysterious operation of wave mechanics on the ether. They spend all their lives in order to produce an incomprehensible masterpiece, and finally in their eighties maybe a thousand-page treatise appears, printed by some vanity press in Cincinnati; and that's the end of it, and of them. Anyway, I gave up on Buddhism.

I floundered for a while; then, about 1962 I read The Myth of Sisyphus and it made quite an impression on me. I thought the philosophical point that book was making, that the meaning of life was in the struggle against the absurdities of existence, actually fit pretty well with the scientific ideas I'd learned over the years from biology, and especially from evolutionary theory. I saw mankind as just another species working its way along the continuum of the unfolding of life, and us individuals as the units that were gradually working out the expression of our genetic potential in evolutionary space-time. So, I thought, the meaning of life lies in being fully human, and as expressive and creative and as free as one can possibly be. And I have tried to live my life according to these precepts ever since, and tried to convey these principles to my colleagues and students; not by preaching about them, for this is not my style, but by holding up my self as an example of the credo.

However, as I have become older, I have slowly come to the conclusion that Camus was also wrong. The Opponent, that game-playing shape-shifter, will make sure that if this is what you want, that you will have insufficient talent, or force of will, or energy, to achieve it. This idea isn't new, either; Herodotus said, "It is the custom of the gods to bring low all things of surpassing greatness." In other words, you are going to fail, and fail over and over again. You are going to influence no one. You will wind up as a bad joke, or a bad caricature of a philosopher. All struggle is folly.

And besides, even the feeble hope I may have had, that my offspring might carry such genes as could contribute to human understanding, has been dashed. My genes have not been expressed and will die with me. Evolution will have to proceed without my having contributed anything to it; not that it will make any real difference, and not that there was really any hope in any sense. Sorry, Albert, I finally heard myself saying, you are wrong; life is meaningless; not only in the general sense, but also in the particular; even the question of suicide, the one you thought was the only important one in philosophy, is fundamentally trivial. Nothing matters, nothing at all.

So that leaves the only other option that I can see: surrender. I have never given up; up until now I have thought that was to my credit; but maybe that's the only solution that makes any sense. At least that way you come up with a kind of draw.

I would like there to be a fourth option; I'd like to be able to choose to lose my mind completely, to go beautifully mad like Lucia; I'm pretty sure I'd pick that, now, if I was sure I could do it. But, I think I'm stuck in this morass of reality. Too bad. Better luck next life, maybe.

So that's how things stand in my head at the moment. A decent life seems impossible to achieve. The choice seems to be between a life that is an obscenity and no life at all. My philosophy of life seems to be reduced to a gloomy quotation of Kafka's: "There is infinite hope, but not for us."

B: Well, I understand what you're saying; but I don't think it's possible to come up with a one-sentence solution, or philosophy of existence, or whatever you want to call it. For you or me or anyone. It seems to me that a decent life can't be planned, it has to be lived; you can't say to yourself, from now on I'm always going to be a better person and never do the bad things I used to do ever again, because I have a complete ethical plan for the rest of my days. I think you have to be out there in the trenches, and make decisions on the spot; some of them are going to be wrong, like deciding to have that last drink, the one that keeps you up all night feeling the bed soaring through space. But given enough experience, maybe it would be possible to make the right decision more often as you got older.

Anyhow, buddy, I'd like to continue this conversation; like all the little chats I have with you, it's been rewarding and thought-provoking. But I do have to leave. I just have time for a quick bite to eat before I head out to the airport. Would you like to join me?

P: No thank you, man, maybe another time. I have things I have to do. Listen, Bruce, have a great trip. I'm going to miss you, really. Let me give you a bear hug before you go.

Vaya con dios, man; say hello to all those beach bunnies for me. Tell them I'll be dreaming of them.

Bruce 6

After lunch, I left for the Texas coast, flying in a diminutive nine-seat plane from our airport to Dallas (with a stop in Oklahoma City), where I caught a Texas International flight to Corpus Christi. I already had my motel reservations, and had left a little card on Miss Freemartin's desk as I always did, to tell her where I would be staying in case anything momentous were to come up.

The day was cloudless, with only a little haze, and I looked out the window of the aircraft at the piedmont gradually falling away toward the Gulf. The drier hill-country steppes with pale green vegetation - thickets of mesquite or prickly-pear cactuses making patchy tufts against the wooly backdrop of grasses and sedges - gave way to a verdant flora of big oaks, their contours softened by Spanish moss, hiding the ground from view. Then, I began to see drowned estuaries, arms of the Gulf extending in and forming muddy bayous; and finally, the land came to an abrupt end, and the parchment sea lapped against little fringes of sand beach. Beyond were pale, smooth bands of earth - barrier islands, guarding towns like Port Lavaca, Seadrift, and Rockport from the ravages of the frequent and powerful waves stirred up by hurricane-force tropical winds. The plane banked to the southwest to follow the coast, and I saw the horizon, an indistinct margin where sky and sea met, like a Mark Rothko painting in two muted colors gradually diminishing into one another.

When I got off the plane in Corpus, the humidity was high, but there was a gusty breeze from the Gulf. The gangly palm trees repeatedly bent over and stood back up, like flags on pliant poles. I rented a little Plymouth convertible from a man in a yellow sport coat and drove through town with the top down, over the causeway across the Laguna Madre, and suddenly in the reddening dusk I was out there, out on the beach and looking off across the Gulf of Mexico. A stronger wind was up out here, and lofty waves were crashing across the sand. I smelled the semen-like odor of the seawater and felt tangled webs of anxiety fall away, as if I were a snake shedding its skin. I felt free, ready to do whatever came to hand that held promise of adventure. I had my tennis racket, my old canvas shoes for hiking in the sand, my new bathing suit (a tight shiny blue one that showed off my rear and my front equally well), an Indian blanket, and a dozen condoms. I was ready for fun, games, and sex if they were there for me, in any of a thousand combinations; I was ready for the unknown.

I checked into my motel, the Ocean Siesta, a flamboyant construction in electric blue poured concrete, with a sheet-metal sign featuring a parabolic wave and a bikini-clad surfer circa 1953 waving at the guests. The clerk was a blond and sincere young man, probably a college student, with a Central Texas accent and an ingratiating manner. He handed over my keys with a toothy grin and said, "Ah hope yawl injoys y'sef!" I waved him a crisp farewell salute and loped over to my cabin. It was small and clean, with the obligatory two double beds; but the great thing about it was that it faced the Gulf. I was less than fifty yards from the beach. Well, first thing tomorrow I'd be out there, but now I'll just relax, I thought. I slipped off my sandy shoes, turned on the TV for a little background noise, opened all the windows, and sank into my fluffy mattress. Ah, such pleasure, and such a long time since I'd felt so totally relaxed.

I found my thoughts drifting back to think about the distasteful events of the past year, beginning with the day of the great blizzard. How far away and how insubstantial they seemed at this time!

Pyke had been right about the ups and downs of marital separation. It had been seven months now, and I had finally begun to adjust. The day after Pyke and I had romped in the snow, school reopened and I went back to work. He was right about hardly anyone showing up for class, too. I think a mood of rebellion had swept across the campus, starting in the dormitories and fraternity houses and spreading by word of mouth across the mall; it snowed, it's gotten really cold, and it's close to Christmas; we've had a hard quarter, and we deserve a break; fuck it, let's not go in today, let's stay in our rooms and play cards, or watch TV, or get laid. But I met my classes, and dutifully lectured to the few who were there, and I doubt that anyone could possibly have known there had been a cataclysm in my life. Damn, I'm a real pro, I thought.

That evening, driving home, I had felt pretty good. I had endured 48 hours without that woman and was still hanging in there. No one knew I'd been forsaken by the woman I'd loved except Pyke, and he wasn't telling anyone. Until I decided to spill the beans to someone else, I was reasonably sure my privacy would be respected.

When I checked the mailbox in my driveway, I felt a momentary sting of rejection when I noticed there was no letter from Viola. Damn the bitch, thought I, do I really mean so little as all that? Then I shrugged it off, and went in to make myself a scanty supper of boiled potatoes, beer, broccoli, and tinned chocolate pudding. Yes, I knew it was somewhat on the starchy side, but I wasn't especially ravenous.

I discovered, then and on later evenings, that I really didn't like eating alone, especially when I was responsible for it all. No one was going to help me make anything, and no one was going to help clean up the kitchen afterwards either.

Sleeping alone wasn't as bad as I had thought. Drinking beer made me pretty tired, and I didn't even need to masturbate. Not yet, anyway.

So the days passed, in a regimented sort of style; wake up, shit, shower, shave, dress, make myself an egg, toast, and some coffee; go in, teach my classes, come home, eat, work on my next day's lectures, wash dishes, watch some TV, and go to sleep. It wasn't so bad, sometimes, when I didn't dwell on it.

My first letter from Viola didn't come for a week. It was postmarked Chicago; so they'd made it after all, curse the luck. One little sheet of cute stationery, pale blue with faint red lines, stylized, smiling little robins in one corner, written on both sides in blue ink. Practically impossible to read. Very chatty it was; it could have been from a sister. Nothing about our past life together and the way it had collapsed, just a statement that she hoped I was well. No address (did she think I'd come looking for them?)

The next day, our separation became general knowledge around the department. I'm not sure how, because I hadn't said anything explicit to anyone; Miss Freemartin had asked me about my wife and I did say I hadn't seen her for a while, and possibly Pyke had made some other oblique remark that she'd been able to piece together into a hypothesis. Anyway, she was the first to say anything to me. It was fairly direct.

"Your wife's left you, hasn't she, Dr. Cahill?"

This, coming out of the blue, first thing in the morning, as I was going through my mail. "Yes, Miss Freemartin, four days ago. How did you know?"

"Let's just say I have my sources." She was half-smirking and half-whimpering. "You poor man, you must be taking it very hard." I shrugged. "How long had you been married?"

"Have, please, Miss Freemartin, no divorce papers have been filed just yet. We have been married for six years. No, we have no children. Yes, the house is in both our names. Yes, I have heard from her, but no, I don't know exactly where she is. Now if you'll excuse me, I need to teach my classes."

For the rest of that day, I dreaded having anyone approach me. They all had that same look - partly sympathetic and partly titillated. Well, I hope I amused them with my story, repeated over and over again. I was given the names of three lawyers and four marriage counselors. The Dean asked me if I wanted any time off; he looked very relieved when I assured him that would not be necessary. Hey, boss, it's not exactly a death in the family; not exactly. In some ways it's even worse, though, because a loved one has gone away and rejected you at the same time. Usually with an aged relative, the two events occur rather far apart, temporally speaking.

All the rest of the day I spent getting more and more disheartened. At home, I didn't even eat, just fell into bed and read my textbooks for two hours. At around 10, I called Pyke, just to shoot the shit for a while. He seemed to know what had happened, whether by my tone of voice or from the hearsay around the building. I think there was someone with him, though, by the guarded way he answered me. So after a time I let him go and tried to get some sleep.

Around midnight the phone rang. I hadn't managed to fall asleep yet. When I picked up the receiver I knew it was Viola even before she spoke; I could tell by the sound of her breathing.

"Hello?"

There was a short pause, and more breathing. "Hey, Bruce, how are you? Did I wake you?" (Was her speech just a bit slurred?)

"I'm not very well, lady. I love you, remember? No, I can't sleep."

"Poor darling. I just wanted to let you know I haven't forgotten you. I'm sorry about what happened."

"Well, so am I. What are you up to? It's about 1:00 where you are, isn't it?"

"Two, actually. We're on Eastern Time here. We're in Fort Wayne, visiting my parents. I'm not sleeping well, either; Arthur snores a lot. I'm downstairs. He'll probably kill me if he finds out I called you."

"Well, I'd have mixed emotions about that. Are you still living in Chicago? Could you give me an address, or a phone number?"

"Bruce, things are in a bit of a flux right now. The job Arthur thought he had in Chicago - an old friend - turned out not to materialize. So we're still looking around. We'll be here for a few days. Don't worry about me, whatever you do. You can call my mother if anything comes up; she'll know where to find me."

"Listen, baby, it sounds like you made a mistake. Don't your parents think so, too? They always liked me. Why don't you come home? I'll be waiting right here."

"Bruce, that's not going to happen. I have to go now. I'll write you a long letter soon, darling. Goodbye, sleep well."

"I love you -" I said, but she'd already hung up. Hell's bells, I thought, I didn't play that very well. I whined, didn't I? Well, I couldn't help myself; I'm weak. But do I really want her back? What if she'd said yes? Maybe that was just a line I was programmed to speak in that particular situation.

I didn't hear from her very often after that. The promised long letter didn't come for a month; it was indeed long, more than forty pages, in a large manila envelope. It gave an impression of having been worked on very hard, and at late hours; smudged ink in several colors, and handwriting that slouched and spindled its way across the page, writing that had obviously been forced onto the paper when she was half asleep.

The letter was oddly detached, written almost as a sort of third-party witness of our marriage. She mostly recalled trivial things, without much regard for chronology, things I had forgotten, telling them in immense detail. For example, exactly how a little paper cup of coleslaw had tasted (metallic and spoiled) when we'd gone to a drive-in after one of our first dates. This letter really confused me. Was I supposed to interpret these events as significant? Were they somehow the hidden keys to the disintegration of our life together?

I sent several more letters to her, care of her parents, but never received another, unless you count a postcard from a resort outside Muskegon, where we'd gone on a weekend trip shortly after our wedding. I couldn't tell from the desultory message whether she was there with Arthur or not.

About six weeks ago, her mother wrote me with the news that Viola and Arthur had broken up. He'd left for somewhere further east, "maybe Pennsylvania." Viola had taken an apartment in a newer part of Ft. Wayne and was living there with another girl. Her mother gave me the address but advised me that Vi had "changed a lot," that she wasn't likely to be the same woman I remembered. I wrote to that address, three weeks ago now, but I haven't heard any more. "I think it's finally over," I said aloud, lying on my soft mattress in south Texas, fifteen hundred miles from my wife.

I fell asleep almost immediately after I said that, and morning came presently; I had a big breakfast (room service, for the first time in my life). In my room, I slipped into a robe, swim trunks, and slippers, then headed for the water. It was a clear morning, and the sky was full of wheeling gulls. I descended down the weatherbeaten wooden steps to the beach. The sun shimmered in the open sky, drumming on my body with a steady warm touch like a lover's. My eyes were like slits in the glare, but I was smiling and feeling good. I moved slowly, like slow dancing, through the moist air; my sandaled feet made tiny crunching sounds in the sand. I unfolded my multicolored blanket like a matador, swinging it around my waist and sending to the ground by releasing it at the last minute and letting it soar. Stepping to the edge, I kicked off my sandals with a couple of dance steps, threw my arms out into space, and dropped to the blanket as if I'd been poleaxed.

The warmth was like being hugged by a warm and willing woman as it built up, permeating my skin and settling deeper into my muscles. I reflected at how transparent human flesh is. Thinking back to my Boy Scout days, I remembered how my hand looked when I shone my flashlight through my fingers; I could see the faces of my fellow campers glowing redly in the tent. Now, I could feel the rays of the sun penetrating deep into me, illuminating the dark cells down inside my being, stirring up those biochemical macromolecules with unaccustomed energies, those energy-packed photons of solar radiation.

I was keeping my eyes closed. I felt rather than saw the light passing through the lids; the heat made me feel completely relaxed, my eyes losing their tenseness as my mouth fell open with a sigh.

And in such moods, thus I passed the first days of my vacation; there was a lot of sun, a little sunburn, some drinking, no hangovers, some tennis, some swimming; no sex, though I'd had meaningful discussions with a few nice unattached ladies. Things were looking good.

Friday, at around 11:30, I came in from sunning myself to get ready for lunch. I'd had another nice chat with my new friend Marybeth Minnifer, a 26-year-old high school teacher from Brownsville, who seemed to enjoy staring at the bulges in my swimsuit; I enjoyed staring at hers, too. Our conversations so far had focused on our philosophies of teaching; I'm not quite sure that she had one, but she agreed with everything I said, even when I brought up some of Pyke's arguments that were in contradiction to my own. We were going to meet in town at a seafood place that had been recommended to us. Things were looking up.

The little red light on my telephone was flashing. Must be a message for me, I thought; I wonder what that could be about. I called the front desk and they told me I'd had a call at around 10:30 from "Mr. Dean Pfaff"; "very important for him to call back," the message read.

I had no idea what that could be about. I know I'd turned my grades in in time. I must have forgotten some essential detail; I trust it'll be something I can take care of on the phone, I thought.

Standing beside the bed, I punched out the number. He answered on the second ring. "Dean," I said, "it's Bruce Cahill." "Oh, thank you for calling back, Bruce," he said, and then, abruptly, I could hardly hear what he was saying. Outside my window, a kid had started gunning and racing the engine of his great hog of a motorcycle. I covered my free ear, but still could only pick out, on the average, roughly every other word the Dean was saying; all that I could tell was that it was something about Pyke.

"I'm having trouble hearing you, Dean," I said; and then, out of a temporary silence, he said, "He's really dead. He killed himself yesterday." More roars from the cycle, then something about a suicide note; finally, I heard him say that a visitation and memorial service were scheduled for tomorrow afternoon, Saturday, the 25th, at the Unitarian Church's meeting hall and could I make it all right.

I found that I was sitting on the bed and nodding into the phone. My fingers and my toes had gone cold, my mouth was dry, and there was a feeling in my stomach as if I'd swallowed a whole orange. Finally, I was able to choke out, "of course;" and I tried to ask the Dean for more details, but when the snarl of the motorcycle quieted for a moment, I heard only a buzz in the earpiece. He'd hung up. All I knew was that Pyke was dead, somehow, and that I was going to head back to pay my respects. Pyke, dead. Those two words just didn't go together; he was a strong, vigorous, and quite young man; yes, he was having difficulties in his life, but that had been true for as long as I had known him, and a lot longer before that. Pyke dead. Did the Dean say something about suicide? How could that be? Well, I suppose it was quite possible. We all have thought about it, after all. He even talked to me about it, in what I took as a sort of intellectual, analytical fashion, only a few days ago. What had I said to him in response? I tried to recall. Did I take him seriously, or did I dismiss what he was saying? Did he take my response in the wrong way? Could I have said something to him, given him a little more help? Oh, God, I remember now, I said to him that I couldn't talk any more, that I had to go to the airport to leave on this dumb vacation. Oh, shit, he's dead and it's all my fault. Or at least partly my fault? Shit. Pyke McKenna is gone forever. Dead, dead.

Outside my window, as I sat staring at the telephone receiver, I heard the cyclist riding off, in a whining roar that faded to silence.

Lieutenant Clower

(A twelve-year veteran of the State Police, Lt. Duane Clower headed the team that found Pyke's body in a remote part of Rainbow Bridge State Park. This statement comes in part from a television interview at the scene and in part from a written report Lt. Clower submitted internally. I am indebted to Lt. Clower's supervisor, Chief Cliff Heimdahl, for permission to quote from it without restriction.)

Following a telephone call from Miss Eleanor Sekkonen, received at 15:12 MDT Thursday, 23 July 1970, our office dispatched a searching party to attempt to locate Mr. Pyke McKenna, reported missing. The missing person, last seen at approximately 07:00 MDT Thursday, 23 July 1970, was a white male, aged approximately fifty years, brown hair and beard, probably wearing bib overalls and boots without a shirt, no distinguishing marks or scars. I called the order in at 15:19 MDT via shortwave radio. The Department personnel designated for the search, with the approval of Chief Heimdahl, were Lt. Floyd Hadding, Cpl. LeRoy Kriegmuller, and myself. The party reached the general store on the eastern edge of the park, from where Miss Sekkonen had called, at 16:19 MDT. Miss Sekkonen then joined them and directed them to the spot where the subject was last seen. Mr. McKenna and Miss Sekkonen, employees of Cimarron State College, had been on a collecting expedition to obtain animals for use in the College's biology program. The police party and Miss Sekkonen proceeded to a high, rocky area of the park, indented with canyons. Searching on foot proceeded north and south of the site where the subject's pickup truck and tent were left, and where Miss Sekkonen indicated he had last been seen. The search was classified as hazardous duty, since numerous fissures and overhanging ledges had to be inspected.

The subject's body was discovered by Cpl. Kriegmuller at 18:43 MDT on 23 July, 1970, at the bottom of a cliff, about one hundred and five feet in height, about one and a half miles west of the park road at its junction with the Wolf Butte Nature Trail and about one hundred yards from the stream, presently dry, known as Ash Brook. It was about four hundred yards from the site of the camp where Mr. McKenna and Miss Sekkonen had spent the previous night. Cpl. Kriegmuller and Lt. Hadding were drawn to the location by noting the activities of crows and ravens in the area. The subject's body, lying face down, could not be clearly seen by the search party from the top of the cliff; the legs and back were almost hidden from view in a wide crack near the base of the canyon wall. An additional difficulty was that an overhanging outcrop of rock almost directly over the site prevented the searchers from easy visual scrutiny of the subject. Nevertheless, Miss Sekkonen was able to make a positive identification.

Lt. Hadding indicated that owing to the lateness of the hour and the roughness of the terrain a helicopter fitted with a block and tackle would have to be deployed in order to raise the body. The helicopter was dispatched from Pawnee Springs; Sgt. Dennis Elder was the pilot. He reached the area at 19:49 MDT. Lt. Hadding descended into the canyon on a harness attached to a cable and maneuvered the subject's remains into a rubberized fabric bag. The body of the subject appeared to have been molested by animals such as coyotes, foxes, and ravens; one hand was badly mangled and several fingers were missing. There was no perceptible trail in the rocky soil from the site of the death to the spot where Miss Sekkonen indicated they had spent the night. An autopsy (completed at 11:23 MDT Friday, 24 July: Number M-71-D023-C003) established that the probable cause of death was massive cranial injury and that the probable time of death was early in the morning of Thursday, 23 July.

During the autopsy, a typewritten document was found in the subject's coveralls pocket which appeared to be a suicide note. The document bears the date of 22 July. The text of the note is appended. Although foul play has not been completely ruled out, the bulk of the evidence suggests to the investigative branch of our division that the subject took his own life. Miss Sekkonen, who reported the missing man to the authorities, is not presently a suspect in the death. This was also the conclusion reached by Mr. Edgar Tarnhofer, coroner of Erdwell County, where the death took place, and submitted in his report of 13 August, 1970 to the Third District Major Crimes Commission, made up of the sheriffs of Erdwell, Centerland, and Muspell counties.

Appendix 1. Text of the note found on Mr. Pyke McKenna's person, 24 July 1970:

July 22, 1970. The world was too cruel. I am no longer fit to live in it. I am lost under all this sky. I can not simplify myself. Play Puccini's I Crisantemi for me.

Coda: The Memorial Service

Saturday morning, under a pall of heavy clouds; humid, with the temperature in the middle 70s. I had no idea where the Unitarian church was, so I looked it up in the telephone book. It turned out to be on East Donner Street, near the northeastern edge of the city limits, only a few blocks from the little shopping center with the Safeway. I put on a grey tweed coat, an unpatterned dark blue tie, and black slacks, and left the house fifteen minutes before the service was scheduled to begin. Turning off Kelsey north and then, after four blocks, east onto Donner, I found the place immediately. Donner was a narrow street and both sides were lined with cars; surely, I thought, all these people are not here to pay tribute to Pyke McKenna; maybe it's bingo night.

I parked the car on a side street and walked up the short flagstone path toward the entrance. The church was smaller than I had anticipated, an unassuming building not much bigger than a big house, of rust-colored brick. The entrance consisted of two narrow columns of overlapping sandstone blocks, roughly laid with a minimum of mortar, flanking two broad glass swinging doors that were etched with designs -- doves, open hands, scrolls -- symbolizing peace; and the word PEACE was etched heavily at the bottom of the left-hand door.

A young man with thick glasses, rather stocky, all in black, greeted me as I passed through the glass doors. He held his hands together, prayer-fashion, at waist level. "Are you here for the McKenna gathering?" he asked me, smiling through closed lips. I nodded, staring at him; I was a little stunned by his choice of words. It carried the connotation of us all getting together for the decorous celebration of a minor holiday. "It's in the S-sanctuary," he said with a slight trace of stutter and a broad gesture, "down the s-staircase at the back of the nave."

I am not an expert on church architecture, but I assumed he want me to walk down the aisle in the center of the meeting hall to the altar at the rear, and that I would find the stairs there. The main hall of the Unitarian church was not fully reminiscent of the equivalent in a Christian one, but echoed it, as if it were trying to be a sort of parody. The main architectural unit was not the pointed Gothic arch, leading the mind upward toward God, but a broad, flat sort of elliptical cross-section cut off at the ends by straight vertical lines; the sort of thing you see in circus tents and yurts. This form was seen in the roof of the main worship area, in the windows high up on the walls, and in indented sconces, lower down, that held not crosses, images of the saints, or crucifixes, but candelabras. The form conveyed, first of all, the broad sweep of the wings of a mother hen (or a dove?), or the cosmic equivalent, encompassing all of Being in its mighty embrace. I was also reminded of great eyes, like those of colossal stone Buddhas in southeast Asian caves; heavy-lidded and narrowed, but still regarding all things in amused tolerance; a sort of heavenly scoutmaster benignly overseeing the antics of his charges. The windows especially gave me this impression, set as they were into deep channels running straight through the thick beige stucco walls.

At the front of the auditorium, directly in the center, was a lectern where the minister, or whatever the Unitarians called him, spoke. A rather ordinary and plain lectern it was, too; no sumptuous velvet altar cloth or other ornamentation, just a simple square wood column in dark oak, fitted with a small brass light with a pull chain. It was not one of those high towers where the clergyman speaks from a position far above his flock, but neither was it flat on the floor, as you would find in a classroom on a college campus. It was raised up on two concrete forms, each about nine inches tall; both were derived from

The Shape, an ellipse with squared-off ends, and the upper one was smaller than the lower, so the speaker could mount to the lectern in two steps.

Behind the lectern and behind a screen with a picture of the sun on it, I found a narrow staircase leading down. This can't be it, I thought first; it's so narrow and dirty, with stuff like mops lining the walls. But in a few seconds I heard voices I recognized, and soon I emerged into the reception room.

It was a surprisingly bright place; the walls were in a high-gloss yellow with white enamel trim, and the sunken ceiling was crowded with fluorescent light fixtures. A mob of people was milling around. I knew most of them, but I never thought that Pyke could bring them out to such a place, especially by merely dying. There were faculty from virtually every department on campus; administrators, Dean Pfaff and the other deans - I think all of them were present; and even, wonder of wonders, President Ogden himself, in the farthest corner, dressed in a black suit that put night to shame. I half expected to see two ravens on his shoulders croaking out "Doom" and "Nevermore."

I began to walk around the room. People were gathered about in small knots, fours and fives, conversing animatedly. The atmosphere didn't seem particularly funereal; it could have been a gallery opening. Many people were smoking, which as an old-line Protestant I found practically sacrilegious.

On a long table at the side of the room had been arranged a meager selection of food and drink. Although I was not hungry enough to eat anything, I couldn't help but notice a lumpy mound of diamond-shaped sandwiches on thin crustless white bread. The filling of these sandwiches was a salmon-colored paté having a few flecks of green; the bread was limp, and appeared moist, as if the sandwiches had been made up years in advance, frozen, and thawed perhaps an hour ago by the caterer.

Two smaller plates of cookies flanked the heap of sandwiches; these were apparently sugar cookies, flat, very pale, and perfectly round, and about the size of a half-dollar. They were thicker than communion wafers, but their color and texture suggested that an eater of one would enjoy a similarly tasteless experience.

At the end of the table was an ornate bowl of punch containing a doughnut-shaped block of melting ice floating in a pinkish, fizzy liquid. In order to have something to hold in my hands as I circulated among the attendees, I ladled a portion of this fluid into a rather plain glass cup with a small, solid, ear-shaped handle. I also took a matching glass saucer with a beaded rim and a single small white napkin having a thin black band near the edge. I sipped the punch; it had a vague, perfumed orange flavor.

I didn't really feel like barging into one of the little enclaves of conversation, but almost everyone was in one. As a result, I found myself walking around the fringes of the room. Once in a while, I'd wave at someone and think about exchanging a few words with them, but most of the time I kept walking clockwise and looking about. Then, near the corner of the room opposite the one I'd come into, I felt a tug at my sleeve; I looked around and there was Miss Freemartin, dressed in a long black frock with a flowered bodice and clutching a puffy lace handkerchief in her left hand. "Oh, Bruce," she said, "isn't it terrible?"

I don't think she had ever addressed me by my first name before. Taking a sip of punch, I agreed that it was. Whatever she was talking about, it certainly was. Pyke's death? Her dress? The punch? My mood? The visitation? I was prepared to agree with any of it. All of it.

We both looked at each other for an agonizing few seconds; then I asked, "Have you been here long?" I don't know why I should have chosen that particular question out of the universe of statements I might have addressed to Miss Freemartin, but she very sensibly ignored it.

"Oh, Bruce, I can't believe Professor McKenna's passed away. Just the other day he came up to me to ask me to type something. So politely he asked; so much like him. I finished it, too, but now he won't ever need it. I can still hear his voice so clearly; and I can still smell him. I'm sorry, I don't know what you must be thinking; but he had a certain smell, it was just his, I could always tell when he'd been around somewhere. Something a little like pipe tobacco and something like fresh fish. Didn't you ever notice?"

"No," I said truthfully, "that's something I never knew about Pyke."

"So many people here; so few of them I know. I suppose I don't get out of our own little set very much. Did Professor McKenna have a family, and are any of them here? He never spoke about them, not to me, anyway. Is that tall woman - she looks something like him - no, that's someone who's with President Ogden. Can you imagine the President here? I didn't know he even knew Professor McKenna. I only saw him once, on stage at a convocation. The President, that is. When my neighbor's nephew graduated from here, back in 1966. I'd forgotten how short he was. My, what a tragedy; Professor McKenna's death, I mean. Where were you when you found out about it? Oh, yes, of course, you were down at the seaside. I was the first to hear, or maybe the second. That nice Officer Clower, the one who was on television, called the Dean's number and asked to speak to the head of the department. I asked who was calling, because the Dean had wanted me to ask that question of all voices I didn't recognize, and he identified himself and said that he was with the major crimes division. And I don't know just why, but when he said that, an image of Professor McKenna popped into my head, and I was sure he was either dead or badly hurt. So I put him through, and in two minutes the Dean came out, absolutely white-faced, and told me the news. Well, the first thing I did was to call Jeannie, over in Agriculture, and then the news just spread like wildfire. You were probably the last to hear. But isn't it terrible, Professor McKenna was so strong and so young … " She broke into sobs at that point, weeping into her lacy handkerchief and holding onto my arm. I patted her on the back with my free hand, on the roll of fat she carried between her shoulder blades, and disengaged myself gently, saying, "Miss Freemartin, let me bring you something to drink."

As I was filling a cup for Miss Freemartin, Jack Dombrowski came up to get a sandwich. He was flushed and apparently a bit drunk. Grinning, he shook my hand; I set down the cup and promptly forgot about it. "Well, well," Jack said, "if it isn't the prodigal. Glad you could make it to our little gathering."

"Funny, Jack, that's the same thing the little minister called it."

"Yes, very funny, quite funny indeed. A tragicomedy, this. The man wanted to go out in a way that would be serious, but look at how the people are responding. I see the little girl he was with couldn't make it. What do you think of that?"

"Little girl?" I hadn't heard anything about the circumstances of Pyke's death yet. No one had told me about Miss Sekkonen.

"Yes, we all have little girl friends, don't we? Or maybe you don't, you're always the exception. But this was Pyke's latest. I'm not sure what he saw in her; she was shorter, uglier, and younger than any he'd drummed up yet. But maybe he was getting a little perverse in his old age. Who knows? Anyhow, she was the last. You'd think she'd be here just to bask in the honor of that title."

I didn't exactly like the turn the conversation was taking, but Jack didn't continue it. He laughed, clapped me on the back, snatched up two or three sandwiches, and left, saying to me, "Enjoy it."

As I turned away from him, I saw in the corner, quite alone, an old woman in a wheelchair. I didn't recognize her at first, but then I saw that it was Hattie Bamberger. I'd hardly seen her at all since our first conversation in the hallway of Murchison Hall, so long ago, when I was a naive job-seeker. She had changed a lot; she was much, much thinner, practically cadaverous, and she looked straight ahead without seeming to see anything; so unlike the vigorous woman of eight years past. I stepped over to say hello. "Dr. Bamberger!" I said in a loud voice, and she looked around with her eyes, rapidly and furtively, as if she was trying to locate a hidden assassin. "Dr. Bamberger," I called, "it's Bruce Cahill! How are you?"

"Bruce," she whispered softly through wrinkled, pinched lips, "Bruce, Bruce Cahill ..." It was apparent that she was trying hard to make sense out of those three syllables, sounds that had once meant something to her, but now were nebulous and obscure, just outside the realm of pure nonsense. Her lips were trembling and her head was bobbing spasmodically.

"Dr. Bamberger, I haven't seen you for so long." I was kneeling now, looking straight into her eyes, which still looked around, avoiding mine. "How are you?"

"I," she whispered, still not looking at me. "Th ... Sh ... Still. Not. I can't ... "

I felt a hand on my shoulder and looked up into the eyes of a young girl in a nurse's cap and cape, a dark-haired girl in a page-boy bob. "She's not very well, sir. I was reading her the paper the other day; she likes to hear the obituaries. When I read the entry for Professor McKenna, she started to cry. I had no idea they were colleagues. The director of the Home thought that she should be taken down here to say goodbye to him. 'All they live for is death,' he said. I don't know if it's a very good idea. We're going to sit at the back of the church so we can take her out quickly if there's a scene."

Just then, there was a loud call for our attention from the doorway leading up to the chapel. It was the young man I had met at the front door. He announced that the service was about to begin upstairs and that we should proceed up there. And, in an unhurried fashion, we all complied; I rode up in the elevator with a few others, including Miss Bamberger and her nurse. As it began to move, Miss Bamberger took my hand in her gaunt and speckled one, clutching it with a surprisingly powerful grip. I looked down and saw her lips moving as she looked at me with a slight smile; she was saying, "Bruce, Bruce Cahill."

We all filed into our seats and sat quietly for a few moments. I had picked a seat near the rear of the room, on the aisle; far away from the center of the action. No one I knew or recognized was sitting near me.

The organ began to play, very softly. It seemed to be something improvised; it certainly wasn't Bach or anything churchy. I was reminded of the kind of portentous music that used to play on radio soap operas I'd listened to as a child with my mother, at home after school.

Then, when we were all settled down completely, the organist struck a dramatic chord and I heard voices, down in the front of the room, singing. After a ragged start, I could tell it was "Since by man came death" from Handel's Messiah. A choir of quite young people, very heavy in the soprano section, was singing:

> Since by man came death
> By man came also the resurrection of the dead.
> For as in Adam all die
> Even so in Christ shall all be made alive.

The chorus sat down, and out of a red-painted door at the left of the stage, or whatever ecclesiastics would call it, came the minister we had seen before. A slight look of disquiet came into his eyes. He mounted the lectern and began to speak, a little breathlessly, but without the slight stutter I'd noticed before.

"I'd like to welcome you all to Pawnee Springs Unitarian-Universalist Church," he said. "My name is David Menlo Sedgwick, and I am the Leader of the Congregation here. I know many of you are not regular parishioners here - this may be one of the very largest gatherings we've ever had in our little church - but I assure you that you are all most welcome.

"We are gathered together to pay tribute to the memory of a fine man, Dr. Pyke G. McKenna. Although I myself was not personally acquainted with Professor McKenna, I have spoken to many of you today and in the past few days and I have seen how deeply you have all felt about him and how deeply moved you all are today. I am sure that Dr. McKenna's spirit is moving among us today, and I am sure that if he could speak to us now, he would say, 'Thank you, friends, for this outpouring of fellowship.'

"Without more ado from me, let me turn this meeting over to Dr. Trevor S. Ogden, the President of Cimarron State College, for a few words of reminiscence about Dr. McKenna. Dr. Ogden?"

There was a hush in the room as Trevor Ogden stood up in the front row of the church. This small neat man had enormous power over an audience that I had seen demonstrated on many occasions and this, it seemed clear, was going to be no exception. I didn't even know at the time that he had ever met Pyke; Pyke hadn't spoken about him to me. He walked deliberately up to the lectern where Rev. Sedgwick was still waiting, holding out his hand in greeting. Ogden ignored him and walked straight up the steps to speak. He looked down at the lectern and folded his hands quietly in front of him as he waited for Sedgwick to retreat, and finally lifted his head to address us. He spoke calculatedly, leaving long pauses between most of his sentences.

"I want to remember Pyke McKenna as he was when he was alive; I don't wish to eulogize him. Pyke would not want a eulogy. Pyke McKenna was a man who loved freedom. He was a man of strong opinions; he was always tolerant of opposing points of view, but he was never willing to remain silent about what he believed in. In a public forum, he spoke his mind without hesitation. He was a quiet man in private; yes, I would say that he was a gentle and a polite man. In his classes he made his points succinctly. I have spoken to many of his present and former students, and their respect for him is universal. He was a gifted man; a man of letters; a scholar. In short, a teacher. A real teacher; a free teacher. He was always a leader in his department and around the campus; he was a good citizen of the college. But more than that, he was a good citizen in our society. He was always more than ready to explain and defend his teaching methods to members of the general public."

Ogden paused, slowly drank about half of a glass of water, and went on. He raised his hands to grasp the lectern firmly by its sides; his voice rose in pitch, taking on a new earnestness.

"We all know only too well that there are few men today who can command the breadth of knowledge and expertise that Pyke McKenna mastered with such seeming ease. It will be hard to find his like again, you will all say. But if Pyke McKenna were here today, he would have this message for each of us; you must carry on for me. You must do as well, no, you must surpass my work. He would say to you, my friends, you must stand up for my goals; each of you must teach as I did. Not in my individual fashion, but with my universal principles. This must be the goal of our lives, to learn our democratic and intellectual tradition as well as we can, and then to pass it on to the next generation. For none of us lives for ever, my friends. Pass it on, I beg of you; pass it on. For all must teach if all are to be free. Carry on for me; I was a free teacher and so must you be. A free teacher."

He spoke the last sentence almost in a whisper, then looked down at the floor, dropped his hands to his sides, and went quickly back to his seat. Sedgwick returned to the podium, popping up like a Punch-and-Judy puppet, and announced, "Now we will be favored by a musical selection, a very popular song of our day, sung for us by our young soprano, Cynthia Merrick, who will be accompanied on the guitar by Spencer Perkins. Kids?"

The two teen-agers rose up out of the choir and performed a version of "Where have all the flowers gone?" about which I will say nothing except that I hope with all my heart that Pyke did not hear it.

"And now," continued Sedgwick, "I think it is most appropriate that we hear from the man who probably knew Pyke McKenna best -- his leader and guide for more than twenty years, the Dean of his Division -- Dr. Jim Pfaff."

The audience muttered as the Dean rose to the podium. I was enbarrassed and a little bit upset at the way Sedgwick had chosen to characterize the Dean's relationship with Pyke. The two men shook hands and exchanged what were apparently warm words; then Pfaff turned around to expound on his subject. First, he took his half-frame glasses out of his vest pocket, polished them with a red handkerchief, and settled them carefully on the rear of his nose. Then, he took a sheaf of papers out of his suit coat pocket. They were folded lengthwise in half, and he smoothed them carefully out on the podium and began to read from the text. He used a voice that I had not heard before from him, a bedtime-story articulation featuring, I fancied, himself as a beloved uncle and us as sleepy recipients, sucking our little thumbs and twirling the locks of our curly hair around delicate tiny fingers.

"My friends, my knowledge of Professor Pyke McKenna goes back to the days just after the second world war, a golden age of this campus if it ever had one. My character, as well as that of Pyke McKenna, was forged in these difficult and exciting days when our society had just come out of a terrible war. And remember, Pyke McKenna was a veteran of that war. He had seen first-hand how terribly strong the enemies of democracy could be, and he and I wanted to make sure that we were doing all that we humanly could to keep our country free from the need to ever fight such a terrible war again.

"Pyke McKenna and I used to sit for hours in my office and discuss how best we could serve our nation and the students that were swarming into our classes, eager to learn what we could teach them. We all worked very hard in those days, and he was one of the hardest workers of the lot. And he confessed to me, then, that he sometimes felt that he was inadequate to deal with the overwhelming responsibility that had been loaded onto his shoulders. But I convinced him that what he thought were inadequacies were useful, because they could focus his intelligence on the job he had to do; and by dint of hard intellectual labor, and practice, he could overcome anything that stood in the way.

"And Pyke McKenna, gradually, became a great teacher. I certainly can't take any credit for that. It all came from inside him, from the great human spirit that was lodged in his mind and body. But I think that if he were here among us, he would say in his very modest fashion that it was because of his friends, his colleagues, down through the years that he drew his strength to go on; to continue through some hard times, both early in his career and later. And we all were happy to be counted among Pyke McKenna's friends; we loved to be on the receiving end of the joyful spirit that he radiated. The man loved his work so much that it was contagious, and the rest of us all tried a little bit harder because Pyke McKenna was there."

He paused, cleared his throat, and took a tiny sip from his glass of water. "Pyke McKenna and I had the same philosophy of education. And it came from the same place, it was forged in the same mill; the tough battles in the trenches on behalf of the tough American students back from the war. And now we're in another tough war, and there will be a new batch of American students back from this war. And they're going to have their own special set of demands, needs that the earlier generation of students didn't have. And because Pyke McKenna is gone, the torch is going to be passed to a newer generation of teachers. Many of you sitting out there are going to be responsible for satisfying the requirements of this new generation of students - not just the war veterans, but those kids that for one reason or another didn't have the opportunity to serve their country overseas. And the kind of education this generation gets, I'm convinced, will decide what kind of America we're going to have. Are we going to be just good enough, or are we going to continue to be the best? It's a big responsibility we have as educators. We have to make sure that our country has winners for their leaders; because we have tough opponents, tougher now even than we had then. So if America is going to remain in the forefront of world leadership, it's up to us, and we have to do it now. Or else, as I see it, we're going to have to sit back and let foreigners dictate our choices to us, and I'm sure none of us really wants that to happen. So, my friends, do it for Pyke McKenna. Go out there and fight for a competitive and an educated America. Pyke would have wanted it that way.

"Now Pyke McKenna was a great teacher, but he was also a great friend. Many times I invited him into my home, and he and my family shared so many wonderful evenings together. He was a great lover of animals, as you know, and he never tired of playing with our beautiful English setters that my wife and I have raised for so many years. He and I, and many others of us, used to have wonderful philosophical conversations that just went on and on. And he certainly taught me a lot about life, and I as well as many others are honored that he gave us an opportunity to be his friends.

"Because of that friendship, several of us wanted to remember him with some kind of a living memorial. After long discussions, we decided to plant a tree for Pyke; we're going to put it right in back of Mundelein Hall. I talked to the good folks down at Paul's Nursery and they decided we ought to put in a Siberian Elm in the fall of this year. Also, we're going to buy some nice redwood furniture, a table and some chairs, and put them under that tree when it gets big enough. We hope it'll be a place where students and others can sit in the shade for years to come, and use it for a place to discuss important matters, or just enjoy themselves. And there'll be a brass plaque there, so everyone who uses that spot can look down and remember our great friend and colleague for a long time into the future, hopefully long after all of us who knew him personally are gone.

"Well, I could go on all day talking about Pyke, but I think you've heard enough from me for now, so I'll turn matters over to the minister. But before I go, I want to thank everyone for coming out to remember Pyke. And remember, Pyke's memory truly lives on in us, so let's discharge our responsibilities the way he would have expected. Thank you very much."

The Dean didn't step down from the podium right away, but removed his glasses, put them back in his pocket, and looked out over the assembly with a half-grin that exposed his upper teeth; then he stepped straight back, without looking, and almost stumbled over Sedgwick, who was hastening back to the podium in order to keep things moving along. He spoke only a few platitudes that I really didn't listen to, and I could tell that the service was going to end; to end without any of the participants raising the points that I felt should have been brought out about what made Pyke a unique and irreplaceable person. My face began to turn red with a kind of queasy embarrassment. I felt a little sick inside that this was all that the leaders of our college and division had seen fit to put together to honor one of the most remarkable men who had ever graced our institution with its presence. Shit, they could have been talking about the man who emptied the rubbish barrels after the football games.

The Unitarian youth choir began to sing "Sweet Beulah Land" --

> "I'm looking now across a river
> Where I've never been before;
> Just a few more days to labor.
> Time don't matter anymore.
>
> "Beulah land, I'm longing for you
> And someday on thee I'll stand.
> Then my home shall be eternal,
> Beulah land, sweet Beulah land."

and the minister raised his arms in benediction. There was a general shuffling in the room, indicating that the service was over and it was time to get on with normal life.

I stood up at once, turned around suddenly, and left the hall via the front door, walking quickly; I think I was the first person out. I even beat Dr. Bamberger and her attendant down the steps. All I wanted to do at that particular moment was get away from the place. As I stepped through the etched glass doors and exited into the world, I took a deep breath and noticed that the weather had become sunny and warm; the morning clouds had blown away and the temperature was just under 90. All in all, the old-timers would say, just about as nice a day as we could ever expect in this town at this time of year. I felt sick.

Head down, fists stuck in my coat pockets, I strode north on Cass Avenue, a narrow tree-lined street of single-family homes that became more modest the farther I walked. I must have seemed to be in quite a hurry; I wanted to tire myself out, work up a sweat - anything to burn the memory of the service away. No, I wasn't angry, not distressed - certainly not - the feeling I had was more akin to nausea; disgust at the failure of the inept tributes we had produced to do any justice to the memory of the existence of the man who had so touched our lives, and disgust at the self-satisfied smugness of the watchers and their apparent satisfaction in having done their human duty by taking part in such a nice inoffensive funeral.

My eyes were burning, partly, I suppose, from lack of sleep, but also from a desire to begin to cry; I rubbed them with both hands, walking blindly for several steps. Then, I began to run, at first slowly in a sort of shuffling dog-trot, dodging children in short pants out riding their plastic tricycles. Old couples seated in porch swings moved their heads slowly from left to right to watch me jogging past. Gradually, I started to increase my speed. Since I was hardly a runner, after a block or two I began to gasp and my lungs hurt, but I forced myself to keep it up. The pain felt good, and my ragged breathing reminded me that I was still alive. The running was mostly downhill, so I was able to keep up a pretty good speed.

After half a dozen uneventful blocks, at the corner of Cass and Cedar I failed to lift my rear foot high enough to clear the curb, and, thrown off balance, I dived forward, my body twisting, into a patch of gravel. I cried out "Shit!" as I fell.

I lay splayed out for a few seconds to catch my breath, then sat painfully up. I had hit with both hands, hard, and they were both badly scraped, with parallel cuts grooved into their heels and palms. My left knee stung, and the leg of my trousers was torn from its knee halfway down the shin; a flag of fabric flapped from the rip. I looked down at myself and tried to brush the superficial dirt from my jacket, and I noticed its left sleeve had also been badly torn, at the elbow, by a slab of sidewalk. "Great," I muttered aloud, "practically my best suit of clothes ruined for the sake of unscheduled exercise." My hair was covered with sweat, matted down on top of my head and dripping down the back.

I rolled over to push myself up, holding my left leg rigidly. When I tried to put weight on that leg, the knee answered with a sting of pain; so I was reduced to a clumsy hobble, but with a little practice I was able to move my limbs briskly and to make good time. I must have really looked a sight now. By this time, however, I had run far enough so that such dwellings along the street were far from the road and quite modest, so I don't think anyone noticed me. I was close to the edge of town and the street was beginning to be less well maintained, the narrow cracks in the asphalt being transformed into ruts with some claim to permanence. In a half-mile or so, I knew, it became a dirt track and then petered out when it met the section road near the railroad switching yard.

I decided to turn and walk west, along a street whose name I couldn't distinguish; the green and white signs at the tops of the corner signposts had been twisted, every one, into unreadable bow tie-shaped ribbons of steel. The sun was sagging toward the horizon, throwing great foreshortened shadows in front of everything. In two or three blocks, I came to the end of the street; behind a pile of cinders and an irregular heap of rusty wheels from rail cars, I saw, slightly raised, the tracks of the branch line of the Santa Fe. Well, fate has brought me to this point, I thought, and who am I to argue with an old lady?

I swung myself up the gravel slope as best as I could, and started to walk down the tracks. Small hissing chirps came from the thickets of tumbleweed - possibly grasshoppers, maybe small birds like dickcissels - but otherwise, everything was quiet. I fell into a shuffling rhythm of fast and slow strides; right foot on a tie, left foot dragged through the gravel between the ties, right foot quickly over the tie and into the gravel beyond it, left foot slowly dragged onto the next tie, right foot back on the tie beyond. It felt good; it felt right. I wasn't thinking, just walking, in a rhythm of pain and relief from pain with just the right amount of self-pity - here I was, far from home, far from my car and the freedom that went with it - like an injured prisoner on a forced march. To solidify the impression, I clasped my hands behind my head as I walked, and kept them there until my elbows and the nape of my neck throbbed. During this process, the rubbing of my wedding ring on two adjacent knuckles of my right hand caused them to begin to blister. I only stopped holding this absurd pose when I stumbled on a tie and twisted my left knee again, giving me a new dose of sharp agonizing pain.

I had been walking through a bleak landscape. The tracks in this part of town ran absolutely straight for as far as I could see; the vanishing point was about a mile and a half away, at the spot where they dropped toward the river valley, where I knew the big trestle bridge was; but I couldn't see that bridge yet. I saw no houses, no humans stirred. To my left was a row of nested, identical warehouses, like Quonset huts; I noted that their roof lines were almost exact parallels to The Shape. To the right was another set of tracks, and beyond that was open farmland - grazing land running right up to the edge of the railroad right-of-way.

I dropped down to one knee for a brief rest, holding my left leg out almost at right angles to my body. Sighting down the tracks, I saw in the distance a tall, square grain elevator with a smaller trapezoidal penthouse on top; a light was visible through a tiny window in the penthouse. I wondered what it would be like to work in such a room, and indeed, what work was even performed there, on top of thousands of tons of winter wheat. Wouldn't the respiration of the grain cause a dangerous reduction in the oxygen content, and an increase in the carbon dioxide level, of the air in the elevator? It might be quite easy to suffocate up there, especially on warm days. Maybe the grain might burst into flames by spontaneous combustion, brought about by the metabolic heat produced by the living kernels. That would be a quick and terrifying death.

What if the penthouse floor, neglected for many years and rotting, should give way, and the man working there fell into the wheat? Would it act like quicksand, drawing him down and smothering him? (And would they be able to sell the grain then, or would they have to dump the lot? Most likely not - his corpse would be treated the same as any other "light filth," insect parts and rat droppings, the small concentrations that are allowable in grain for human consumption. His mass would be quite small relative to the mass of the grain.) Or would he be able, after falling, to swim over to the wall and escape via some sort of ladder? Was someone working there now, watching me slowly shuffling down the tracks? Is he armed with a high-powered rifle - is that his function? And is he ready to gun me down the minute I cross an invisible boundary onto the grain storage company's property?

Heedless of danger, I struggled back to my feet and continued to walk. The perspiration had largely evaporated from my hair now; I reached up and felt the cowlicks sticking out in stiff bristly mats. My feet were being rubbed raw in my nice black leather shoes, which I hadn't really worn often enough to break in; and besides, they were obviously never designed for such treatment. The novelty of the pain was beginning to wear thin, and I was starting to think again, a dangerous thing to do, because I was thinking of Pyke and his horrible end and his appalling funeral. I was thinking that I had to stop walking soon, and get off these tracks, and go back to work again - or else I was going to have to kill myself; to walk over to the rail bridge, throw myself off the trestle and break my neck on the concrete basin of the river below. Such a hard decision to make.

I had almost decided to remain alive, solely on the basis that I didn't want to force my friends and associates to endure, so soon, another dreadful funeral, when I heard a rustling in the tumbleweed brush to the right of the tracks. I stopped walking, held my breath, and looked toward where I had heard the sound coming. My first thought was that it had been a snake. I took another step, and the agitated sound returned, this time accompanied by a guttural hiss. Oh, Lord, I thought, not a rattlesnake, I really don't want to die this way; and I backed up slowly, looking around for some sort of weapon. All I could find was a short piece of iron pipe, less than a foot in length, sawn roughly off at one end and having an elbow joint at the other. I picked this up and held it at the sawn end, feeling quite unprotected, but safer than if I'd had nothing at all. My heart was pounding so loud I could almost hear it, and my feet and hands felt like ice. I waited, unmoving, almost unbreathing, a minute or two to let whatever it was move away and save face, then took a few cautious steps forward.

Again, I heard the noise. And this time I saw what was making it; it looked like a very large rat. All I could see was the snout, projecting out from behind a weed. It was flat on the ground, and the animal was opening its jaws and hissing in my general direction; it moved its head from side to side over the gravel. It didn't seem to be able to see me; at least, it didn't fix its eyes on me. I made a step closer, a little frightened but curious at the odd behavior. I thought it might be trapped, or possibly suffering from rabies. At any rate, it didn't seem predisposed to attack.

I saw, finally, by bending down for a close look, that it was a badger. My breathing, like its own, was now coming in ragged gasps. By now I was only a few feet away. I could clearly see its yellow teeth and its dirty, matted fur; on its striped head, its eyes were glazed, the pupils almost indistinguishable; it seemed to be blind. The hissing became more continual, the waving of the head more violent; then, it reached out with its front feet and tried to run away, twisting more of its body into view; and I saw - oh, my God! - I saw its hindquarters, horribly torn and bloody; and its entrails ribboning out, swollen and fly-blown, extending back a distance perhaps twice its body's length; and its useless, crushed hind legs being dragged along. Had the thing been hit by a train?

I made a blind decision. I plunged into the brush; I found the head; I swung the pipe down, once, and then again, crushing its brains to a bloody pulp. Then, I threw the pipe away, as far as I could, ran to the other side of the tracks, sat down, swung my head between my legs, and vomited into the gravel.

I sat there for some time in the same position, gasping for breath. I was spent in every way; sick, tired, hurt, and mentally exhausted. But I was finally beginning to think, to think without stopping. The horror of the badger's fate and the action I had taken to end its suffering had forced my mind back on track, so to speak. First of all, I said, I have to stop this self-flagellation. I have to go back to my car, go home, take a shower, and rest. I have to do it now. Yes, only one day after my official vacation and still I am not rested. Your body and your mind need respite, I said to myself; yes, you have obligations, but all of them can wait a bit. Do not open your briefcase, do not answer the telephone. You are injured and you are very weary, but you must go on 'fore the Lord comes to carry you away, away; no more sorrow and sadness and trouble there'll be; there'll be peace in the valley for you, someday; but not just yet.

I pushed myself up from the track and scrabbled down the incline like a crab, holding myself up with two arms and my good leg until I slid into a standing, wobbly position at the bottom of the slope. I had no idea where I was. It was moving on toward sunset and there were no landmarks I recognized. I walked through an old field of long grass and came up behind a few small houses. None of them showed any lights, so I took a chance and walked between two of them, out into a narrow L-shaped street corner with no sidewalks and no street lights. There was no one about, it seemed, so I walked toward the east, away from the setting sun, for I knew this was where I needed to go, in general, to find my car.

About a block further down, I saw an old lady walking in the same direction I was. I forced myself into a painful trot in order to catch up to her and ask her where I was. She must have heard me running, because she turned around to face me, wearing a frightened look. She was black. "Excuse me," I asked, "can you tell me what street this is?" "Lor', child," she said, "but you skeered me. I'm not used to bein' run up on. This here's Quivira, and them lights over there's Nineteenth. I bet you a long way from you home." "Yes," I replied, "but I'm on my way back now. Thanks for the directions."

Nineteenth and Quivira, wow. I'd never been in this part of town, certainly not on foot. I had no idea how I'd got so far away from Donner and Cass. I estimated it was nearly a two-mile walk. Well, I thought, nothing to do but to do it.

I turned left on Nineteenth, a three-lane street with a lot of traffic. I hobbled past a mix of old houses and small businesses; liquor stores, bowling alleys, pawnshops, beauticians. Deep laughter came from the interiors of the frequent bars. Every face I saw was black and I must have looked like an escaped madman, crippled besides; I wondered if I was going to make it.

A car pulled up alongside and the driver blew a soft tap on the horn. No, I said, I'm not going to look, I'm just going to keep walking. Then, I heard a female voice calling my name; I looked at the car and, leaning out her rolled-down window, there was Ellen!

"How are you?" she said. "You look a mess. What happened?"

"I fell down. What are you doing in this neighborhood?"

"Just driving downtown; I thought I'd see a movie. I saw you - at least I thought it was you - from across the street, so I turned around. You want a ride?"

Man, I thought, God exists. An angel of mercy sent just when I need one. I got into her car, and she looked at me oddly. She seemed to be shrinking back, as if from an odd odor, which I no doubt was emitting - several kinds of odd odors, in point of fact.

"Are you all right? Are you sure you just fell down?"

"Well, it's a long story. Did you go to the thing for Pyke? I went for a long walk afterwards, and fell down, and I started feeling sick. But you don't want to hear about it. I was walking back to my car."

"Where is your car?"

"It's back near the church. Ellen - if you don't mind -- could you just take me home? I can ride the bus over and pick up my car tomorrow. I don't really feel like driving now."

She agreed, I folded myself painfully into her front seat, and we headed back across town to my house. Man, was I glad to be with her. I sat as far away from her as I could, pressing my back against the right-hand door; I didn't want to press my vile stench upon her. She looked straight ahead, looking a little upward through the top of the windshield. "You quite sure you're OK?" she asked. "You haven't been drinking, have you?"

"No, but maybe I should have done that. I couldn't be any worse off."

"Did you get in a fight?"

"Hell, no. What kind of a street punk do you think I am? Don't answer that. What did you think of the funeral?"

"Well, I don't know. It didn't seem to have much to do with Pyke. It seemed a bit manufactured."

"I hated the thing. I got really depressed, even before it started. By the time it was over I was ready to scream. I ran out the door; I didn't want to talk to anybody."

"I noticed. You ran out like you'd been stung by a bee."

We passed the entrance to the college, and crossed the bridge over the river and the tracks. I looked back in the direction I'd been walking. No one would ever know, I thought, how close I had come to leaping from those self-same tracks a few minutes ago.

We pulled up to my door. All the lights were off in the house and only a yellow porch light was on. "Well, here we are," Ellen said.

I paused with my hand on the door handle. "Would you be able to come in for a moment? I'd like to offer you a glass of wine. I need to clean myself up, but it won't take me very long."

"All right; the movie doesn't start for almost a half-hour. No wine though, I'm driving. Would you like to come with me?"

That offer surprised me. Ellen, I thought, was living with an M.S. student named Brock Williams, a rangy, stalwart-jawed Californian with a booming laugh to match her own. She brushed her hair off her ears, nervously, with both hands, as I looked at her.

"Well," I said, "I might; what's playing?"

She blushed slightly. "I was going to 'Topaz,' you know, the new Hitchcock. have you seen it?"

"No; I'd heard both good things and bad things about it. But let's go, I'm curious. Give me ten minutes to shower and change my clothes. There's Coke in the refrigerator."

Well, we did go to the movie. She liked it; I didn't. I suppose I'm really not very intellectual when it comes to movies. I prefer escapist stuff like Westerns and science fiction, and this dark story, full of betrayal, violent death, and vengeance, left me somewhat subdued. We went right back to my house when it was over.

We sat in her car in my driveway for a few minutes. Neither of us said very much. I made no move to get out, nor did I invite her in. Impulsively, I put my hand on the back of her neck, pressing down on her soft black hair. "I suppose I'd better go in," I said, but stayed where I was.

"Oh, that does feel good," Ellen said, turning to face me. She took my other hand in both of hers. "Thanks for coming with me, Bruce. I wasn't looking for you tonight, but I've been thinking about you."

"How are you and your boyfriend getting along?"

"Who, you mean Brock?" She snorted a half-laugh. "That man's in love with himself." She let go my hand, closed her eyes, and leaned back against her door. "He's about to graduate, and he's been pressuring me to give up my job here and go away with him. Trail along after him, like a good wife - except he doesn't want to be married to me, of course. He's going to Los Angeles -he's going into management, with some big oil company. No, I want to stay here," she said, looking down to the floor and then looking back up at me, "with my work - and with my friends."

I let go of her neck and held both her hands in mine. "Ellen, I'd be honored to be a better friend of yours. I feel close to you, and have for some time. I like being with you very much." I was trying to keep my voice from breaking. My throat felt very dry and I kept swallowing over and over. "Unfortunately, right now I'm afraid I'm not very good company. My wife left last winter, but my house is still full of her. And now Pyke is gone, a man who was closer to me than any brother. I feel like a wounded animal, one that's been hit by a train and can't understand what's happening to it." She reacted to my simile by gasping a little and squeezing my hands tighter. "But I'm getting better, really I am. I started today to really think about myself and how I should position myself with regard to the rest of my life. I'd like to talk to you about that, as a friend, sometime soon. But right now, I think I need a rest. So I'll go into my house now, and I promise to call you in a day or two."

She surged across the seat to mine, embraced me, and buried her face in my chest. "Oh, Bruce, that sounds so good to me. I want to be a close friend; I need to talk to someone, preferably a man, and I'll be a willing listener to whatever you need to say, too." She looked up, her eyes glistening; she was smiling like La Gioconda.

I hugged her tighter, and we kissed; a rough first kiss, somewhat like that of a pair of absolute beginners, not knowing quite how to proceed, how hard to push; but also like that of two veterans of failed love, who know quite well how to begin and also when to stop.

I opened the door then, not speaking further, and stepped out into the moonlight, and waved at her as she backed out and drove away; and the night was still after she left, dense and humid. I stood in the darkness, arms at my sides, tired and spent; thinking of her, and a badger lying dead, and Pyke McKenna likewise, and I started to laugh; yes, an involuntary laugh with an edge of tears to it, a laugh like that you would emit at a performance of King Lear if the scenery fell behind the blinded Gloucester to reveal a stagehand with his pants down.

And I went into my house, and fell into my bed half-undressed, and I slept, God did I sleep.

Eleanor

(Eleanor Sekkonen graduated this June from Cimarron State with a major in biology and a minor in mathematics. She is a short girl, barely five feet tall, with short dark hair; I would call her plump. An extraordinary student, unusually precocious in her ability to grasp and articulate complex ideas, at the moment she wants only to go on for a master's degree in secondary education, although to me she would be definite Ph.D. material. At the time of Pyke's death, she was a 19-year-old sophomore. She was probably the last person to see Pyke alive.)

Dr. McKenna and I got along surprisingly well, I thought, considering the difference in our philosophies of life. We met when I started arguing with him in class. I thought that some of the sweeping statements he would typically make while lecturing were not very scientific and had little place in the context of a course on biology, so I began to speak out. I was careful to be specific with my questions, and not to give him a chance to respond in generalities. I caught him in quite a number of factual errors. Although he was superficially reasonable in his responses, I could tell that it bothered him when I continued to press him.

He tried all of the traditional methods to intimidate me; long silences, public humiliation before my classmates ("Miss Sekkonen, please shut up"), holding me up as a straw man for his arguments ("People such as Miss Sekkonen won't agree with this, but..."), and so on, but I would not be silenced, nor did I show anger.

We continued our discussions outside of class, in the hallways, out on the mall, in his office, over cups of weak tea in the student union; it was exciting for me to feel like a colleague of his and to talk on an equal footing. At times his presence would cause me to become quite carried away rhetorically and I would find myself winging off in flights of argumentation that I never dreamed I was capable of. During these debates I would feel my heart pounding and I knew I was blushing; I'd watch Dr. McKenna leaning back in his chair, taking it all in, smiling out of one side of his mouth and looking very amused; but it didn't bother me in the slightest. It was a tremendous source of fun for both of us, a game whose rules we had invented as we went along, and consequently of which we were the supreme masters. I think we laughed together more than anything else. He and I would both adduce outrageous arguments to support our extreme views of the truth as we saw it, and both of us recognized these for what they were, as pieces in the intellectual chess game we were playing, not worth anything in terms of who might prevail, but just sacrifices to divert the opponent and possibly get him to lose concentration on something more serious.

It was not just science we disputed about, although that was what we both seemed to have the most antipodean differences over. I recall that we had a long discussion over Russian literature that lasted, off and on, for several days. I was amazed to find that he had such an encyclopedic knowledge of Russian novels and poetry; it put mine to shame, although I had been devouring it since I was twelve years old. I've read The Brothers Karamazov three times, Crime and Punishment twice. I esteem Dostoyevsky, obviously, and Dr. McKenna couldn't stand him, called him an unwashed and perverted reprobate. He extolled the "cosmic virtues" of Tolstoy, whom I really have no strong feelings about. I never wanted to read Anna Karenina or War and Peace over again. For the sake of argument, though, I called Tolstoy and insufferable and self-righteous prig. I had Dr. McKenna at a disadvantage there, because I had just read Troyat's biography, which had just come out, and I could quote chapter and verse.

So it was fun to have those contumacious discussions, and I learned a lot about Russian literature that I hadn't had time to become familiar with on my own, especially poetry, from Dr. McKenna, who had memorized long stretches of Pushkin in the original; and I had to admit it sounded glorious, leaving the translations far back in the dust.

In return for Dr. McKenna's gift of Russian, I helped him learn to curse and swear in Finnish. My people, like many Finns, were late immigrants to the U. S.; my grandparents came over just before World War I. My father has joked that his father and uncle, who knew no English, wanted to go to the Minnesota lake country which was so like their homeland, but they got on the wrong train out of Chicago and wound up in Texas. I don't believe it, though, because there are a large number of Finnish immigrants in the Panhandle, as well as around here, and they all seem to have immigrated between 1900 and 1920. Sometimes, it even seems as if we're all related, or at least come from the same districts of Finland. As a result, there hasn't been sufficient time to forget all of the language from the old country. The cusswords are the last to be lost anyway, I think, and Finnish is particularly rich in them. I love the way they sound, and Dr. McKenna found them fascinating. He had a good ear for the way languages sound, and I pronounced him summa cum laude in the subject.

I don›t want to give the impression that we did nothing but quarrel, or curse, because that isn›t correct at all. We had a common set of fundamental organizing principles for our lives; the duty to seek the path of truth wherever it might lead, the nobility of a life of struggle well lived (not only in a human but in an evolutionary context), and the ineffable beauty of nature in its largest and in its smallest manifestations. I think it would be correct to say that we became valued colleagues.

As we grew to know each other better, I noticed that Dr. McKenna would ask my opinions about many matters related to his teaching. He would do so in such a way that it might appear that he was merely trying to draw me into an untenable position, and he would never overtly admit that I might have come up with a good idea, but I didn't fail to observe that many of my suggestions were not only taken to heart but put into practice. For example, I suggested to him that using three-dimensional models of molecules such as DNA, enzymes, and structural proteins like keratin would help the students to see how cells are organized. He said to me at the time that it was a grotesquely silly idea, that the cell was too complex for that; the models that could be used for display purposes in a classroom were far too large, and would give a false notion of the scale of the processes that were taking place. He said it would be like putting a real baby into a dollhouse and using that system to try to explain the life of a family to someone who'd never seen a human being. But soon after that, he did begin to use models, although not in the way I had anticipated; he folded up pieces of cardboard or sheets of paper, origami-fashion, linked them together, and manipulated them around inside of transparent bags, the kind with built-in gloves. He suspended them from fishing line, which he glued to the top of the bag. It was a delightful concept. The bag represented a cell and his models were organelles, like mitochondria, or the cell nucleus, or something else. They were brightly and beautifully painted with high-gloss enamels and it was easy to see even in the back of the room what they represented. He kept the bag inflated with air from a gas cylinder; he told the class he'd thought about using a helium-air mixture so that the bag would just float at eye level, but he decided it would be too costly and too fussy. So although it was my suggestion that set him off, he twisted it around and, I think, did a better job.

Outside of the classroom and the discussions we had around the campus, I suppose we weren't really close friends. I only saw his apartment once, for a few minutes, when we stopped off there on our way to pick up some plant specimens that he thought we could find growing alongside the railroad right-of-way west of town. The decor of the place was disturbing to me. I didn't see any books, or records, or the normal stuff you'd expect an intellectual to have around his flat. The walls and the shelves and the top of every cabinet and table and dresser was covered with a hodgepodge of junk. A lot of it was obscene, either violent or pornographic, and the rest of it was just tawdry.

Examples; he had a poster of a naked woman, the top half of her, looking out with an erotic grin, and coming out from her breasts were the barrels of two pistols, flashing red shots at you. Another poster was of a chimpanzee sticking its finger up its nose. Also a big poster of a human head, this one was from a biological supply house, I think, with a face on the right half and just the flayed muscles and bones on the left. He had candles shaped like cocks, and a pillow that looked like a woman's pelvis; at least it had panties on. There was a lot more, but you get the idea.

Also, he insisted on feeding his snake while I was there. I forgot to mention this pet of his; it seemed to fit in well with the rest of the things he kept around. He kept it in the kitchen, in an aquarium with a cover of wire mesh. He cautioned me not to go too close (I wasn't about to do that!) because I would make it nervous. It was a boa, a rather small one, he said, although it looked plenty large to me. According to him, she was a female and her name was Helga; she ate only once a week and today was the day. He told me that she had just finished shedding her skin, a two-week process during which she couldn't be moved or touched. Probably, he said, she still couldn't see because her eyes were affected by the skin-shedding process, but that didn't matter because snakes relied on chemoreceptors to find their prey; in other words, they could smell it.

He stepped across the kitchen and got a storage canister, a metal one, the kind you keep flour or sugar in, and reached in and pulled out a mouse. The poor thing struggled and tried to get away or to bite Dr. McKenna's finger, but it was hopeless. It was all but dead and it didn't even know it. He held it by the base of the tail and dropped it through a little hinged gate in the mesh cover of the cage.

The poor mouse barely had a chance to stand up on its feet when the snake lunged from the corner of the aquarium and sank its fangs into it, and then, faster than I thought a cold-blooded animal could move, it wrapped the mouse in its coils and started to squeeze the life out of it. Whenever the mouse would try to struggle, its poor eyes bulging out in fright, the boa would squeeze down just a little tighter. It took maybe five minutes for it all to be over. Then, the snake just let it drop, swung around with its jaws wide open, and started to swallow its meal, head first. I stopped watching at this point. Dr. McKenna said it might take an hour or so for her to get it down; I was willing to take his word for it. So we left.

I was glad to get out of there; I was feeling a little bit sick. At least he didn't insist on discussing what we had just seen. I had the feeling that he was just a little bit ashamed of the way his apartment looked; I divined from things that he'd said obliquely, that his material life had been going to hell over the past year or two and that he'd given away a lot of his possessions, nice things, to friends. So I assume that this was what he couldn't get rid of.

And so now I suppose we must talk about the last days of Pyke McKenna, the last days I or anyone saw him alive. Still after a year or two it makes me feel nervous and upset to talk or think about it. Sometimes a day or more will go by and I manage not to, but then it all comes back again. At least I don't start crying anymore in the middle of what I am doing; it took me at least six months to get over that.

It was right after the end of summer school; the last exams were on that Thursday, the 16th. I stopped in on Monday to see what my grade was. Actually, I knew damn well what it was going to be, but I just wanted to see Dr. McKenna before either he or I left for some indeterminate time. For one thing, my family wanted to see me; they live in Lubbock, and I really don't like that town at all, but unfortunately that's where I have to go to see them. So I had promised to go back home for a week; I thought that would be enough time to see all my relatives. My father and mother both come from big families, and I must have 30 first cousins. I'm sure I could never pass a matching test on their names and faces, especially since they're growing and changing all the time. Also, my great-grandmother was still alive, although very sick. She had just turned 93. She spent all her time in bed, and had forgotten all the English she ever knew, which was never very much, and just called weakly in Finnish to her daughter, my grandmother, to bring her some water or to wipe her bottom. Except, toward the end, it was usually not even a word, but my grandmother knew from the tone of it what she wanted. I never knew whether she was going to live between one visit and the next. For the last five years of her life I'd go to see her but she never recognized me, I don't think. Usually, she just stared as I rattled on about the things I'd been doing. Her hollow eyes stared at me out of her wrinkled, papery, yellow face. Once in a while she would move her lips as if she was trying to say something; and once, last year, she did manage to say very quietly, in Finnish, "dead...dead."

So in a way I really wasn't looking forward to going home, but I wasn't thinking overtly about this when I went up to Dr. McKenna's office late that afternoon. It was hot and humid, and I felt a fine sheen of sweat spreading over me as I walked the two blocks from the dormitory to Murphy Hall. The elevator was out of order, as usual, so I climbed slowly up to his fourth-floor lair, stopping frequently to sip on a can of 7-Up I bought from the machine in the lobby.

Amazingly, he was in. He didn't have the grades posted, but that didn't surprise me; it was only the second day past the deadline, and I think it was a question of principle with Dr. McKenna always to be late, at least for deadlines imposed by others. I ambled around the corner to see that the door of his office was open; he was sitting at his desk, wearing a sleeveless T-shirt and cut-off jeans, and barefoot. He was actually working on those very grades. He greeted me cheerfully, as usual; although he was smiling broadly, he said to me, "What the hell do you want, runt?" Playing along, I bowed low, salaamed, and said, "O mighty one, thou whose scabbed knees I am unworthy to scrape, I seek after my grade, knowing I am unworthy but hoping for a scrap of kindness to be cast my way by virtue of thy nearly infinite mercy." (We talked like that, really, we did, it would have been really embarrassing if anyone had been listening.) He laughed vociferously, swinging his head down toward his knees, then stopped, looked at me seriously, and said that my score was three standard deviations above the mean, and what did I expect him to do? I replied that unless he was a more capricious grader than the average professor, that meant I had gotten an A. He nodded slowly, licked his finger, and made an imaginary mark in the air.

Then he said, quite seriously, "You're the best. You know you are. You're the best I ever taught." I raised my eyebrows, and he said, even more seriously, with a chill in his voice, "Believe it, kid. You're the one. All you need now is the will, and you can achieve honor. Unfortunately, coming up with that is the hard part. The talent, you inherit with the genes. The will, you have to struggle for; no one is born with it; there's no survival value in beating your brains out against abstractions."

He raised his right hand to his lips and tapped them slowly, as if he was trying to think of just the right way to phrase something. "The problem of knowledge is not to enjoy it, but to endure the process of finding it. Because only new knowledge will reward you for having discovered it. And while it is not true that all the easy-to-find truths have already been recognized, you still have to be very lucky to have those pure moments of insight; most of the time, you have to sweat and blunder and make mistakes and fail utterly before you finally turn down the right path in the maze and find out something new about nature. Even then, most likely no one you know will be very impressed with your findings, because if they are really new they require a certain amount of background knowledge to appreciate; and this being an age of specialization, the experts making the discoveries are going to be far from each other on average. And furthermore, more than likely no one but you will ever know if you've lived up to your expectations. The greater you turn out to be, the greater is the sense of failure; only an idiot is smug about his life's work. Einstein and Leonardo, for example, both died saying that their lives had been nothing but failures."

I thought about that speech for a while, and asked, "And what about you? Are you satisfied with your life's work?" He said, "Good God, no. I never had enough talent, to begin with. All my efforts have been utterly superficial. I didn't have good judgment; I always seemed to pick projects that were either too trivial or too difficult. I never finished anything to my satisfaction. I tried hard, but that's nothing to be proud of; any moron can say that."

I said, "I can't believe what I'm hearing. You are the greatest teacher I've had in fourteen years of schooling. You have a brilliant mind, and you have no doubt influenced hundreds of students from your classes over the last however many years. No one who ever took a class from you will ever forget you."

He pinched his eyes shut with his fingers, and said, "But that's not important. A teacher's influence is gone after a generation, at most. The only real success in science is success in research, the discovery of new facts about nature and the passing on of these facts to one's peers and to future generations of scientists. I have failed irredeemably in this area; I have published no new facts or concepts; my name is not known to my peers; I am nothing but a failure."

So, as I was not feeling too happy about the way the conversation was developing, I just said to him, "OK, Leonardo; I understand you. Like all but one or two scientists in every decade, you've come up short. Meanwhile, while you're being too hard on yourself, our lives go on. What are you up to this summer?" With a long exhalation of breath, he replied, "I'm thinking about spending the rest of the summer in the wilderness. It's about forty days until classes start again; that seems like about the right amount of time to spend fasting and meditating. Take a vow of silence, not speak a single word to anyone. Maybe I'll collect material for next year's lab classes, or maybe I'll just spend the summer staring at trees, or ant's nests, or rock formations, or clouds."

I said, "That sounds better than what I have planned. I'm going to go home to Texas and make myself thoroughly disagreeable to my relatives, not one of whom has ever had an original thought, or any thought at all about anything not related to food, sex, hunting, or fishing. I may watch my great-grandmother die. Probably, I'll go to the public library and sit there day after day in air-conditioned comfort reading nineteenth-century European fiction."

He held his finger up in the air as I was midway through my speech, as if he'd just thought of something and wanted to be sure he remembered it, and then said, "Actually, maybe I can help make part of your summer worthwhile. The department has money that has to be spent on class-related work by the end of the fiscal year, that is, by July 30. If you want, you can be immediately placed on the state payroll for the next two weeks and help me collect specimens for next year's lab classes. Do you like to catch lizards, or wade around in two feet of mud in stream bottoms collecting filter-feeding insects? If you do, I can offer you a job, paying the minimum wage, for maybe as much as ten days!"

That proposition gave me pause. I'd already more or less made arrangements to meet one of my cousins, who was going to make the long drive up from Texas to meet me at the dormitory and drive me back. But I didn't see any real problem to delay my visit for two weeks. My mother would make me feel guilty, but I was beginning to learn to deal with that. My father would be pleased that my expensive college education was beginning to pay some slight dividends in the form of actual wages printed out on a paycheck.

So I tentatively agreed. I did ask him if there would be anyone else to help us out, because I didn't relish the thought of netting tarantulas or bats all by myself. But he just gave me a withering look, and said, "This is not your home state, where oil royalties have enriched the state university system to the point where they don't know how to spend the money they have. Here, we have only winter wheat, which is worth about ten percent by volume what crude oil is, and requires more labor to harvest. So it's going to be just you and me, kid; or just me, I can always buy nine gallons of Early Times and tell the state comptroller I need it to preserve my specimens in."

Well, I made up my mind right then and told him that I would help him out. He gave me a big, big smile and said that was excellent, and that we should start as soon as possible. "You are on the payroll as of this instant. By the way, you should disabuse yourself of the notion that you are going to be paid by the hour, babe; this is a lump-sum job. You are going to earn $128 in cash Yankee money, and we will work until I say we are done, or until the stroke of midnight on the 30th, whichever comes first. Is that still OK with you?" I sighed a little, but I said that it was. He said, "Right. Today is Monday. I have to finish my grading tomorrow morning, but I'll decide what we need to bring along with us in the afternoon, and get a pickup from the garage, and call you at the dormitory sometime after 2. I expect we will want to leave then, so we can get some work done Tuesday before it gets dark. It's about a forty-five minute drive out to Rainbow Bridge, which is probably the best place for us to find a variety of animals. We'll come back here then, and we'll head back out there again before dawn on Wednesday."

I took my leave of him then. That night, in the dorm, I was one of the few remaining girls left, since all the exams had been given and most of the students were already gone. I slept poorly, partly because of the food, which was hot dogs again, but also because I was excited and nervous about going out with Dr. McKenna. I wanted to do well, but I was afraid that he'd be diasppointed, and maybe even yell at me because I was so inexperienced and squeamish. I had no idea what he expected me to do.

I had a dream just before morning, that we (Dr. McKenna and I) were lost in a great round hall, made of huge logs. It was dark, and lit with torches, and no one could be seen, but we could hear distant rumblings and roarings like the sounds I imagined would be made by sleeping giants. Once in a while, also, the floor would tremble as if an earthquake was about to break out. I was holding Dr. McKenna's hand very tightly. It seemed as if we were walking around and around in circles, coming back always to places we'd already been. Then, we found a small room off to one side, pitch black, but at least it seemed as if it'd be a place where we could rest. And then, it seemed that we had been sleeping in the room, and woke up, and stepped out of the room to find that it was no longer in a dark hall, but in an open glade with great oaks; and we saw the iron gates of a mighty stone castle, just barely visible in the distance. I wanted to go up to see it, but Dr. McKenna said no, that it was too dangerous; but I pulled free of his hand anyway, and ran over to the gates. As I looked back I saw him disappearing; not into the distance, but like he was fading away in the air. He was reaching out his hands to me, as if he was asking me to save him. I was very frightened, and ran back to him; but he had completely disappeared. And then when I turned back to the gates, they were gone also, and in their place was an evil-looking giant, maybe thirty feet high and with long tusks, coming toward me, drooling, with a platter and knife and fork! And that was so terrifying that I woke up, sitting right up in bed, my heart beating like a tom-tom.

There was no way I could get back to sleep after that dream, so I got dressed and went downstairs and sat around in the reception room of the dorm, reading and playing solitaire. At about noon I got a blanket off my bed and lay down on the lawn in front of the main doors, just lay there doing nothing, watching the people walk by. Finally, in the early afternoon, Dr. McKenna showed up, driving a beat-up red Ford pickup with the Cimarron seal on the doors. He was dressed for action in his coveralls, striped t-shirt, and hiking boots. Bouncing out of the cab, he paced over to where I was lying down and dived face down into the grass beside me, and then, I am amazed to relate, he grabbed me around the neck and kissed me on the lips. "Good afternoon, darling," he said, "ready for some high times in the high country?" I was too surprised to say much of anything. He wanted to get a bite to eat, which was fine with me, so we went over to Lloyd's and he had a bowl of chili. It seemed that he was very nervous; he fiddled with his spoon, kept fidgeting, drumming his fingers on the table, and kept humming; I recall hearing "Begin the Beguine" over and over again. I had a chicken club sandwich. He picked up the check, saying, "Paid for by the project."

And then, we were out on the road and heading north toward the park. It was a beautiful day, clear and dry, with the temperature in the low 80s. Dr. McKenna was not very talkative, which was fine with me. I was having a good time just looking out the window and watching the scenery roll by.

"I don't know if you've ever been to Rainbow Bridge before," he finally said, raising his eyebrows at me. I shook my head no. "It's a remarkable spot. It's essentially one, extensively branched, box canyon, so that although the whole thing is only a little over a mile long, if you walked in and out of all the individual clefts, you'd wind up walking about twenty miles. At the bottom of the canyon are caves and sinkholes leached out of the limestone, some well explored and others inaccessible or very dangerous. And then, of course, the bridge itself - a stone arch about two hundred feet long, spanning the two sides of one of the ravines, left there by a geological accident a hundred and sixty million years ago - a flow of volcanic lava was deposited over a limestone hill at the bottom of the sea, and then when the land rose at the end of the Devonian, the limestone eroded away and left the bridge. It's all very beautiful. The wind has a special quality as it blows down the canyons, sighing in a high, keening voice, like that of ghosts. It's really a most magical place."

I looked at him skeptically across the front seat. "Magic," he repeated, glancing at me; "if only magic existed and could be controlled. At one time everyone believed in it, and everyone knew someone who was good at causing things to happen by its aid. Magic was as real to those people as money is to us."

He took his hands off the wheel and let the truck steer itself. "If I have enough faith, I can will this vehicle to go where I wish. I can even make it leave the earth and fly through space!"

DEGREES OF FREEDOM

The wheels started to run off the road; we were riding on the shoulder. Dr. McKenna kept looking straight ahead, with his hands in his lap, smiling an idiot grin. I panicked, grabbed the wheel, and steered us back up onto the pavement. "Alas," he sighed, still smiling in the same manner but now staring at me, "I detect the presence of one who disbelieves. I was just about to master the art of flying through space. I was beginning to acquire sufficient faith in magic. Now I must begin again." And he finally began to steer normally. If this was a joke, I thought, it wasn't very funny; but he merely continued to smile, look straight ahead, and drive down the road. For the first time, I began to wonder whether I should have taken this job.

A few minutes later, a brown metal sign appeared pointing off to the right. This was the road to Rainbow Bridge. It was a dirt road, and a strong wind had come up, blowing dust right at us; we drove straight into it. I could smell the musty odor of dry earth penetrating into the compartment where we sat.

The road meandered among boulders and rock outcroppings, and skirted occasional woodlots of pines. "Western White Pines: someone planted those here," Dr. McKenna said. "They don't grow in this vicinity normally; they start becoming common about three hundred miles west of here. But so far, they're doing all right." Just then, as we swung around a curve, we startled three deer that had been feeding alongside the road. The first one, apparently a young male with rudimentary antlers, leaped directly into our path and stopped there, frozen in fright. Dr. McKenna shouted "Hoo-boy!" and swerved to the right to miss him, and hit the brakes; the deer finally bounded away, across the road and down a ravine, out of sight. The other two deer, females, were directly opposite my window. I was close enough to hear them snorting, confused, as they tried to decide whether to follow the first or not; finally, they took off in the opposite direction, up the hill, and disappeared into some brush.

"Well," Dr. McKenna said, "want to go after those?" I've got enough rope to make a couple of lassos. They'd make nice specimens for Anatomy 231, don't you think?"

"I had in mind pursuing something smaller, like butterflies."

"Spoil-sport. You're no fun at all. I should have brought your grandma."

"Hey, any of my male relatives would be happy to chase those things. In fact, if they'd been along, all three of those deer would probably have been gut-shot long before now."

But we were back up on the road and continuing to drive toward the main part of the park. Finally, we pulled into a fenced area with a few campsites, picnic tables and signboards; the parking lot was just a few marked spaces on the asphalt. We were the only ones around. I got out and stretched; the first thing I saw was a sign shaped like an arrow that said "Canyon Trail."

It turned out that there was a fenced trail all the way around the rim of the canyon near the campsite. The wind was picking up stronger, but Dr. McKenna said we needed to walk around a bit to check out the territory, so we set out to walk part of the trail. I pulled my scarf around my face to protect myself from the blowing grit. Dr. McKenna was right, after all; it was magical. We looked down into gorges that averaged, I suppose, about a hundred and fifty feet deep. The few scraggly trees that grew in the bottom of the chasms, sometimes next to huge rocks that dwarfed them, were so small that they made it look even deeper. At the top of the canyon, the trees were larger, but those near the edge often leaned at a precarious angle into the abyss.

The rocky soil at the top of the canyon was reddish-brown, but down farther were fairly well-defined layers of pinks, tans, and white; and at some spots, you could see about halfway down into the canyon a narrow band of bright violet rock. I asked Dr. McKenna what made it that color and, looking at me as if I'd asked him some deeply injurious personal question about his childhood religious beliefs, he said he didn't know. Sticking up from the middle of some of the ravines were narrow, sometimes practically knife-edged rock formations, many of them almost pure white. They glistened in the sun; they must have been practically unadulterated quartz. These rocks were weathered into fantastic shapes; some looked like ocean liners, complete with funnels; others looked like heads of Indians. There was one that resembled the Sphinx. In other spots, there were pinnacles, almost like towers, often with large boulders balanced at the very top.

The whole time, cliff swallows and swifts were buzzing across the canyon, soaring from one side of the gullies to the other, making quite a racket with their batlike calls. They were dive-bombing us as we stirred up insects for them. It made me laugh.

We were on top of the bridge, Rainbow Bridge, before I realized it. It was wider than I had imagined, and I was almost to the middle before I looked left and right and figured out where I was. I came to a sudden halt; I felt a strange, unsettled sensation as if I were somewhere I had no business being, or as if the thing was going to collapse with me on it. Dr. McKenna said, "Don't worry, that bridge is strong enough to stand up to a mighty powerful earthquake, and maybe even to the end of the world, or at least to the end of mankind." He told me that years ago, back in the territorial days, both Erdwell and Centerland counties wanted the park, and that a compromise was struck so that the county line ran right through the middle of the bridge. He thought maybe someday one jurisdiction or the other might decide to charge a fee for crossing it, and set up a toll booth.

After about an hour, we came back to the truck and each had a bottle of soda pop, Coke, from Dr. McKenna's cooler. Then he said, "Right. Enough goofing off. We're going to get some work done this afternoon. I'm going to take the nets over to the pond and seine up some small fish. It's about half a mile from here, over in the next ravine. Don't come looking for me, because I do this naked.

"What I want you to do is trap ground squirrels. There are two ways to do it. First is with nooses. This is very simple; you take a cord with a lasso end, loop it around the hole, then unroll the cord thirty feet or so and sit quietly until the gopher sticks his head up to look around. Then you yank on the cord, and if you're lucky, you've got him. If not, you go to another hole and try again.

"The other way is with these traps. They work basically the same way; you set the trap over the hole, secure it in place with a stake, and if the squirrel comes out and touches the trigger, these little spring steel clamps snap around his body.

"When you get one, you drop it into this killing jar." He showed me a wide-mouthed jug, maybe a gallon and a half in capacity, with some wire mesh in the bottom. "It's got cyanide gas in it right now. Just let me check to make sure there's enough."

He knelt down, unscrewed the lid, and stuck his nose into the jar and took a whiff! I couldn't believe it, and shrieked out, "What are you doing? Are you crazy or something?" He looked back with a contemptuous grin, and said, "Hey, man, no sweat. I'm a lot bigger than a gopher. It's going to take more than a few micrograms of some toxic chemical to do me in."

He set the jar on the ground next to me, stood up, stretched, and took a deep breath. Then he shook his head rapidly back and forth. "All the same, the damn stuff does give you a buzz. I don't recommend that you try it. You're a lot smaller than me. Also, when you drop the gopher in, don't leave the top off for any longer than you have to."

We loaded up and he drove me a half-mile or so to an open field. Pulling off the road, he stopped the pickup, but left the engine running. He said, "I'll leave you here for now. There are hundreds of ground squirrels in this area; I'll let you learn how to find their holes. Just watch, you'll find plenty of them. You've got five traps and three cords, so you should be kept plenty busy.

"The jar will hold about thirty of the little dudes; I hope you can get at least twenty. That'd be plenty of material for the 231 lab. I'll be back just before sunset to drive us back."

So he left me, driving the truck off in a cloud of dust. I was left alone, just me and my traps.

I hadn't exactly bargained on this. I obviously hadn't thought things through; what did I think I'd be doing, setting live traps for cockroaches? Having to handle cute little mammals and cruelly put them to death, and to watch their last agonies as they suffocated inside a glassed-in prison, was not what I'd expected. Oh well, I thought, maybe I won't be very good at this, and he'll have to fire me.

It was very quiet in the field after Dr. McKenna left; there was no wind at all, and the only sounds were the buzzing of insects and the far-off whistles of Western Meadowlarks. I decided I'd carry all of my paraphernalia to the middle of the field, sit quietly for a while, and decide where to set up. I climbed to the top of a small mound and sat in the open sun, looking around. Tomorrow, I decided, I'd definitely bring a hat to keep the sun from baking my brains out.

I looked around for ground squirrels, but could see none. Was this a test Dr. McKenna had set me, or another pointless joke? Maybe he was trying to test my resourcefulness. I decided I'd look for movements in the grass, and focused my attention just on the patterns the leaves of grass made against the background. Amazingly, this worked. When I got used to looking for it, I saw the characteristic movement that grass makes when a little animal is pulling it over to feed on the seed head. Once I knew what it looked like, I could see it happening all around. Now all I had to do was to find their holes, and I soon figured out the easiest procedure; look for the grass movement nearest me, move toward it until I startled the animal, and watch where it took off for. Then follow the vector of its path; it was never very far away to the little hillock with the almost-vertical hole.

I set my spring traps first, and then strung out one cord noose. There was no action for some time, maybe fifteen minutes; I just sat there, looking all around for something to happen. It was very quiet, although I did notice a black pickup truck with four guys in it (two in the front and two in the back) driving past. I'm pretty sure they didn't see me. I assumed at the time that they worked in the park, because they didn't look much like your average nature lover. Then everything started to happen at once. I looked up to see a squirrel poking out of my cord-trap hole; I was so excited I practically stood up to yank the noose. I missed, of course; but at the same instant I heard two spring traps pop. Damn, I got some, I thought to myself.

Checking out the first, I found the little victim trembling at the lip of his hole, caught by the leg. Blood was trickling down over his foot and onto the ground. As I approached, he looked away from me and scrabbled uselessly with his front feet. I would have liked to have let him go, but it was obvious that he wouldn't have survived anyway. His leg seemed to be broken. "The kindest thing for you," I said to the uncomprehending victim, "is the jar." And, pulling the stake out of the ground, I picked up the trap with him in it and held it at arm's length; I carried him over to the glass vessel where he'd be spending his final moments; and, without watching, I unscrewed the lid and dropped him in.

With an afflicted heart, I returned to the other sprung trap; in this one, the gopher was caught by the chest. His little ribs were practically caved in and he was hardly able to breathe. "You too," I said, and condemned him to the same fate; but this time I watched what happened. He took a deep breath of poisoned air, and all his little legs jerked out, rigid; his neck jerked in a couple of spasms; then he took a second breath and died. His limbs relaxed and he clasped his fellow casualty in a final, eternal embrace.

I went back to the field, but my heart was no longer in my work. I set all my spring traps and emptied them promptly when they went off, but I didn't pull the string on any more gophers; I wasn't willing to be personally, directly involved in their deaths. I was like an electrician who'd work on the electric chair, adjust the amperage and voltage to make sure the condemned criminal would die, but wouldn't pull the switch with his own hands.

Dr. McKenna came back just before sunset, exuberant, announcing record catches of small fish. He asked me how I'd done and all I said was "Twelve." He looked a bit disappointed, but said that maybe I'd do better tomorrow.

In the truck, on the way home, I was pretty quiet; finally, I got up the nerve to ask him if I could work on something different tomorrow; maybe try to trap some insects or fish; something cold-blooded. He laughed shortly, and said, "Sure. Whatever you like. We can switch sites. I did bring some insect nets."

When he dropped me off at the dorm, he said, "We have to get a very early start tomorrow. Most animals are more active around dawn and dusk. In order to get there around sunrise, I'll be back at 5:30." I groaned. "We'll work hard in the morning, then take three or four hours break around midday. It'll be very civilized. Quite continental, actually. I'll see you bright and early."

That night, I had another frightful dream. This time, I was with Dr. McKenna in a land of misty snow. We seemed to be in a kind of park, a beautiful 18th-century garden of the sort I would imagine might be found in the capital of some ideal European monarchy, maybe Paris. The place was decked out as for a sort of festival; the trees were hung about with strands of tiny white bulbs that shone through the fog, and the benches were covered in wonderful gold brocaded fabrics. But I felt that something was wrong; I could see macabre shapes - not animal, not human, not mechanical, but having qualities of all - moving around at the limit of my vision, and I could hear ghastly cackling laughter far away. Dr. McKenna didn't seem to share any of my fear; in fact, he was cheerful and sunny as I had never seen him before. He held my hand and we danced through the park, and he swept me into the air and kissed me as if we were the happiest of lovers. He sang joyous, hilarious old songs from his childhood that I had never heard; and although I tried to laugh and share in his delight, something filled me with apprehension.

We were sitting together on a bench, and he was holding me so tightly I gasped for breath; in fact, I was sitting on his lap. Then unfortunate things started to happen. The beings I had seen and heard before started to come closer; they snarled and cursed at us. At first they just moved in and retreated, but soon they became bolder. One of them, a huge bipedal monster with the face of a hog, the legs of a horse, and the arms of a baboon, threw a stone at Dr. McKenna; it hit him right in the forehead and bounced away. But he only laughed, saying, "I couldn't feel that at all!" I became very afraid, pulled away from his grasp, and tried to hide behind the bench. Another creature came out of the fog, a thing like a toad, carrying a heavy club in its clawed forefeet. It struck Dr. McKenna over the head. I screamed in terror, but again he said to me, "They can't hurt me; I felt nothing."

More and more of the horrible things kept swarming out of the shadows to attack Dr. McKenna; I couldn't bear to watch as they assaulted him, but nothing happened; it all seemed like an amusing game to him.

Finally, a blind old woman came up to him. She was dirty and stank; her face was hairy and her feet were bleeding and wrapped in tattered pieces of carpet. For some reason, I had to watch her; she was dressed in brownish rags, and leaning on a crooked cane, but in her palsied hand she carried a dagger made out of a sharpened wooden stake. Dr. McKenna seemed to recognize her. She addressed him, saying, "It is wrong to feel hate, but it is wrong to ignore those you have caused to feel pain. My body has been wracked with fire for years because of you. I will have my revenge!" And she leaped on him, and he was helpless to ward off her blow; the dagger entered his heart and passed through his back; and he fell forward, sightless eyes staring, dead.

I woke up, screaming and crying; I found myself in the arms of Cathy, the head resident, who had heard me wailing in the middle of the night. She asked me if I was all right, and as soon as I could regain my composure I told her, "I had the most horrifying dream," and told her to go back to sleep; but I stayed awake all the rest of the night, my brain full of the grisly images of the nightmare.

Around 5:15, I staggered out of bed and dressed. I remembered to bring a hat. I went down to the front hall and stood there, waiting; I pressed my nose up against the door. Right on time, he was there, the truck's headlamps carving a cone of light out of the night, and I sprinted out into the cool darkness to sit in the cab with him. The echoes of the dream were still with me, and I felt a pang of terror as I ran through the dark. Although it was not cold at all, my teeth were chattering when I reached the safety of the truck.

"Hello, sport," he said, "you seem to be energetic this morning."

"Just couldn't wait to earn some more money," I said. "How are you?"

"Could be worse, I suppose. Want some coffee? There's some in the Thermos. Also a couple of jelly doughnuts. They were out of Danish."

So we drove into the crimson rising sun, illuminating a fringe of horizon-hugging vermilion clouds as it rose. There was absolutely no one else on the road. We returned to our familiar parking spot and got ready for the day's work.

"Today I'd like you to concentrate on trapping insects," he said. "I brought a variety of nets and traps for this purpose. I'll show you how they all work. First of all, we have the light trap. This is a tiny battery-operated lamp that puts out the wavelengths that attract most species, and is bright enough to overwhelm their perceptions when they get close enough. This is called, by the way, the "area of dazzle." Even in broad daylight, this thing works pretty well. The lamp is here, at the top, under this conical glass screen; the insect flies into this gap and winds up inside this funnel, and it is then overcome by the vapors of chloroform rising up from the killing jar. Just pull out the legs and set it up in the open. It should be good for all morning, but if the light goes out I brought an extra battery. I think you'll get mainly moths with this, but you never know.

"Here are some adhesive traps; they're very simple, just pieces of cardboard folded into a star-shaped pattern. Smear these with the stuff in this jar, a mixture of sugar and stale beer, set them on the ground with a stone on top, and I guarantee you they'll be covered with ants, beetles, and God knows what else in an hour or two. Pull them off periodically with tweezers and put them into these polystyrene boxes; we'll sort through them later, maybe tomorrow. I heard it might rain tonight, and if it does we need something to keep us occupied so we can earn the state's money.

"These beakers with a little apple juice in the bottom are known as pitfall traps. Take this spoon and dig down into the soil far enough so that you can bury the beaker; leave the rim level with the surface of the ground. Put these in places where there's some grass. Also, if you can, arrange some stones or pieces of wood tepee-fashion over the top to keep birds or lizards from cleaning you out in a hurry.

"And finally, we have nets. I brought three, of different mesh sizes. You should be able to trap butterflies, dragonflies, and - by dragging the surface of the pond - some water-striders or corexid beetles. When you've trapped some, hold them in the net and empty it into these killing jars - just like yesterday's, only smaller.

"Of course, you should feel free to use your own ingenuity to collect these specimens. Darwin used to catch beetles with his bare hands. I like to catch insects; you never know what unusual specimens might turn up. The year before last, out here, I found a katydid that as far as I could tell shouldn't have made it out of Europe; who knows what it was doing in the exact center of North America? I tell you, nature is like a fathomless ocean, surging with mystery."

He walked me over to the pond where he'd trapped fish the previous day and left me alone again. I felt like an absurd commando in some one-sided interspecies war, with my battery of nets and traps, but I felt a lot better about today's assignment than yesterday's. I don't know why I was so squeamish about killing mammals, when insects were just as alive and just as beautiful and useful, from the standpoint of evolution; but I couldn't help the way I felt. I was happy to leave to Dr. McKenna the responsibility for taking up a collection of ground squirrels. That was what he intended to do today, since I had performed so poorly on that assignment.

The morning passed quickly. Insects are everywhere, of course, and in huge numbers. Dr. McKenna told me that there were probably at least the same number of insects for every person in the world, as there are people in the world; amazing, but I could well believe it. I suppose I trapped a thousand of them that morning, but even if I had got a thousand times as many I wouldn't even have made a dent in even the numbers that were just in the vicinity of Rainbow Bridge.

Probably around 11 (I didn't have a watch), he came over to check out my hoard. He was very impressed with the number of species I'd collected. I was glad that he seemed to be satisified with my work, because I don't think he was very happy with what I'd accomplished yesterday.

He'd brought a heavy green blanket from the truck and spread it out on the ground by the pond; we took a break for something to eat. He'd brought sausage sandwiches, homemade yogurt, stuffed raw mushrooms, cookies, and more Cokes. It all tasted very good and I felt exceptionally contented as I stretched out for a rest, maybe even a nap.

Dr. McKenna lay down beside me. I was looking straight up, into the gathering clouds, and he was lying on his side, facing the water. I wondered, idly, if he was going to try to kiss me again, and what I was going to do about it if he did. Suddenly, he sat up with a start. He looked over into the pond and said, "Did you see that, or hear it?" I shook my head and asked what. "Just keep looking out there, about a foot," he said, and crawled to the edge. Keeping his head low, he raised his right arm and slowly moved it to the water's edge, forming his hand into a claw.

Nothing happened for almost a minute. I was hardly breathing, and Dr. McKenna hadn't moved. Then, just for an instant, an animal stuck itself up out of the water. It looked like a tongue poking up through the surface. That was all Dr. McKenna needed; he shot out his hand and grabbed the thing, and then said "Ya-hoo!," laughed, and stood up, pulling it out of the water. It was a snake, an amazingly violet-colored thing with a cream-colored belly, maybe four feet long. Dr. McKenna had hold of it just behind the head; he was still laughing, and said, "This is the biggest one I've ever seen!"

I didn't know what to do. I was shrinking back, afraid. He said, "Come on, kid; help me kill it!" Meanwhile, it was thrashing around, wrapping itself around Dr. McKenna's arm. I still didn't know what to do. He yelled out, "The formaldehyde! The needle and the formaldehyde! Fill up the 5-cc syringe and bring it to me!"

I ran back to his knapsack and rummaged around, and finally found what he wanted in a side pouch. He was still yelling, but almost laughing; telling me he was losing circulation in his arm and that he couldn't hold on much longer. I assumed he was joking, but I had no idea how strong a snake of that sort could be. I'd certainly seen his boa squeeze the life out of the poor mouse he fed it. I was trembling so much I could hardly unscrew the formaldehyde bottle, but somehow I managed to fill up the syringe without sticking myself, and ran back to where he was standing. He held his arm out, with the snake wrapped entirely around it, and told me, "Inject it! Right up behind the head!" But somehow, I couldn't; not that I was too squeamish to do it, though I was feeling just a little bit sick; but I was afraid I'd slip and plunge it into Dr. McKenna's arm. So after I had tried some ineffectual thrusts and half-hearted stabs, he said, "Oh, Christ, give it to me," and took it away from me with his left hand and held the barrel with his fingers and put his thumb behind the plunger. Then he stuck the snake in the back, and pumped the solution in quickly, so that some of it actually spurted back out as the flesh bulged up around the needle. And Dr. McKenna's face took on the most awful expression as he made the injection; his teeth were clenched in a horrible grin and his eyes were bulging. I was horrified, really; I had my hands jammed into my mouth to keep from screaming.

For a moment, it didn't seem as if much was happening; the snake was still wrapped around him, and he was staring at his arm with his eyes still open wide as if to say, "Well? Hurry up," and then gradually the snake came loose. It started at the tail, where the tip made a couple of twitches and then started to relax, and unwound gradually and dropped off his arm and pointed at the ground. And then the tail throbbed about three times, and then it was like all the life went out of the whole animal at once; like one second it was alive and strong, and the next second it was just a sack of meat.

Dr. McKenna looked like he was sorry he'd had to kill it. He sighed, sat down on the ground, and started to peel its dead body from his arm. It had been grabbing him pretty tightly; his whole forearm was banded with red and white. His face, that had been so frenzied a few moments before, was cast down and he had a dejected hangdog look as if he'd lost a lifelong friend. He looked up at me and said very quietly, almost in a whisper, "Please get the bucket of FAE solution from the truck, and also a gallon jar."

It took me about six or seven minutes to walk back and find what he wanted, a big blue metal can with a retractable plastic spout, labeled "formaldehyde - ethanol - acetic acid, 5-10-5%." It was very heavy and I wondered why he couldn't have carried the snake to it, but I had been given instructions. I lugged it back to where he was sitting. He had put the snake on his lap, stretched out at full length, and was stroking it very gently with long smooth strokes. His eyes had a melancholy, oblivious look; his mouth was open and he was making soft murmuring sounds. When I banged the pail down beside him, he seemed to come to his senses; he picked up the snake and inserted it, very gently, tail first, into the jar. With gentle motions, he coiled it up perfectly; when he was done, he looked down from above and muttered something that might have been "So be it." Then he poured enough formaldehyde mixture in to just cover the snake completely, screwed on the lid, turned around and sat back down on the blanket. "I'm very tired all of a sudden," he announced, "and I think we should take something of a long break from our work. I'm going around to the other side of the pond to lie down, and you can do what you want. I think I'll come back here around three, but if I'm not back exactly by then, just give me a shout. I'm a light sleeper."

Well, that was all right with me, I decided. I really wasn't exactly sure what time it was, but I was tired after last night's almost sleepless night and a fairly hard morning of work. I pulled the blanket over to a little shrub that provided a bit of shade and lay down for a rest.

Unsurprisingly, I went right to sleep, and luckily, I had no dreams. Only once, after I'd been asleep for maybe an hour, I thought I heard something or someone breathing heavily, almost growling, above my head; but I opened my eyes quickly, and looked around, and nothing was there, so I must have imagined it.

I must have slept for a long time, because when I finally woke up for good the sun was low in the sky and it was considerably cooler. Clouds were forming in the west, also. As I looked up, I saw Dr. McKenna sitting on the blanket, peeling the bark off a branch. He looked down on me, very tenderly, as if I was a small child that he loved and was taking care of; and he said, "My dear, it is time for proletarian toil once again. I have trapped enough gophers, I think, and I believe I shall wander around the edges of the pond with some nets, looking for frogs mostly. You may continue with your insect collecting, if that would be acceptable to you."

So I carried on with my trapping and netting, sometimes down by the pond and sometimes up on the sides of the ravine, and he went to the other side of the pond, squatting in the long grass with his nets, waiting; and every five minutes or so he would strike, and once in a while he would come up with a live frog. Then he would return in triumph to the formaldehyde jar, the one already containing the snake, and drop it in. There would be a brief splashing, and then it would be over until he got the next victim.

After a half-hour or so, I noticed it was beginning to get dark, and in the sky I noticed quite a distinct, dark squall line, with heavy purple clouds behind it. Dr. McKenna didn't seem to have noticed it; he was crouching down at the edge of the water, surveying the surface. I shouted at him, "Hey! You think we might be in for a storm?"

He looked up at the sky, and said, "Holy shit, kid, this is going to be a big one. Look at the lightning in those clouds, and look how fast they're coming. We'd better get the hell out of here! Drop the nets, forget the jars -- just run!" And we both set out for the truck, dashing as fast as we could go. Dr. McKenna was able to run a little faster than me, but my fear helped me to cover the ground at a good clip, also.

It began to look as if he was right about the storm. It got suddenly much colder and darker, and a stubborn breeze whipped up behind. My hat flew off, but I wasn't about to stop to pick it up. The trees leaned away from the wind, bowing their heads over and over, like penitents at the Wailing Wall; the grass pirouetted in whirlpool patterns against the ground. I looked up to the sky and saw that it had become filled with gyrating, basin-shaped clouds that were unmistakably green; a dark, bilious green like that of dirty oil spilled into sand. Dr. McKenna shouted back, "We'll be lucky if we get out of this without a God-damn tornado!"

Then rain started to fall out of the boiling clouds, heavy drops like a barrage of mortar shells splattering into the dust, leaving craters of mud from which silty dribbles jutted out like an octopus's legs. And the practically continuous lightning, flaring from cloud to cloud, illuminated the landscape in incandescent orange, a landscape from which all the color had already been drained by the darkness of the clouds. The drops came faster and faster, but the pickup was in sight now, its image bouncing up and down in my vision as my head bobbed around from my frantic running.

We got to the truck just as the heavens really opened up. I have never seen anything like it. Imagine twenty men with five-gallon pails, throwing water at you just as fast as they possibly can from every direction, and maybe you'll have some idea of how it felt. It was coming down so hard that it stung, like hundreds of little bullets pelting into your flesh. Dr. McKenna was a few strides ahead of me, so he got into the pickup maybe five seconds sooner, at the most; but he was still reasonably dry, just wet on his head, shoulders, and feet, and I was practically soaked.

Both of us were gasping our lungs out. Dr. McKenna dug around in his pocket for the keys, saying, "At least we might be able to get out of here tonight. I'd sure hate to be trapped out in this weather."

He stepped on the starter and the engine ground for a few seconds, but wouldn't catch. He repeated the process two or three more times, but the effect was the same. Dr. McKenna began to be agitated; his eyes bulged out and his breath was coming in gasps. Meanwhile, the rain was coming down even harder. Again, he ground the starter. "Come ON!" He shouted the second word with a yell that rattled the windows. "Start, you bastard! You piece of excrement!" He was now screaming incoherently. Water was pouring off the windshield like someone was spraying it on with a fire hose. The engine wouldn't, just wouldn't start. The starter gave a few more ineffectual grinds; Dr. McKenna stamped so hard on the gas pedal that I thought his foot was going through the firewall. Finally, when he turned the key, there was nothing but a click. "The God-damn points are wet," he shouted, "Either that or the fucking battery's dead. God damn this fucking college to hell. How the fuck they can be so fucking short-sighted ... Son of a bitch, here we are sitting unprotected in an antique vehicle in the middle of a God-damn hurricane ... "

He stopped cursing and reached up and touched the side of his head. "And now the God-damn roof leaks! Jesus Christ, first we're about to drown and now we've got the God-damn Chinese water torture."

I began to notice it, too. I looked up and saw quite a stream of water dribbling into the cab. "Look," I said, "It's coming in over here too." "The fucking roof must be rusted out," he said, "and it's soaking through the roof matting. Goddamn it, I'm not going to sit here and get slowly drenched. I brought my tent, and it's a hell of a lot more waterproof than this fucking vehicle is."

He opened the door a crack, and the light came on. Big drops of water fell slowly off it. "This is what we're going to do. The tent is in the truck box, inside its stuff bag. I'm going to run back there and grab it, it and its stakes, and then bring them right back in here. We're going to partly unroll the tent, as much as we can, and get inside it, both of us, the upper parts of our bodies. Then we're going to open your door and get out, and use the tent as an umbrella, and run as fast as we can to higher ground, where we might be drier; and I'm going to put up the frame from the inside. Then maybe we can stay more or less dry until this blows over, and maybe the truck will start if we can dry out the points. Ready?"

He opened the door wide. The rain pelted down in a continuous hiss. In only a second or two, it seemed, he was back, dragging a mass of wet nylon canvas behind him. He slammed the door and plopped the wet mass across my legs. "It's not so bad. This is going to work! The cover is soaked, but the tent's going to be OK."

He unzipped the stuff bag, peeled it off, and tossed it out the window. The tent began to expand until it took up almost all the space in the cab. He had to maneuver the whole thing around several times until he figured out which side was which, and how we were going to position ourselves inside. He got a flashlight off the floor of the truck cab; amazingly, it worked. "We'll use this to see where we're going," he said. Finally, we were ready; I flung my door open, and jumped out into a puddle; he followed and slammed the door. I couldn't see a thing, but he had his head poked partly out of the zipper opening so he could direct us. "This way," he shouted, and I ran along blindly behind as he led us out of the parking lot and toward the camping area. We must have looked like an imaginary animal, four-legged and armored in a strange shining coat, with a single yellow eye affixing its beam to the earth.

Suddenly, I was down on the ground. I'd tripped over something, and as I looked down I saw in the weak glow of flashlight large stones, apparently surrounding a cooking pit. It was one of those I'd stumbled over. "Get up," said Dr. McKenna, "we're practically there. There's a wooden platform right over here."

It was true, we'd found one of the campsites, less than ten paces from the cook pit where I'd fallen. We threw ourselves down onto the platform; it was practically dry. Dr. McKenna expertly manipulated the tent stakes, and in a twinkling we were inside a nice pyramid-shaped enclosure; not exactly warm, and not completely dry, but better off than we were before. The wind was still howling, but it wasn't raining quite as hard as it had been.

After a minute, Dr. McKenna said, "Well, it looks as if we're going to be stuck here. Not to worry, though, I'm prepared for this. I brought some blankets, and if they're not too wet we'll be able to sleep." I must have winced. "Yes, my dear," he said sarcastically, "You'll have to sleep in close proximity to me, a man you're not married to, unless you're prepared to sleep out in that stuff outside, or in the dripping truck. Because, my dear, we're stuck. It's up to you, because I sure as hell ain't going out there again after I get the blankets." And without waiting for me to answer, he threw open the tent fly and headed off at a dead run for the truck, which must have been a good thirty yards away. I tried my best to hold the fly shut with my hands, but some water did come in and got part of the floor of the tent wet. It was still raining, but now the main problem, I thought, was the wind, which was howling so strongly I was afraid it was going to pick up the tent, with me in it, and dump it over the edge of the canyon.

In less than a minute, he was back, dragging rather than carrying a big plastic bag. Inside the tent, he said, "Man, are we lucky. All four of these blankets are dry except for this one little corner of one, that got wet because there was a tear in the bag. Look at these things! What joy, civilization is such joy -- look! Delightful, fuzzy pieces of fabric that we can use to keep ourselves warm and dry. Mankind thinks of everything. Look, we even have a lantern. Two sources of light; what a fucking bonus."

He unwrapped the blankets from the plastic bag, and passed two of them over to me. Man, did I need them; I was soaked and shivering, and I wrapped myself up in them completely. I took off my wet shoes (my socks, surpisingly, were still pretty dry) and shrank back into the warmth. I must have looked absurd, like some furry vegetable with a face; but at least I was drying out. I looked over to where Dr. McKenna was unrolling his blankets. He was pretty wet, but despite everything he didn't seem yet to be as soaked as I was. I was surprised to hear him let out a glad cry; "Glory be to God!" He said. "I thought I'd forgotten this. I'm glad I remembered to wrap this up in the blankets. What luck that we have this ambrosial fluid at hand, just when we need it." He waved a full fifth bottle of Jack Daniel's at me, grinning like a fish-eating pussycat. "Do you drink this stuff?" He asked. I shook my head with a shudder; I don't even like beer, and he knew that. "Too bad," he went on, "It's one of America's noble products. I certainly intend to put it to good use at this particular contemptible confluence of events, you may be sure." And, true to his words, he snapped the seal at the top of the bottle and started to drink it, taking long draughts right out of the bottle. as he moaned and gasped with pleasure like a drowning man suddenly breathing air again.

The rain continued outside, rattling on the tent walls. The wind had died down considerably and I was no longer worried that we were going to blow away. We were still dry, too; being on a wooden platform had kept us from standing in water. The sun had gone down, and it was totally dark outside. The red light of the lantern cast everything in the tent into eerie shadow. I'd never been in a place where there were no permanent electric lights at all, and I was beginning to get frightened. I was at the mercy of the weather and of Dr. McKenna; I literally could not escape from this little square of nylon canvas, not now, and I had no idea when I would be free. It looked as if I was going to have to spend all night with an apparently somewhat unstable person, who was now drinking heavily besides. Twenty minutes had gone by since he opened the bottle and he had consumed maybe a third of it, six or eight drinks of whiskey. Yes, he was a very big man, but shouldn't that amount of alcohol have been sufficient to make him thoroughly drunk? I didn't remember the graphs I'd seen in my health classes, but I knew that one glass of beer was enough to make me feel dizzy and shaky. And even assuming he weighed twice as much as me, and could perhaps tolerate twice as much alcohol per pound of body weight, shouldn't he have drunk enough now to be about to pass out into a dazed slumber?

It didn't appear to be so. He was still taking pulls on the bottle every few minutes, and now he was starting to act intoxicated. First he began laughing to himself, little giggles at first and then real guffaws. And he never even looked over to me while it was going on. I didn't dare ask him what was so funny; I just shrank deeper into my cocoon of blankets and retreated farther into the corner of the tent.

Next he rolled over on his side, facing away from me, and started to mutter to himself under his breath. I couldn't catch any of what he was saying. It sounded like a stream of cursing.

Then he sat right up, suddenly. His eyes were wide and red. He looked straight at me and took another deep gulp of liquor, spilling some down the side of his face. The bottle was about half empty now.

He wiped off his beard with his left hand and addressed me in a loud voice. "Isn't this some fuck of a life?" I just trembled, deep in my blankets, at what seemed like a rhetorical question; but it seemed he wanted me to answer. "I'm asking you why this is any better than decomposing in the grave, or even roasting in some comic-book hell. I'm asking you to tell me! You little shit, you have no idea; you're so fucking young you've probably never even thought about the dread of existence." He paused for a long time, staring at me wildly, and took another drink. Then he said, calmly and seriously, "Nobody has any

DEGREES OF FREEDOM

right to be as young as you are. You are one pathetic piece of shit, just dropped out of the asshole of being, still fresh enough to stink. I really hate the sight of the likes of you."

I was really trembling now, and it was not from being wet. He was weaving back and forth in the middle of his blanket, holding the bottle. The red beacon of the flashlight scattered murky shadows across his long face. He looked up at me coldly, and said very slowly and seriously, without slurring his words at all, "I have an overwhelming desire to press something long and firm into your yielding flesh. You little shit, if you won't let me fuck you, I may have to kill you."

That made me even more scared. I shrank back into the corner of the tent as far as I could. I pulled the corner of the blanket up, around my mouth so he couldn't see my lower lip trembling. I was starting to feel like I wanted to vomit.

He said, "Look, you don't need all the romantic preliminaries, do you - candlelight dinner, flowers, dancing cheek to cheek? All that bullshit? It's simple, as I see it. You're a fresh piece of shit, why do you need it? You should be ready, hot and ready on a moment's notice. Clear, clean, and straightforward." What scared me even more was that there was no irony at all in the way he said this. He was scowling as if he was returning defective merchandise. I felt like he was really getting ready to kill me.

He got up on his knees, facing me, and unzipped his fly. "Here it is," he said, pulling out his penis. I had never seen anything like it before; it was shaped like a club and purplish-red in color. "What could be more straightforward, straight and forward, get it; than this? Life is short but my cock is long. I wish I could say that in Latin. I'm feeling horny as a little toad, and you're here with me staring at my nakedness, and I know you want it too, I can smell it; so let's not waste any more time."

He started to crawl forward and reach for me. I started to cry out, "No! Get away from me!" and tried to get out of the tent, but he grabbed my leg and dragged me toward him. I kept struggling and kicking, and his hand slipped down to my foot, and I was able to pull out of my sock, leaving it behind in his grasp. I lunged out of the door, hoping to get to where I could run away from him in the darkness, but he grabbed my belt as I was standing up in the doorway and pulled me back on top of him. One of the tent pieces must have broken, then, because I could feel myself getting smothered in the canvas; I couldn't see anything. I was gasping for breath because he was squeezing me so tight. I could feel that hard penis pressing into my flesh.

I kept flailing out and kicking, but he was too strong for me. The horrible thing was to hear him laughing as I kept hitting away at him. His foul breath was blowing into my face, making me feel sick. Then he got me turned around and had my right arm pinned behind my back, and his right hand was pulling, hard, at my hair, and he was biting and tearing at my chest with his teeth. It hurt me, badly. The pain was like a violet curtain passing back and forth in front of my eyes. I kept hitting him with my left arm, but I had almost no strength left. And my legs seemed paralyzed, and they were pinned under his heavy thighs besides. So I became terrified; this was beginning to look like the end of my life. I had really thought at first I was going to be able to fight him off, but now things looked really hopeless. I just started screaming and crying, I was completely out of control. I don't remember what I said to him or even if I was saying anything in words. I've never been so hysterical in my life!

And then, gradually, I could hardly believe it, he started to let me go. He let go of my hair first. I think he said something like, "Shit, this is not really worth it." He shoved me away from him, really hard, and finally I was loose. I didn't run out of the tent; my legs were too weak for me to do anything but collapse into my blanket, sobbing and gasping and not daring to look up for fear he'd come after me again.

I kept hiding my eyes, and kept sobbing for a long time. Finally I was able to look up. Sometime, he must have put the stake up, since I had room to move around again. It was so quiet in the tent. He was still there, but he was curled up into a ball in the other corner; his head was buried in his arms; I think he was asleep, but I didn't dare make any noise. He'd pulled his trousers and shirt off at some point, but he still had his undershorts on, and his big hairy legs and bottom were stuck out toward me. The trousers were rolled up and stuck under his belly. He was still wearing his heavy wet grey wool socks.

I hardly dared to breathe, let alone try to make a break for it, for fear he was just playing possum and was looking for some excuse to attack me again.

Besides, it was still raining, though not as hard as before. I heard him making a noise like snoring, and I moved as quietly as I could toward the tent fly, keeping as much room between him and me as I could. I kept trying to think what would be the best thing to do; I'm sure he could run faster than me, and besides he had the key to the truck, so I couldn't drive away, either, even if I could somehow get away from him, open the door, and get into the cab before he woke up; and even assuming that the engine had dried out enough to start, which seemed pretty dubious. So I decided maybe the best thing for me to do was just to lie there, and keep an eye on him, and hope somehow he would sleep off this violent fit that had come over him.

I was so constantly afraid that I thought my teeth would never stop chattering, but somehow, I must have slept for a while. Then, he woke me up by shaking me by the shoulders. I snapped my eyes open; it was light enough to see. I shrank back from him in terror, but he had calmed down completely. He had put on his overalls, but he wasn't wearing his shirt. He was smiling sheepishly, and said, "Hey, I'm really, really sorry. I had a lot to drink. I haven't ever acted that way before. Let me go out and make some coffee, and if you can possibly forgive me maybe we can talk. O.K.?"

Well, I didn't say anything, but at least he wasn't attacking me any more. I felt a lot better. Because I was still so very tired, I went back to sleep again as soon as he went outside; I figured he'd be back in a few minutes to tell me the coffee was ready.

I slept for what seemed like a long time, and then I thought I heard a rooster crow. That's a strange thing to hear out this way, I thought, and woke up wondering why Dr. McKenna hadn't come back to get me. I rubbed my eyes, stretched, and rolled out of the tent. The sun was well up in the sky and it was very clear and dry; there was almost no sign of the storm. Dr. McKenna was nowhere to be seen; the coffee pot was on the stove but it didn't seem to have been heated up. I stood up and walked over to the stove and put my hand on the pot. It was cold. I opened it up; there was coffee in the basket but no water in the bottom. The spoon was sitting right on the stove grill as if he'd just left to get some water; but the water spigot was only about forty yards away, I could see it clearly from where I stood.

So where had he gone? The truck was still sitting there where we'd left it. Well, my first thought was that I really hadn't been sleeping as long as I thought, and that maybe he'd just gone into the brush to relieve himself.

After a couple of minutes, I decided there was no need for me to wait for him to come back and make the coffee. I really needed it and besides I was really hungry. So I filled the pot from the spigot, turned on the stove, and started to rummage around to see what we had to eat. There wasn't a hell of a lot. Half a loaf of white bread, four eggs, no butter, no juice, no sausages or bacon; a couple of little boxes of cereal, but no milk and no sugar. It was a good thing I liked my coffee black. I brought back what there was, broke the eggs into a frying pan and scrambled them; there was no grease for the pan so they stuck and burned. I scraped them out onto a plate, picked out some of the bigger black spots, cut the whole mess in half and jammed my half between three slices of bread, and bolted it down with generous gulps of coffee. Luckily that tasted good.

After I'd finished all this, there was still no sign of Dr. McKenna. I began to be worried. Had he wandered off and fallen somewhere and hurt himself? I thought I'd better search for him.

He wasn't around the immediate vicinity of the campsite, that was certain. I thought maybe he'd walked over to the pond to collect all of our traps and the rest of the stuff we'd left behind in the downpour, so I headed off in that direction; but it was so muddy that I gave up, just hiking up to the top of the ridge. I could tell that he was nowhere in sight over there, either.

As I walked back to the truck, I began to feel increasingly alarmed. He must have fallen, I thought, and injured himself so that he can't call for help. I decide the canyon was the place most likely for that to have happened, so I set out on the trail, looking down into the gorge and calling his name every few seconds. My shouts came back to me as echoes; it was as if an invisible doppelgänger with my voice was helping me look for him on the other side of the ravine. I walked as far around the rim as I thought he could have gone in the few minutes he'd been away, but there was no sign of him. My next thought was that maybe he had gone to the pond after all, and fallen in and drowned. It was a crazy notion but I couldn't think of anything better at the time; so I walked clear back over to the pond and walked clear around it in the soggy muck, sinking up to my knees in spots. Again, nothing.

I was really at my wit's end as I walked back again. Crazy thoughts started going through my head. Was he hiding in the truck box for a joke? No. Did someone come by, and had he ridden off with them to get help, without telling me? I looked in the road for tire tracks; there were some, but they looked like ours. I knelt down in the mud to try to compare the tread patterns, but I really couldn't tell anything. Had he fallen into the toilet and drowned? I checked both the men's and ladies' rooms, using the lantern, but didn't see any human hands projecting above the surface of the sewage. No, I didn't probe about with a long stick to make sure. Had he been killed by a grizzly, and dragged off to its den to feed its cubs? Not likely; there was no tell-tale trail of blood leading away from the campsite, and besides, he told me the last grizzly in the state was shot a hundred years ago. Aliens from outer space? No, I could find no scorch marks in the earth, no circular depressions in the wet grass, could smell no nameless sulphurous odors.

I don't know how long I spent trying to find Dr. McKenna. I retraced my steps to all the places he could possibly have been, and I kept racing back to the truck to sit and wait, too; I thought he might be out looking for me, having somehow missed me while I was away seeking him, and I'd better stick close to the last place he'd seen me. And I kept calling for him until my voice became hoarse, calling his name over and over into the empty surroundings, until it sounded like the raving of some mad fool. But of course, nothing happened.

It must have been well along in the afternoon when another visitor's car arrived in the park. It was a young black couple, from Pawnee Springs, as it turned out. They were happy to help me when I explained my problem. The young man even drove me all around the park, but of course there was no sign of Dr. McKenna anywhere. So I concluded I'd better notify the police, and the young fellow drove me over to the little grocery just outside the park limits, back in the direction of where we'd seen the deer.

And I guess you know all the rest; it was all in the newspaper, and on the radio and even on TV. It was harrowing, of course, all of it; the police were so callous in the way they approached the search. Here I was practically in tears, and they were just going their way like a troop of boy scouts or boot camp buck privates with walkie-talkies. You'd think they would have been more excited; I would have thought this would be a case that would enhance their reputations.

And then, amazingly, they found the body and, while one of them held me by the arm so I wouldn't fall in, I had to lean over the edge of the gorge to identify Dr. McKenna; all I could see - oh, God! - was his arm and shoulder and part of his head, but I could tell for sure it was him because he was just wearing his overalls without his shirt. I'll never forget that sight if I live to be a thousand; he was so dead, unmistakably and irreversibly dead, so short a time after he had been alive and happy, and then so drunk and trying to rape me - but still, he was alive, then! Excuse me --

The frightening helicopter too, like some furious insect, and that man going down into the canyon and wrestling in the white dust with Dr. McKenna's body as if it were a sack of coal - I watched all of that. I still dream of the -

No, I can't talk about it any more.

And then, the aftermath; having to tell my story over and over, to reporters, to the sheriff's investigators - every one of whom stank of cheap cigars - and then all my friends and relatives had to know. I was getting ready to scream from the pain. I didn't realize how much Dr. McKenna had meant to me and how alone I felt when he was gone. It felt as if my whole world had been destroyed in flames; that all the men and women and children and birds and animals had died, that the sun had darkened and there were no stars in the sky because the earth was covered with smoke. It was like God had died.

You're lucky, you know it, Dr. Cahill? This is it, this is the last time I'm going to tell this story to anyone. I'll refer the curious to your book, after it comes out.

Yet, I still can't understand just what it was that happened that day. It's not a neat and tidy story to me, not at all. I cannot believe that Dr. McKenna wanted to kill himself. I mean, I saw him, the way he looked at me in the tent. That was not the face of someone bent on self-destruction. He wanted me to forgive him, and I would have, and I think he knew I would. For a moment, I admit, I wasn't sure; I felt like taking revenge, I admit. But my heart wasn't that unforgiving. No real damage had been done to me; I was scared, but it was no big deal.

So what happened to him after he left the tent? I have racked my brains to figure that one out. There are several possibilities. Maybe he just wandered off, still pretty hung over, and just fell; or maybe, just maybe, someone grabbed him and killed him.

Remember, there were a lot of people who hated him. Anybody could have followed him to that spot and waited for him to be alone for a moment, and jumped him. Maybe those tire tracks I saw were those of the killers. Maybe they were the four guys in the black truck I saw the day before; they might have been checking out what he was up to.

Of course, we have to explain the note. I wondered from the beginning why it was typed; I figured maybe the killers planted it on him. The first half of the note is so banal, with stereotyped complaints about life's inequity, and even a misspelled word, which in all my experience of Dr. McKenna I never knew him to perpetrate. But then there is the second half, with its insightful remark about simplifying himself, and the reference to a very obscure composition by Puccini. I doubt if we can attribute such rarefied esthetic sensibilities to Dr. McKenna's murderers. No, it must have been written by him.

So, if he was in fact murdered, why was he carrying it around? The only explanation I can come up with, and I find it hard to believe myself, is that he wrote the note for "practice." I think he was thinking about suicide, and that this was a draft he'd written; maybe it gave him a thrill, somehow, to know that he had on his person a note that he might be able to use someday, in some form, to justify a self-inflicted death.

Oh, damn it, Dr. Cahill, I am so thoroughly and heartily sick of this speculation. I really can't stand it any more. We will never know. For God's sake, let's let the man rest, and let's get on with our own lives. What he did for us will live in us forever; let's make our lives monuments to him. It's what he would have wanted, don't you think?

Dr. Cahill, I must tell you; I think I'm going to fail if I try this. I don't really, deep in my heart, think that there will ever be anyone again like him. Never in the history of the human race. Damn it, Pyke McKenna, why did you have to die?

Bruce 7

So this is it, Pyke McKenna. This is your book, and it's the only one you're ever likely to have; and I know you wouldn't be satisfied, and I know I'm not. I don't know whether I know you any better - I certainly know a lot more about who you once were - but I still don't think I have you quite figured out. But this is it. I'm done with it; it's not finished, but it is done. And I have done it, all by myself; finally come to the last of it, I've done it all. I know this is the same excuse used by all other no-talent failures, but I've done my best, as God is my judge I have.

    October 15, 1972, 11:37 p.m., I'm sitting in my office typing this, I want desperately to be done with this thankless project, get the accursed thing off the desk top and into the desk drawer where it belongs. At least in that selfsame drawer I still have something left in the bottle of Mexican brandy I always keep in there, for emergencies just like this. This is the first such exigency, Pyke, but I knew it'd happen sooner or later. This evening, ten ounces of the brandy gone, that's a lot for a little guy like me, I'm going to be irretrievably hung over tomorrow because I'm not quite done drinking it yet. More than half of it left, for the next emergency like this, may I be old and gray before it takes place.

    But now, at last, this manuscript is virtually concluded, after two-plus years of constant labor. This is it, this is really the end of it all. Now is the time for the post-natal letdown. I haven't got the stomach to take it to an agent, the wretched thing isn't literature, isn't biography, isn't history, why the hell did I think anyone would ever want to read it? Everyone I show it to says it's too episodic, too fragmented, too forced, too clumsy. Well, blast it to hell. I know I'm not Faulkner or Samuel Eliot fucking Morison, I'm just a provincial biologist with something he thinks he ought to do for a friend.

Damn you, anyway, two years you've been gone and I still can't think of you without choking up. I don't want to go into my old age blubbering sentimentally about an old colleague; I want to burn it out of me and get on with my life. I thought this book would do it for me, but obviously it hasn't. I'm just going to put the damn thing in the drawer and let it decompose for a while. Maybe the extra time will help me get over this. I hoped time, as the hoary expression would have it, would heal all wounds; after almost three years, the wound of my divorce isn't completely scarred over yet, the way you told me it would be, even though it's getting there; but the empty space left by your departure only two years ago is still around, it feels like a lost limb.

I sit in my office, it's not too hot to do so this time of year, watching the electric fan you gave me go around and around. I fixed the squeaks, Pyke, really, it wasn't that hard, a few drops of oil really do wonders, even if that could be considered squandering a synthetic chemical and playing into the hands of the petrochemical interests. At least I haven't bought one of those new fancy multi-speed ones in the pastel plastic cases. Man, you would have hated those.

I still have the basket you gave me, of course. It's been sitting, empty, on my bookshelf, but I think I'll start putting it to use. That's what your great-grandmother would have wanted, I'm sure. Maybe I'll keep my rubber boots in it, the ones I use for splashing around in the river, collecting seeds of water plants in the fall. That would be an honest sort of thing to do with it.

There's someone new in your office, Pyke, a new Ph.D. from Iowa State, not there at this minute, of course, but he'll be there tomorrow, a molecular biologist with moist lips, double chin, fine, graying hair, and thick glasses. When he smiles, his eyes disappear into the folds of his cheeks. He whistles, Pyke, it's maddening, the guy can go on constantly whistling for ten minutes without ever generating a melodic passage. He's mad for biopolymers, Pyke, not Bartok, or Baudelaire, or Bergson, just loves to talk about unwinding of

DNA and molecular rheology. Rheology, not theology, but you'd never know it from the reverential tone he adopts.

That's the new thing, biophysics, big money in it from medical foundations and federal agencies. Centrally important to modern biology, they call it, in their pompous editorials in Science, looks like the new Nixon administration is going to buy into it in a big way.

Yes, Pyke, he's going to win again, George McGovern has made no headway in his efforts to sway the masses. Cambodia never happened, the Watergate Hotel break-in never happened, My Lai was a myth. Vietnam, like Prohibition, has been a Noble Experiment in democracy; war by committee, by public relations exercises. California Man is going to outcompete Prairie Man again. How long is it going to take us slow-witted Midwesterners to figure out that we haven't got the stuff to compete with those slick-assed bicoastal advertising agency jet-setters. Such a thing must have happened to the Neanderthals once the Cro-Magnons moved in with their fire and pottery and flint arrows.

Damn it, Pyke, you left us when we most needed you. Just at the time when what you were saying was finally getting through to people, you were taken away. Were you really so discouraged that you killed yourself? I suppose that is always possible. God knows you were depressed the last few times I talked to you. But somehow, it's still hard for me to believe that you could really do it.

Or is Miss Sekkonen's theory, that you were jumped by someone with a grudge and taken off and croaked, is that the correct one? That seems pretty cinematic to me, even though there were a lot of people who hated your guts.

That Eleanor, now, I am wondering about her. How closely does her account of what happened in the tent, that last night of your life, how does that match up with the truth? We really only have her word for how you acted toward her, and how she behaved in response, and the consequences of your disappearance and death. She is such a bright and imaginative girl and I wonder how much of what she told the state police and me is actually true. She really comes out of this event looking like the innocent victimized lamb.

I have considered a nasty little nagging alternative scenario; that she belted you with a rock in the middle of the night after you made advances on her (whether brought about by your being drunk or not, whether she gave any sign that she wanted you or not, we shall never know), and panicked when you appeared to be dead, and drove the pickup back to Pawnee Springs and typed out your note and drove back and found you still out cold and dragged you through the darkness and pushed you off a cliff and waited until morning to efface the marks of your body having been dragged and finally, that afternoon, called the cops in a simulated panic; is that the truth? Was she somehow able to muster up the superhuman strength that would have been required to drag a 260-pound load, more than twice her own weight, the quarter-mile from the tent to the spot where she would have had to shove it over the cliff? And could she really have sat there, calmly, all those hours, watching the sun mount up in the sky and waiting for the right moment to phone the pigs? But it had rained hard the night before. Wouldn't that mean that the body, if it was dragged, would have to be covered in heavy mud -- and wouldn't that have been noticed by the police?

I don't know what to think about the various options, and I suppose no one should really give a damn. McKenna is dead for sure now and we have to go on by ourselves. You would have wanted it that way, right? I hear you speaking to me now, just like you do to Linda Norquist in her dreams, but as far as I know I'm still awake. I hear you saying, for Christ's sake, Bruce, stop wasting your time. You are a big kid now. It's time you started earning your keep as a state employee and a professional biologist. Get your ass off that chair and put that sentimental bullshit aside, and start thinking about science. It's too late for me now, not that I ever had a chance anyway, but you are still young enough and fresh enough that you might do something worthwhile. Teach your damn classes, do enough to keep the Dean off your ass, but think! Get out and look at the prairie; it's magical! Look beyond the thousands of acres of cattle-grazing pasture and irrigated wheatfields, and think about what used to be here; think about lost, wild America beating in the heart of every pronghorn and meadowlark and every leaf of buffalo grass. Don't let it die, Bruce. Don't let the last scraps of wildness be lost and beaten out of every college student, don't let the sirens of money and development seduce them all. Give the future a chance to live in harmony with the land, show them that this is the only way it can be done over the long term. You have to do it. Someone has to do it. It's your responsibility.

Pyke, I promise I'll think about it. But it's a big assignment. It doesn't have to be done tomorrow. Give me a break, Pyke, I must go to sleep now. I haven't been thinking about my professional responsibilities just recently. I was remembering what you said to me, late one night, about six years ago, as we'd finished off the last of a fifth of Scotch. We had just finished laughing for a solid minute and we were feeling like great buddies and all of a sudden you turned to me and you said, "I sure as hell ain't going to say I love you, Jack." Well, me neither, pal, you in your grave or what, I ain't going to say that to you.

But God damn it, Pyke, you've got to give me a break. In this world of horseshit, I needed what you had to give me. You made it possible for me to live as a man in this wretched thing we call a life. By the way, I'm really going to try to change myself further. I have decided that all my life I've been a person that things happen to, and I just stand back and let them happen. I've got to learn to be more aggressive and to fight for the things I need. But long before I started to feel that way, you changed me, in much more important ways. I would have followed you to the ends of the planet if you'd asked me. But that wasn't your style, was it, Pyke? You had to be the Goddamn bodhisattva, to lead me just so far, and then let me go on my own, while you wandered off in search of another disciple to lead out of samsara. Well, here I am, master, half way between enlightenment and hell, and no place to go. Did you give up on me, or did you just think I had to make it on my own? Well, I sure as hell don't know what to do now. You really left me in the lurch. Maybe I need another drink.

Damn, am I tired. I keep rubbing my eyes and it just feels like salt water is falling into them. I've got to finish this. What to do? Maybe I should go wandering off, like you, in search of an impressionable young undergraduate to lead astray, or to have her lead me astray. That sounds like an interesting proposition. But I should probably really update my **vita** and set out in search of another job. Yes, I realize this is probably the worst time in history for a Ph.D. biologist to look for work. But how can I continue to let Cimarron State drag me down?

If I am going to survive as a professional scientist, I have to go somewhere where my colleagues believe in the dignity of scientific work. I need a position where what I say means something; I can't go on only being tolerated, as an amusing but sometimes annoying aberration, from year to year. I can't stay here where all the company men, all the yes-men, go on year after year uncomplaining and unquestioning. I might as well be dead as to be a full professor here. I'd be better off in private industry, or the EPA, they must be in need of scientists who understand the natural ecosystem. Yes, that's what I'll do, just as soon as I finish typing out this book, I'll get out the old CV and bring it up to date. No, I've got to get some rest. I'll do it tomorrow.

Oh, shit, Pyke, it's no use. I can't put it off. I can't lie any more. I did love you, more than anyone else in the world. I am so alone and I feel so helpless with you gone. It's like you left me half-alive. I come up the stairs trying to believe that you are going to peer around the corner, flash your devilish smile, and say to me, "I haven't seen you for a while. Have you been on sabbatical, or what?"

I sit in my office, and I watch the fan you gave me go around and around, and I feel the air blowing against my face, and I think about the molecules of your decomposing body, drifting through the soil just as those air molecules are drifting around in space, at a rate that is slower, but just as efficient in the long run. Strong grown-up men don't cry, right, Pyke? Well, I did, damn you, the day I got back, after you were found dead, I closed the door to my office and I covered my face and pounded the desk top and the tears just wouldn't stop. I've tried to forget it, not to admit it even to myself, until now. But that was the only time; even at your memorial service I didn't, luckily I didn't have to make a speech, only I felt so choked up that my throat hurt like I had a bad case of strep, and I was gasping, and my heart was pounding, and I couldn't speak or hardly breathe.

Damn you to hell, why did you have to up and die on me? I'm going home now, and that's final. I'm exhausted. I loved you, Pyke McKenna. There, I've said it again after I said I wasn't going to. It just exploded out of me both times. I've said it and it's true; I have never loved anyone the way I loved you. Let it go at that.

DEGREES OF FREEDOM

Pyke, I've been going out with Ellen, but I don't know what's going to come of it. We seem to be two hurt people who are too much like each other to really fit together. She and I both cared for you, though; yes, we admitted it to each other yesterday, we both loved you; and that has been a sort of common ground from which we both draw strength. I hope you'd have approved our friendship; I know she meant a great deal to you.

Pyke, just one last thought; maybe your death was, after all, about love, just as your life was the working through, the embodiment, of your definition of it; first, the generation of it from nothing, like the love you feel when you see a new baby; and then the glory of having it, sharing with all of your old and new friends; and the struggle to understand it while the beauty of it is still rich and new, and then to keep it alive when it begins to fade and lose its luster; and finally the letting go, letting your friends who loved you transfer some of that love to each other. That way, love can continue to grow and need not shrink to nothing as we age. Is this what you were trying to tell me, master? I can see why I didn't understand it until this last moment, the moment when I was at the extremity of my senses. It helps to explain some things, I suppose; why we continue to go on living in the face of misery and why we continue to need other human beings long past the time when mere biology, mere reproductive gene-shuffling, is no longer important.

We learn as we grow old, and we also teach those around us, this ultimate lesson; that love grows, it never grows old. It's something to hold in my mind for a moment, Pyke; it makes sense right now. But let me think about it for a while, let me sleep on it, and I'll see how it stands up in the cold air tomorrow morning.

I'm going, now. I'm going to stand up in fifteen seconds, and turn out the light, and leave this book behind forever. This is really the end, now, I mean it. Nothing could be better to close this exercise than the words of our mutual friend, Linda Norquist; Pyke, baby - God rest your lovely soul.